DANARKO SAGA

Danarko
Ecalain
Carni
Kuriva
Phan'stra

CARNI

Danarko Saga
Book Three

Maxina Storibrook

Silver Grove Publications, LLC

ISBN-13: 978-1-948869-07-2

CARNI
Author: Maxina Storibrook
Publisher: Silver Grove Publications, LLC
www.maxinastoribrook.com

Paragraph break uses Bergamot Ornaments from dafont.com.

This author is part of the Silver Grove Publications (SGP) family. If you have any questions or wish to browse our other SGP authors, please visit our website for books, products, and submission guidelines. You can also contact SGP for bulk discounts for libraries, stores, and more.

www.silvergrovepublications.com

DEDICATION

Without an editor, a book will never be as good as it can be. There would be so many plot holes and errors that I would be embarrassed to show my face to the world again. Two extraordinary women in my life stepped up in my time of need and took up this important mantle: Werui (Aunt) Barbara Dean and Megan Lynch.

Carni is the diamond it is today because of you. Thank you so much from the bottom of my heart!

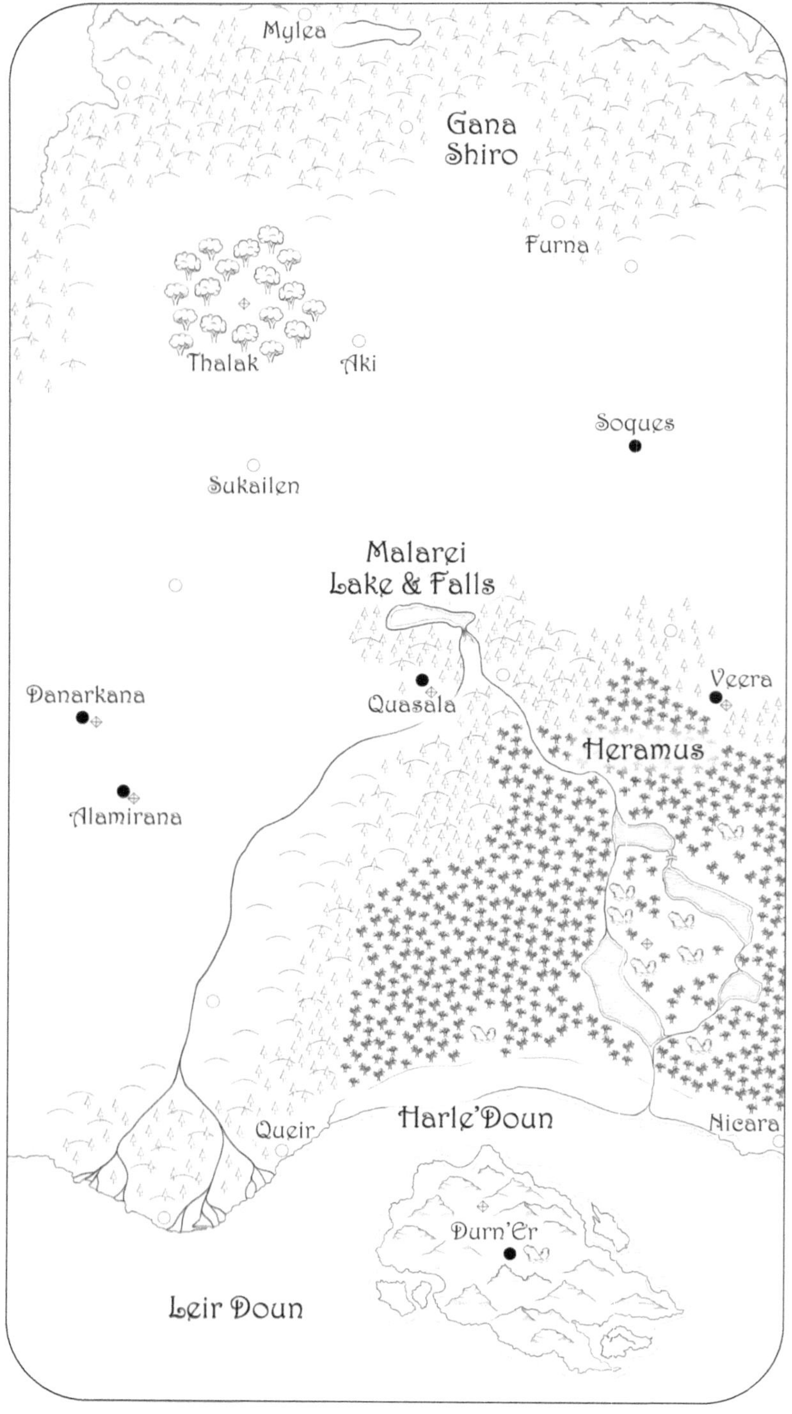

Mylea
Gana Shiro
Furna
Thalak
Aki
Soques
Sukailen
Malarei Lake & Falls
Danarkana
Quasala
Veera
Heramus
Alamirana
Queir
Harle'Doun
Nicara
Durn'Er
Leir Doun

CONTENTS

Chapter 1
Carni's Will

"I have to leave, Shaniel."

His breathing stops. He can't let her go. She had watched one of her friends *die*; she is still grieving over that loss. Crossing his arms, he stubbornly announces, "No. I won't let you go."

The chestnut-haired elf huffs, irritated at him. "I need to figure out what is going on with me, Shaniel. This is the only way; Carni might hold the answers I *need* right now."

Carni.

He pales. He had told Mara about his little sister, Nirvinia, but he hadn't told her everything. He cannot allow her to go into Carni without a trained Corridor Traveler; if she does, she might end up in the same place Nirvinia had died.

"No," he whispers, his arms falling to his sides. "I won't let you put yourself in danger."

Mara grits her teeth. "I'm putting everyone in danger just by *being* here! At least let me go somewhere where I know there is absolutely no one I can hurt and where I can get my own head screwed on straight! There's too much here that is triggering these-these memory things. It's driving me mad."

Shaniel stares at her in horror. He had never personally met any of the vessels who had started the recollection phase, but he has read the reports and knows it has never ended well. "Mara – "

"Please, Shaniel," she interrupts him, her voice barely above a whisper. She touches his shoulder, and that simple contact sends a *zing* of power across his skin. "I promise I will come back. Just... let me go."

His vision blurs. He cannot stop her, but maybe...

maybe he can still help her. "Promise me one thing, then."

Mara's eyes flit over his shoulder, distracted. "Anything," she quickly says as her fingers reach for something in the air beside her. He cannot help the brief sense of awe when she finds one of the fissures in the membrane separating their realm from Carni.

"If you need my help, call for me," he rushes, pulling his unique reki out of his pocket. *It's a small price to pay for her safety*, he thinks to himself as he hands over the customized communication device. The key and lock emblem glimmer with his Source one last time before sparking to life in her hand.

She stares at it, shocked. "I can't take this," she says, shoving it back at him.

He looks away from her. "I can get another. Just… stay safe. Don't – "

He barely keeps the sob at bay. All he can see is his sister at the bottom of that ravine, her hair white from the dream-eater's influence and her body torn to ribbons by the night terror's claws.

"I won't. I promise." There is a slight pause. "You would have been an awesome brother."

His eyes widen. He automatically reaches for Mara, but the portal is already gone. He collapses to his knees, his sister's final rasped words coming back to haunt him.

"You're… pretty awesome, brother."

"What… did I just do?" he whispers, appalled at himself. *Now… now Mara is in Carni. What if she becomes eiv'ra, like Nirvinia did? What if she falls into the Nightmare Pit and runs into a cerberus or a night terror? I'm not awesome. I'm horrible.*

"Shaniel!" Still caught in the downward spiral of his thoughts, he turns to the voice of his friend and comrade. Aeserast stares at the look of horror and desolation on the laig'hius's face as Darion approaches. "What happened?"

"Aeserast," he breathes, touching the top of his head as his vision suddenly sharpens. For the first time in decades, a tear slides down his cheek. "I think I screwed up…"

Now I know how Aeserast feels whenever he makes a mistake. I'm never teasing him about it again.

Darion glances around. "Where is Mara?"

Shaniel trembles at the Eleth'Lord's question. He suspects the Alkinian has strong feelings for the young Danarko, and Shaniel has seen what he is like when he loses his temper. His voice is barely a breath as he admits, "I let her go through the portal…"

"Do you know where she opened it?" Aeserast demands, and Shaniel can hear the hope in his voice.

He squeezes his eyes shut, wishing he isn't the one reporting this terrifying news – especially to Aeserast and Darion. They have already been through so much. "She… walked in. It's my fault. I shouldn't have let her go…"

There is a brief pause. The back of his neck tingles as Aeserast's Source permeates the air. Shaniel already knows what he will find, though; Mara had been here for several minutes trying to find a fissure. Her Source will be on almost every crack and tear in the membrane in this alley.

"Shaniel, how long had she been hunting for an opening?"

"A while," he responds immediately, shaking his head. "But… it doesn't matter, Aeserast. She went to *Carni*."

"Why the Corridor Realm?" Darion's voice is clipped.

Shaniel stares at the ground, avoiding their gazes. "She said Carni might hold the answers she needs. I gave her my reki, though. Maybe… maybe we can track her through that?"

"Did you remove the tracking blocker from it?"

Darion's simple question sends another spear of self-deprecation through Shaniel. He presses his palms against his eyes as if that will help him. "Carc'ra… no."

Aeserast's power recedes, and Shaniel's ears twitch at

the sound of his exasperated huff. "Nothing. She could be *anywhere*. Perhaps we can search for her Source signature from the Tower of Discord."

"She is still wearing the Alamiran crest; it will mask her Source for as long as she keeps it on." Darion's statement has Shaniel pressing his palms even harder against his face.

"We need to find her; who knows what that realm will do to her?" Suddenly, the Creation'Lord breathes, "The *portals.*"

Shaniel hisses reflexively, his head whipping up to stare at Aeserast. Mara has translocation sickness; not only that, but merely going through the portals has been consistently making her memories *worse*. "If Mara has been having trouble with just translocation, who knows what being in Carni will do to her over an extended amount of time?" He grits his teeth. *I really did screw up. Why didn't I think of this* before *she had left?! She is heading directly into what could be causing these memory lapses!*

"We need to find her immediately."

Shaniel glances at the elf, startled by the grim tone and dark look in his jade green eyes. The air visibly glows around him as he temporarily loses control over his enormous amount of Source. Gold flecks glimmer in the jade-green haze.

"Settle down, Eleth'Lord," a familiar authoritative voice orders. They turn to see Twyla standing at the entrance to the alleyway with Timian beside her. Her eyes swirl with the influence of the Corridor Realm. "She is safe for the time being."

Darion steps toward her, his expression mirroring a dark thundercloud. Timian holds out his hand, stopping him. "Twyla informed me that Mara suspects the Corridor Realm has been causing her to remember faster than her mind can process the memories, so she went to confront whatever it is the Will wanted from her."

"Tell me where she is," Darion growls.

His threatening tone shocks everyone but Timian, who turns to the Creation'Lord as if Darion hadn't spoken at all. "Search for her. If you find her, report to Twyla and I immediately; do not pull her out of Carni without our express permission."

"If you do, the consequences could prove fatal," Twyla whispers, her face twisting up in guilt. "I wanted Mara to speak with you before leaving, but she had already set her mind. What I do know is the Will has already influenced her path."

Shaniel's breath hitches. Nothing good ever happens when Carni's Will is involved; it is how many wanderers have become eiv'ra and never returned to the material worlds again. "But… she is in her material form," he argues. "If we don't help her, she could *die.*"

Darion's knuckles turn white.

Timian remains unnervingly calm. "Shaniel, if you wish, you may accompany Aeserast and Darion to the Tower of Discord. Report to me when they find her." His eyes flick to Aeserast. "If the Tower's Ghost appears, I request an immediate report."

"Of course." Aeserast's hand is already reaching forward. Within seconds, a swirling oval of warped air floats above the ground.

Shaniel scrambles to his feet as Aeserast and Darion step through the portal. Glancing between the Time'Lord and the Alkinian duir'ne, he confesses in a low voice, "I messed up. I let her go."

A frown creases Timian's brow. Before he can respond, Twyla smiles and reassures him, "You would not have been able to stop her even if you had tried, Common'Lord. Carni's Will would have pulled her into its realm one way or another; it is better that she went willingly."

Shaniel nods before stepping through the portal, barely registering the sensation of passing through the bubble-like membrane. His foot lands on one of the gears that make up the ballroom-sized clock; a faintly glowing mist partially obscures the giant hour, minute, and second hands ticking across the surface.

He takes a steadying breath, catching the unmistakable smell of metal gears, damp air, and the sweet scent that permeates the Tower of Discord. Glancing up, he is not surprised to see the starless 'sky' of the Treavaun, which is one of the dark, twisted sections of Carni.

Aeserast sits on the middle of the clock face, his legs crossed and his eyes closed as his Source forms a protective bubble around him. Darion stands to the side, running his hand absently through the sentient lavender-white swirls twining about him.

"Any luck?" Shaniel murmurs, eyeing the scrying sorcerer.

Darion shakes his head. "Myst, have you sensed any disturbances in Carni?" the Eleth'Lord asks the swirling mist.

"*No.*" The androgynous voice echoes through their heads. Shaniel shivers as he feels the mist creeping over his arms and legs. "*Even the Tower is quiet.*"

Aeserast huffs, opening his eyes. "Nothing. Not even my net found her." The transparent orb surrounding him dissolves as he stands up. He sways, unstable on his feet.

Recognizing the telltale signs of the half-Respoura using too much of his Source, Shaniel leaps forward and catches his friend. "You've been doing this more often, Aeserast," he grumbles, helping him to the huge Xharos rune for the number twelve on the edge of the clock. A stone bridge extends outward over the abyss, ending at a floating door on the other side.

Aeserast smiles ruefully. "I haven't had you around to keep me in check."

Shaniel grunts, not saying anything as they cross the bridge. Darion opens the door, revealing Alkinian-style living quarters with smooth, seamless walls and curved chairs. Shaniel leads Aeserast to the sleek couch before heading to the kitchen. Darion paces restlessly.

"The tea is — "

"I know." Shaniel opens a cabinet, pulling out Aeserast's special Source-boosting pods and heating a cup of water. "Is Aihalia still living here?"

"She manipulated her own section of Carni to create a separate unit for herself, but there is a door in the back that connects our living quarters," Aeserast explains as Shaniel walks into the living room. "You should visit more."

Shaniel's face scrunches in displeasure as he sets the cup in front of Aeserast. "No, thanks. Not when she's still here."

Aeserast sighs heavily. "She promised she wouldn't feed you another potion, Shaniel." Shaniel slumps on the couch next to him, stretching his arms along the back as Aeserast sips at his tea. "I will return to searching for her in a moment."

"Rest, Aeserast," Shaniel encourages. "You're as bad as Mara."

Darion paces back and forth, not saying a word.

—— ◆ ——

"Danti…"

"*What is it now?*"

"I'm so hungry…"

"*I can't help you with that!*"

Mara groans, her feet dragging on the glimmering crystal pathway. She cannot tell how much time has passed since she had woken up with no memory in this strange place. Her surroundings are a myriad of twisting swirls and colorful patterns; the pathway is the only solid object as far as she can see, and even that isn't very reassuring as the path is made out of semi-transparent crystal that glimmers with multi-faceted rainbow colors.

She had given up trying to determine whether the swirls are close to her or not; even when she veers to the edge of the pathway, the crystal merely expands in that direction as the swirls warp and dance.

She shivers, suddenly cold. "D-Danti?" she chatters, tucking her silver-edged black robe around herself to try to stay warm. The lightweight clothes underneath aren't helping. "What's going on?"

"*I don't know.*" She is always disconcerted when the disjointed voice in her head uses her own voice. "*We should – find shelter.*"

"You think I haven't been doing that?" she shoots back. Her foot catches on something, and she sprawls across the crystal pathway. Twisting around, she glares at the shattered device she had accidentally dropped when she had woken up in this strange realm. The gold key and lock etched on the shattered pieces glint as if mocking her. "That's the third time I've seen that! Is this pathway just a huge loop?!"

The surrounding swirls pulse with an odd light as they twist and dance. She thumps her head against the pathway, her stomach clenching in hunger. She is so exhausted. How long has she been walking? Minutes? *Hours?* She can't tell.

She rolls onto her back, staring into the sky. Huge swaths of blue and purple arc above her like the aurora borealis. She knows what 'northern lights' are, but she has absolutely no recollection of a specific memory. Has she actually seen it before, or did she learn it through a textbook?

"Amnesia sucks," she mutters, watching the colors morph and change. Now, it is a dark blue sky with tiny pinpoints of light as the green, white, and purple aurora dances across it. "Maybe we're dreaming, Danti."

"*I don't know.*"

"Maybe you're not real. Maybe I'm just crazy." Her stomach rumbles loudly, and she places her hand over the unhappy gurgle. "I'm hungry enough to be hallucinating…"

She closes her eyes, imagining a delicious guldon pasta basted in Alkinian ale. She doesn't remember ever eating it, but right then, she doesn't care. The thought of any type of food makes her mouth water.

Inhaling, she catches the delicious aroma of baking bread and seafood. She stands up and fights the dizziness as she takes a few steps forward, but her shaking legs give out from underneath her. She barely feels the pain of her knees striking the crystal pathway as her vision blurs.

In the distance, she can see the pathway leading into a forest. Something moves at the edge, but it is too far away for her to make out what it is. She blinks a couple times to clear her vision, but it doesn't work. She pushes herself up and staggers forward.

"*Rest*," Danti urges, sounding frantic. "*You will collapse.*"

"But it's right there," Mara mumbles, her eyes sliding out of focus.

"*You are so — stubborn.*"

"You've said that already," she huffs, rubbing her eyes. She squints at the trees. "Is that… fruit?"

"*Watch out!*"

Mara stumbles, sprawling on the pathway yet again. She glances down to see the broken device; the key and lock glint again, *definitely* mocking her. "Now you're just messing with me," she weakly accuses the swirls, her head resting on her arm. She can't get up; she has no more strength.

She slips into unconsciousness, unable to resist the temptation of sleep any longer. She welcomes the blissful sensation of not feeling the biting hunger or bone-weary exhaustion from before.

Time slips by, unmeasurable as she drifts through the darkness of her own mind. After a while, she sees a purplish-blue film in front of her. It glows weakly in the encroaching darkness. She reaches forward to touch it, but something wet pressing against her lips rouses her out of the strange dream.

She reflexively swallows, and the water eases her parched throat. She gasps, opening her eyes to see a ten-year-old girl holding a flask in her hands. She tilts her head to the side, and her dark, wavy hair slides over her shoulder. She blinks, her ocean blue eyes wide and innocent.

"Hello," she greets, her grin exposing a row of white teeth.

"H-hello," Mara responds, her eyes flitting around the room warily. "Where am I?"

"Our village!" The girl puts the flask down before handing over a plate laden with fruit. "We found you collapsed on the path. It isn't good for those of the material realms to sleep in Carni, you know."

"I… didn't know," Mara admits warily.

"Most people don't." She leans forward. "What's your name?"

Making a split second decision, she decides to go with the name Danti had given her when they had woken up in this strange place. "Mara."

The girl's head tilts to the side in curiosity. "Like half of a whole? That's a strange name." Before Mara can say anything, she gestures at the food. "Please help yourself, Mara!"

"Thank you," Mara says, picking up one of the fruits and raising it to her lips.

"*Don't eat that,*" Danti suddenly orders.

Mara frowns. Why not? She is so hungry. Her stomach growls in agreeance.

"You can eat it," the little girl says, an odd smile on her face. "It is not fruit of Carni; it's from Alkina."

Mara stares at the fruit intensely. "Why is that important?"

The girl's smile never falters. "The food in Carni is addictive, and too much of it can kill a material body." She stands up, brushing off her patchwork dress as if there is dust on it. "But that is not Carni's food; it is Alkina's food. It should be good for you."

Should be.

Mara swallows hard, staring at the fruit again. *I'm too hungry for this,* she finally thinks, taking a bite. A sweet yet harsh taste floods her mouth as the soft meat of the fruit practically melts on her tongue.

"Take your time," the girl encourages, giggling as Mara digs into the fruit. "Once you are done, you are welcome to leave."

"Thank you," Mara quickly says around a mouthful as the girl leaves, shutting the door behind herself.

Mara polishes off the platter of food in record time. Finally sated, she glances around the small hut. A bed is in the corner, and a desk lined with different handmade dolls rests along the wall.

She folds the blanket that had been covering her and places it on the desk before heading for the door the girl had used. As soon as she steps outside, she is greeted with an odd yet beautiful sight.

The familiar crystal pathway is overgrown with oddly shaped flowers and edged by green trees laced with glowing gold veins. She stares into the woods surrounding the path, spotting more huts blending in with the vegetation. The buildings themselves are a light brown with green and gold vegetation growing across them.

"Hello?" Mara calls out, glancing around. "Where did she go…?" she murmurs half to herself, stepping onto the overgrown path in search of the mysterious girl.

A silvery pulse radiates out from her foot. She staggers, startled by it.

"Hehe…"

Mara turns in the direction of the giggle. The small huts are gone. "Who's there?"

"Who's there? Who's there?" a little girl's voice mimics.

"But of course she doesn't know who's here!"

"Duh! She fell asleep in Carni!" This time, it is a little boy.

"She is *still* asleep. Can't you tell by that look on her face?" Yet another child's voice.

"Why did she fall asleep, though? It is bad to fall asleep here if you are not trained."

Mara rubs her temple; the children talk as though she cannot hear them. Maybe she really *is* hearing voices in her head.

"Is she all right? She doesn't look well."

"Who knows?"

"*I* don't know."

"I don't think she knows, either."

She feels a feathery touch across her arm and a tug at her robe. *It can't all be in my head,* she thinks to herself. *There must be children here, and they're messing with me.* "Who are you?"

"I think she hears us!"

"No way! Only Voyana's favorites can hear us!"

"Maybe she is an Ecalain...?"

"E-Ecalain?" Mara repeats, confused. She feels as if she should know that word.

Softly-glowing ocean blue eyes stare at her. Mara staggers backward to see it is the girl from the hut hanging upside-down in the tree, her legs hooked around the limb. Her dress falls to her hips, revealing snug black pants underneath.

The girl blinks several times, her wavy hair swaying with her. "You can see me out here?"

"Of course," Mara snaps, suddenly irritated. "Why do you think I can't?"

"No one except for the Ecalain and Ecalauna should be able to see me outside of my house unless I want them to." Her eyes dilate. "What family are you from?"

Mara's lips part, a single word on the tip of her tongue.

She reflexively touches her throat to find an oversized pendant. "I…"

The girl focuses on the necklace. Her eyes widen as she drops from the branch, somehow twisting in the air to land on her feet. "That's Darion's pendant!"

Five other children with odd features suddenly appear. One is a boy who looks like he has wolf ears and a tail. "Are you Mage Danarko?" he asks, a look of awe on his face.

Something nags at the back of her mind at that name. She knows it; she…

A red-haired girl with bright green eyes scoffs at him. "Who else could she be? Darion gave that necklace to her, after all."

The girl who had helped Mara takes a small step forward. "Are you Lost?"

Mara stares blankly at her. "Uh… yeah, I guess. I've been trying to find my way out for a while now."

"She's Lost…"

"It's good we found her!"

"The nightmares would have eaten her."

"We should take her to Darion. He's probably looking for her."

"Um…" Mara glances between the rambling children, confused. "I'm sorry, but… who's Darion?"

All six children stop and stare at her. "You don't remember him, do you?" the wavy-haired girl whispers, her ocean blue eyes narrowing.

Mara slowly shakes her head.

Five of the children gasp and scramble away from her as if she had turned into a monster. The girl who had asked the question is the only one who remains still.

"More than Lost… she has Forgotten!"

"What do we do now…"

"Someone who has Forgotten will attract the Storms!"

"Quiet!" the girl orders, and the other children go

silent. "I will wake her."

"No! Don't do it!" the little wolf-boy exclaims, grabbing the girl's arm. "The last time you took someone to Auntie, they tried to hurt her!"

"Auntie doesn't like it when we interfere," the red-haired girl whispers.

"We should not disrupt Auntie's plans," another boy reiterates.

"She was brought *here*, though," the blue-eyed girl argues. "That means Auntie wanted her to be here."

"Um… who is this person you're talking about?" Mara asks hesitantly.

The girl beams at her. "Auntie! She can help people like you." She frowns and tilts her head to the side. "Are you feeling all right?"

Mara takes a deep, steadying breath. "Yeah," she lies. In reality, she feels dizzy and lethargic; despite waking up only a little while ago, she has the urge to go back to sleep.

The girl watches her for another moment before taking her hand and tugging her down the path. "We can see Auntie after you sleep," she says firmly. "You can stay at my place; it's safe for people like you."

"People like me?" Mara repeats, feeling a headache creeping over her temple.

The girl nods. "People from the material realms. If you sleep just anywhere, you could easily lose *all* of your memories, not just some. You have to be careful about that."

Mara stares at the little girl. *She doesn't know, then,* she realizes.

"We should not tell her; we do not know her intentions," Danti murmurs into her mind, and she quietly agrees. The less this girl knows about their situation, the better – especially if knowledge of their situation will actually bring danger on them.

The little hut appears through the trees, and within a minute, they are inside the small room. The girl fluffs some pillows and unfolds the blanket before turning to Mara with a grin. "Here you go!"

"Thank you, um…" A pang of guilt shoots through her. "I'm sorry. What's your name?"

She giggles. "I like the word lunesh!" She pirouettes on her foot before sitting down on her bed. "A traveling mage called me that once, and I loved it so much that I wanted it to be my name."

"Lunesh…" Mara repeats slowly, intuitively knowing it means *moon's flower*. "It's very pretty. So what do you do here?"

"I play," she answers simply. "I also sing and dance. What about you?"

Mara mulls over it, but her mind draws a blank. She shrugs nonchalantly, trying to brush off the question. "Nothing… much."

"You like fighting."

She stares at Lunesh. "What?"

Lunesh nods. "You fight a lot – at least, that's what Auntie tells us. You like punching and kicking. It makes you feel good."

Mara takes a slow breath, utterly confused. "How do you know so much about me?"

"Auntie knows you. She watches you."

A chill slides down Mara's spine. *"We should leave,"* Danti murmurs, alarmed.

No kidding, Mara thinks, unnerved. She glances at the door, wondering if she can slip out unnoticed later that night.

The little girl tucks herself into her bed. "Sleep well, Mara," Lunesh mumbles, yawning and closing her eyes.

"Y-you, too, Lunesh," she stammers, laying down. Her mind swirls with questions, one of them being why Lunesh is calling her the name Danti calls her despite seeming to know her real identity. Is her name actually Mara? If that is the case, does the meaning behind it apply to her?

Is she only half of something else?

Despite her swirling thoughts and her desire to leave, sleep overtakes her. Her dreams consist of a blackness so complete she cannot help but wonder if there is anything beyond the swallowing darkness.

"Wake up, Mara."

Her eyes pop open at Danti's mental prodding. She glances at the still form on the bed.

"She is asleep. Now is our time."

Mara stands up, slinking out the door. The forest is still bright, looking as it had the first time she had walked out of the small hut. She steps onto the pathway, wondering which way she needs to go to leave.

A silvery ripple extends from her foot.

Suddenly, she is no longer in the forest. Unsettled, she glances around her surroundings. The sky is now covered in churning bluish-purple clouds, looking as though it is about to storm. The crystal pathway glistens darkly, the refracting colors more ominous than before. In the distance, there is a definitive shape to this strange land as the pathway slopes down into a canyon.

She approaches the dark ravine, inquisitive. "This place sure is odd, isn't it, Danti?" she starts conversationally in an attempt to ignore the foreboding atmosphere.

"I have a bad feeling…" Again, it speaks in her voice.

"Don't go that way."

Mara whirls around to see Lunesh. This time, though, she isn't smiling. Reflexively, Mara raises her fists to guard her face. "How did you follow me?"

Her lips part, her expression so desolate that Mara has a hard time believing this girl is a child. "You have forgotten everything, haven't you?"

"Answer me."

She points at the dark canyon. "You don't want to go there." She splays her fingers wide. "Follow me."

Mara glances back at the steep cliffs edging the pathway. "Why not? What is it?"

"The Nightmare Pit."

Uneasiness slides down her spine like cold slime. "Where will you take me?"

"To see Auntie." The girl touches Mara's hand, ignoring her confused look as she pulls her down the pathway away from the ravine. When Lunesh's left foot hits the pathway, a gold ring pulses outward.

They are back in the forest with the gold-veined trees.

"Who is Auntie?" Mara asks warily as they pass drooping branches made out of glowing yellow, pink, orange, purple, and blue vines.

"Auntie is Auntie!" she answers cryptically, tugging Mara through the glowing forest.

Some of the colorful vines and branches brush against her, and she feels an odd tingling sensation throughout her body. Glancing behind them, she frowns at the blackened vines.

Did *she* do that?

Mara's eyes are drawn down the pathway where the vines are thicker. When she pushes them aside, she glimpses black residue wherever she touches them. She looks behind them once again to see the first set of blackened branches disintegrating. "Lunesh, I think – "

"Here we are!" Lunesh lets Mara's hand go. She glimpses the same black mark on the girl's hand before she can hide it. She grins at Mara's appalled expression. "I look forward to seeing you again in the future!"

"Lunesh, your hand – "

"I'm fine, Mara." Lunesh gives her that odd knowing smile again. "Have fun with Auntie."

The girl walks back down the path, shifting her arm in front of her – but not before Mara sees the black mark spreading along her arm.

Mara stares at her hand, noticing a gold-tinted film that slowly turns black. Her hand shakes as it falls off like ash. "Danti…"

"*I don't know.*"

Mara grits her teeth as the crumbling vines pop into her head. Had she really done that? What had caused it?

Is that going to happen to Lunesh, too?

Mara turns around to follow after the girl. She cannot let her die.

A gold hand wraps around her arm, stopping her. "*Lunesh will be fine,*" a woman murmurs behind her, although it sounds more like she is speaking to her mind.

"Who are you?" Mara's voice trembles. "What's happening to me?"

"*There is no need to fear me, fletchling,*" she says. "*You are merely Lost and have Forgotten yourself. One of the realm's children brought you here so I can awaken your memories once again.*"

Mara's arm is released. Whirling around, she stares at the solid gold tree with drooping gold vines. The hand that had held her arm is turned upward, beckoning her forward. "*Allow me to assist you in Remembering.*"

An odd shock goes through her, and she feels the hairs on the back of her neck rise. Alarmed, Mara asks Danti out loud, "Are you all right?"

She feels it hesitate. "*Yes,*" it finally admits.

"*Take my hand, fletchling. Allow me to show you this realm.*"

"*Do not take — her hand,*" Danti suddenly exclaims, sounding frantic.

Mara takes another step back. "No."

The hand jerks as if physically injured by the rejection. "*Do you desire to remember on your own, then, Essence?*"

"*Yes.*" Mara is surprised at the firm, assertive tone. She opens her mouth to ask why she is calling her 'Essence', but the woman's arm is already receding behind the vines.

"*So be it. You are on your own, fletchling. Thana baro.*"

Chapter 2
Down the 'Terror Pit

Mara takes another step back, and a ring of silver courses out from her. Suddenly, she is standing inside the ravine of the Nightmare Pit. Lunesh stares at her, her eyes wide as she cradles her blackening arm. "Why didn't you accept Auntie's help?"

Mara collapses on her knees next to Lunesh, horrified. Her hands hover over the girl's arm, wishing she could help but afraid to touch her in case she makes it worse. "Lunesh, I'm so sorry…"

Lunesh stares at her impassively. "You should not apologize for what you are, Mara."

Mara meets the girl's ocean blue eyes. There is no emotion in the child's face. "What are you talking about, Lunesh?"

"You are who you are; you cannot control your own nature."

Mara shakes her head. "You aren't making any sense. How-how do we stop this?"

Lunesh smiles, but there is no warmth behind it. "I'm not important; I am just one of Carni's random creations, created from the thoughts and wishes of others. I don't matter."

"You matter to me." Silvery tears splash onto the pathway between them.

Lunesh's eyes soften at this. She touches Mara's face, a genuine smile lighting her features brilliantly. "Thank you, Mara, but you should not have followed me into the night terror's den."

A shadow looms over them. Mara falls backward, eyes wide as she stares at the enormous, blob-like, black creature standing behind Lunesh. It opens its mouth, exposing rows upon rows of sharp teeth coated in dry blood. Scraps of cloth are caught between those sharp points.

"You need to remember why you are here; I am not important."

The monster snaps its teeth around Lunesh, and she disappears in a pouf of gold dust.

Mara stares in horror as the monster shakes its head at the sudden explosion. It blinks bloody eyes at her before snarling menacingly.

An icy rage surges through her, clearing her head and taking over. A dark cloud encompasses her as she stands up; silvery lightning crackles in the cloud like a brewing storm.

"You… will pay," she breathes, clenching her hand inside the black cloud. A curved black blade edged with silver sparks forms in her hand.

She doesn't think. She charges at the creature, leaping into the air and slashing downward. The creature shrieks, exploding in a mess of black goo.

Mara lands in a crouch. Slowly exhaling, she releases the blade; it dematerializes and blows away on an invisible current. Staring at the destruction around her, she remembers what Lunesh had said about her: she loves fighting.

Everything that has happened to her until that point rushes through her mind. Growing frustrated on the crystal pathway; the plants turning black at her touch; Lunesh's contaminated arm; her sudden instinctive desire to destroy the creature that had eaten Lunesh.

Am I a… killer?

An odd purple current washes over her, feeling oddly familiar. Even Danti reacts to it, and silver sparks dance around her protectively. For the briefest of moments, Mara remembers a pair of purple eyes twisted in pain as they stare at her.

What did I do to him?

Collapsing to her knees, she stares at the darkened

crystal pathway in horror. The slashed night terror's remains mock her. She can tell Danti is struggling to find something to say to help her feel better.

Maybe she really is crazy; maybe that is why she is Lost.

<hr>

Shaniel rubs Aeserast's shoulders as the Creation'Lord sips on another cup of Source-aiding tea. "I apologize," he rasps to the pacing elf. "I will try again in a moment."

Darion shakes his head. "There is nothing more that you can do." Despite his own words, though, he grits his teeth.

Shaniel sighs, sitting next to Aeserast on the couch. "Take my Source."

Aeserast stares at Shaniel, appalled. "No, Shaniel! I will not do that to you again."

Shaniel grabs Aeserast's free hand, clenching it tightly. "This is my fault; I let Mara walk through that portal. It's been over a day, Aeserast! She could be in serious danger right now."

Aeserast slowly shakes his head, whispering, "Shaniel, I will not break my promise to you."

Shaniel glares at Aeserast. "You know I can take it, Ace. Just like old times, remember?" He smiles tightly.

Aeserast stares into Shaniel's eyes for a long moment. "You are staying here until you are better," he orders the laig'hius.

Shaniel waves his hand dismissively. "As long as it's only your potions I'm drinking. No more of Aihalia's."

Aeserast nods mutely, setting his cup on the oblong table and taking off his robe. He folds it neatly as Shaniel stretches out on the couch, hugging one of the throw pillows to his chest.

Darion frowns; he has read reports on what happens when Aeserast takes Source from another, and it isn't pretty. "Are you sure this is wise?"

"No," Shaniel instantly replies, grinning. "But where's the fun in that?"

Aeserast's palm covers Shaniel's forehead and eyes, pushing him down. "After this, I am giving you the nastiest revitalizing concoction I can make."

"Gonna kill me twice, then? I see how it is."

Aeserast's fingers constrict around Shaniel's head. "This is not funny, Shaniel," he whispers, closing his eyes.

Shaniel touches Aeserast's hand on his forehead. Darion can see the smirk on his lips. "Just do it, Ace."

"... Again with that name."

Shaniel's smirk twists into a pained grimace. He grips the pillow tightly, and his nails rip into the tough cloth. He grunts, his other hand wrapping tightly around Aeserast's wrist.

Aeserast yanks his friend's hand down, gritting his teeth as the laig'hius's claws dig into his leg, instead. Inhaling slowly, he breathes, "I apologize."

Shaniel goes limp.

Aeserast expels his breath, releasing Shaniel's forehead. He pushes the red-streaked black hair out of the way, checking his friend's state. Satisfied with whatever he found, he stands up and heads for the door.

Darion glances between Shaniel and Aeserast, his eyes wide. "What was that?"

"You know what it was, Darion. Now let us finish this so I can help him."

Darion follows Aeserast across the bridge, his fists clenching. "Aeserast, I have read the reports. Is Shaniel – "

"No."

Darion grabs Aeserast's arm. "Then explain, because the only way I know how you take Source is you yank it out all at once."

"That's exactly what I did!" Aeserast exclaims, whirling to face Darion. "I took all of it, Darion, and left him hanging on by a thread. He is barely alive right now. I need to finish this so I can give him back his Source, else he really *will* be dead."

Shocked by the tears on his friend's face, he releases the Creation'Lord's arm. He is too stunned to stop the fey-elf from whirling back to the clock tower and storming to the middle. When he feels the blast of energy, though, his eyes widen.

Aeserast really *had* taken Shaniel's Source.

The magenta energy mixes and swirls in the air before expanding rapidly, searching across the realm for a single telltale Source. Stretching it as far as he can, Aeserast clenches his fist.

Darion can feel the net of power tighten.

"Found her," Aeserast gasps, falling to his knees as the power returns to him. His eyes are open yet unfocused as he sees the area where Mara is. "Just inside the border of a Treavaun area on the outer edges of the night terror pit. She doesn't seem to be in danger, but – Darion, wait! Timian's report!"

Darion's hand is already through the portal. He shoots a cold look at Aeserast. "Fix Shaniel, Aeserast. If he is not back to his annoying ways by the time I return with Mara, I am tossing you into the Hariana myself."

He disappears through the portal.

Aeserast struggles to his feet, shuffling across the bridge. Myst floats about him, condensing just enough to help him along. "Thank you," he murmurs to his youngest creation as he opens his door. Making it back to the couch where Shaniel lies, he collapses onto his knees.

"I apologize, old friend," Aeserast whispers, his voice hoarse as he pushes back Shaniel's hair once again. "I told you I would not do it again, yet… I did."

Pressing his palm against Shaniel's forehead, he shoves Shaniel's Source and the remainder of his own back into the empty hole he had left in his friend's mind, forcing them to swirl together. It is impossible for them to merge completely, but they can be mixed much like granules of salt and sugar.

For a brief, terrifying moment, the Source rejects its new home, fighting its way back into Aeserast. It finally settles down, repairing itself within seconds.

Shaniel's eyes flutter open. He stares dazedly at Aeserast for a moment before grinning sleepily. "See? That wasn't too – "

Aeserast collapses.

Cursing colorfully, Shaniel fumbles to catch him so his head doesn't strike the table. Examining his own Source, he discovers that it had changed once again and leans more to purple than before. Even worse than that, he knows intuitively Aeserast had nearly depleted himself in order to bring Shaniel back from Eleth's doorstep.

"You idiot!" he roars at the unconscious Aeserast. "Don't give me *everything* you have! Who's the srui now? Huh?!" He glances down the hallway. "Aihalia! Are you here?"

———— ♦ ————

Darion falls through the swirling sky.

"*Carc'ra!*" he swears, twisting around in the air; he does not see the glimmering Carni's Path beneath him. He gathers his Source about him and reaches out, trying to slow his descent by grabbing onto the half-formed Carni Matter surrounding him. The particles shrink away, leaving him nothing to manipulate.

Of all of the things to happen in a Treavaun, this has to be one of the worst.

Glimpsing the crystal pathway far beneath him, he squints at the discrepancy. Night terror guts discolor the usually bright pathway, and a black-clothed Alkinian woman kneels in the middle of it all. He watches in horror as the night terror's head trembles, reforming via the Carni particles gathering about it. He clears his mind of any thought of it, but it still reforms.

Mara must be thinking about it.

"Mara! Do not focus on it!" he yells, no longer worried for himself.

The young elf whirls around and sees the black blob amassing on Carni's Path. Staggering back, she reaches into the sparking black cloud surrounding her and withdraws a Source-created blade.

Thank goodness Carni Matter is responding to her, *at least.*

She hesitates before attacking, looking uncertain.

"Attack it!" he yells, frantic. Reaching out one more time, he attempts to slow his fall.

Mara jerks in surprise, her eyes flicking up to him. The freshly reformed night terror uses this moment to attack, and she barely manages to block its sharp claws.

If I am going out this way, I might as well save Mara, Darion thinks grimly, amassing his Source into the shape of a blade without using the surrounding Voyana and Carni Matter. A *zing* races through his hand and arm as he grabs the hilt of the jade green Source blade, colored differently than its usual runkare-state of emerald.

He points the blade down, ready to chop the night terror in half.

Unbidden, Carni Matter forms beneath him, slowing his fall. He takes advantage of it, stabbing the night terror's head on his descent and cleaving it down the middle.

The crystalline path trembles at its roar.

The Carni Matter separates, revealing the black goo on the inside. However, Darion had been unable to completely cut the creature in half, which is the only way to truly kill a creation from this realm.

Catching sight of Mara through the reforming gash down the middle of the creature, he barks, "Run!"

For a split second, their eyes lock. Her expression swirls with terror, guilt, and uncertainty, but she pivots on her foot and sprints down the path. An odd silvery ring radiates out from her footfall, and he instantly regrets his words as she vanishes via Carni's manipulation of the path under her feet.

Mara gasps for air, finally slowing down. She glances over her shoulder, but she doesn't see anything. The path had changed again since that silvery ring, and she begins to wonder if it is connected to her thoughts — after all, she had been thinking of how she wanted to get out of there.

She leans over, resting her hands on her knees as she catches her breath. Who had that man been? Does he know her? Is her name *actually* Mara — which, according to Danti and Lunesh, means 'half of a whole'? If that is the case, where is her other half?

"Hello, Mara."

Mara whirls around, her eyes wide. Lunesh stands on the pathway, but she looks older. She smiles warmly at Mara, tilting her head to the side so her wavy hair shifts and slides almost like water. Her eyes glow a faint purplish color in the surrounding gloom.

"L-Lunesh!" Mara exclaims, relief coursing through her. "How are you still alive? What happened to you?"

"Oh, no. I died." Lunesh examines her red nails. Her eyes flick up to Mara. "And it was your fault."

Mara's face whitens. "How are you here, then? I mean, you look older…" She fights to come up with a logical explanation to what is happening around her.

Lunesh ignores the question. Holding out her hand, she admits, "I'll forgive you if you come with me."

Mara immediately takes Lunesh's hand. A shock races through her arm, and she yanks her hand back. "Who are you?"

Lunesh's face twists up in a smirk. "Your worst nightmare," she whispers, disappearing in a gold pouf.

Mara's eyes widen. She whirls around, searching for the imposter. "Where did you go?" she demands.

"Right here," Lunesh whispers in her ear.

Blinding pain shoots through Mara's side. Her breathing hitches as she looks down to see a bloody curved sword protruding from her. A pretty stone falls out of her pocket; the design of a gateway glimmers briefly before the stone strikes the path, cracking down the middle.

She can feel Danti trembling in unexplainable terror at the sight of that sword. "Why… did you do this?" Mara hears herself say, and she intuitively knows Danti had somehow managed to speak out loud through her.

The fake Lunesh twists the sword even deeper into the wound, and Mara groans. "Because it is your worst fear – dying the same way as your original self."

"I think… you got… the wrong person," Mara rasps, but she feels Danti recognize something in the imposter's words.

"That's impossible," the fake Lunesh whispers, her lips barely touching Mara's ear. "One of you is Lost, the other is Awake; I merely took the fear from the one who is Awake."

Danti.

The imposter pulls out the sword, glancing down the pathway in irritation as Mara collapses to her knees. "Great," she grumbles. "He always ruins the fun."

Mara wraps her hand around her side, trying to stop the bleeding. She draws in one breath after another, trying to keep her system from going into shock; however, something about the wound is triggering something deep, deep within her. Some… some type of memory, perhaps?

------◆------

Blood spills down her side in an endless stream. The stones around her are stained red, splattered with the result of what had happened. "Wh-why…" she asks weakly as the girl pulls the sword out of her stomach.

"Because you did nothing when my sister died at your relatives' hands."

———◆———

Mara refocuses on the hand in front of her face, enraptured by the red liquid.

"Mara!"

She looks up, dazed. The bronze-haired elf that had fallen from the sky is running toward her. His expression turns to horror at the sight of her bloody fingers. He collapses on his knees in front of her, his eyes wide.

"Do you… want to kill me, too?" she forces out, laughing weakly. "It seems like… everyone else does. I guess it's… retribution… for what happened."

"What happened?" he asks, reaching forward to take her hand.

A spike of fear shoots through her. "Don't touch me!" she snaps, falling backward and wincing as her wound sends another sharp pang through her. "I-I don't want you to disappear like she did."

"You cannot hurt me," he says soothingly, holding his hand out. "Please, allow me to help you."

She shakes her head. "No. I'll corrupt you, too, just like I did with Lunesh."

He frowns. "Carni's creation? What happened to her?"

She averts her eyes. *He had known her*, she thinks. *He will definitely want to kill me.* Maybe she deserves it, though; at least she can confess her crime this way. "When I… touched her, her skin blackened. Then that monster ate her."

The elf shakes his head. "Lunesh cannot die. She is Carni's creation; she would have melded back into Carni only to be recreated near Carni's Will."

She hesitantly looks back into his brilliant jade-green eyes. "Really?"

He nods, eyeing her wound once again. His gaze hardens. "Please, Mara. Allow me to examine your wound."

Her hand covers it reflexively. "How… how do you know to call me that?"

He gives her a quizzical look. "That is your name." Realization dawns on his face. "You… do not remember me, do you?"

She pauses, wondering if she should admit it or not. However, her silence answers his question.

He exhales slowly, holding out his hand. "My name is Darion; I am one of your friends. Please, Mara, allow me to examine your wound. Injuries in Carni can be fatal if not treated immediately."

She recognizes the name; according to Lunesh and the other children, this is the one who had given her the amulet around her throat. "How… how did you find me?"

"You broke the stone; I had given that to you in case you were ever in danger, just like now." He points to the broken stone beside her. "I want to help you, Mara."

She takes a shaky breath. "What should I do?"

"Lie back for now; I need to look at it." He places a hand on her shoulder, guiding her into a prone position before slowly pulling up the hem of her shirt. He examines the wound near her hip bone; the snug terular shifts out of the way to expose the stab wound that had been created by the Carni creature's Source-weapon. She watches him for a moment, noticing the skin tighten around his eyes in worry.

"If it's that serious, why didn't you just check it?" she asks.

"Carni is odd," he murmurs absently. A green mist covers her side, and she feels an odd sensation as it pulls the wound closed. "If I had tried to forcefully check your wound or attempted to heal it without your permission, it could have made it worse."

Her vision slides out of focus. "This place is so weird," she mumbles. "I can't figure out how to leave, and I don't even remember why I came here."

She feels his hand cup her cheek. *So warm*, she finds herself thinking as she presses her cheek against his palm, sighing. She doesn't know why, but she feels as if he had done something like this before.

"Mara, do not fall asleep. You need to stay awake!"

"Nngh…"

"Carc'ra." He lifts her up, and she hisses as her wound pulls. She curls around it protectively, shifting against him. She takes in his musky scent, recognizing it. "Hang on, Mara. I will not let you die."

"It is all right, Mara. We will keep you safe," she hears him say in her head. She knows it is Danti, but at the same time, she also knows he had said that to her once, as well. A frazzled edge of a memory tickles her consciousness as she grips his shirt tightly. She buries her face against his shirt, her breathing ragged.

She can trust this man; she knows she can.

As soon as he is out of the churning dark skies and back underneath the lazy colorful swirls, he reaches forward with his fingers and finds one of the many tiny rips in the membrane leading to Blazhreia. He focuses, trying to find one emanating the signature reading of Cerlail Academy.

There.

He grabs the tiny tear, easing open the portal by coating the edges with his Source. Mara hisses in pain from the jostling motion, and he is momentarily distracted as her fingers dig into his shoulder.

The portal trembles.

Bracing himself, he steps through with Mara before it can collapse, ready for resistance from the realm that is trying to imprison her. He passes through with surprising ease, staggering onto the teal grey stone. He stares at the familiar chamber, horror sinking in.

Teal pillars border the oversized chamber that can hold an army. Flickering, smokeless flames hover within metal-banded torches anchored to each pillar and along the walls; the ceiling above is too high for the light to illuminate the arched dome above them. An enormous gate stands ominously on the other side of the chamber, intricate carvings decorating the exterior and depicting the creation myth of the Chamber itself.

"Elethanos…" he breathes, horrified as Mara's fingers loosen on his shirt, her consciousness fading.

A tug on Darion's sleeve turns his gaze down to see a seven-year-old, auburn-haired girl with brilliant emerald eyes staring intently at Mara.

"*She is not dead. Why is she here?*" Even though the girl's lips do not move, her voice echoes throughout the chamber.

"Elethanos, get a couch and a medical kit together for me," Darion quickly orders the girl, stepping around her. "While you are at it, analyze the portal I came through. It was rerouted from Cerlail Academy, and I want to know who or what caused that."

"*Of course.*" The little girl touches the edge of the portal, closing her eyes. An archway forms around the portal, anchoring it in place as the embodiment of the Chamber itself examines the teleportation hole.

A bright red blob pushes out of the floor, morphing into a couch. A round end table pops up next to it, and the box on top bounces a little from the sudden halt of the morphed unit.

Darion quickly sets Mara on the couch, noticing her pale complexion. "Alert Mornak of my arrival, and tell him to – "

"*I already informed him. He is grabbing the box now.*"

"Thank you." He kneels next to the couch and pushes Mara's hair back. A cold sweat dampens her brow. Her eyes are out of focus as she struggles to look at him. "Hang in there, Mara."

He opens the box next to him, pulling on a pair of

sterile gloves before rolling up her shirt and examining the wound. Before he even needs to ask, a globe of white light pops out of the ground, rising into a floor lamp. He grits his teeth in recognition of the sword wound, already knowing it is too deep for him to heal on his own.

Creeeaaak.

Standing up, he whirls around and faces the monstrous gate creaking open. The thin slit widens, revealing the top of the ceiling hundreds of yards above him. Even more carvings depict the abstract lore surrounding the chamber – one that even the eons-old Alkinian species has not been able to fully decipher.

The flames on the torches twist and dance, turning blue-grey.

"She is not dead yet, Elethavi!" Darion shouts at the Death Gate. "What are you doing?"

The huge gate continues to creak open. However, the scene on the other side is not one of the landscapes or rooms Darion has seen; it is a swirling, churning blue-grey mass.

The rebirth vortex.

He exhales in relief. Glancing over his shoulder, he eyes Mara; she is still stable. Glimpsing the anchored portal at the other side of the room, though, he frowns. "Elethavi, shift the anchor out of the way for the – "

Something slams through him, leaving his entire body tingling. He coughs, staggering forward as he glimpses the soul rocket into Mara.

"Carc'ra," Darion hisses as the huge gate groans shut. The flames on the torches return to their flickering yellow color. Kneeling next to Mara once again, he cups her face and peers into her mind, searching for the ejected soul so he can extract it and toss it into whatever realm Elethanos had locked the entrance onto for the reborn entity.

A silvery barrier blocks him, stopping his search.

"*Let me pass,*" he demands, directly addressing the

Essence. *"That spirit does not belong here; it needs its own body."*

"This is not – a rebirth." Two fragmented bits of conversations are stitched together to form the disjointed sentence. *"Please wait – a little longer."* He bites back his surprise at the surprisingly curt tone as he withdraws.

He picks up the blood-clotting salve and quickly smears it onto Mara's side before carefully rubbing it in. She doesn't react when he slides his hand around to her back, applying more to the other side. Without looking up, he knows his wiry-framed assistant is standing at the entrance to the hall that leads to his living quarters.

"M-my 'Lord," Mornak stammers, nervously shifting a metal box in his hands. The muffled *clack* of stones echoes oddly in the Chamber. He is dressed in his usual dark brown leather knee-length jacket and black pants, both custom-made in Garnesh. He pushes his mousy brown hair back to expose his rounded ears.

"Summon the Life'Lord, Creation'Lord, and Time'Lord. Make sure to snap the stones in that order." Darion rubs a numbing salve over Mara's side in preparation to stitch the wounds closed. The red-haired little girl skips over and picks up a clear string and a needle, threading it together before handing it to him. "Thank you, Elethanos. Please prepare to provide more extensive medical devices for Lilly."

"Of course."

Mornak shoves his glasses more firmly onto his face before snapping the appropriate stones in the designated order. Walking over, he pushes back his hair from his weathered face and stares at the injured girl in morbid curiosity. "Is she going to die?"

"Not if I can help it," Darion growls, finishing with the stitches on the front wound. He glances at the humanoid form of Elethanos hiding behind Mornak's legs. "Elehanos, help me roll her over so I can stitch the back."

She nods. The couch's cushions churn; it carefully

cradles Mara as it rolls her onto her stomach before settling back down into a normal couch. Darion finishes the rudimentary stitches, once again wishing he could master the healing art like Lilly.

Expelling his breath, he takes the proffered damp towel from Elethanos, giving the little girl a tight smile. "Thank you for your assistance, Elethanos. What did you find out about the portal?"

"*Carni's Will manipulated it*," she explains. Mornak frowns, eyeing the anchored teleportation hole off to the side. "*It seems as though Elethavi had alerted Carni's Will of the upcoming vortex, and Carni's Will manipulated the destination of the teleportation hole to bring the Essence's Vessel here for the ejection.*"

"That pesky Will is getting in our way at every turn," Darion grumbles. "You may release the anchor."

"*Of course.*" The arch around the portal collapses inward, caving the entire unit until the swirling mass of warped air is no longer there. The rubble from the archway sinks into the ground, melding back into the malleable Chamber.

Another portal opens, and Lilly steps through. She immediately walks over to Darion and the couch. "What's wrong, Darion? You never – " She gasps as soon as she peers over the couch and sees Mara. "What happened to her?"

"A dream-eater found her," he informs her. "Mara did not have any memories, so I am guessing it tapped into the Essence's fears. It escaped before I had caught up to her."

"This girl is always getting the worst injuries possible," Lilly murmurs as she examines the wound. "It looks to be a sword wound… Shaniel would know the type based off the cut."

"Mornak, pull the Common'Lord's stone," Darion orders. He winces as he remembers that the laig'hius had given his reki to Mara. "Never mind; let us just hope he will come through with Aeserast."

Before he is even finished speaking, Shaniel stumbles through a sloppily-made portal with Aeserast in tow. "I apologize, Shaniel…" the Creation'Lord murmurs, looking exhausted.

"Quit saying that already," Shaniel growls. "I'm more frustrated at what you did than anything else. Did you find her, Darion?"

Darion's eyes flick back and forth between the two of them, thinking it a bit backward with who is supporting the other. *At least they are both all right.* "Shaniel, I need you to inspect this wound and tell me what kind of weapon made it. Aeserast, the rebirth vortex formed shortly after I arrived, and an entity shot into Mara. Are you able to identify it?"

Lilly's hands jerk away from Mara. She gives Darion a look that could snuff out the eternal flames of Elethanos. "And when were you going to tell *me* about that?"

Shaniel helps Aeserast to the couch. A chair quickly bubbles out of the ground, and he sits down with a huff. "Thank you, Elethanos," he says appreciatively as he touches Mara's temple.

Shaniel leans over Mara's stomach, frowning as he examines the wound. "This was made by a salev'i." He glances at Darion in alarm. "Don't tell me a dream-eater got a hold of her."

"I am afraid one did," he murmurs softly.

"Shaniel, your Source signature changed again. Please hold still as I update the logs."

Shaniel slaps his palm against his forehead, shooting an exasperated look at Aeserast. "Sera, sera. While you're at it, can you make Aeserast's tea? He needs about a gallon of it."

Aeserast shakes his head, withdrawing his hand. "I will be fine, Shaniel. As for Mara, the Essence is shielding me from seeing anything; it is even hiding the extra presence."

Darion glances back and forth between Shaniel and Aeserast, wanting to ask exactly what happened. Shaniel's Source is different, and Aeserast seems to be completely depleted.

Just then, Timian appears in the Chamber. He rushes over, concern etched on his face as he catches sight of Lilly and Mara. "What happened?" he demands, his voice curt.

"Mara was stabbed by a dream-eater," Darion informs him. Before he can finish, Lilly suddenly pulls back from her examination to stare at the wound. "Why did you stop? The internal wounds are – "

"She is healing herself," Lilly whispers in shock. "Look."

A brilliant lapis blue Source overlaps the rudimentary stitches, reinforcing them while creating its own stitches. Within seconds, the wound is sealed shut.

"Impossible," Darion breathes, his breath hitching at the sight.

He knows of only one person from Eleth who has that particular Source color.

Chapter 3
Blue Flame

Her father gives her a brilliant smile as she clenches the woman's shirt. "Father, is Lyra really living with us?"

"Yes," he says, chuckling. "Lyra, would you mind staying with her for a bit? I must speak with Akalius again."

"Of course not, Your Majesty." The laig'hius kneels next to the little girl. Her gold wolf eyes glint as her long blonde hair shifts over her shoulder, unbound. "What would you like to do now, Your Highness?"

"Teach me how to do that thing you do!" she thrusts her fist out, a big grin on her face. "You know, like this!"

Lyra laughs, patting her head. "Do you mean fight? I do not believe that is befitting of someone of your age and status, Your Highness. Just allow me to protect you."

She grins, happy. "Does that mean we will also be able to play a lot?"

Lyra smiles. "If that is what you desire, Your Highness, then yes."

"Yay!"

———◆———

Mara doesn't know whose life is flashing through her mind, but she knows it isn't her own. Still lingering on the edge of the last dream, she barely registers an unfamiliar voice inside her mind.

"Whatever have these uncouth creations done to you?! By the flow, this is terrible. Allow me fix that memory impairment on you. Poor thing; no wonder your mind was a mess when I came in."

With just a touch by this new presence, something shatters in her mind.

Memories flood her consciousness, overwhelming both

her and the new presence. Mara quickly recognizes them, though: they are hers and the Essence's memories that she had remembered up to that point. She groans, clutching her now pounding head.

"Mara." A light touch has her staring into two sleepy jade green eyes. "Are you all right?"

"Darion?" Her eyes flit around, taking in her surroundings. She is on top of a dark blue comforter on a king-sized bed. Four posts hold up a sheer black drape wrapped around the horizontal bars of the canopy bed. Darion is slumped on a chair next to her, his hair unkempt as if he had fallen asleep. "Where are we?"

"Elethanos." She frowns at the Xharos name for the Death Chamber. "Do you... remember anything?"

She rubs her temple, wishing the pounding headache would abate. "Yeah, somewhat. Why are we here?"

"I was going to take you to Cerlail Academy, but Carni's Will – the sentient portion of the realm – interfered and manipulated my portal." He hesitates for a moment before asking, "How much do you remember? Do you... feel different?"

She closes her eyes for a moment, relaxing her head on the pillows. "Honestly, I probably remember more than I should." She watches him for a brief moment before admitting, "I seriously thought I had killed Lunesh. She isn't really... dead, is she? Will she remember me if I see her again?"

Darion nods. "The official name for her and those like her is 'Carni's Creation.' The realm created her based off the desires of those who wandered on Carni's Path, and she is virtually indestructible; she herself is based off the image of Rinali Alamir when she had been younger. She would have been reduced to Carni Matter before coalescing again inside of Carn'ien."

She takes a deep breath. "I met an older version of her before you showed up. Was that... also her?"

"No. It was a dream-eater," Darion informs her. "It takes your worst fears and attacks you with them to break you down. They are from the Treavaun, which are the twisted, warped portions of Carni."

Her fingers brush over her shirt. "The wound was so real…"

"It *is* real. You were stabbed, Mara." Mara pales, and he reaches across to touch her hand. "Just rest – "

A lapis blue Source sparks between them, almost as if trying to slap away his hand. He jerks back as Mara's eyes widen.

"Th-that wasn't me!" she exclaims, quickly examining her mind. "There's – "

She is cut off as the blue presence unexpectedly yanks her consciousness to the back of her own mind. Mara wrestles with the presence, trying to regain control of her body.

Darion watches her ease upright, touching her side lightly. "What were you about to say, Mara?"

"*Darion, that isn't me!*" Mara screams, but it doesn't reach him.

Blue-ringed gold eyes blink in surprise at him. "Darion, I do believe you are getting a bit rusty with your Source identification." She speaks in a smooth, authoritative tone.

Darion stills, noticing the change in her voice and the odd way she now holds herself. "Who are you?"

Relief courses through Mara. He knows something else is controlling her body. Now he can –

"Oh, the *tragedy*," she breathes, her hand covering her mouth in a gasp as a playful smile lights her lips. "My own former guard does not even recognize me… that is truly a shame."

Darion straightens. His lips part in shock as he slowly exhales a single phrase. "Your Highness."

Mara's thoughts come to a screeching halt. Darion knows the person using her body. Even worse, he had called her *Your Highness*, a title reserved only for someone who is an Ecalain.

She smiles sweetly at him. "It has been a long time," she murmurs in Old Xharos.

He averts his gaze, closing his eyes briefly in pain. "I apologize, Your Highness."

Mara watches the interaction from the back of her own mind, momentarily too stunned to vie for control. Who is she? Is she the one Darion had guarded before he had become a Highlord? A spike of jealousy shoots through her. Based off his expression, there is more between them than he had originally let on. What kind of relationship had they *really* been in?

She chuckles, noticing Mara's churning thoughts. "It seems as though Mara has a lot of questions now." Her smile softens. "I already knew, Darion. I could sense her power on you."

Darion sighs, looking slightly uncomfortable. "I made a vow to you, though. I – "

Her sharp voice cuts him off. "And I died. I have told you repeatedly to forget that promise, Darion. It is invalid now. Move on." She eases her legs over the side of the bed, resting a hand on his shoulder for balance. She examines the hand with a strange curiosity. "I thought having a body would have been odd. Six thousand years, Darion, and I feel as comfortable as if I have not been trapped in Eleth."

He stares at her for a moment before whispering, "What will happen to Mara?"

If Mara could, she would grit her teeth and snap that *nothing* would happen to her; that it is this person who has something to worry about.

"I do not know," she answers, her voice as soft as Darion's. "However, I would like your assistance to see – "

"*Ohhh, no, you don't,*" Mara snaps, her temper flaring. Her Source wraps around the pretty lapis blue, restraining the ocean of power. "*This is* my *body.*"

40

Mara's hand constricts on Darion's shoulder as her teeth grind together. She exhales slowly, silvery sparks flitting about the black tendrils curling around her.

"M-Mara?" Darion stammers, his eyes wide at the sudden flux of power.

"I'm glad you recognize *me*," she snaps, standing up. She shifts her weight a bit, feeling heavier. "I only have enough room in my head for one; two if you count the Essence! I refuse to put up with another – "

The lapis blue power shoves Mara aside a second time. Irritated, she grumbles to Darion, "This fletchling is oddly stubborn; I do not understand the choices of my other half."

The Essence, which had remained out of the way until now, sparks defensively. "*Mara – was born – Ecalain. I found the perfect – vessel.*"

"Born Ecalain? How surprising…"

Mara has a nagging feeling she knows who this is, but she doesn't want to admit it. "*Traitor,*" she snaps at the Essence. "*I thought you would be helping me.*"

It remains silent.

Darion sighs, already seeing an issue with the two women. "Much has changed since you had – "

"Of course it has." She steps toward the door, wincing as her side pulls painfully. She covers it with her hand, gasping. "What… happened?"

An image of a dark-haired girl with reddish-purple eyes holding Gameleth flashes through Mara's mind. Mara recognizes the older version of Lunesh, and it takes her a moment to remember what Darion had said. That memory is of a possessed Rinali.

Ignoring her own questions, she takes advantage of the moment and shoves the distracted woman out of control. She takes a deep, steadying breath, managing the pain easily enough.

"*You stay there and let* me *handle my body,*" she orders the lapis blue ocean, keeping a tighter hold on her mind now that she knows this… spirit can control her much like the Dark Warrior possesses bodies.

"Mara was stabbed by a dream-eater. It most likely pulled the fear from the Essence, though, and not her," Darion finishes explaining, not even noticing the switch this time as Mara keeps her Source from sparking in irritation. "The Life'Lord, Lilly, has been monitoring her vitals for the past few hours."

"Darion, give me a moment alone, please."

He frowns. "I do not believe that is wise. Mara's wound – "

"I *know* my wound needs treatment, but Darion, this pesky woman is taking control of my body without per-mission." She glares at him. "I don't care who she is; she needs to learn her place."

"*How dare you speak of me like that!*"

Darion sighs, not hearing the intruder's response. "I will let you… get acquainted." Pausing at the door, he glances at her. "I will be outside. If you need me, just call."

Mara nods as the door clicks closed. For once, the stranger is shocked enough that she does not hound Mara or try to fight for control.

Sitting down on the edge of the bed, Mara speaks directly to the owner of the blue Source. "*Listen up; this is my body, so we play by* my *rules. I remain in control, you stay in the back. The only way you're allowed to control my body is if I allow it.*"

She *feels* the discontent rolling off of her. "*You do realize you are putting yourself in danger, correct? I myself have died of a wound exactly like that one. You should have the Jethel'Launa look at it.*"

Mara ignores the archaic Xharos title for the Life'Lord for the time being. "*Not until we're finished. Who are you?*"

Indignation rolls off of her. "*Have you truly not figured it out?*" At Mara's lack of an answer, she huffs, "*I am*

Duir'raz'ne Eliara Alamir, daughter of Shokain and Rhea Alamir. You?" This last part has a tinge of arrogance, as if she is expecting Mara to grovel now that she knows the ancient spirit's identity.

Mara takes a breath, settling her own nerves. Her suspicions had been correct; it is the oldest of the four Ancient Sisters inside her head right now. However, the name of Eliara's father surprises her. *"Mara Danarko, voi'duir'stra of Quasala and goindun of the Northern Dragon Clan."* After a moment of hesitation, she adds, *"Daughter of Shokain and Ezra Danarko."*

A tremor of fear and shock radiates through Mara. *"Danarko?"* the duir'raz'ne repeats, uneasy.

Mara frowns. *First the Da'ruha, now her…* "What's wrong with my last name?" she murmurs out loud to herself, confused.

"It was a member of the Danarko family that betrayed my mother and destroyed our family."

Mara goes silent at this, not knowing what to say. How do you give your condolences to someone when your family name is the same as someone who had demolished everything you had loved? *"I… didn't know."*

"I am certain they must be different," Eliara interrupts, pushing against Mara's mind in an attempt to gain control. *"I need to speak with Darion again."*

"No." Mara shoves her back. The Essence helps her keep the ancient duir'ne from taking over this time. *"This is my body; you will follow by my rules."*

"But I am the duir'raz'ne!"

"And you've been dead for six thousand years," Mara snarls out loud, unable to keep the words in. "Times have changed, princess."

Darion knocks on the door before peering in. "Is everything all right, Mara?"

She gives him a tight-lipped smile, momentarily distracted. "Just fine." She feels a sudden push at her mind, though she expects it this time. The Essence rears up, forming a smooth wall and blocking Eliara from taking over again. *"If you had tried that a year ago, I might have actually fallen for it. Your lovely sister taught me how to keep people from controlling me, though. If you keep trying that move, I'll stop being nice."*

"Kyrina is alive?" Eliara asks, excited. *"This is wonderful! Perhaps we can — "*

"Wrong sister. Was sarcasm not invented six thousand years ago?"

Eliara goes quiet, shamed by her own ignorance. Mara welcomes the silence; she had only recently gotten used to the Essence's chatter. Now she has another voice to deal with.

Darion watches her in concern, catching the eye-roll. "Is everything going well between the two of you?"

"What do you think?" she demands. "A six thousand year-old princess thinks she has the right to show up and take over my body."

"Ah…"

The conversation he had with Eliara when she had first woken up comes back. She narrows her eyes at him. "Were you two — "

"Darion, is she awake?" a familiar voice demands outside.

He turns to Lilly. "Yes; we figured out who came through the rebirth vortex," he explains before opening the door to allow Aeserast and Lilly in. "Though it is a bit disconcerting."

Lilly stares hard at Mara. "Who is in control?"

Mara snorts. Eliara is appalled at the sound. "Me, of course. You think I'd let some ghost possess me?"

Aeserast gives her a relieved yet tired smile. "I am glad you are all right, Mara. We were concerned."

Hope sparks within Mara. "Do you think you could remove this extra voice in my head, Aeserast? She's really annoying. Her Source is the blue one."

"*Show respect! I am higher ranked than you!*"

"*Oh, really? Twyla, another Ecalain, refers to me like I'm the same rank as her — and she's duir'ne.*"

"What's happening?" Aeserast asks warily as he sits in the chair next to the bed.

Mara smirks at the grumbling duir'raz'ne. "Oh, getting to know Eliara."

Darion exhales in exasperation as Aeserast's and Lilly's mouths drop open in shock. "The duir'raz'ne?" Lilly breathes. "But… how?"

"Don't ask me." Mara shrugs. "However, there is one thing I gotta say about her: I thought she would be nicer. This is a bit of a disappointment."

"*You uncouth fletchling,*" Eliara mutters. "*You are the one who shoved me to the back of your mind.*"

"You *are the one who is trying to take over like the Da'ruha; it doesn't take rocket science to figure out why I'm not too fond of people trying to invade my head.*"

"*That… was not my intention.*"

Aeserast watches Mara scowl at her clenched hands. "Mara, you should at least try to get along with her," he says gently. "At least until we figure out what is going on."

She meets his eyes briefly before unclenching her fists. "You're right."

He reaches forward and touches her temple. Another splitting pain shoots through her head as she feels him on the outskirts of her mind. He pulls back quickly. "Luckily, the extra presence is not straining your mind. However, if both of you keep fighting, it *will* cause damage."

Mara nods, not saying anything else as he stands up. Seeing him move slowly, she frowns in concern. "Are you all right, Aeserast?"

He gives her a tight-lipped smile. "I will be; I just overexerted myself while we were looking for you."

Darion accompanies Aeserast out of the room, assisting the Creation'Lord down the hallway. Lilly sighs as she sits down.

"What's really wrong with him, Lilly?" Mara asks, recognizing the disapproving look the Alkinian has – after all, she usually makes that face at *her*.

Lilly shakes her head. "He was not lying when he said he had overexerted himself. You know of his Respoura blood, yes?"

Mara nods. Respoura is a type of fey that requires a constant circulation of Source throughout their system in order to survive; if they do not do this, their bodies will shut down, and they will die. His sister had taken some of Mara's own extraneous Source to sustain herself and keep her fey blood from killing her.

"He has the same ability to withdraw Source as Aihalia," Lilly explains as she presses on Mara's shoulder to have her lie down. "However, because he doesn't need to pull in Source from external locations in order to live, he does not know how to… moderate it, you could say."

"What happens when he uses it?" Mara asks as Lilly rolls up her shirt to examine the wound. When the Highlord doesn't respond, Mara wraps her hand around the elf's wrist. "Lilly, tell me what happens."

"He pulls out everything," she whispers, not looking at Mara. "He had done that to Shaniel in their search for you."

Alarmed, Mara tries to sit upright, but Lilly keeps her prone. "Where's Shaniel? Is he okay?" Mara demands.

"He is fine," Lilly reassures her. "In fact, he is doing better than Aeserast; when the Creation'Lord had finished, he had put the remainder of his power and Shaniel's back into him. He is doing well."

Mara thumps her head against the pillow, glaring at the ceiling. "And they call *me* an idiot. Where is he now?"

"He returned to the Academy with Timian to deliver the report on the situation." Lilly frowns as she examines the wound. "What have you done since waking up?"

"Um." She racks her brain. "Eliara tried leaving the room, but I took back over and sat down. After that, you came in."

"How odd…" Her hand presses firmly against Mara's side, and the mage winces. "Hold perfectly still."

Tiny pricks take Mara off guard, but it is the painful jab like a needle into her side that startles a grunt of pain out of her. "Wh-what are you doing?!"

"Your body absorbed the stitches too fast. I'm reapplying them before your wounds reopen even more than they have."

Mara's breath comes short and fast as the sensation continues; she grows dizzy, unable to focus on the blonde woman above her. At this point, she is unable to stop Eliara from taking over.

"Done," Lilly says, withdrawing her hand. Red stains her fingers. She pulls out a cloth from her pocket and wipes away the blood as she examines Mara's face. "My apologies; I forgot you did not like that sensation."

"It is all right." She closes her eyes, taking a deep breath. She smiles weakly at Lilly. "I am afraid holding together the wound via Source-stitching will not work, though. The fear the dream-eater had reenacted was strong; it had even shaken me when I realized what it was."

Lilly freezes, staring at Mara's blue-ringed gold eyes. "You… are not Mara," she whispers in realization.

"No, I am not." Her eyes slide closed. "Mara passed out during the stitching; she is fine, though. I think I shall rest a bit myself…"

Lilly watches Mara breath deeply, fast asleep now. "It truly is disconcerting," she murmurs, her eyes creasing in worry. "I wonder how Ezra will deal with this…"

Shaking off her concern for her friend, Lilly quietly makes her way to the door. A whimper from the bed has her turning around, though, just as Mara's face scrunches in pain. Her hand covers the wound. "Why?" she breathes, already in the throws of a nightmare.

Lilly's eyes widen as she realizes why the wound keeps reopening. Sure, dream-eater inflicted wounds last for as long as the recipient remains in that stupor, but Mara had been asleep after Lilly had finished stitching it closed.

But *Eliara* hadn't.

"No," she breathes, sitting back down and examining the wound yet again. The stitching is being chipped away by the blue and silver Sources. The Essence and Eliara, most likely — both of which have memories of similar wounds.

"Mara, wake up," Lilly urges, shaking the mage's shoulder. Realizing she is addressing the wrong person, she strokes back Mara's hair and prepares herself for the next words. "Your Highness, you need to wake up. You are causing the stitches to tear apart."

The girl's eyes open, revealing two beautiful gold eyes. "Lilly?" Mara mumbles, hissing as her side twinges. "Wh-why does it still hurt? Didn't you fix it?"

"I did, but because the duir'raz'ne and the Essence have each encountered wounds like this, it tears open the stitches anytime they dwell on the wound," she explains quickly, examining the wound yet again. Sure enough, the stitching is nearly completely gone. "I need you to stay awake for this."

Mara takes a deep breath, suddenly wide awake. "Eliara, too?"

A sense of foreboding creeps through the chief medical advisor. "She is still asleep?" Mara nods. "Wake her up. Now."

Mara closes her eyes, mentally prodding the sphere of lapis blue. *"Rise and shine, Your Highness."*

"Why is it you refer to me appropriately when I most desire quiet?"

"Quit dreaming. We need you awake."

Pain shoots through Mara's side as the Life'Lord's hands press directly onto the wound. A choked cry of pain slips past her lips as her insides burn. Mara can't even ask why she isn't stitching it closed anymore; she squeezes her eyes shut, biting the base of her thumb to help distract her. She barely even feels her teeth digging into her skin.

"I apologize," Lilly whispers. "Just a little longer."

"Hurry," Mara forces out, biting her hand harder to keep from screaming. Within seconds, she tastes the coppery twang of blood.

She feels someone stroke her hair back, dabbing at her damp brow. The pain abates, and she focuses on the voices above her. "…had reopened, and stitches weren't working. I had to cauterize the wounds."

"You should have called for me. I would have helped," Darion reprimands the Life'Lord lightly, his hand still on Mara's forehead. "Mara, are you all right?"

She unclamps her jaw from around her hand, the pain of that momentarily distracting her. "Yeah," she rasps. She feels the pain in her hand abate as Lilly heals it easily enough, reconnecting the damaged tissue. Staring at her now-healed hand, she frowns. "Why can't you do this to the wound?"

"Dream-eater inflicted wounds work much like a neivir wound, but the thing still cutting into you is the memory itself." She turns to Darion. "She *needs* to be taken back to the material realms, Darion."

He shakes his head. "We cannot do that until we are certain she is not still eiv'ra."

"She has her *memory*, though! That should be good enough, right?"

"Not always." Aeserast stands at the entrance to the room, his face grim. "The worst I have seen is when they know *who* they are, but they do not have any aspirations. We cannot be certain until Mara herself can tell us what it is she needs in order to leave Carni."

Mara stares at her guardian in bafflement. "We're in Elethanos, though. That's not in Carni, is it?"

"It is to an extent," Darion explains softly. "It is a common misunderstanding."

Mara huffs. "Weird. I'm fine, though; I feel a lot better than earlier."

Aeserast gazes at her, his eyes devoid of emotion. For a chilling moment, Mara is reminded of the dream-eater who had posed itself as Lunesh. "Can you tell me why you came into Carni, then? Why you wandered Carni's Path for two solid days before we found you? Did you find the answers you sought?"

"I…" Her mind blanks. Why *had* she been walking through Carni? *That's right… I wanted answers. I thought Carni was causing my memory lapses.* Frowning, she realizes she hasn't had a single recollection since being there – but then again, she had completely forgotten who she was until Eliara had broken the memory impairment.

If Carni had originally been making the memories worse, then why did she forget everything when she went there? Wouldn't the memories have progressively over-whelmed her?

"Just as I feared." Aeserast looks at Lilly again. "She is not leaving Carni until she figures out who she is. Taking her back into the physical realms could leave her permanently eiv'ra."

Lilly crosses her arms, giving Aeserast a disbelieving look. "Carni Wanderers are all so strange," she grumbles, glancing at Mara. "I want you to stay awake for a few hours; that should help the wound heal enough so it doesn't reopen again while you sleep."

Mara nods, still confused. A strange breeze enters the room, sending a chill down her spine.

Darion frowns, standing up straight and tilting his head toward the door. "Elethanos, why did you not alert me of Elethavi opening again?"

"*Shaniel is conversing with him,*" a young girl's voice explains, the sound echoing through the room. There is a thrum of happiness in the tone.

Darion sighs. "I see." He glances between Lilly and Mara. "Is she healed enough to walk?"

Lilly nods. "As long as she doesn't move too abruptly."

"I will help her to the Chamber, then; go on without us."

Lilly tilts her head out of curiosity as Aeserast gives a knowing smile. The Dream'Lord already suspects who is in the Chamber.

After they leave, Darion holds his hand out to Mara. "Come; I am sure you are tired of these four walls."

"Just… a bit," she admits, smiling ruefully as she squeezes his fingers tightly. She feels Eliara's discomfort in the back of her mind.

"Elethanos, please take the special bottle on the back right shelf of the cellar into the Chamber. You know the one," Darion calls out seemingly to no one.

"*Of course.*" Again, the little girl's voice echoes around them. "*How many glasses?*"

He glances at Mara. "Five for now." He tucks her hand against his side. "Do you have a question, Mara?"

Taking a deep breath, she asks, "What does being eiv'ra mean?"

They step into the hall. "Eiv'ra means 'lost' in Xharos. It is typically an individual with no purpose in life wandering the Corridor Realm. Those who have studied Carni know that once someone enters the Corridor Realm, they must have a clear goal in mind else they will become eiv'ra. If they become eiv'ra, they must discover what it is they desire most of all; if not, then they will forever wonder what their purpose in life is." He pauses for a moment, not looking at her. "Many who become eiv'ra do not return to the material realms such as Blazhreia or Alkina. If they do, they live aimless lives, never sure of their purpose in existing."

"Huh." Mara doesn't know what to make of that. "What makes it different than regular uncertainty?"

He raises an eyebrow. "With normal uncertainty, someone can eventually find what they love if they try different things. When they become eiv'ra, the uncertainty becomes a part of them; they will doubt their very existence. They will never be able to truly enjoy anything ever again."

"Oh." She bites her lip. "Am I really... eiv'ra?"

"Can you tell me what you want most of all, no matter the consequences?"

Mara doesn't respond. *What... what do I want? I went to Carni wanting answers, but it seems as if I'm just asking even more questions than before.*

"We can converse on this later; I have a guest from Eleth who I believe you would be interested in meeting."

Snapped out of her melancholic reverie, Mara frowns at him. "From Eleth? They can't come out of the Death Realm, can they?"

"To a certain extent, yes," Darion explains as they pass by a modern-looking kitchen that looks out of place against the teal stone walls. "I have had many from Eleth visit me within the Chamber, though that is as far as they can go. Elethanos brands those from Eleth with a sigil so that if they do escape, it will still be relatively easy for me to find them."

"What about the Da'ruha?" Mara asks as they approach an open door on the other side of a large common area. She senses Eliara's curiosity on the topic.

Darion looks uncomfortable at this. "She seems to know where the anti-tracking areas are and flees there first. Unfortunately, I have to be inside of Elethanos to be able to track her, so when I get a solid lock from here, she may not still be at the location once I arrive."

"That's no fun." They step into the large chamber, and Mara's eyes immediately go to the ceiling where the light from the open gate dimly illuminates the arched dome for the briefest of moments. The monolithic gate creaks closed, shutting off the light to the intricately carved murals on the ceiling. Darkness creeps down the teal grey pillars, trying to encroach on the blue-grey flickering flames lighting the room. *This place is huge*, she thinks, amazed.

Lilly huffs, demanding in a curt tone, "You named your daughter Mara instead of Ariela like you had previously agreed upon. Why?"

"I, uh… it was going to be Riley! But Ezra said that's not a fitting name for a girl, so…"

"Mara! Look who's here to visit!" Shaniel calls out as Mara shifts her gaze ahead of them. As soon as she sees the hazelnut-haired man, she freezes.

It is her father.

Chapter 4
Eleth's Visitors

Shaniel continues, not noticing Mara's stupefied state. "She's pretty great at Siege. She even taught *me* a few tricks."

Shokain scratches the back of his head self-consciously as he grins at her. "Is that so? I'm glad you still play." His smile falters at her stunned expression. "H-hey, now. It's just me."

"Daddy?" she breathes, her hand covering her mouth as her vision blurs. She senses Eliara's shock at seeing Shokain and is briefly distracted; why is the ancient princess shocked at seeing Mara's father?

Shokain gives her a lopsided grin. "Hey, baby girl. You're all grown up now, aren't you? I've heard you're training under – whoa, easy there!"

She hugs him tightly, disguising her tears against his slate grey tunic. He smells like the cold, damp stone of the Chamber. He rubs her back, and she feels his rumbling laugh. She feels like a little girl again, back when he used to tell her stories about the spectacular engineer.

"I missed you, Mara," he murmurs, resting his head against hers. He sways back and forth, rocking her the best he can.

"I-I missed you, too," she chokes out, her fingers curling in the shirt. "I still – I still have that book you made us. The one with all those stories."

"Truly? That's good." He pats her hair, beaming at her as he sits on the couch. "Look at you! You're turning into a fine young lady, aren't you? Are you still training hard?"

She nods, quickly swiping away her tears as she laughs. "I think Darion is the only one I can't beat yet." Hope sparks within her. "Have you... have you seen..."

He sobers. "Darion told me. I'm searching for him every day in Eleth, but it is hard; that place is as big as all the *realms* combined. It is a wonder I find an Eleth gateway so frequently in my travels." He takes her hand, patting it firmly. "Don't worry, though! As soon as I find him, I'll have Darion bring you here. Come to think of it, how is your mother doing? I haven't seen her in a long time."

Darion rubs the back of his neck self-consciously, turning away. Mara nearly laughs at him as she tells her father, "She's doing great, though she's always busy. She works under Lilly at Cerlail Academy."

"That's good, at least." Shokain takes a deep breath, blinking as he stares at Mara a little harder. Suddenly, he turns to Darion in alarm. "Darion, Mara isn't the only one in her body. I think something is possessing her."

Everyone stares at him in dumbfounded shock.

"Um…" Mara starts, a bit self-conscious. "I'm guessing you don't know. I'm the Essence's vessel."

He narrows his eyes at her. "I knew about that; Darion told me a few months ago. It explains why you had been born with two Sources." He stares into her eyes – no, he stares *through* her. "However, it doesn't explain what the *blue* Source is."

Mara fiddles with the edge of her shirt. "That would be Eliara, the duir'raz'ne. She kinda… launched into me when I got here."

Shokain stares at her before guffawing loudly. "Impossible!" he exclaims. However, when her expression doesn't change, his laughter dies. "Wait… you're serious?!" He glances at Darion. "How could you let such a large soul like an Ancient Sister launch into my daughter?"

"Shokain, please settle down," Darion says, glancing at Mara. "I understand your concerns, but Mara *is* the Essence's Vessel, which means she was already containing part of the duir'raz'ne within her."

"That doesn't mean I can't be concerned," Shokain

grumbles, his eyes slanting to the ground.

Eliara stirs at this motion. *"He is your father?"* she asks almost rhetorically, unnerved.

Her question surprises Mara; she thought their conversation would have made it obvious. *"Yeah. Why?"*

"It is nothing. I merely wanted confirmation." She recedes into the depths of Mara's mind, content as an observer for the time being.

Mara frowns; the duir'raz'ne's actions are getting odder and odder by the minute.

Shokain examines his daughter's face closely. "Is something the matter, Mara?"

"No, not really. Eliara just asked a random question," Mara passes it off, still trying to figure out why the ancient duir'ne is acting so strangely. *"We need to talk about this later; I'm getting tired of you reacting over obvious things like this."*

"I agree. Darion also has some explaining to do."

Surprised, Mara's eyes flick to Darion. He is watching her, a calculating look on his face. She turns back to her father. "So… what's Eleth like, Dad?"

Shokain looks crestfallen. "'Dad'? What happened to 'Daddy'? Are you getting too old for that?"

The others chuckle as Mara plasters a smile on her face. "N-no, it's just – I'm almost seventeen, Dad."

"But you called me Daddy when you came in here…" he mumbles almost to himself. "What is this, only emotional moments will make you call me that now?"

"Da-Daddy, please," Mara begs, her cheeks flushing a bright red.

He smirks at her, patting her head. "I do not mind, Mara. I'm just messing with you."

She rubs her temple, thoroughly embarrassed now. She can't be mad at him, though. After all, he hasn't seen her for nearly six years. "Um, Dad… I have a question."

"Fire away, baby girl."

"Would you… would you play a game of Siege with

me?"

His smile is blindingly brilliant. "Of course I will. Darion, could you grab the board and playing pieces?"

Darion gives the man a gentle smile. "Of course, old friend."

Within minutes, Mara is sitting across from her father, staring at the most complex city layout she has seen as of yet for this game. Her brows scrunch together as she hesitantly asks, "Are the rules... the same?"

"Oh!" Shokain knocks his fist against his palm. "That's right; you know the old version. Darion and I hammered out the game mechanics; we added two more pieces to the board, as well as a few extra rules."

Darion sits next to Mara in a newly-materialized chair. He reaches across her to pick up the mage with the red spot on its chest. "Do you remember when I told you about the red mages before your flight to Thalak?"

"Yeah." Mara swallows the guilt that rises up at the thought of his injured hands on the balcony overlooking Quasala. Despite his reassurance that he does not blame her, she had still hurt him.

"Shokain and I integrated the Red Mage and Commander pieces into the game board; they both have unique abilities," he explains, giving her a reassuring smile.

He sets the piece down before continuing with his explanation, and Mara listens intently. According to what he is saying, not much has changed; the Red Mages and Commanders are the most powerful pieces and have a few additional rules surrounding them, but other than that, it is still the strategy game she loves. She finds it neat that they had implemented cards to make it easier to keep everything organized; she remembers playing the game without cards and choosing which troops to place rather than randomly drawing them. However, despite the explanation, *playing* the game shows her how much the two new pieces influence the entire board.

Huffing, she leans back in irritation. "You… win again."

Shokain guffaws loudly. "You don't have to sound so desolate about it, Mara! Come; one more round before I have to leave."

Her heart wrenches. "L-leave? But you just got here."

Shaniel, who had been speaking with Aeserast and Lilly on the couch next to the gamers, reaches over and pats her shoulder. "He can't stay here forever, Mara."

Her eyes drop to the board. She stares at the nicely hand-drawn design of a tree. "I know, but…" She takes a deep breath, regaining her composure. "I didn't realize you had to leave so soon."

Shokain reaches across the game board and pats her hand, nearly causing her to drop the cards. "I'm sure we can play again in the future." He drills a hole into Darion. "Perhaps *next time*, Ezra can be here, as well."

Darion exhales slowly, shooting the man a sidelong glare. "We have already discussed this, Shokain. She is not coming here."

Shokain hangs his head. "Not even for a little bit…?"

"Not today."

"Fine," Shokain breathes. A hairline crack is forming between the two monolithic gates. "Seems as though it's time for me to leave, anyway… perhaps next time, I can partake of my lovely wife's company." He shoots Darion a pointed glare.

Mara stands up with him, mixed emotions swirling inside of her. "Y-you're leaving now?"

He steps around the table and hugs her tightly. "I love you, Mara," he whispers. He grips her shoulder tightly, grinning. "Let's keep this visit from your mother, all right? I'm sure she would be upset if she knew you visited me without her." He kisses her forehead.

Mara narrows her eyes. "Why can't you see Mom?"

He gives her a sad smile. "It has more to do with me

being dead than anything else. We fear if she sees me now, she may never want to leave this Chamber, and I cannot have her do that to herself – or Darion, for that matter."

Mara glances at the Death'Lord and is surprised at his thunderous look. "If she tries to do that, I will toss her back to Cerlail Academy and refuse her entry again."

Shokain winces. "See? If that happens, I won't be able to see her again until she passes into Eleth! I don't want that."

"Oh, I see now." Mara glances at the gate. The air in the archway ripples like water to reveal a familiar scenery on the other side: the edge of the Heramus. The warped trees begin a few feet away from a group of three individuals. Everything beyond the gate is a monotonous grey; the only distinguishing features on the individuals are two pairs of wolf ears and a laser gun on the patrolling soldier. The male laig'hius has pitch black hair and black wolf ears while the female's complexion is significantly lighter. "Who are they?"

He grins, pulling on Mara's hand and guiding her to the widening gate. The others follow, though they do not seem as surprised by the sight of people on the other side. "Come, come! I'll introduce you."

The laig'hius's black ears twitch, and he turns around to reveal pale features. He beams at Darion before stepping through. "It is good to see you, old friend."

"And you, as well," Darion admits, bowing to the newcomer. "How is Eleth treating you?"

"All right," he says. The laig'hius woman with lighter wolf ears turns to the gate, and the young man glances at them. "It would be better if it was not so *grey*. I am beginning to dislike the lack of color."

Darion rubs his jaw. "I have heard that a lot… I wish I could help." He nods to the laig'hius woman as she steps through. Her hair remains a light grey as her blue eyes snap to Mara. "Akalius. I assume you are faring well."

"I am." Her eyes briefly flick to Shokain before settling on Mara again. "Is this your daughter?"

"It is!" Shokain puffs out his chest, proudly announcing, "Mara Ariela Danarko, my beautiful daughter!"

Akalius bows deeply. "It is my honor to meet you, Duir'ne Mara. My name is Akalius; a long time ago, I was once in service to the Alamiran family." She gestures to Phan. "Same with my brother."

Their other companion steps through, his greyscale attire gaining color to reveal a tan and brown outfit like that of the Veeran guards. His hair gains a dark blonde, almost bronze sheen to it, and his eyes are sky blue. He gives everyone a friendly smile. "Hello; I hope I'm not intruding."

"Of course not, Kael," Darion says, beckoning him in. "Mara, this is Kimala's brother, Kael Brunet."

Mara's eyes widen. She glances back and forth between the Veeran guard who is her cousin and Darion. *If anything, they* look like siblings, she thinks to herself. *Though the blue eyes are the same as Kimala's.*

"*They* are *siblings*," Eliara whispers in her mind, also surprised by Kael's appearance – though in a different way. "*He must not remember his past lives yet. If a soul is in Eleth long enough, they can potentially start remembering their previous lifetimes.*"

"*That's weird*," Mara confesses, forcing a smile on her face. "It's nice to meet you, Kael."

He holds out his hand, and she shakes it, feeling that odd cool touch just like she had with her father. "Is Kimala well?" he asks, sounding almost earnest.

She nods. "Great, actually. She's an intermediate medic at Cerlail Academy; she works directly under Lilly. In fact, I wouldn't be alive today if it wasn't for her tincture that stops Hemius."

His hand tightens around hers as he stares intensely at her face. "You have Hemius?"

60

Mara smiles lopsidedly. "Seems that way." She glances at Darion. "Um…"

The Eleth'Lord catches on quickly. "Do you want me to get Kimala?" he asks the deceased guard.

Kael rubs his chin, thoughtful. He gives Mara a sidelong look. "How has she dealt with my passing? Has she moved on?"

Mara fidgets. "Um, well…" she stammers, feeling a little guilty that she doesn't know how to answer this seemingly simple question.

Lilly steps forward, placing a hand on Mara's shoulder. "She has. She keeps your memory close, though; it is what drives her forward. We have nearly found the secret behind this blasted blight, and it is all thanks to your sister's unparalleled mind." She gives him a small smile. "She will be turning seventeen this month."

Kael relaxes, his smile coming more easily. "Then no. I do not want to interrupt her studies in case our reunion will only reopen old wounds." He glances at Mara, looking torn. "But… could you give her a hug for her birthday from me and tell her I'm proud of what she has done? I don't know how close you two are, but…"

"I will," Mara quickly says. She doesn't care how awkward *that* will be. She knows hearing her brother's words will mean a lot to the medic.

Shokain hugs her again. "Give a hug to your mother for me," he murmurs, kissing her forehead. "Tell her I'll see her soon enough."

She gives him a quizzical look. "But… you just told me not to tell her."

Akalius snorts, rolling her eyes as Shokain rubs the back of his neck. "You're contradicting yourself as always."

"Give me a break! I miss my wife, but I know she won't stop nagging Darion if she knows I've been here and wasn't told about it!"

Three sets of chuckles echo through the chamber as

they pass through the rippling film separating the two dimensions of the living and the dead. The monolithic gate shuts behind her father, blocking his smiling face as he waves goodbye one last time.

I will not cry, she reprimands herself as her eyes sting, and her vision wobbles. *Darion said I can visit again.*

It still doesn't change the facts, though.

She turns to the half-hidden entryway into the living quarters of Elethanos. Entering the first room, she notices the couch and immediately eases herself onto it.

Lilly is right behind her, concern creasing her face. "Is it hurting again?"

"A little," Mara admits. "More like an ache than anything else."

Lilly examines the wound. "It seems fine for now; try to stay up for a little longer."

Mara nods as Darion enters the room. She opens her mouth to thank him for earlier when Eliara suddenly demands, *"Let me speak with him. I need to know something."*

Mara's jaw snaps shut in irritation. *"You can't wait five minutes, can you? All you can think of is yourself."*

"How dare you assume that of me," she huffs, indignant. *"You should show more respect, fletchling. We are dealing with matters far above your comprehension."*

"Well, excuse me for wanting to thank him before we started talking business again! What if that had been your father? Wouldn't you have wanted to speak with him for a bit?"

Eliara hesitates, shocked at the venom in Mara's tone. *"That is exactly what I want to speak with him about,"* she admits softly.

Mara's temper flares. *"You are so selfish and self-centered."*

"I am not!" Eliara cries, fighting for control. *"I must know about my family and what happened. It is imperative we find out sooner rather than later!"*

"Zip it, princess."

Darion frowns at the face Mara makes at the cushion

next to her. "What is the matter, Mara?"

"I wanted to thank you," Mara says sincerely, smiling at him. "It meant a lot. I never knew how to ask about it, though."

His eyes soften. "You are most welcome."

Mara's smile wobbles. Eliara's sharp tone completely ruins the sentimental moment, though. *"I need to speak to him!"*

Mara's temper flares. Both Lilly and Darion raise their eyebrows as her Source crackles around her. Unbeknownst to them, though, it is the Essence who restrains Eliara in the back of her mind, keeping the foreign presence from taking her over.

"You're more annoying than the Da'ruha herself," she snarls at the blue ocean of power, smothering her growing, yet irrational fear of the ancient duir'raz'ne possessing her.

"You do not understand, fletchling," Eliara snaps. *"Leave this matter in our hands; It will take but a moment. Allow me to speak to him."*

"After everything you pulled?" Mara says, incredulous. *"You won't even let me thank him properly. Forget it."*

"You... you... welp!"

"Is that the best insult you have for me?"

Lilly and Darion stare at Mara, intuitively knowing the mage is arguing with Eliara based off of the silver-sparked dark cloud surrounding her. "I shall leave this one to you, Darion," Lilly murmurs, resting her hand temporarily on the Eleth'Lord's shoulder before exiting the room.

Darion sits next to Mara. "You should at least *try* to get along with her, Mara. Your dissent with one another is not helping your body heal."

"You think I don't get that?" Mara's Source briefly flares up. "She's the one demanding to speak with you and trying to control me in order to do it! Seriously, Darion, I don't know what's so good about her. She's done nothing but leave a bad impression on me."

"You are the same," Eliara snaps back. *"Not allowing me to speak with Darion, giving me no freedom whatsoever, and even shoving me aside like I am disposable. It is no wonder your last name is* Danarko."

The last word is spit out with so much venom that Mara's head spins. She leans back against the couch, unsure of everything yet again. Without even thinking, she whispers, "What's so wrong about my name?"

"Ah… I see now. Mara, I know how you feel about it, but please allow me to speak to her."

A spear of pure panic races through her as she remembers the cloying sensation of the Dark Warrior controlling her body. Eliara must have gotten a glimpse of the previous vessel's experience, as well, as she suddenly goes perfectly silent and still. "No. I can't."

Darion takes Mara's hand. She can barely look at him. "It is all right, Mara. She is not like the Da'ruha; she will relinquish control back to you."

"It's not that I won't," Mara whispers, a silvery tear slipping down her cheek. "I *can't*, Darion. I-it's too ingrained in me at this point. Even the Essence can't stand the thought of anyone but me being in control."

Eliara's shock is mirrored on Darion's face. He is the first to recover, though. "Would you be all right with relaying whatever she says, then?"

Mara nods, averting her gaze. "I can do that much."

He tugs on her hands, urging her to follow him. "Come with me, then. I am sure her questions are of the type that need to be asked behind closed doors."

They step into another room with a couch and chairs. Along the back wall is a desk with notebooks lining the top. Darion shuts the door behind them before saying in a clear voice to the room, "Elethanos, soundproof the room and shift the location to an inaccessible area."

The floor trembles, feeling like a small earthquake. Mara stares at Darion, suddenly uneasy about all of this.

64

What is so important about their topic that he must isolate them from everything and everyone?

"Why did you do that?" Mara asks, glancing at the wall that the door had been on. There is no trace of the entrance.

Darion sits in one of the chairs, gesturing to the one across from him. "Not many know of mine and Eliara's past, and I would prefer to keep it that way."

He doesn't call her 'Highness' or 'duir'raz'ne.' No, he calls her by her first name. Not only that, but Eliara doesn't make a snide comment about disrespect or titles like she has been doing with Mara.

"What were you two?" she whispers.

Darion frowns. "Mara, that is not important right – "

"It's important to me!" Her fingers curl into fists as she stares at the floor. "Was she part of the royal family you had guarded before becoming a Highlord?"

"Yes."

Her fingers go limp. She collapses in the seat across from him, expelling all of her breath. "That… answers my questions."

He eyes her quizzically. "You do not wish to know more?"

She gives him a blank look. "I do, but I can ask those later. So what's all of this about my last name? She's been acting weird ever since I told her." Hesitating, she admits, "Even the Dark Warrior acted oddly."

Darion leans forward, resting his elbows on his knees. "Let me begin by addressing Eliara's concern. *That* family died out millennia ago, Your Highness, and Mara's father was given the family name to try to clear the stigma surrounding it."

Mara isn't the only one confused at Darion's words. "*If the Danarko line died out, then why* is *there still a stigma? It has been over five thousand years, after all,*" Eliara says. After a moment of hesitation, Mara repeats it.

Darion shakes his head. "We do not know; there may have been rumors that turned into exaggerated legends. The truth was warped through too many retellings, and that particular Ecalain family were eventually referred to as the Titans because of their immense power. Many of the Alamir family – especially those residing in the Neka city Olympus – were often referred to as Olympians." He sighs. "The entire Danarko family was villainized, even those who did not cause trouble."

"*What about Mother?*" Eliara asks, alarmed. Mara barely manages to relay the question as her head spins at the almost casual mention of the famous Greek gods. To think that the common mythical tale on Earth actually stemmed from six thousand years ago on *Alkina* is unfathomable. It means the Greek gods had been elves, not deities.

She notices Darion watching her closely, concerned. "Mara, if this is too much – "

"I'm fine. What happened to her mother, Darion?"

"She died of heartbreak when her husband passed away before her. It was before they knew Kyrina had still been alive but after the initial destruction of the Da'ruha."

"*What happened afterward?*" Mara hesitates at the soft question, not sure if she is to repeat it.

Darion takes a deep breath, rubbing his face. "I will admit, I have not spoken of this to anyone for centuries; I have even forgotten many of the smaller details." He gives Mara a tight smile. "As you now know, I had been an Alamiran guard. More specifically, I had been assigned to Eliara. We had fallen in love and were to be wed after her eighteenth birthday, which is the Alkinian tradition."

"*I kept telling him to find someone else,*" Eliara comments snarkily. "*After all, I was* dead. *However, every time he told me he found someone and was going to retire, I ended up meeting her – and not in a good way.*"

Mara's mouth goes dry. "So… you and Eliara…"

"Not anymore." He winces at his own words.

"*Oh, for Voyana's sake!*" Eliara snaps. "*Tell that srui he needs to get over that vow. It is invalid now.*"

Mara's brow furrows, recognizing this from when she had first woken up to Eliara's chatter. "She's wanting you to forget about a… vow? She says it's invalid."

Darion rubs the back of his neck, not looking at Mara. "When I became her guard, I took an oath to protect her with my life. When she died, I made a vow over her grave that if she ever came back, I would protect her until my last dying breath."

Mara doesn't catch Eliara's grumbled comment as everything clicks together. "That's why you're always protecting me," she whispers, feeling a little desolate. "You… you felt like you needed to protect me because of the Essence, which is a part of Eliara."

"*But it isn't! Just look at this thing.*" Eliara prods the silvery Source with a single lapis blue tendril; the silver sparks rear up indignantly. "*It may have been a part of me once before, but it has evolved to survive on its own. I cannot even connect with it anymore.*"

Darion shakes his head, oblivious to the commentary going on inside her mind. "No, Mara. I did not protect you because of her." He notices the silver sparks playing about Mara's shoulders. "What is she saying?"

Mara rubs her temple, her head aching as the Essence throws nasty quips back at the duir'raz'ne. "Would you two stop it? This is getting so weird…"

Darion watches her inquisitively. She sighs, admitting, "Eliara is saying she and the Essence can't merge back together because they're too different now. The Essence is not too upset about it, either. It's actually *regretting* ever putting up with Eliara in the beginning." Mara's face scrunches up as she says to the Essence out loud, "It's one thing for me to dislike her, but it's kind of weird for you, Danti."

The sparks around her tame, racing along her arms in

a caress. The Essence hums happily, "*I like — that name.*" Mara chuckles at its response.

"Danti?" Darion repeats, quizzical.

"It's what I had called the Essence when I had that weird amnesia spell," Mara admits, smiling sheepishly. "So… what happened after Eliara died?"

Darion sighs. "We discovered that Rinali had been possessed and died under the manipulator's control, though we could not determine the identity of the manipulator when we tossed it into Hariana; Your Highness would know it as Tartarus. Around the same time Rinali reincarnated, the prisoner broke out of Hariana and possessed her again. Since then, we have been unable to completely separate them without risk of damaging either one of their cores."

"*How can you not know who it is?*" Eliara demands, her voice sharper than Mara anticipated.

As soon as Mara repeats her question, Darion grits his teeth. "Apparently, whoever it is had been in some type of energy-rich area before she had died, and it had altered her. We cannot examine her mind for risk of possession, as that seems to be her main skill."

"So the Da'ruha *is* female?" Mara asks.

"We have determined that much." He hesitates. "We have theories on who it could be, though, based off the signature Source readings and a few historical references over time."

"Who?" Mara doesn't think; the question pops out of her mouth before Eliara's response.

"*Morrigan,*" the ancient duir'ne whispers.

Mara frowns. She may be a history nerd, but by what she knows of Morrigan, she is a Celtic goddess of war and battle often associated with having multiple identities, one most commonly being the crow. "Wait a minute. You're not talking about… well… Earth's Morrigan, right?"

Darion shakes his head in disbelief, and Mara relaxes.

"You are as sharp as ever. The Da'ruha, as we call the spirit possessing Rinali, relishes in battles; we first suspected her real name when Earth had what was called the Tuatha dé Danann, and she was referred to directly *as* Morrigan. In fact, that was the longest she had lasted inside a body; it took us a long time to hunt her down throughout the realms. She had started wars, wreaked destruction, and even brought civilizations to their knees. However, during that specific time, we knew Rinali had been in Eleth, as I had conversed with her several times on how to capture the entity who had possessed her."

"But... who *is* Morrigan?" Mara asks, utterly confused. "What does it have to do with *me*?"

"*Everything, fletchling,*" Eliara whispers. "*Morrigan's father was a Danarko, a radical group of Ecalain who thought to control the lesser species of the realms. Cronus thought differently than his family — but not in a good way. He was ostracized along with his wife and two children: Morrigan and Aion. When Aion died from an accident, Morrigan misunderstood and went ballistic, blaming the Alamir family. We had to lock her away because she killed my cousins.*"

"K-Killed them?" Mara repeats, aghast.

"*Family feuds gone to the extreme. Mother and Father wanted nothing of the conflict, so they left and started their own life — much like Cronus Danarko had done with his wife, Lilith. However, when my cousins were involved in the accident that had killed Aion, Mother and Father had to intervene between the two Ecalain families. They did not know how much I knew, though, despite being so young at the time; this had all happened before I even met Darion.*"

"Eliara, what are you telling her now?" Darion demands, irritated. "Stop. You are overwhelming her."

"I-I'm all right." Mara doesn't sound convincing even to her own ears. "I just... need a bit of clarification. So Cronus was a Danarko who deserted his own family but ended up in the middle of the family feud anyway?"

Darion straightens in his seat, instantly recognizing

the names. "Ah, Cronus. He was Eliara's uncle and Rhea's brother; he took on the name of his wife and was disowned by his family. Did she tell you about his daughters?"

She nods, still trying to comprehend everything. "One of his daughters died from a freak accident, so Morrigan killed the Alamirs involved in the incident out of a misunderstanding?"

"Yes; she was locked in prison for her crime. She went missing shortly before Rinali was possessed, but we could never verify if she had died or if the corrupted Source signature really was hers."

"Corrupted…?" Mara repeats, uneasy.

Darion nods. "Morrigan's Source had been a bright, vivid orange. However, as you know, the Da'ruha's is blood-red. An individual's Source cannot change that drastically in a – " Suddenly, Darion stops, his eyes widening as he comes to some type of realization. "Of course."

"What is it? Did you find out something?" Mara asks, curious.

"Aeserast had to utilize Shaniel's Source to search for you," Darion explains, rubbing his jaw. "However, he is not familiar with withdrawing another's Source in moderate amounts; as a consequence, he yanks all of the Source out at once."

A tremble goes through Mara as the Essence shrinks back in fear. Mara rubs her arms, mumbling, "Lilly told me about that. Wouldn't that kill someone?"

"Normally… yes." He gives Mara a grim look. "However, Aeserast also knows how to put that Source *back*. When he does, some of his own Source mixes into it, thus changing the chemistry of the biochemical."

"Which changes the color," Mara says, connecting the dots. "So Shaniel's Source is a different color now?"

Darion nods. "A little. But as for the Da'ruha, hers had changed exponentially; it might be a stretch, but perhaps Morrigan had been coexisting within an individual with a dark red Source, thus altering her *own* chemical makeup."

"That would mean her mind would be altered, as well," Eliara argues. *"She would be thinking more like her main host."*

Mara frowns. "She's saying Morrigan's mind would have been altered, too. Does this mean Shaniel is more like… Aeserast, then?"

Darion rubs his chin. "Truthfully, ever since the incident, I have noticed they have even more similarities between them. It is drastically different from when they had first met, that is for sure; Aeserast had never broken the rules, and Shaniel – "

His lips part in a silent exclamation.

"It all makes sense," he murmurs, walking to the desk to grab a notebook and a pen. He scribbles something down as Mara slumps in her chair, mulling over everything they had been talking about.

Geez, it's like history is repeating itself, Mara thinks. *Eliara is back, Morrigan is probably hunting for her to finish what she had started, and Darion…*

A thought crosses her mind that nearly makes her giggle. "Darion."

He glances at her. "Ah, my apologies. Do you have a question?"

"Yeah, just one." She fights the smirk, barely keeping her face straight as she asks, "So I kissed a six thousand year old man?"

His reddening cheeks make up for the duir'raz'ne's infuriated screeches inside her mind.

Chapter 5
Ripped Apart

Darion watches Mara doze on the couch, worried he dumped too much information on her all at once while she is still recovering. Mornak walks up to him, glancing briefly at the girl. "My 'Lord, we need to speak."

Darion uncrosses his arms, restraining a resigned sigh. He knew this day would come; Mornak has been filling in for him too long, and now the assistant is sick of the job. It happens to all of his assistants, sadly enough; it is part of the reason why he is still the Eleth'Lord after all of this time. "Mornak, I apologize for making you – "

"Please let me speak." Mornak smirks at Darion's taken aback expression. "I am not upset with filling in for you; quite the opposite! I am enjoying myself here. Elethanos and I have great philosophical conversations on a daily basis."

Darion stares at his assistant, confused. "If you are not resigning, then… what are you saying?"

"Allow me to move in," Mornak says cheerily, a big grin on his face. "Elethanos has agreed to create a work room for me as long as I have permission from you. This way, anytime you do have to leave, you do not have to come to my lab; I will already be here! Not only that, but this will give me an excellent chance to study even more about Elethanos and the Elethavi."

"Are you sure this is what you want?" Darion asks, incredulous. "You do not know how to create a portal yet, Mornak. You will be completely isolated."

Mornak shrugs. "Quite honestly, it's a relief to be here; many in the city are beginning to find out that I work for a Highlord despite how secretive I am about it, and they are becoming aggressive. The last time I returned to my lab, all of my tinctures had been smashed, and some of my books had been destroyed. Luckily, I had brought the important ones with me, but still. I am no longer welcome in Garnesh, Darion."

Darion glimpses a swish of red hair behind the wiry man. "What do you think, Elethanos?"

"The company would be nice," the little girl whispers, the words coming directly from her lips in a rare show of quietness. "Conversations with Mornak are enlightening. I enjoy telling him about the realms and Eleth."

"If that is what you want, then so be it." Darion frowns. "Do not hesitate to contact me if you need me, though."

Mornak waves his hand, brushing aside his concern. "Bah. Nonsense! You need to take care of your lovely lady over there." He winks at Darion. "This will give you a chance to spend more time with her, too. Win, win, if I do say so myself!"

Darion's cheeks flush a little at this. "Mornak, that was not my – "

"I know, I know." Mornak pats Darion's shoulder, his face growing serious. "But you *do* need to protect her, right? This gives you a chance to do so."

"What have you been telling him, Elethanos?" Darion snaps half-heartedly, running his fingers through his hair. Elethanos hides behind Mornak, sticking her tongue out at Darion. He sighs. "Tell the others to meet me in the chamber; I need to speak with them. Mornak, please keep an eye on Mara. If you see any changes, notify me immediately."

Mornak bows from the waist, a big grin plastered on his face. "Of course, my 'Lord."

By the time Darion walks into the main chamber, Aeserast, Lilly, and Shaniel are already sitting on the bright red furniture. Darion settles into the armchair, linking his hands together as he begins, "I shall be quick, as I know it is getting late."

Within minutes, Darion shares his findings with the other Highlords. They stare at him as if he is going crazy.

"I'm not sure if I'm understanding this right," Shaniel admits, scratching the back of his red-spiked black hair. "You think that some ancient soul from *before Rinali* is the Dark Warrior?"

"Darion, we have already ruled out Morrigan being the Da'ruha," Aeserast says, exasperated. "Their Source signatures are too different."

"Elethanos, manifest a physical comparison chart on the last three changes with Shaniel's Source signature," Darion orders.

"Of course."

Aeserast frowns. "What does this have to do with the Dark Warrior?"

"Everything." Grey papers materialize on the table in front of him. He picks up the first and the last one, his expression turning grim. "Aeserast, be honest. How many times have you withdrawn Shaniel's Source?"

Aeserast pales as Shaniel shakes his head defensively. "Don't blame him for anything. I – "

"I am not asking as a Highlord," Darion interrupts the laig'hius. He stares directly at Aeserast. "I am asking as a scientist and theorist. How many times have you completely withdrawn Shaniel's Source into your own body, Aeserast?"

"Three times," Aeserast whispers, averting his gaze. "The... first time had been when he had been stabbed by a dream-eater. I pulled his consciousness out so he would stop triggering the wound to reopen as Aihalia and I healed it."

"There was not a report on that one," Lilly murmurs, disconcerted.

"How *could* I write a report on that one?" Aeserast snaps, his temper flaring. "It was when Aihalia gave him that blasted transfiguration potion; we fought, and I...

kicked him out. When I hadn't heard a single word from him for over a week, I went looking only to find him nearly dead on Carni's Path – and it was all *my* fault."

"Settle down, Aeserast," Darion urges, noticing Lilly's rattled expression. His eyes flit to Shaniel; he is oddly calm, even for him. "Like I said, I am not reporting you. However… I do believe you should look at these."

He hands the two sheets of paper over.

Aeserast and Shaniel stare at them. "What are these?" the Creation'Lord asks, his voice shaking ever so slightly.

"Do you remember when Elethanos had to update her logs on Shaniel's Source readings?" They nod. "That means his Source signature had changed drastically enough since the last time he had been here that Elethanos did not initially recognize him."

Aeserast's eyes widen slowly. "So… you're saying…"

"Aeserast's little Source-grabbing technique is actually changing my biochemical signature," Shaniel finishes grimly.

The two of them share a look, finally realizing what is happening.

Aeserast's fingers tangle in his hair. "I never meant to *alter* anything! Perhaps I can figure out a solution to reverse the effects and revert – "

"We can figure that out later, Aeserast." Shaniel props his elbows on his knees. "What does this have to do with the Da'ruha being Morrigan?"

"Her core could have been residing in another and was influenced by it," Aeserast breathes, horror crashing down on him. "It has been proven that individuals with similar nari can sync their biochemicals and meld them together in a special state of runkare, but this is taking it to an entirely different level, Darion. If this is what happened to her, then the one who had housed her will have a similar Source signature – but they will be even *more* powerful than the Da'ruha."

Darion nods. "Shaniel, would you deliver a report directly to Timian? Make sure only he receives it."

Shaniel nods, standing up. He pauses next to Aeserast. "Don't beat yourself up over me," he reassures the Creation'Lord, grinning. "We're both alive, right? That's all that matters."

"Srui."

Shaniel's grin turns wolfish. "Looks like I'm not the only one affected; careful with the temper, Aeserast. One of us needs to be the level-headed one."

Aeserast expels his breath in a whoosh as Shaniel disappears through a portal. He glances at the doorway leading to the residential chambers. "How did she deal with all of the information?"

Darion shrugs. "I am not quite sure; I have not checked her mental state yet."

"I can do that." Aeserast stands up, walking to the entryway into Darion's living room. He sits on the edge of the grey couch. A shock of red hair pokes up from behind the arm rest. "Hello, Elethanos," he greets, keeping his voice low so he does not wake Mara.

"*Hello.*" The little girl eyes the slumbering mage. "*Are you going to look at what is unseen again?*"

Aeserast nods as he brushes Mara's hair out of her face. For a split moment, he wonders if it is significantly longer than when she had come into Carni. Surely, the Corridor Realm has not already begun affecting her biological makeup.

"*Be careful,*" Elethanos suddenly warns. "*Her mind is sensitive right now; any more additions to it may strain her mental capacities.*"

"They aren't already strained?"

"*Not yet.*"

Aeserast stares at Elethanos for a moment, surprised. It is phenomenal that Mara's mind is not being strained despite having two relatively large entities residing within her at the same time. "I will be careful."

He places two fingers on the side of her temple, merely peering into her mind to check on the progress. Earlier when he had done this, he had been met with the surreal sight of three different Sources orbiting one another. Now, the black one looks as if it is attempting to devour the new lapis blue Source; it is completely wrapped around the blue, reminding him eerily of a possession — only in this sense, it is reversed.

Darion's earlier comment has him confused, though. If two Source cores in extremely close proximity to one another can end up mixing together even if their nari is different, why isn't this happening with Mara's and Eliara's Sources? In fact, how come Mara's Source and the Essence haven't merged yet?

Examining the three different Sources once again, he watches how the silver one reacts with the black and the blue. Oddly enough, it is almost as if the silver Source is *repelled* by the other two, and the blue and black migrate toward one another. Despite there being more blue than black, the black one is the dominating presence.

Mara must be mentally stronger than Eliara.

Just as the thought pops into his head, the silver Source touches his consciousness lingering on the outskirts of Mara's mind. He decides to take advantage of the contact and asks, *"Why is Mara's Source doing that to Eliara?"*

"They are trying to — meld," it responds. *"However, they — differ too much. They will never — become one — this way."*

"What about you, though? I am sure you heard our conversation. Why haven't you melded with Mara?"

"You are half right. Mara is — mentally stronger than — Eliara, but — that does not influence — this merging. We are merely — opposites. Opposites cannot merge."

Aeserast withdraws, left with more questions. He returns to the others in the main chamber. "They seem to be too different from one another to reside in the same body, honestly. It's almost like watching two bulls vie for dominance." He shrugs. "We will have to see how things progress."

Lilly rubs her chin in concern. "The dissent between them might stint the healing process. I still do not agree with us remaining here; she would already be healed if we were at the Academy."

Darion shakes his head. "We will do no such thing; she remains here until she is healed."

Aeserast glances at the doorway, a small frown creasing his brow. While he agrees with Darion, he cannot help but worry for the young mage. Even with basic treatment, the wounds should not be reopening.

Just what had she seen in the Treavaun?

———◆———

"Oh, little duir'ne, come out to play..." Rinali sing-songs. Eliara covers her mouth, trying to muffle her gasps for air. "How I always wanted a sister to play rough with. This is fun."

Eliara closes her eyes. She does not know what had happened to her sister in the time she had been spending with Artemis; her aunt's reports had said nothing of Rinali's murderous mood. What had changed?

"I found you, First Heir."

Rinali is suddenly in front of her, a wild grin on her face. Her eyes churn a deep blood red, completely obscuring the beautiful ocean blue.

Eliara barely sees the scythe as it cuts toward her. Her sword appears unbidden and stops the blade, shoving back on the Source-created weapon.

Rinali eyes the floating blade with curiosity. Grinning, she grabs it and shoves her sick-looking Source into the blue blade, listening to the ear-splitting shriek it emits as it is corrupted.

"No!" Eliara grasps the hilt of her other blue salev'i.

She will not let this evil creature contaminate her sacred blades.

Rinali is no longer smiling. "You cannot defeat me; you are too weak. All of you are too weak."

Her once-exquisite blue sword digs into her stomach, pinning her against the tree. Red liquid splatters the flowers around her, and they glow a soft silvery blue before returning to normal.

"I shall let you see your betrothed one last time," Rinali whispers, smiling sweetly. "I am sure he would die to say goodbye."

Eliara moans as Rinali yanks the sword out. She slumps to the ground, gasping for breath. "Why are you doing this, sister?"

"Why?" Rinali sneers. "Your family took everything from me, so I wanted to reciprocate."

———•◆•———

Mara groans, on the edge of the nasty dream. Pain shoots through her abdomen and she hisses, touching the wound on her stomach. It is slick and warm.

Cracking open her eyes, she stares at the thick, red liquid. Her breathing hisses in and out as she blinks rapidly, trying to register what had happened. The prominent color stands out from the grey couch, making it easy to discern how much blood she has lost so far.

Sitting up, she cries out as her stomach throbs. *Definitely real*, she realizes, grimacing. "*What did you do?*" she demands the half-dazed Eliara.

"*Me? How could I have done anything? I was asleep, same as you.*"

Mara grits her teeth, fighting through the pain as she staggers to the door. Her hand leaves a bloody streak as she stumbles into the hall, using the wall to support herself. She sees Darion in the kitchen, grinning as he makes something that smells suspiciously like breakfast. Aeserast and Lilly are at the bar, both with a glass in their hands.

"H-help," she rasps, collapsing to her knees. The pain is almost unbearable; she feels as if the sword is still in her side, slicing into her.

Somehow, Darion hears her over the noise of the kitchen. His eyes widen in horror as he sprints to her side. "Lilly! Get over here!"

The Life'Lord hurries over, her hands already glowing as she tries to stop the bleeding. Darion touches Mara's face; she feels him at the edge of her mind, trying to figure out what is wrong just as Eliara slips into control. She is in too much pain to care at that moment.

"I think... we were dreaming of my death," Eliara huffs, grabbing Darion's hand. "When we woke up, she — she was bleeding. I cannot stop it this time, though. It is as if it is enchanted like my kareia."

Lilly shakes her head. "It's as she says. It is scarily like Gamerog's cut. We *need* to teleport her, Darion."

Darion holds Mara's hand tightly, torn.

"Do not transport her," Eliara rasps, her hand constricting around his. "The consequences are too — "

She coughs, and coppery blood fills her mouth. Mara can feel both of their consciousnesses slipping away.

"No... portal..." Eliara forces out before going limp.

Mara sinks into blackness so complete it swallows the very light of the silvery Source around her. She tries to block out the pain, to isolate herself so she can think past it. However, it is as if the very wound is in her mental self, not just her body. She focuses even harder, blocking out anything and everything that could possibly flare up the memory of that incident. If she doesn't think about it, maybe it won't hurt as badly.

Suddenly, she is ripped free of the comforting nest she had made for herself. She gathers the darkness around her the best she can, hoping it will be able to protect her from the blinding pain she now feels in her mind as well as her very being. This ripped state reminds her of something, though she cannot remember exactly what it is. All she knows is pain and darkness – though even that fades away as she loses consciousness for what feels like an eternity yet a few seconds at the same time.

Rubbing her throbbing head, she blearily opens her eyes and stares at the dark, swirling colors of Carni's sky. She feels as if she had landed pretty hard, but…

Where had she fallen *from*?

She slowly eases into a seated position. "Eliara, what happened back there?" she asks the annoying duir'raz'ne. "One minute, we were dreaming, and the next, I was bleeding out."

No response.

Frowning, Mara reexamines herself. Her eyes widen as she discovers that not only the ancient presence is gone, but so is the Essence. Something… *else* is wrong, too.

She looks down at herself, patting her arms, sides, stomach, and legs. Solid, but oddly unfamiliar. She looks more closely at her clothes, though, noticing that despite them being the same design as what she had been wearing before – her normal sparring shirt and pants with her mage robe – they are *completely black*. Not even her robe has its usual silvery border and pattern on the back denoting her chosen field.

"Hey, Essence –" She stops herself, suddenly realizing *how much* she had grown used to the Essence's presence within her mind. Despite how annoying it had been, it had always been there to aide and assist her even when she didn't want it. She had taken its presence for granted, never expecting a day like this to happen; she thought she had to put up with the pestering, fragmented voice for the rest of her life.

Now, though, she is completely alone inside her head.

She takes a shaky breath. Even though she had only grown conscious of it a year ago, it feels much, much longer – most likely as a result of sharing so many memories with it. She shivers, feeling cold in the emptiness of her own mind.

"What… should I do…?" she breathes, wrapping her arms around herself. Where should she go? Should she try thinking of a location, or perhaps a person? Since she is in Carni, her thoughts will lead her to her destination.

Getting to her feet, she begins walking down the crystal pathway – Carni's Path – only to stop mid-step. Aeserast's cold, flat words come back to haunt her. Darion's question rings through her head.

"Can you tell me what you want most of all, no matter the consequences?"

She tucks her black robe more tightly around herself. She still doesn't know the answer to that. Squeezing her eyes shut, she scours her own consciousness, trying to figure out the answer.

A thought slowly forms in her head. It is a concept, something she has always held close to herself; something she has lived and abided by as though it is law, but she has never had to put it into words. She… she needs…

"Mara?"

Her head snaps up. She grins at Lunesh, suddenly hopeful. "Lunesh! Thank goodness. I-I don't know what happened to me; I suddenly woke up here. Maybe – "

Mara stops herself, her smile freezing on her face. *Wait. This girl looks like the one that had attacked me.* Her memory of her amnesiac time in the swirling realm is a fog, but she still remembers most of it. *How do I know she won't try to kill me again?*

Lunesh frowns, her head tilting to the side. "You seem… different, Mara. Did something happen?"

"I don't know." Mara doesn't even try to hide the wary tone in her voice. She narrows her eyes. "Are you the real Lunesh, or are you some dream-eater?"

She grins slyly. "Ahhh, so you figured it out. It seems

as though you are Awake, albeit still Lost, little Alkinian."

Mara sinks into a crouch. "Awake is all I need to be," she exclaims as a salev'i materializes in her hand. She is not surprised to see it is completely black from pommel to blade, comprised solely of her dark Source.

The dream-eater's eyes widen as she – no, *it* stares at the sword. "I stabbed you with that blade!"

"Yeah, you did." She practices a couple swings with it, feeling the balance. "Why are you so surprised?"

"That was your deepest fear!" it argues. "I *saw* it in your mind. The sword, the wound, everything!"

"You're wrong," Mara whispers, her smile bitter. "You saw the Essence's fear; it seemed to be remembering things when I wasn't. I guess that's the benefit of having two minds in the same body."

It narrows its eyes at her. "You are alone now, though."

"Yup." Mara points her sword at the dream-eater. "The thing I fear the most isn't as simple as me dying; in fact, I'd take that any day over what I truly fear."

The dream-eater bares its teeth. "What is it that you fear, mortal?"

"Something you can't pit against me as easily as stabbing me, that's for sure." Mara's Source-created blade whistles through the air, too fast for the eye to see.

The dream-eater barely manages to leap to the side, avoiding the attack. It dodges, swerves, and twists out of the way, looking almost like a dancer as it narrowly escapes the edge of Mara's blade.

"Hold still," Mara snarls, following up a slash with a punch. "You need to pay for hurting the Essence like that."

"Tell me what it is you fear, then," it taunts, grinning. The dark hair shifts over its shoulders, and for a split second, Mara nearly recognizes who else this figure reminds her of. The name is on the tip of her tongue...

Mara tries to punch it, but it dodges yet again. It grabs

her wrist and gasps in surprise just as Mara feels a creeping sensation migrating up her arm. She yanks back, feeling as though she had been violated.

The dream-eater backs away, looking disconcerted at something. "That... that cannot be your fear. It must be something else."

"Huh." She shakes out her arm, dispelling the numbing tingle. "Care to share? I've always been curious."

It gapes at her. "But you have been boasting this entire time about – "

"Has no one heard of bluffing?" Mara exclaims to the sky. "First Eliara, now *you*. Seriously! Even the Essence knows more about daily banter than you!"

"Do not make a fool out of me, Alkinian," it snarls, holding its arms out as if it is ready to fight.

"Tell me, then." Mara straightens, turning to the dream-eater. "Can you show me my 'deepest fear,' or is it impossible for you to manifest?"

The dream-eater's form wobbles, trying to take shape. She watches curiously as it morphs into Shokain with a sword wound in his chest, and then Aeserast with burn marks. It keeps flitting through different people, different injuries. Mara watches it impassively; her suspicion is proven with its attempt.

She is afraid of watching her friends die.

However, the biggest issue is the second part of the fear; the part she hates to admit but is too true to ignore. She is afraid that *she* will inflict those injuries, that *she* will be the reason they die.

There is no real way to express that from an external source without manipulating her psychologically.

Finally, it settles back onto Lunesh's form. *No, not Lunesh*, Mara realizes, finally recognizing the older girl from an old, old memory she had glimpsed inside of Eliara. *This is the Da'ruha.*

That realization dredges up other questions, though.

While Lunesh had been mirrored after the younger Rinali, this dream-eater seems to be mimicking the older version – the version that had been possessed. But how is it able to pull that form together? Are dream-eaters created from people's *nightmares* while Carni's Creations such as Lunesh were created from wishes?

"You are strong," the dream-eater hisses, baring her teeth. "But you are Lost. You do not even have a *purpose*. You will fail."

"Even if I fail and remain here for the rest of my life, at least my friends will be safe," Mara murmurs, smiling tiredly. "So, in a sense, I'm preventing my deepest fear from ever happening."

The dream-eater flinches back as if she had splashed acid onto it.

"But I *will* defeat you." She raises her hand. A pitch black sphere of raw energy forms, twisting and twining on itself. "Even if I have to wander Carni forever."

Suddenly, the dream-eater takes a new shape – herself. "You are a strange Alkinian," it says, smirking as it raises its hand. A twin orb appears. "Either way, I will destroy you."

Mara stares at it, a chill sliding down her spine. On the rare nights she did not dream of a vessel, she had nightmares about fighting herself. This is eerily like one of those dreams.

Watching the doppelgänger's orb approaching her, she holds out her hand and wraps her Source around it. It snuffs it out of existence.

"I'm actually curious," she says, trying to cover up her own fear. "Do you think you can top my nightmares, dream-eater? I'd love to see the worst you can throw at me."

Even the dream-eater looks rattled. Emitting a shout, it charges forward and swings at her with a black blade.

Mara fends it off, surprised to find her doppelgänger

is more skilled than she had anticipated. She smiles grimly as she puts everything she has into the fight, giving and receiving an equal amount of injuries.

Each time the sword nicks her or the dream-eater touches her, she grows weaker and weaker. It is already too late when Mara realizes what is happening.

It is somehow weakening her.

Staggering on the crystal pathway, she forms one of her notorious 'rose bombs.' It streaks at the dream-eater, blowing up in its face. It tumbles across the pathway, sprawling over the crystal.

Mara limps away, putting distance between her and the creature. A weak black pulse emits from one of her footfalls. She pauses, vaguely recognizing something similar happening when she had been out here with the Essence. She glances behind her.

The dream-eater is nowhere to be seen.

Taking a steady deep breath, she trudges forward. *I need to find somewhere safe to rest*, she thinks grimly. *It took too much of my strength. I need to moderate my…*

She blinks, coming to a stop as realization crashes down on her.

I'm not in my own body.

Her breathing hitches. Now she knows why she had felt odd when she had woken up; whatever 'body' she is currently in is not her own. How will Eliara manage her Hemius without her? Will the Essence continue to keep it from spreading? What had her departure done?

An even worse thought flits across her mind. *My body isn't… dead, is it?*

She closes her eyes, shaking her head. *Safety first*, she schools herself, her mind filled with concern for the Essence and, in a roundabout way, Eliara. *I need to get somewhere safe so I can return quickly.*

She walks across the path, growing more and more concerned as the dreary swirls darken. The last time she had been in an area with a sky like this, she had run into trouble. *This must be a Treavaun area*, she thinks, remembering the term Darion and Aeserast had used. *I wonder why I keep ending up in these places when all I want is to be somewhere safe.*

The sky rumbles ominously at her thoughts.

Chapter 6
A Fragile Mind

Eliara groans, her head throbbing painfully. She feels as if a part of her has been ripped out, leaving a gaping hole in her consciousness. "Mara, something is wrong…" she murmurs. Hearing her own words out loud snaps her wide awake.

She stares at the cushion in front of her, memorizing every thread with intricate detail. Not moving, she glances beyond it to examine the smooth walls and soft blue panels emitting a relaxing light.

She curls her fingers, clenching and unclenching her hands to confirm she really is the one in control. Taking a shaking breath, she turns inward; if Mara catches her in control, she might go ballistic. The mage knows much more than she does about mind manipulation, whether she likes to admit it or not.

Instead of finding the familiar ball of tendrils curled within the silvery cocoon of threads, she encounters a terrifying sight. The Essence twitches, sparking every now and then as if in pain. It looks even more damaged than before, the ends of each of the vine-like strands frazzled and frayed. There is a hole in the middle where Mara's Source used to rest, displaying the damage wrought from the poor mage somehow being ripped out of her own mind.

"No…" she breathes, sitting up in bed. She clutches her head as a painful jab shoots through it, and her right eye swirls with odd purplish colors. No doubt all of this is the result of the previous inhabitant's sudden absence; she is surprised the body is functioning as well as it is for her.

If anyone should have been ripped out, it should have been me, she thinks, trying to think past the throbbing in her head and neck. *She was in so much pain when the wound reopened, though, that she had withdrawn into her own core, leaving me in control... maybe that is why?*

A soft rap on the door precedes it opening to reveal a haggard Darion. He exhales in relief when he sees her sitting upright. "Mara."

A spear goes through her heart once again at hearing the mage's name on his lips. She had told him to move on, but it does not mean her feelings for him are completely gone. Her eyes water, suddenly feeling as if all of this is her fault. "Darion..."

"Thank the flow you are awake. When you collapsed, we could not wake you. Aeserast nor I could see if you were all right, either."

She closes her eyes, unable to look at him. "It is not all right."

He sits in the chair next to the bed. "What do you mean, Mara?"

"She is gone." She covers her mouth – no, *Mara's* mouth. She is an intruder. "Carni – Carni must have ripped her out when you transported us." She winces as another lance of pain shoots through her mind. "The Essence is fragmented, and I-I do not know how to fix it."

He stills. "Who is gone?"

"Mara." Her hands drop into her lap as a single tear races down her cheek. Sure, she finds the impudent, arrogant elf intolerable, but she would have never wished the mage to be cast out of her own body.

"Mara?" Darion breathes, appalled. "She... is gone?"

"I will help find her," she says, ignoring the sharp pain in her shoulder as she grabs his hand. Her heart aches to see the desolate look on his face. "I will do everything in my power to – "

She coughs wetly, and a coppery taste floods her mouth. Eyes wide, she touches the corner of her lip.

Her fingers come away slick with blood.

Another pain shoots through her shoulder and head, though this time, it is accompanied by an even sharper pain in her chest. She coughs breathlessly, and her lungs contract painfully from the motion.

Another lance of pain pierces her head. She loses consciousness.

The next thing she knows, she is flat on her back. A grim-faced Lilly and worried Aeserast stand over her, several odd-looking machines on either side of the medical cot.

"What… happened?" she rasps, her fingers twitching involuntarily. Her blurred vision slowly clears.

"The Hemius reactivated, and you had a seizure," Lilly says softly, cupping Eliara's head between her hands.

"He-Hemius?" Eliara repeats slowly, her brow creasing. She remembers that word from Elethanos when Mara had been speaking with Kael. "What… is that?"

Aeserast frowns, glancing at Darion. "It is Eliara," the Death'Lord says simply.

"Ah." Aeserast clears his throat before explaining, "It is a substance the Dark Warrior had created; it infects the body and kills an individual from the inside. Mara was infected with it, but the Essence always protected her."

Eliara's head turns to the side, her eyes unfocused as she stares over Darion's shoulder. "The Essence was damaged when Mara was ripped out. I think it… tore a hole through its central processes. It will take a while for it to repair itself."

"We do not have a while." Lilly glances over Eliara with a clinical eye. "We stopped that seizure, but the Hemius has already wrapped itself around both of her lungs and has a firm hold in her brain. The only way to sedate it at this point is to seal it – but it might also seal the Essence."

"Mara was ripped out?" Aeserast asks Darion as Eliara's eyes slide closed. "Where is she, then?"

"Eliara thinks Carni did it," he answers, gritting his

teeth.

"Calm down, Darion." Aeserast rests a hand on his shoulder. "We will find her."

"Aeserast?" Eliara murmurs, barely able to speak louder than a breath. "Would you check on the Essence? I am worried about it…"

She feels him on the edge of her mind. Shock radiates from him when he finds the fractured silvery Source, and he quickly withdraws.

"How is it still there?" he breathes his eyes wide.

Eliara's consciousness begins to fade. "Do not let it disappear…"

They stare at the still form of Mara-but-not-Mara. Darion and Lilly turn to Aeserast. "How bad?" Lilly asks.

"It's completely fragmented," he whispers, shaking his head. "There is a hole in the middle where the core should be. It is phenomenal it is holding itself together."

"Or perhaps," Darion murmurs, "that is where Mara's Source had been."

They stare at him. "That… no way," Aeserast rejects the notion. "If that's the case, then it should have blown apart when she had been ripped out!"

"She passed out before we transported her," Darion points out. "Eliara had been in control at that time. Perhaps when that happened, Mara had pulled away from the Essence just enough so it was not destroyed."

Lilly nods. "It is certainly possible; I have seen it happen before when trying to pull apart different souls in a possession."

Aeserast grips his hair, spinning in a tight half-circle. "But if Mara really did get ripped out of her own body, that means she is *still in Carni.*"

The situation finally crashes down on the other two Highlords. "Mara must still be eiv'ra," Darion breathes in horror. "There is no telling where Carni's Will will guide her."

"That interfering Will," Aeserast snarls, already reaching forward. "I will speak to it directly and demand to know why it is doing this to her."

"Wait, Aeserast." Darion halts the suddenly impulsive Creation'Lord. "Timian has given us explicit orders not to speak directly to Carni's Will without prior consent. If you disobey him – "

"We don't have *time* for permission! You saw what a day did to her; she has already been gone for *three days now.* By the time we receive permission, she could become eiv'ra permanently!" Aeserast yells, his fingers clenching so tightly that his knuckles turn white.

"Go."

They turn toward the door. Timian stands there, his face a dark thundercloud. "Speak to the Will, Aeserast; find out where Mara is. I will handle things from this side."

Aeserast wordlessly reaches forward with an access stone in his hand and yanks open a portal. It glows a blinding lavender as he uses a bit too much of his Source to open it. Within seconds, he is gone.

Darion meets Timian's gaze. The Time'Lord sighs. "At least wait until the duir'raz'ne awakens before you leave, Darion."

Darion dips his head respectfully. "Yes, sir."

Lilly strokes the young mage's brow, still unable to believe Mara is not in her body at the moment. "She is sweating… the Hemius is still active. If I seal it, it must be now." She glances at Timian, hesitating. "However, if you believe it is not necessary – "

"Do it." Timian stops next to the cot, looking conflicted. "The duir'raz'ne is strong, but I am afraid managing this will be too much for her weakened state. She has not used her own Source in centuries. Being in Eleth for so long could have dulled her skills."

Lilly nods, pulling out her reki and thumbing through her contacts. She sends urgent messages to three of her most trusted coworkers, knowing she will need assistance putting the seal on the girl's mind.

"Darion, a word," Timian says softly. They step to the corner of the room in order to be out of the way. "This is a critical time; no one else must know of this occurrence. If the Da'ruha were to hear of Mara's weakened state, she may try to take advantage of it."

"But Her Highness is back. Her power may be reduced, but –"

"She has never been strong enough to fight off her own sister," Timian interrupts, grim. "Especially now after millennia of being inside of Eleth with only a third of her original power. You must find Mara quickly, Darion; only she can bring the Essence back to full strength, and only she can fend off the Dark Warrior."

"You are not telling me everything, ruicov." Darion narrows his eyes, using the Xharos term for 'grandfather.'

The Time'Lord smiles, the crinkles around his eyes making him look much older than his frozen age of forty-five. "Where would be the fun in that?" His smile falls as his expression turns serious once again. "Some things are best left in the dark, Darion."

Darion gives him a hard look before returning to Lilly's side. Timian slips out of the room just as the medical assistants rush in with emergency surgery gear.

— ◆ —

Aeserast steps through the portal into a blindingly bright sphere. He squints, unable to see through the shining Voyana encapsulating the center of the entire realm – Carni's Will.

Even though he has always known how to access the Will, he has never done it until now. He pushes aside draping vines heavy with Voyana and Carni Matter, wading through the yellow-gold water infused with the biochemical.

He can feel the massive amount of energy pulsing around him, brushing against his arms in the form of vines and completely soaking his robe. It doesn't feel claustrophobic, though. Taking a deep breath, he has to remind himself that he is not approaching Carni Alamir herself – just the pseudo-consciousness of the realm her remnant energy had created to mirror the ancient Alamir sister.

He pauses outside the final curtain of vines of mixed Voyana and Source. He is not sure what to expect beyond those tendrils; a girl in the image of the deceased Ancient Sister, or simply a glowing figure, considering the realm is made of a unique matter that can take on the form of anything around it.

"What is it you seek, little Ecalauna?" a voice whispers from behind the vines.

He jumps, startled. He berates himself for the action; of course the realm recognizes him. He has been residing within it for centuries. "I am searching for Mara Danarko. She was – "

"Ah, my precious eiv'ra. She will be safe."

Aeserast grits his teeth, holding back his sharp retort at that casually mentioned fact. "Please tell me where she is so I may protect her and guide her home."

"She must Find who she is," Carni's Will whispers. "Do not follow her recklessly; she must learn. If she does not, then her power will consume her, and she will be no more."

Aeserast stares at a particular pulsing vine. "What do you mean by that?"

A low chuckle emerges from the vines. There is a slosh of something moving behind the curtain, and the vines sway at the ripples racing through the water. "You are certainly inquisitive. Mara is special; in order to fully develop her powers, she must become Lost in order to Find herself again. Give her time, Creation'Lord."

He mulls over this. "How will I know when to help her?"

"The bells only toll once." His eyes widen as a glowing hand emerges, holding a black per'lusa flower. "When it does, send the silent guard of a forgotten time. He will know how to bring her home."

He carefully takes the flower, feeling Mara's trademark Source signature emanating from it. It disintegrates, and black sand sifts between his fingers to fall into the water.

A hand runs through his hair. He freezes, not daring to look up. "And *you* will know best how to deal with what will happen next."

He closes his eyes briefly as the hand withdraws. "But what will happen? Who..." Opening his eyes, he finds himself on a ticking clock face. Myst twines around his legs as the countless clocks along the Tower of Discord's surface tick out of rhythm of one another.

"Who is the guard?" he finishes, confused by the Will's cryptic words.

———◆———

Eliara stirs, waking up slowly to see familiar bronze hair and vivid green eyes – the same green eyes that had entranced her millennia ago. Her lips part as a single name slips out before she even thinks about it.

"Darius..."

Those green eyes turn away from her. "You know I do not go by that name any longer."

She exhales slowly. "I know. I apologize." She barely has the strength to turn her head to look at the closed door. "Why do I feel so heavy?"

"It is most likely the seal Lilly and the others placed on you to restrict the movement of the Hemius." Darion leans forward to brush his fingers across Eliara's forehead. "It seems to be working, although Lilly wants to keep monitoring it. It is only sealing rapid movement; the

Hemius is still active."

Eliara's vision blurs. "Why did you never tell me my sister had done this to the land?"

"I knew it would upset you," he murmurs, his voice as soft as hers. "You should rest for now; you will need your strength later. We need you to pretend to be Mara; we cannot let the Da'ruha know she is not currently in her body."

"Does the... Da'ruha... fear her that much?" Eliara hesitates over her sister's once-respected title. Despite almost six thousand years passing by, she still has a hard time believing that the title that had once referred to the Sister who had overseen the Ruha Coven has become synonymous with something so *evil*.

Darion nods. "She has been unable to possess Mara's mind, and whenever they have clashed, Mara has been the one to win. The only thing Mara has been unable to do is capture and imprison the Dark Warrior herself."

Eliara frowns. "Dark... Warrior?" she repeats, confused. "But – "

"Lost in translation over the millennia," Darion quickly explains, his smile tight. "Timian even instigated some of it in order to differentiate between the Da'ruha from your time and the Da'ruha of present day."

"I see." She glances around the room, feeling empty. She feels as though she is the one who is eiv'ra, not Mara. "Then you must find her, Darion. I will do my best here."

He hesitates before squeezing her hand tightly. "I will bring her back, Your Highness."

"Wait." Her hand constricts around his, keeping him from leaving. "I need to know. Do you..."

He pulls his hand free, and her arm drops onto the bed. "I... apologize, Your Highness."

Eliara smiles in relief, feeling some of the tightness in her chest loosen. "I am glad you are moving on, Darius."

He glances out the window overlooking Quasala, but

not before she sees that pained look again. "I never knew how to bring it up."

"I could tell, though," she murmurs, her eyes drifting closed yet again. "You have that look on your face anytime you see her or talk about her. Find her, Darius, and protect *her*. She is more important than me; I am but an old soul weary of all the pain you have been put through."

She cannot let him know that her heart aches at these words; despite always telling him to find another, she still loves him dearly, albeit in a slightly different way than millennia ago. For a brief moment, she resents Eleth for ejecting her into the body of the one he cares about. Could there not have been another?!

The sliding door opens, and a familiar face walks in. Eliara's eyes widen, her lips parting in surprise. "Mo – "

"Ezra." Darion quickly steps in the way of the blonde woman, stopping her. "You know what Lilly said; she needs to rest."

"That's my *daughter*, Darion!" Ezra snaps, gesturing wildly to Eliara. "You should know that I will not listen to anyone who tries to keep me from Mara!"

Eliara quickly snaps her jaw shut, her mind whirling. *First her father, now her mother,* she thinks, feeling a little dizzy. *Why do Mara's parents look like mine?! Not only that, but Shokain even shares my father's name!*

Ezra pushes past Darion, sitting down in the vacant seat and gently resting her hand on Eliara's fingers. "Sweetie, how are – " The woman's breath sucks in. She stares at Eliara, uncertainty and wariness flitting across her features.

She knows, Eliara realizes. *Somehow, she knows I am not her daughter.*

"Who are you?" she demands, her voice quivering as she withdraws her hand. She glances at Darion. "Where is Mara? Who is this?"

Darion sighs heavily. "Of course you would find out."

He glances at Eliara. "This is Mara's mother, Ezra Danarko. Ezra, this is… Eliara Alamir. Mara is still in Carni; we are searching for her now."

A multitude of emotions flit across Ezra's face. "Is Mara all right?" she finally asks. "She isn't… Lost, is she?"

Darion doesn't answer her question. "Aeserast is currently searching for her; I am leaving to help him. Please assist Her Highness in any way she needs and do not tell anyone of Mara's state. We cannot risk the Da'ruha finding out."

Ezra nods, her expression full of determination. "If there is anything else I can do, please let me know."

Darion glances at Eliara once more. He hesitates before bowing his head respectfully. "I will return soon with Mara, Your Highness."

"Thana baro," Eliara whispers, watching him leave. Her eyes flit back to Ezra; she is still rattled at the similarities between this woman and her own mother.

Perhaps this is the reason why I have been unable to speak with her for the past century, she thinks gloomily. *She had been reborn with no memory, just like any other regular soul.*

"By the sounds of it, Your Highness needs a crash course on how to be Mara until they return," Ezra comments, sounding calmer than Eliara expected.

"Please, call me Eliara," the duir'raz'ne murmurs, sighing heavily. "I think it would be best for me to remain here, though, since I am nothing like the girl."

"Nonsense." Ezra pats Eliara's hand, startling her. "You should be able to enjoy yourself just as much as the rest of us, Eliara. I heard from Lilly's assistant that they had to place a seal over the Hemius, but as long as you're careful, you should be able to walk around and explore the Academy."

Eliara gives the woman a wavering, hesitant smile. "That sounds lovely, but I do not wish to impose on Mara's social life."

Ezra snorts. "My daughter thought of nothing but studying; everyone who knows her will think she is under strict orders not to strain herself. They won't think much about it." She smiles encouragingly at Eliara. "Are you feeling up to a brief tour?"

Eliara hesitates. On one hand, she wants to spend more time with Ezra; the Alkinian gives off the same calming aura that her own mother had. However, she cannot help but feel that Mara will be furious if she finds out she had been roaming around impersonating her.

"Only… for a bit," Eliara finally concedes, pushing herself upright. "I do not want to anger Mara too much. She can be quite…" She searches for a nicer word; she is pretty sure the girl's mother will not appreciate her bad-mouthing her daughter.

"Stubborn? Aggressive? Doesn't listen?" Ezra smirks at Eliara's shocked expression. "It's my own fault she's that way. I caused her to grow up faster when her father died; I was an emotional wreck for over a year, so she had to learn fast how to manage a household. She got that stubborn streak from her father, but she learned how to *use* it when she had to order me to take care of myself." Ezra sighs. "Looking back on it now, though, I am quite ashamed of myself. I really should have taken better care of her; she was in a lot of pain from her father's death, too. She never got to properly mourn over that loss."

"I can understand that," Eliara whispers, her mind flashing to Darion. Her visitations probably never helped him move on properly, either. "So… you know of Mara's hardheadedness?"

Ezra laughs, helping Eliara stand up. "Do I *know* it. She also has a problem with authority – which, I don't doubt, you have already experienced."

"She never listened to me," Eliara grumbles, her voice barely a breath. "Even when I desired to ask the Eleth'Lord questions, she claimed she couldn't let me have control. I wanted to make things simpler."

Ezra's eyes soften. "Ah, now that's different. Mara was nearly possessed by the Dark Warrior less than a year ago. Ever since then, the Essence has been giving the psychiatric team a hard time whenever she goes in for her weekly evaluations. Even Aeserast, the Creation'Lord, sometimes has difficulty checking on her." Ezra hooks her arm with Eliara's. "Mara hasn't outright said it, but we all think it's influenced by the Essence losing so many of the previous vessels that way."

"She did say something like that…" Eliara murmurs as they walk out of the hospital room. The off-white glow of the corridor is gentle on her eyes as they follow the curving hallway. "So this is Cerlail Academy? Darion has only ever told me about it."

Ezra nods, leading her down the empty hallway. "We're currently in the medical wing. This is where I work; Mara studies in the tactical and sorceral wings."

Eliara wrinkles her nose. "I do not believe I can fake her studies. I know more about the medical field and plant life than plotting and attacking."

Ezra gives her a sideways glance. "Really? How interesting. Perhaps we can converse on the differences between medical techniques used in your time compared to modern day."

Eliara smiles, relaxing a little. "I am a bit rusty, but I would enjoy that."

They walk down the hall in silence together. Eliara tenses when a young-looking Alkinian in a white robe approaches Ezra, but the individual doesn't pay her any heed as he prattles on about a recent patient he had been taking notes on.

Ezra frowns. "You are right. They should not have used that technique before clearing his mental state. I will speak with the medic advisor and check on the patient myself."

"Thank you, Advisor Danarko." He bows before hurrying off.

As soon as he is out of sight, Eliara comments, "I will admit, I am a bit surprised he did not address me."

Ezra shrugs. "Mara does not involve herself with the medical field unless she has to; however, she does have a bit of knowledge on the topic which had been acquired through the Essence's large knowledge supply. Not only that, but my assistants understand not to address her directly, as she hates being called by any titles."

Eliara glances at Ezra, startled by this. "Titles? What sort of titles would she be called?"

"Voi'duir'stra, Goindun, Your Grace... a few know she is the Essence, as well, and have called her Your Highness." Ezra winces. "She tends to get very flustered over the titles and has everyone calling her by her first name regardless of where they are on the social ladder. I have been unable to convince her that it is just their culture to follow the social ranking, and it is nothing personal."

Eliara mulls over this, now curious. "You speak as though Mara is not from here."

"Shokain and I raised her on Earth." Ezra falls silent as someone exits one of the rooms ahead of them. His light blue robe shifts as if a breeze is pushing it off to the side, and the pattern across it is that of a gusty cloud or air current. "Ah, 'Lord Tyson; perfect timing. Could you take a message to Timian that Mara is awake?"

The man turns to them. His smile is friendly as he looks at Eliara. "It is good to know you are doing well, Mara. It was quite a scare when your Hemius went rampant."

Eliara gives a tight smile, not quite sure how Mara would respond. However, she knows she has to say something. "Thank you."

He bows deeply. "I shall inform the Time'Lord immediately, Medic Advisor Ezra. In the meantime, take it easy, Your Hi – Mara," he quickly corrects, flashing Eliara one last embarrassed smile before turning on his heel and striding down the corridor.

"Who was that?" Eliara asks softly, unsure how to respond to the Ecalauna's correction of the title he is supposed to use.

"Air'Lord Tyson Mills," Ezra whispers. "Mara met him right before she went to Carni, so he doesn't know her that well. The other Highlords must have informed him of her preferences, though, which is for the best." Ezra sighs. "In the meantime, I need to check on the patient from that report."

Eliara glances at her. "Who is the patient?"

"Mara had known him; his name is Evan Shasta. When we received him during the Toratheia, he was in a critical state, and we have been helping him regain his health since then. Mara had met him before, though I am... not quite sure the circumstances behind it." Ezra scratches her neck in embarrassment. "As far as I could gather, he helped her escape from Alamirana, but by doing so, he was locked up in a phobia manifestation chamber for going against his own family. They let him out for Toratheia and even healed him a bit, but the damage was already done."

"That is horrible," Eliara whispers, appalled. "Who would do such a thing?"

Ezra shakes her head. "We're not fully sure. According to what they found in Dounta when they had rescued Mara, Naiya had been manipulated and was puppeteered several times; even her Source was being controlled. Ever since finding trace remnants of the Da'ruha's Source in her body, we're now under the suspicion that she wasn't the mastermind behind Mara's first kidnapping." She glances at Eliara. "My apologies; I didn't mean to – "

"Do not fret about it." She smiles reassuringly at the medic advisor. "As for Evan, how is his state now?"

"Stable." Reaching the end of the hall, Ezra holds out

her hand over the panel. The doors slide open to reveal a platform. "His brother, Jayden, tends to study inside of his hospital room. They keep each other occupied; a lot of times, Jayden will read to his brother, as he is still having trouble with his vision."

Eliara follows the medic onto the platform and watches the woman place her hand on the orb near the entrance. She jumps a little as the platform rises, surprised at the technology. She glimpses outside the window as they ascend, and she is drawn in by the sprawling city.

"Is that... Quasala?" she breathes, amazed. "It has grown so large..."

Ezra chuckles. "It was a tiny village when you were around, wasn't it? One of the first?" Eliara nods. "It's the hub of culture now. I noticed you seemed surprised when the platform moved, too."

Eliara shrugs self-consciously. "I did not expect such advanced technology utilizing Source, but I suppose it should not be a surprise."

The platform slows as Ezra pulls her hand away. They disembark and walk along the glass windows of the building. Eliara stares out the window, unable to tear her gaze away from the vibrant colors of the living world.

"Here we are." Ezra pauses by a door. She glances at Eliara. "Are you ready?"

She reflexively swallows. *Mara had known this person,* she thinks, suddenly unsure. *What if he realizes I am not her?* "Is it truly all right for me to go in there?"

"Of course." She waves her hand in front of the control panel and opens the door before Eliara can object. "Perhaps seeing you will help both of them feel more at ease."

Eliara hesitantly follows Ezra into the room. It is plain like her own, although different objects had been brought in to accommodate a longer stay, such as an end table next to the bed, a dresser, and even a writing desk.

A young man sits upright in the bed, a book open in his lap. His sandy blonde hair is pushed back from his face, exposing small scrapes along his forehead and around his eyes. Clear bandages protect his neck, and even his arms and wrists are covered with the healing adhesive.

Next to the hospital bed, a younger version of him plays on a tablet, looking like an excited child with a new toy. He glances up to reveal sky blue eyes just like his brother, although his face looks younger and much more innocent. He beams at Eliara. "Mara, you're here! Look at what the medical assistant gave me; it has a lot of books in it, and some of them are in languages I don't know!"

The young man in the medical bed chuckles at his brother. "I know you are not used to them, but please be careful, Jayden. They are not as sturdy as physical books."

"Yes, Evan." The boy returns to flipping through the pages of whatever book he is reading on the device.

The young man turns to them and gives Eliara a self-conscious smile that wobbles. "I am glad you are all right, Mara. When I heard you went to the Underground Castle, I feared the worst; I myself do not remember much of that place." He glances at Jayden. "I am glad you brought my brother here, though; we never wanted him to be exposed to what the others were planning."

Jayden glances at his brother, frowning. "Are you talking about what they did to you, Evan? That was really mean of Desdemona. Why won't Rath punish her?"

"He likes Desdemona; she's his favorite." Evan sighs, smiling at the others hopelessly. "I cannot thank you enough for taking us under your care. I apologize for any trouble this has put on you."

"No worries." Ezra walks up to his bedside and taps a panel over the end table. A couple holographic screens appear, and she reads over Evan's medical charts. "I was informed you were given rejuvenating eye drops before your mental state was checked, which is not the typical procedure. How are you feeling?"

Evan seems surprised at the woman's bluntness. "Better than yesterday, actually," he admits as he taps the book in his lap. "I'm beginning to see the words, and the headaches are getting better."

"And mentally?" she persists. "Are you still seeing the shadows?"

He shakes his head. "Not for the past two days; it… has been a relief. Having the lights on has reduced my anxiety, as well."

Ezra exhales her breath, satisfied with the responses. "If you start to see them again, let one of us know *immediately*, Evan. We want you to feel safe here."

He nods. "Of course. Thank you for all of your care, Ezra." He turns to Eliara, giving her a self-conscious smile. "Now you know I went a little crazy."

"What happened?" Eliara whispers, unable to hold back her morbid curiosity.

Evan's eyes drop to the book. "I was placed in a phobia manifestation chamber for long spurts of time. It was pitch black; I-I couldn't see anything. It drove me insane, and things… happened. I kept seeing these strange shapes." He shivers, his fingers scratching at the bandages on his arm. He stops, gripping his wrist tightly. "When I was brought out right before the Toratheia, it turned out I had somehow damaged my eyes beyond what Salanski could heal. The medics here have been helping, though, and I can now see general shapes and color. If I hold certain solid objects closer, I can see some detail."

Eliara examines the book in his lap; the text is larger than a regular book. "How close do you have to hold it?"

He lifts the book, bringing the text a couple inches away from his nose. "I can somewhat read from this distance. It's still difficult, but… it's a start."

Ezra pats his shoulder. "You have already improved so much, Evan; do not feel bad about the progress. In the meantime, make sure to rest. Excessive eyestrain can impede its ability to heal."

He smiles weakly at her. "Thank you, Medic Danarko." He nods in Eliara's general direction, though she can now tell that he is not fully focusing on her. "I look forward to catching up with you later, Mara."

"Rest well," Eliara whispers as she and Ezra exit the room. The door shuts behind them. "What had been done to him was truly awful."

Ezra nods as they continue down the hall. "We have been taking care of him since the night of the Toratheia Ball. We were worried he wouldn't regain his sanity *or* his sight when we had initially brought him in." She smiles at Eliara. "He is determined to help us now, though, after he is healed enough."

But is it that easy? Eliara wonders as they walk through the medical wing. *He had been a prisoner, yes, but he had also been one of them. Who is to say he is not a spy of a sort?*

An odd breeze brushes by her, sending an odd chill down her spine.

Turning around, Eliara glances down the corridor just in time to see a door several feet away sliding shut. *It must have been that*, she brushes off in her mind, continuing down the corridor with Ezra.

Chapter 7
Creeping Darkness

Mara's feet drag across the dark pathway; she feels as though she has been walking for *days*. Her eyes droop, and she can barely focus on the path in front of her as she shuffles one foot in front of the other. *I need somewhere safe to rest*, she thinks to herself, repeating the silent phrase over and over in her mind as the ominous swirls above her churn like angry waves on a stormy ocean.

But what is safe in the Treavaun?

If only she had her sword. She would feel so much better traversing this strange, twisted land if she had a more trustworthy weapon than her Source, which is unpredictable at best. It doesn't help that she feels as if most of her energy had been siphoned off from the fight with the dream-eater. No matter how many times she pauses on the pathway to rest, she is not regaining her strength.

Squinting, she stares ahead at the vague forms swimming into focus. Are those... huts?

Her breath catches. They are; not only that, but they look exactly like the ones that had been in the forest with Lunesh and the other Carni Children.

She staggers into the village, glancing around. "Is anyone here? Hello?" she calls out, hearing the desperation in her hoarse voice.

Two ocean blue eyes peer around a building. "Mage Mara?" a quiet voice whispers, surprised.

"Lunesh?" Mara stops, uncertain. Is this little girl *really* Lunesh, or is she another dream-eater? "Why are you here?"

"Auntie sent me here to retrieve those of us who wandered too far from her forest," Lunesh says, stepping out from behind the building. Her hands are clasped behind her back. "I'm the oldest, so it is my duty to look for them and bring them home."

Mara does not approach the girl. She looks about ten years old – the same as the Lunesh she had known in the Will's Forest – but the dream-eaters can take on any form. "How do I know you are the real Lunesh and not some dream-eater?"

Lunesh's eyes widen and her hand goes to her mouth. "Dream-eaters are scary… please tell me you haven't fought one, Mara! They will take your Source like a Respoura, but they don't need it, so they let Voyana take it away."

Mara leans against a building. "Too late for that."

Lunesh quickly backs away from her, looking terrified.

Mara frowns, glancing behind her. There is nothing there. "What's wrong, Lunesh?"

"If you fought one, that means your Source levels are low," she whispers, hugging her arms to herself and shivering. "When *your* Source is low, it's dangerous."

Mara stares at her for a long moment, vaguely remembering Lunesh's blackened hand. It looks fine now. "What happened when I had touched you? Why did your hand turn black?"

Lunesh shakes her head. "That is not important; that needed to happen. However, I do believe you need to leave, Mara."

Mara laughs desolately, glancing around. "Where am I supposed to go?" She slumps to the ground, leaning her head against the hut. "I was looking for somewhere safe for me to recover after a fight I had with a dream-eater. It was the same one that had stabbed me."

Lunesh doesn't move closer. "You… were stabbed?"

The mage nods. "A lot has happened since we last saw each other; after you vanished, I fought a night terror and ran away when Darion showed up because I didn't recognize him. A dream-eater stabbed me before he could catch up, and then… well, during the healing process, I think I was yanked out of my body." She frowns. "How come I have a physical form even though I don't have a body? I don't get it."

"Carni Matter is malleable and often acts on its own," Lunesh explains, cautiously sitting down. "It binds itself to your Source in order to give you some semblance of a body while you are here. However, if your Source is drained away, it will make you feel weaker because now there is less substance to give you a physical form, so it expends more effort on your part to hold your form together without aide." She pauses. "It is phenomenal you are able to do it so well on your own. Are you sure you are not part shadow elemental?"

Mara tilts her head to the side, looking at Lunesh. "Never knew there's such a thing as that," she admits.

"Oh, yes." Lunesh grins, flashing her perfectly white teeth at her. "It is quite fascinating, really; sometimes, when an elemental's core is broken, they actually reform inside of a person to regenerate. Because of their injury, they don't remember that they are an elemental. It is quite a surprise to them when their physical form dies, but they find themselves in a semi-corporeal form."

Mara mulls over this. "Do those elementals ever… regroup here, in Carni?"

Lunesh nods. "Normally, it is the unknown or shadow elementals who end up here. There are a couple floating around."

"Is Thanos here?" she asks quietly, hope creeping up even though she tries to keep it at bay. She doesn't want to have them bashed.

Lunesh watches her for a moment before admitting, "Yes." At Mara's sudden look of determination, she continues in a rush, "But do not go looking for him, Mara! You can easily disrupt the process of his reformation if you try to find him."

Mara's head thumps against the wooden wall. She stares at the dreary sky, her emotions swirling. *He's alive*, she reassures herself. *I just… can't see him right now.* "Will he be all right? Is it safe for him here despite the Treavaun?"

Lunesh nods. "As long as he is in his elemental form, he will be fine." She smiles secretively. "He is in the safest place in all of Carni: Auntie's forest."

"The Carn'ien," Mara murmurs, closing her eyes. *I had been so close to him, and I didn't even know…*

"Do not be upset if you could not sense him," Lunesh reassures her, guessing correctly on her swirling thoughts. "Auntie had cocooned him in her power to protect him. He is special, after all."

Mara frowns. "Special how?"

"He will once again be the protector of the reborn Da'neka."

Mara stares at Lunesh, her breath whooshing out. "So you knew Hope had been Kyrina," she murmurs, grimly smug that the Essence can't stop her from talking about it this time.

Lunesh giggles. "Of course we did! Kyrina is connected to Voyana just as we are. We know whenever she is reborn."

Mara narrows her eyes. "Do you tell the Highlords?"

Lunesh shakes her head. "Of course not. We do not like to interfere with the material realms; the Ecalauna manage their sectors, and we manage ours. The only ones we are in direct contact with is the Creation'Lord, who oversees the Tower of Discord, and the Eleth'Lord, because he often travels Carni on a whim."

"On… a whim?" Mara repeats, aghast. Why would Darion do something so seemingly dangerous like that?

"He goes deep into the Treavaun and meditates in the Danti Cauerr'ien, or he might make a pilgrimage to the cliffs overlooking Hariana," Lunesh explains, not seeing anything wrong with the Eleth'Lord's actions. "He lets us visit him and Elethanos on occasion, as well."

"You mean Carni's Children, right?" Mara clarifies, and Lunesh nods. "But… I'm still confused. Why would Darion do such a dangerous thing?"

"He believes it is atonement for his crimes," Lunesh says abstractly. "Auntie has tried telling him that the past is no longer relevant, and he should stop punishing himself for it. He does not listen."

Something nags at Mara's mind. She has seen a dark, brooding look or an immense sadness on the Eleth'Lord's face more often than she cared to admit. "What crimes?"

Lunesh pauses, watching her. "It is not my place to say," she whispers, standing up and brushing off her clothes. "If you would like to know the answer to that, ask him directly. In the meantime, I must resume searching for the missing Children."

"Lunesh?"

"Yes, Mara?"

"Please be careful." She gives the young-looking girl a worried smile. "Don't… get eaten again, okay?"

Lunesh gives her a bright smile. "I won't!" She skips around a building.

Mara struggles to her feet, shuffling over to peek around the corner. Despite having no place to hide, the girl is nowhere to be seen.

She takes a deep breath. She doesn't feel any better than when she had sat down, which is disconcerting; Source is supposed to regenerate over time, right? Why doesn't it seem as if hers is? *I guess I have no choice but to move forward*, she thinks, walking down the same road Lunesh had traversed.

Soon enough, she is out of the small village and slowly trudging across Carni's Path once again. She stares at the ground, watching the dim pathway shimmer with dull, muted colors.

Something ahead flashes brightly, drawing her eyes

upward. Her brow furrows at the slight incline; when had she started trekking up a hill?

A bright pulse lightens the area briefly, revealing patches of dead grass on the hill-like incline. Squinting, she picks up her pace; she knows that glow. Only one other thing has had that particular signature.

Beneath her, bright green veins pulse within the dark crystal. She ascends the hill, watching as the veins thicken and pulse. As she walks over them, she feels herself gaining energy and feeling better than before. She glances back in wonder, but there are no glowing veins. *They must have led me here*, she rationalizes.

Topping the hill, she gasps at the sight. A colorful forest sprawls in front of her, the overall light blue glow banishing the surrounding darkness. Lime-green grass precedes the glowing trees, illuminating the valley the forest is nestled in.

Mara staggers forward, nearly falling down the sudden slope. She stares at the tall grass, slowly reaching out and touching the knee-high plant. It radiates with raw energy similar to the Essence but... not.

Glancing behind her once again, she notices the surrounding darkness is closing in. She watches in horror as several tendrils of grass dim before blackening, wilting before her eyes. She hurries through the field, racing for the safety of the trees.

Despite the glowing plant life, Mara is not over-whelmed with the light. She briefly pauses by a light blue per'lusa flower, awed by the bright yet soothing colors in this forest. The blue rose-like flower forms a single teardrop on the tip of each of its petals. With a start, she realizes where she is.

The Danti Cauerr'ien.

Supposedly, the Silver Mirrored Forest is a copy of the forest that had been wiped out by the Da'ruha shortly after Eliara had died. She sees why it is called Danti, though; despite everything having a vibrant color, it seems to be overlaid with a bright, almost silvery glow. She has never seen pictures of it, but now she understands why; no recording device can do this place justice.

If this is the Cauerr'ien, then I should be safe here, Mara thinks, trudging down the grassy path. She meanders through the forest, admiring the glowing trees and exquisite flowers. Her breathing slowly deepens as she begins to feel lethargic. She rests her hand against a tree and pauses for a brief moment in hopes of shaking off the sudden bout of tiredness.

The light brown bark underneath her hand turns black.

She stares at it in sickening realization as black veins stretch outward from the obvious handprint, tainting the once beautiful tree. *It wasn't the Treavaun encroaching on the forest,* she thinks, feeling a little nauseated. *It was* me.

"You there! What are you doing here? It's dangerous."

Whirling around, she subtly shifts in front of the tree, hoping to hide the destruction she had brought upon it.

An elf dressed in a purple-banded silver robe stands a few feet away. His purple shoulder boards and robe pattern designate him as a specialty researcher, although Mara does not recognize the design on the shoulders to determine what he studies. However, based off his current location inside the forest, it most likely has something to do with this place.

"I-I'm sorry," she quickly apologizes, but then winces. If he really is from the Academy, he might catch on that she isn't from Alkina or Blazhreia based off of her dialect. "I'm just trying to find a safe place to rest until my friends find me."

He frowns, tilting his head to the side. "You're not in your corporeal form. What happened to your body?"

She laughs nervously. "That's…"

"Zain, I need the reader; the flowers seem to be reacting to something." An elfin woman with dyed bright blue hair steps around a tree, looking at the man in irritation. However, as soon as she sees Mara, her hand flies to her mouth. "Oh, you poor thing! Are you eiv'ra?"

Mara glances between them, recognizing the woman's robe, as well. It is silver like the man's, but the edging is gold. Gold patterns and shoulder boards decorate the fabric. She is the Chief Wizard of the sorceral wing at Cerlail Academy, Vierna Lunawer.

She will definitely recognize me, Mara mentally panics. *I wonder how much trouble I'll get into for this...*

Vierna squints at her, rubbing her chin. "That looks like an Academy robe, but it's completely black... Who are you? Do you attend Cerlail Academy?"

"Uh..." Mara's eyes flit around, looking for a way out. All high-ranked Academy officials know her Source signature simply because of her training on the rooftop stadium; however, the woman doesn't seem to recognize her without the Essence's added signature energy. While it will be good for her to be found and taken back to her body, what will they say about her Source suddenly tainting the ancient Danti Cauerr'ien?

Zain focuses on something above Mara's shoulder. He frowns in confusion. "Vierna, look. There's something on the tree behind her."

Carc'ra! It must be spreading, she thinks, plastering a smile on her face. "You seem busy. I won't take up any more of your time."

Vierna's eyes sharpen on her. "Tell me. Did you do that to the tree? Who are you?"

"No one," Mara mutters, backing up. She glimpses the blackened ground where she had been standing; her robe had hidden the darkening plant life until she had shifted. *Bad move!*

Vierna glances down, seeing darkness where there used to be a glow. She staggers back, alarmed. "Wh-what is that?"

Mara takes this opportunity to run. She sprints through the woods, heading deeper into the Cauerr'ien. Tripping over a root, she grabs the side of a tree to steady herself. When she pulls away her hand, a black handprint remains. Tiny veins branch out from it, creeping over the glowing bark.

Her breath comes in short gasps. She swallows hard, her mind swirling with doubt and questions. The Danti Cauerr'ien has been around for thousands of years; nothing has ever managed to destroy it, and scientists have been trying to harness its power for centuries.

She managed to taint it within minutes of arriving.

Am I evil? It is the same question she has been asking herself ever since Codi died. *Am I the one who causes all of my friends to suffer? Is that… is that why my Source is black?*

She had read once that Source color is based off how the biochemical interacts with the body and the mind. Most individuals with a cool-colored Source are calm and caring, while those with warm colors are passionate or exuberant. Black Sources are extremely rare, and even the researchers at Cerlail Academy only have five documented individuals including herself who have ever had a black Source. All five accounts do not seem to have anything in common, either.

She sees a break in the trees. *The exit!* She sprints forward, hoping to leave the forest before she completely destroys it with her Source.

However, as soon as her foot sinks into the shifting, dark blue surface, she realizes her mistake. Her momentum propels her forward, and she staggers several feet into the lake. By the time she manages to stop herself, she is already waist-deep in the water.

She glares at the shore. How is the slope so steep for such a calm body of water? Wading to the embankment, she climbs out, weighed down by her soaked clothes. She shivers, cursing her bad luck and wondering how she feels cold in her Carni-manifested form.

Taking off her robe, she rings it out the best she can. She stoically watches the droplets of water strike the glowing ground, turning it black. She spreads out her damp robe, laying on top of it. She glares up at the dark purple and blue clouds.

"My life is a mess," she grumbles out loud. She can imagine the Essence's fragmented affirmation. Covering her face with a hand, she sighs. All she had wanted was a place to rest before she returned to the others.

I'll go back and find Vierna and Zain, she thinks guiltily. *Apologize properly about the forest and explain what had happened. Maybe they can take me back to Darion and the others.*

She stares at the swirling dark clouds, disturbed by the sharp contrast between the sky and the glowing, serene forest. Twisting so her body is parallel with the lake, she turns her head and gazes over the water.

The blue liquid gently swells and recedes as if moved by an invisible tide. Tiny ripples appear in the water, radiating outward only to disappear and reappear somewhere else. Mara has the crazy thought of invisible spirits dancing across the surface, pirouetting in the air only to land and cause one of those ripples. She can almost see those dancing forms; faint outlines of deep blue, just like the water.

She blinks sleepily, staring directly into the face of one of these sprites. It is leaning over the water, staring at her curiously. After a moment, it turns and skips across the surface; its footfalls leave behind ripples that quickly fade.

Mara rubs her eyes. Is she starting to hallucinate? Looking out onto the water, though, she *knows* those creatures are not alive; they radiate the same power as the surrounding forest.

They must be a part of the Danti Cauerr'ien, she realizes, watching the dancers skip across the water. They do not have a true form, only a mere outline; she can see where their hair flows behind them and the vague shape of their bodies, but nothing more.

Their dancing is almost melodic. She rests her head on her arm, lulled by the graceful movements. Her eyes drift shut as she watches the dancers leap across the water. Soon, she is dozing, oblivious to her surroundings.

———◆———

She sits on an embankment overlooking the dark blue water, humming a slightly familiar tune as she fingers the black tunic. A brown belt fastens it snugly around her waist as her foot taps out a rhythm on the water's surface. Her beige pants end just above her bare feet, and at that particular moment, she doesn't really care what happened to her shoes.

Shoving her unbound hair out of her face, she glances up at the churning purple sky. She doesn't know where she is, but then again, she doesn't have an urge to find out. She gazes at the glowing trees, serene in this quiet forest by the lake. There is no such thing as time; she is at peace. She could stay here forever.

"You…"

She looks down, strangely not surprised to see her reflection is different than her own appearance. A girl who looks like her gazes back; she wears a light blue dress, and her long, hazelnut hair creates beautiful waves over the soft-looking fabric.

"What is it you desire?" the reflection asks.

Mara stares at her, her humming coming to a stop. A frown mars the pretty elfin features of the reflection. "I…" Mara starts, thinking, *I want my friends to be safe. That's why I'm here; to protect them from me.* She cannot bring herself to tell the reflection, though. She stares over the lake, wondering how long she has been here. Minutes? Hours? Surely not days, though. She cannot tell from the surrounding forest or ever-dark sky.

"You know what you desire, do you not?"

She sighs, staring up at the sky. "Yes, I do. But… it's also the reason why I'm here."

"Tell me."

She glances at the reflection. "To protect them from me."

The reflection shakes her head. "That is not what you desire, though."

Mara frowns. "Yes, it is."

"You desire to protect them, do you not? You desire to stand by their side with no fear for their safety." The reflection smiles. "But if you wish to continue believing the other is your true desire, then so be it."

"No… you're right." Mara stares at her hand. "I don't want to be afraid anymore. This is *my* power, right? I shouldn't be so afraid of it."

"That which we cherish is often what we fear the most. Do not be afraid of yourself, Mara; you have already defeated your inner doubt. Now banish the fear and solidify your desires."

Mara stares at the reflection, trying to get a good look at the girl's eyes. Two brilliant lapis blue rings encircle the gold irises. "Who are you?"

"You know who I was," she answers cryptically. "But you will also determine who I will be."

———◆———

Vierna stares at the analysis screen, not blinking. After a few moments, Zain clears his throat. "Chief, the results aren't going to change even if you keep staring at them."

"Run another diagnostic," she commands, thrusting the device back at her assistant. "It must have read improperly."

"This is the third reading, though…"

She knows that, but she is having a hard time believing what the black Source is doing to the ancient forest that has withstood the deepest, darkest portion of the Treavaun. For the longest time, it has provided a haven for anyone seeking sanctuary in this dangerous part of Carni.

The foreign Source is *devouring* it.

At first, she had thought it was residual from the odd yet familiar Alkinian who had come through here. However, after examining the Source for over an hour, she had picked up on the unmistakable readings of the foreign energy converting the external Source into another version of itself, thus expanding and growing much like Voyana does.

This Source is doing what I have been trying to do for years, she thinks mournfully as the glowing flower they had been analyzing for the past hour turns black before her very eyes. *No one has been able to completely master energy restructuring, though. Only Voyana itself can do this, and even with* that, *it was with pollution, which is —*

"A form of chemical reactions," she breathes, whirling on Zain. "I want you to log everything that you read with the scanner, Zain. We're going to break down what this thing is doing so we can replicate it and utilize it."

Zain's eyes are locked onto the flower. "Uh… Chief, you might want to look at that first."

She glances at the flower, irritated. "Yeah, it's turning black. I get… that…" Her mouth falls open.

The flower crumbles, disintegrating into a pile of black sand. It slowly shifts over the ground, moving to the next flower and repeating the process.

Vierna pushes her assistant away from the black sand. Despite being in a Treavaun, the Danti Cauerr'ien is reportedly the safest place in all of Carni other than the Will's Forest. Even the sealed Tower of Discord is more dangerous than this place. She had never imagined anything could happen in the presence of the lingering duir'raz'ne's Source. But here it is, staring her in the face.

"Change of plans. Pull out the anchoring unit and

open a portal; we need to report this to the Highlords."

Zain glances at his superior, startled at the insatiably curious Chief Wizard's sudden switch in tone. "It's just after the forest's Source, right? We should be safe."

"I'm… not so sure about that."

Please tell me I'm wrong, she hopes as she helps her assistant set up the emergency portal unit; neither of them know how to properly open or close portals, so they use the external rift opener. By pouring their Source into it, it opens and temporarily anchors a portal long enough for them to step through.

Zain pulls two metallic boxes out of his bag; they are about eight inches all around and covered in gears and seams. He turns a few dials before setting them on the ground about a yard apart from one another. He digs around in the bag before turning to Vierna, who is rapidly packing their supplies. "Chief, I need the portal's controller."

Vierna freezes. "Oops…"

Zain sighs. "You packed it already, didn't you?"

She sets down the bag, digging the square unit out and handing it over to him. "Is it already charged?"

He nods, fiddling with the controls. "Just need to flip on the switches." He reaches for the side of the box but hesitates.

"Hurry up, Zain. I don't want to know if that stuff eats other Sources, too."

"I think it does," he breathes, his face pale as he backs away from the unit.

The black sand creeps over the box, and they both hear it creak as if a huge weight had settled on it. The entire unit breaks apart, and for a fleeting second, they see Zain's crème Source churn around the modulator core before being encompassed by the black sand.

"Carc'ra," Vierna breathes. "Run!"

They sprint down the pathway, glancing over their

shoulders as they watch the sand encompass the second box.

Zain stumbles, his foot sinking into a pile of black sand creeping across the ground in front of him. He yells in horror, scrambling out of it and frantically shaking his foot to dispel the sand.

"Zain!" Vierna cries, terrified for her assistant.

Zain stops his frenzied movements, confused as the condensed Source falls off. It slowly shifts to a glowing green blade of grass, encompassing it like the black sand had done to the flowers in the clearing behind them. "I… think it only attacks external Source."

Scientific curiosity sparking once again, Vierna forms a small glowing pink orb on the tip of her finger. Without a second thought, she lowers it to the black sand.

"Chief, don't take my word for it!" Zain exclaims, panicking all over again.

The black sand roils, clamoring for the Source. She feels an odd shock of recognition as it touches her finger, delicately plucking off the small Source orb and withdrawing.

Frowning, she straightens. "Do you remember which way that Alkinian eiv'ra went?"

Zain glances around, suddenly uneasy. "I think she went toward the lake. Why?"

"This Source feels the same as hers." She rubs her chin. "I *know* I have sensed this Source before, but where?"

Zain pales. "You mean *she* is the one doing this?"

"Quite possibly."

Chapter 8
Discovery

Eliara stares out the window, a forgotten journal on her lap. It has been nearly four days since she has seen Darion, and she grows more and more concerned as the days pass by. What if he and Aeserast never find Mara? What will happen to her and the Essence? Will the Da'ruha find her? What will she do if that happens?

Taking a deep breath, Eliara focuses on the page. However, the black ink blurs with the lines. She is terrified of the answers to all of these questions; if she does see her sister again, will she be able to fight her off? She couldn't before because they had been family. Now, though, there is a six thousand year gap between them. She is also not at full strength, so her sister can potentially be more powerful than her.

She sighs, closing the journal. Fretting will get her nowhere. Standing up, she puts the journal and pen on her night stand before walking to the dresser. Pulling out Mara's usual drab attire of a snug black shirt with brown pants, she begins to change only to pause to stare in the mirror.

The terular fits over her like a half-top with spaghetti straps; most likely Mara's influence to keep it out of the way when she is dressing. The thin, clear band on her wrist hides the extensive Hemius blemishes across her body, but it does not disguise the faint scar running from her right shoulder down to her left hipbone. Another scar sits above her left hip, looking like a sword had run her through.

She touches the scar, remembering it reopening multiple times in Elethanos. When she had asked Ezra about it, she had explained that Mara had been shot by a neivir bullet; they had to cut open the wound to pull out the shards. Because both Ezra and Surana had been out of practice and had no time to retrieve the medic in town, the healing job had left a scar. Eliara cannot ignore that it lines up with the wound that had killed her nearly six thousand years ago.

Taking a shaky breath, she eyes the diagonal cut. This one is from a fight with the Da'ruha earlier that month; Mara had been slashed by Gameleth across her torso, and her terular had kept her from immediately bleeding out.

Eliara feels a little nauseated at the knowledge that her once-beautiful sword had caused such nasty wounds on the young Alkinian.

She finishes dressing, her sober mood making her moves slow and methodical. Timian currently has Gameleth under his care; he is monitoring it closely in case the Da'ruha tries to summon it back to her since she still has the sheath. Gamerog, though, is in Mara's closet; Eliara has a hard time looking at the tainted blade.

Maybe I can purify it, she thinks while swirling on Mara's robe. *I am sure she will appreciate that.*

She gathers her courage and opens the closet door. She already knows Mara does not go in here often; it is full of nice clothes and dresses that were most likely bought *for* her. She stares at a long-sleeved, sheer blue shirt for a brief moment.

Has Darion seen her in any of these?

She shakes away the thought, grabbing the hilt of the sword in the corner of the closet. Pain bites into her palm, and she feels a little sick as she senses the reddish-purple Source deep within the sword. However, she also finds Mara's Source nearly doubling the Da'ruha's power.

She pauses, staring at her family crest on the sword. Even with her power drastically reduced, she is still more powerful than Mara. However, according to what she is sensing within her old sword, Mara has been 'feeding' it more than she should be able to.

"My precious Gamlein," she whispers its original name, her fingers brushing over the hilt. "You have been through so much, haven't you?"

The blade vibrates, singing mournfully; it remembers her.

"Has Mara been treating you well?" she asks softly as she sits on the edge of the bed, stroking the metal scabbard.

The sword emits several short high-pitched rings that sound like chirps. She smiles, recognizing it; the kareia is happy with its new owner. Suddenly, it releases a slow, drawn out sound ending on a higher pitch.

Unsheathing the stained sword, she stares at the floating Old Xharos runes on its surface. *Mara eruka'ring* lingers on the surface, with Mara's name being the rune for 'half of a whole.' She frowns, but ignores this for now; she has known the meaning of Mara's name in Old Xharos, but she never thought Gamerog – formerly known as Gamlein – would directly call her this.

"She is still in Carni," she answers the kareia's question. "Darion went to find her, so I am sure she will return soon enough." She runs her finger down the flat of the blade. "In the meantime, allow me to clean you up; I am sure Mara will appreciate that."

It thrums happily, and she feels the blade press against her fingers. She smiles, sheathing the sword and walking back to the dresser. Strapping on the sword belt, she pauses for a brief moment to finger the silvery design edging the belt.

Darion had made this.

Her emotions swirl within her. It is one thing to know he has moved on from her romantically and is courting other women, but it is another to *see* it firsthand. Taking a deep breath, she shoves her feelings aside and gently straps Gamerog to her side. This way, she can work on banishing the tainted Source throughout the day so she does not have to worry about collapsing from exerting too much of her limited abilities.

She exits the room and walks down the now-familiar corridors of the Quasalan palace. Lilly and Timian had insisted that she should pretend to be Mara until Darion and Aeserast return with her, and they have been helping her with this seemingly impossible task.

Ezra walks down the hall. Spotting her, she smiles. "Mara, would you mind helping me out for a bit?"

"Sure thing, Mo – Mom," Eliara stammers. She still has trouble calling her 'Mom' instead of 'Mother,' which is what she is used to calling her own mother. "What is it?"

"Kimala is having trouble with that healing spell," Ezra says in a low voice. The medic advisor has asked for her help with medical advice ever since she learned that Eliara's techniques are more student-friendly than the advanced medical textbooks, thus making it easier to train Kimala. "Could you explain it to me again? Your description is better than my own."

Eliara nods. "Of course." She glances around. "In here?" she asks, gesturing to an empty reading room.

Ezra nods eagerly. Once they sit down, though, she notices Gamerog on the duir'ne's hip and raises an eyebrow in surprise. "Why are you carrying that with you?"

"It *was* originally my sword," she says dryly, her thumb hooking around the hilt. "I am trying to clean the Source stains, and the best way for me to do that is to keep it on me. I figured it will only take me a couple of days if I do it this way."

Ezra stares at her, stunned. "No one has been able to purify that blade before."

Eliara frowns. "That is odd. Mara seemed to be doing a fantastic job before; the blade is two-thirds cleaned of the Da'ruha's Source."

"Mara?" Ezra repeats, rubbing her jaw. "I wonder if

the kareia was taking it without her realizing it… It's quite possible. She has been having a hard time confining her Source, so a good portion has been visible. The kareia could have been sapping at it to help mitigate it."

"That would explain the large amount of Source I sense in the blade," Eliara admits. "I will not strain myself, though."

She smiles at Eliara. "I know you won't; you seem to know your limits better than Mara did."

Eliara chuckles. "Indeed." She relishes in this moment where she can let her guise drop; trying to mimic Mara's dialect and speech patterns is tiring. She tends to stay in her room the majority of the time, not wanting to slip up and give herself away. Luckily, Mara used to do the same – only she had studied, not drawn or written.

She proceeds to explain her version of the complicated healing spell to the medic advisor again. Once she is finished with the explanation, she sighs deeply.

Ezra gives her a concerned look. "What is it, Your Highness?"

"This is probably quite odd, knowing your daughter is in Carni while someone else inhabits her body." She hangs her head. "I do not know if I can keep up this ruse much longer. So many people know Mara much better than I, so I am afraid to merely walk down the corridor."

"You have been doing great these past few days," Ezra reassures her. "Not only that, but by wearing that sword, you will look even more like her. She was nearly inseparable from it."

Eliara tilts her head to the side in curiosity. "Why was she not wearing it in Carni, then?"

Ezra hesitates for a moment. "Right before she left, we were afraid she might do something… brash with it, so we wouldn't let her put it back on."

"Darion told me about the vessels who committed suicide," Eliara whispers, her eyes dropping to the ground.

"While I do not agree with their methods of coping with whatever the Essence had put them through, I do not believe Mara would have been one of them. She is too stubborn."

Ezra laughs. "You're right about that." She stands up and gestures for the duir'raz'ne to follow her. "Come with me to see Kimala. She and Mara never got along too well, much like actual sisters, but I'm sure she has been worried about your well-being."

Eliara frowns. "I got along quite well with my sisters."

Ezra gives her an odd look. "Things have changed a bit," she tries to explain. "Nowadays, siblings tend to argue and bicker a lot, but they're still close. They will drive one another crazy at times, too. Mara always antagonized Kimala because she is quite funny when worked up." Ezra smiles ruefully. "Actually, you might get along well with her. She is tein'stra, but she acts more like a duir'ne. She is promised to Alec Roanoak."

"Ah, such a nice young man," Eliara immediately comments, smiling. "He wanted to duel me the other day, though; I had to pretend I had already overstrained myself to get out of it. I am certain Mara's fighting style is not the same as my own."

"You would be surprised." Ezra opens the door for her, following her down the hallway. "She knows a lot of different fighting techniques because of Shaniel, Darion, Aeserast, and Riley all tutoring her. Plus, there is the Essence's knowledge base to take into consideration. You can probably get away with more than you think."

Eliara smiles shakily. "I would not want to impose on her social life, though." Seeing someone approach, she mentally panics as she tries to act impassive like Mara.

Alec falls into step with them, smiling easily. "Good morning. Are you headed to the Academy today, Ezra?"

Ezra nods. "I'm teaching Kimala another advanced field technique. Want to join?"

Alec shakes his head. "Not today. My father wants me to practice for the upcoming fall festival's ritual, since I will be turning eighteen." He rolls his eyes. "I find it slightly ridiculous that we have two customs. Sometimes, I wish we would catch up with the rest of the world."

Eliara cannot help the slight frown furrowing her brow. Ezra notices and chuckles. "Have you not heard yet? Even though you come of age at sixteen, there is the Alkinian coming of age at eighteen that is also celebrated. Most Alkinian-accepting countries follow the Alkinian's coming of age time, but Quasala is a bit different; here, one will come of age at sixteen, but will not be able to take the throne or any other important duties until eighteen."

"I find it ridiculous," Alec comments, not finding it odd in the slightest that Ezra had to explain their customs to her daughter. "If we cannot perform the truly important tasks until we are eighteen, then make *that* the true coming of age time."

Eliara clears her throat, daring to speak. She does her best to mimic Mara's Common accent. "Maybe… maybe it's in place to help ease the child into adulthood? I mean, it *is* kind of a harsh transition between having someone support you the whole way to suddenly being tossed out and told to fend for yourself."

Alec stares at her, and for a brief moment, she fears he had seen through her ruse. Suddenly, he grins. "I never thought of it that way! You really do have an interesting way of looking at things, Mara. That makes more sense." He waves to them. "I'll see you later. Please tell Kimala I will meet her for dinner."

Ezra chuckles as Alec disappears down the corridor again. "See? Not too hard."

Eliara glances at her. "I did not know that logically thinking things through with an analytical standpoint is a… different way of thinking here."

Ezra shakes her head. "It's not that. Mara grew up on

Earth, so she knows those customs better than Saheir's or Alkina's. Because of that, everyone thinks she has an odd way of thinking and speaking. She's a very straightforward kind of girl; and, by the looks of it… so are you." She gives Eliara an odd look. "One thing that I'm noticing is how similarly you both actually do think. It is kind of spooky."

Eliara raises an eyebrow. "Perhaps it is meant to be that way."

"Maybe."

The walk to Cerlail Academy is slow and steady. Eliara takes in as much of Quasala as she can; the last time she had been in this city was when it had been a tiny village in the middle of a forest. She is amazed that the same village has turned into the capital of the continent and home of the country's leader.

The three main buildings of Cerlail Academy stretch high above the city, serving as a landmark. She recognizes vague Alkinian structure in those buildings, but something about the tactical wing reminds her of the old history books of the time before Voyana's explosion when Alkinian cities had been full of polluting machinery. The buildings had been straight, uniform, and edged, much like the tactical wing is now. She has yet to gather the courage to walk into the building for fear it will collapse on her.

As they cross the center field between the three buildings, a man with odd wolf-like ears and a weathered face approaches them. His black master mage robe swirls about him, staying out of the way of his feet while the tactical wing's symbol shimmers in the late morning light.

"Good morning." He beams at them before focusing on Eliara. "Say, Mara, when do you think you will be well enough to continue your classes? I spoke with Lilly, and she claims you are doing better than expected."

A spear of panic shoots through Eliara. *This must be Headmaster Gerard Folion*, she realizes, carefully schooling her expression. She glances at Ezra, who only smiles warmly at her. "I-I don't know yet," Eliara says, again trying her best to mimic Mara's speech patterns. Luckily, Ezra has been having her practice on a daily basis. "Mom and I are heading to the medical wing now. Maybe after another checkup, I can get a date on when I can resume my studies."

Folion's brow furrows. His eyes narrow as his gaze pierces into Eliara. "Resume? Are you not even reading the textbooks I gave you, Mara?"

Ezra links her arm with Eliara, distracting the headmaster from the young mage's panicked expression. "Oh, she is; I have to pull the textbooks out from underneath her nose on a daily basis! I'll let you know about when she can attend your classes, Gerard. Right now, though, we need to see Lilly."

Ezra pulls Eliara toward the curved, crème colored building. Eliara glances back at Folion, giving him a tight smile. "I apologize," she quickly says.

Folion's frown deepens as they enter the medical wing.

"I think he knows," Eliara whispers to Ezra as they head for the platform door.

As soon as they step into the transportation unit, Ezra places her hand on the glowing orb. The door quickly slides shut, and the platform ascends smoothly. "If he does, then he does. It isn't like he will tell everyone; he will most likely go to Timian or one of the other Highlords to see if they know anything. He knows you just came back from Carni."

Eliara slowly exhales. "I still do not believe this is a good idea..."

"Don't worry about it." The platform stops and the doors slide open. Ezra links her arm with Eliara's once again, pulling her out of the elevator.

Eliara stares out the windows as they walk down the corridor. The view of the sprawling city shifts to the inner triangle of the Academy. Crystal pathways connect the three towering buildings on multiple levels as individuals on Source boards coast on Voyana currents to their destination, providing multiple ways for someone to go from one spot to the next.

"Just so you know, Mara does have a bit of medical knowledge," Ezra explains in a low voice as they near their destination. "Kimala won't find it odd if you directly explain some concepts, but do not try to *show* her. Mara had the knowledge but not the ability to perform the majority of them."

Eliara nods, thoughtful. "Was the Essence that resourceful?"

Ezra gives her an odd look. "Mara was constantly calling it a 'knowledge pit.' I'm surprised you haven't been conversing with it yourself."

Eliara gives a nervous laugh. "Ah, well… because of what happened…"

Ezra pats Eliara's arm. "No need to explain. I know you can't tell me everything; I'll just pester Mara when she gets back."

Eliara smiles apologetically. "I wish I could say more; you are so easy to talk to."

"I'd hope so!" Ezra opens the door to a study room. "I'm your mother!"

Eliara pauses. *She only said that because of where we are,* she tells herself, but she cannot help the warm feeling inside her chest. Ezra truly reminds her of her own mother, Rhea Alamir – though Ezra seems to know a lot more about daily common life than her mother ever had.

Kimala glances up, giving Eliara a concerned look. "Are you feeling any better, Mara?"

Eliara nods mutely. She feels as though the blonde girl is the most likely out of everyone to find out her true identity next.

"About that technique, Ezra… I don't think I got it right. How does it go again?" Kimala asks the medic advisor, missing Eliara's look of discomfort.

Ezra smiles reassuringly at Kimala. "It's a tricky one; honestly, I didn't expect you to get the hang of it so quickly." She sits with Kimala at the table. "First, you have to sedate the patient with…"

Eliara tunes them out as she walks to the window overlooking the innards of Cerlail Academy's medical wing. The study is situated over a main thoroughfare of interconnected pathways leading to multiple levels and sectors of the building. Medics, interns, and trainees hurry to their next destination, all of them dressed in either off-white or white robes with colored bands denoting their rank and specialization.

She sighs. Her fingers itch to open one of the various medical books lying about the study, but she isn't sure if Mara would do the same. *Why must I be inside the single vessel who studies the exact opposite as me?* she mourns yet again, resting her forehead against the glass. She closes her eyes to the cool sensation. Of all the things she had dreamed of experiencing if she ever made it out of Eleth – the colors, smells, sensations, temperatures – this is definitely not one of them. Eleth is bland and plain, but at that moment, she would prefer to be inside her muted room than inside the body of a girl who would rather fight and argue than heal and nurture.

Eliara fingers the Alamiran crest around her throat, still surprised it has not been destroyed yet. Even though she had told Darion to find another to love because of her untimely demise, it is still odd watching him choose another over her – especially one as uncouth as Mara. If it had been Kimala, she would have understood; Kimala seems much more refined and ladylike. But Mara… Mara is so completely different. She does not see how Ezra can compare her to her daughter.

"Thinking about Darion again?"

Kimala's question startles her. She glances over with

wide eyes, her cheeks inadvertently flushing a little. "N-no! Of course not," she tries to cover up. She berates herself, remembering she is in Mara's body – but then registering Kimala's words. *Why would Mara think of Darion? Does she have feelings for him, as well?*

Kimala rolls her eyes. "Come on, Mara. You were fiddling with that crest he gave you, and you only do that when you seem to be thinking of him. You can't hide it anymore, you know; I know you like him."

Eliara's breathing nearly stops. She knows Ezra is watching her, catching every nuance; the woman knows her daughter's micro-expressions better than anyone else.

She shrugs, keeping her face as neutral as possible. She turns to the window again, dropping her hands to her sides. "It's not that. He's just been gone for a while."

"He *is* the Death'Lord," Kimala points out dryly as she scribbles something in her notebook. "He has a job outside of obsessing over you."

"What is that supposed to mean?" pops out of her mouth before she can stop it.

Luckily, Mara must have the same bad habit because Kimala groans and rolls her eyes. "Seriously, Mara? Open your *eyes*! He's obviously been courting you these past few months." She pauses, noticing her cousin's silence. "I apologize... I wasn't thinking. You are probably still grieving."

Eliara looks at the floor, avoiding Kimala's gaze. She has no clue what the girl is talking about; had Mara been in love with another? Did that person recently die?

Pivoting on her heel, she feels the now-familiar *swish* of the intermediate mage robe about her ankles as she strides to the door. She doesn't understand why the girl acts so tough when she has obviously been hurt in the past – but *what* hurt her? Why does she find it necessary to take on the world by herself? What does she feel like she has to *prove* – and to who?

Her head throbs; she needs to sit down. She doesn't

know anything *about* Mara, so she should stop attempting to live her life.

Kimala stands up, distraught for some reason. She grabs Eliara's arm. "Mara, I – " She stops, gasping at something.

Surprised by the sudden touch, Eliara yanks her arm free. "I'm returning to – "

"Who are you?"

Startled, she meets Kimala's wary, frightened eyes. Eliara can understand the first emotion, but why is the medic *scared* of her?

Ezra slowly rises to her feet, glancing between them. "Looks like the charade is up. Do you want me to explain?"

Eliara shakes her head, avoiding their gazes. She doesn't bother with the dialect anymore. "I… I just need to sit down. I am getting another headache."

Ezra's eyebrows snap together in concern. "They seem to be getting more frequent… I'll get Lilly. We might need to check the progress of the Hemius." She hesitates. "Will you be all right here?"

Eliara gives Mara's mother a wavering smile. "Of course. I am certain Kimala will take care of me."

Ezra nods, leaving the two girls to stare at one another. Eliara eases into the vacated chair as Kimala sinks back into her own.

"You're obviously not the Dark Warrior, else everyone would be freaking out," Kimala begins, her eyes narrowed. *Again with that name,* Eliara grumbles inwardly. *I despise that translation.* "Who are you? What happened to Mara?"

Eliara releases an exhausted sigh. "Darion is currently in Carni looking for her. She was ripped from her own body when they tried to bring her back to Cerlail Academy after our merging went wrong." She examines the girl for a moment. "As for who I am, you cannot tell anyone other than Ezra and the Ecalauna. Understand?"

Kimala nods. When Eliara continues to stare, she

stammers, "U-understood."

Eliara hesitates for a brief moment. The more people who know her true identity, the more she is at risk of discovery from her corrupted, possessed sister. However, she also feels as though the girl will stop at nothing to figure out who she is until she has the knowledge, which can be more disastrous than simply telling her.

"I am Duir'raz'ne Eliara, daughter of Adul'ne Alamir," she whispers, unable to look at Kimala. "I was merging with Mara when we were torn apart while crossing a teleportation hole. Since waking up, I have been having issues controlling the Hemius. I am trying to maintain it until she returns, as only she knows how to stop the spread within her own body."

Kimala's eyes grow wider the longer Eliara speaks. At this last part, though, she leans forward with a serious expression. "Her Hemius is active again? That's not good. You should not strain – "

"Far from it." Eliara smiles weakly. "That is why I have remained in the palace most of this time under the pretext of studying. Jethel'Lord Lilly placed a sealing spell on the Hemius to limit its progress, but I have been restricted from certain activities that could potentially strain the body. At times, even the walk to the Academy is too much for me to handle."

Kimala slowly leans back in her chair. "I see." Biting her lip, she winces. "About Darion… could you keep it a secret, please? Most don't actually know she likes him, so…"

Eliara smiles wryly. "I shall take it to the Elethavi with me. I am curious, though. Did someone else she love recently die?"

Kimala shrugs. "His name was Lyon. I don't know if she liked him that way, but she cared a lot for him. She was pretty torn up when he died a few weeks ago; *I* think that's why she went into Carni. He was an elemental, after all, so maybe he went there to regather himself."

"I see." Eliara leans back in the chair, resting her throbbing head against the side cushion. "Perhaps she will eventually learn how to move past that pain."

Kimala remains silent, watching Eliara rest. After a while, she opens her notebook and begins scribbling down some notes, coming up with another idea on how to combat Hemius infections.

Chapter 9
Danti Cauerr'ien

Darion delicately sips from the purple and blue teacup, looking out of place on the circular chair in the Creation'Lord's living room. His bag rests at his feet, revealing his intention to stay as long as he needs to in order to find Mara.

Aeserast pinches the bridge of his nose, his other hand tightly clenching his own cup of Source replenishing tea. "You should be with Her Highness, not babysitting me."

"She will be safe with the others." He takes another sip of his tea, giving Aeserast a knowing look. "You, on the other hand, have no such support at the moment."

Aeserast glares at him. "What if the Da'ruha shows up? Can Ezra and the others really fend *her* off?"

"Ezra, Kimala, Folion, and all of the Highlords have my summons stone," Darion answers calmly, setting his cup down. "If anything does happen, they will be able to contact me."

"The Will has already told me how to find Mara, Darion. I do not need your assistance." Aeserast stares into his cup gloomily. Despite his words, he still hasn't figured out who the 'silent guard of a forgotten time' is or how to find him.

"Of course you do." Darion pats Aeserast's back, nearly causing the half-fey to spill his tea. "If you collapse again, you need someone to drag you off that blasted Tower since Shaniel stayed at the Academy."

Aeserast sighs, relenting to his friend's persistence. "There is… one thing that the Will had said that I am still confused about."

When Aeserast doesn't continue, Darion asks gently, "What was it?"

Aeserast shakes his head. "The Will said I will need to send the 'silent guard of a forgotten time' to retrieve Mara once the Tower tolls. Only he will know how to properly bring her back without her permanently becoming eiv'ra."

Darion rests his chin in his hand, heavily leaning on the counter. "Silent guard of a forgotten time…" he repeats, mulling over the phrase. His eyes flit to Aeserast. "Do you know who this guard might be?"

Aeserast huffs, frustrated. "I don't! And because of that, I am worried to send anyone for fear they might bring her back the 'wrong' way, whatever that is."

"Aeserast. When has it ever been good that the Will interferes?"

"… Never."

"Exactly." Darion pats his back. "I do not care what that ancient ball of artificial intelligence has to say about who rescues Mara; I will go after her myself. It has already been a week."

Aeserast hangs his head. "It isn't good to go against Carni's Will, though."

"And it is not good to go *with* it, either. We cannot win either way, Aeserast. The only thing we *can* do is hope for the best." He stands up, taking their empty teacups into the kitchen.

Aeserast rests his cheek on the cool countertop, staring at the wall that leads into the hallway. A silhouette stretches across it, looking as though a tree is casting a shadow onto the wall. One of his recent artificial creations, Puck, has gotten it into his head to "steal" shadows from things in the material realms and place them along his walls. In reality, he is simply manipulating Carni to reenact the shadows, making it a game to see how best he can startle the Creation'Lord. He will have to speak with the elusive, free-spirited humanoid – if he can track him down again. Ever since Puck had developed his own thought and speech process, Aeserast had let him roam about as an independent creature – but he feels like he should have kept Puck closer to home to teach him a few more manners.

"Come; let us search for Mara," Darion beckons, heading for the door.

Aeserast groans. "We have to wait, Darion. That's what the Will said."

"As I said before, I do not care about the Will's opinion. I – "

Donnnnng.

Darion staggers, gripping the counter tightly as the ground shakes from the vibration of innumerable clocks tolling at once. Aeserast's eyes widen, recognizing the sign the Will had spoken of. The ground stabilizes, and they exchange glances before darting out onto the clock face.

"I have never heard of the Tower tolling only once like that," Darion murmurs grimly. "It must mean something terrible."

"I don't know," Aeserast huffs, coming to a stop in the middle of the huge clock face decorating the top of the Tower. His most recent creation of wind and water elements mixed with Gaian Voyana, Myst, twines around his ankles. "Myst, clear off the Tower; I need to see the surface."

As soon as the creation sifts off the main design, Aeserast stares at the positioning of the hands. "Midnight… or noon? That means…"

"It foretells the future of all the realms," a familiar cryptic voice exclaims.

Aeserast straightens, turning to face the glowing form of the Tower of Discord's "ghost." Her features are shrouded in the bright glow, disguising any recognizable traits.

"The Will told me it would be in relation to Mara," Aeserast tells her, ignoring Darion's defensive posture. "Is that true?"

"The young eiv'ra has discovered a new part of herself," the ghost responds cryptically. "She must find another before returning to her other half."

Darion frowns. "What does that even mean?"

"Who is the silent guard of a forgotten time that the Will had spoken of?" Aeserast asks, stepping toward her.

She tilts her head to the side, and Aeserast can sense her smile. "He will find her; he has already set his mind to it. Follow the darkness, and it shall lead you to the light."

She takes a step back.

"One more, please," Aeserast begs, desperate. She pauses, waiting. "Is Mara safe?"

She resumes backing to the edge of the Tower. "As long as she Finds what she is looking for, she will be able to join with the Other. Only then will she have a chance."

She steps over the edge of the Tower, falling through the invisible barrier that rings the edge. Aeserast sighs heavily as she disappears.

Darion stares at him, appalled. "You let her jump."

"She does it every time." Aeserast returns to the middle of the clock face, sitting down with his legs crossed. "She doesn't actually fall, either; she just... walks down the side."

Darion attempts to peer past the invisible barrier keeping him from falling over the edge. Sure enough, he can see the glowing form walking down the side of the Tower, which makes it look like she is falling in slow motion. "She was more cryptic than Elethanos ever is. What are you doing?"

"Looking for Mara." Aeserast closes his eyes.

"I thought she had to find something."

"Whatever it is, she found it."

"But... that woman..."

"She gave us the answers: Mara found the first portion of whatever it is she's looking for, and now the silent guard – whoever he is – will be going to retrieve her." He opens one eye, peering at Darion. "Now may I concentrate, or do you have more questions?"

Darion huffs, walking across the bridge to Aeserast's living quarters.

Aeserast once again searches for Mara. He centralizes his breathing, scanning as much of Carni as he possibly can in one go. The ghost's words echo through his head.

Follow the darkness, and it shall lead you to the light.

Grimly, he changes his search to only the Treavaun areas. The dark, roiling, corrupted Carni Matter churns about, disturbed by something. He delves deeper than he normally goes, risking being ripped out of his own body as he scours the deepest crevices of the desolate corners of Carni.

A faint silver spark pulses weakly in a sea of black sand.

His eyes pop open to see Darion approaching him, his bag slung over his shoulder. "She is in the Silver Mirrored Forest," he breathes, standing up quickly. "Something is wrong, though. We need to alert Timian and – Darion, wait!"

"I will not," Darion snaps, his hand already warping as he reaches into one of Carni's multitude of tiny membrane rifts. "If Mara is in danger, then I shall protect her."

"Don't, Darion! The guard – "

"I will keep her safe."

Aeserast stares at the spot where Darion had stepped through a hastily-made portal. His thoughts swirl around, unfiltered after everything he has seen in this past week.

The silent guard of a forgotten time… were they talking about Darion? But he couldn't possibly be, right?

However, in the contract book accessible only to those of Ecalauna or Ecalain-ranked individuals, there is no record of when Darion had contracted in or anything of his past. Remembering Darion's brief interactions with Eliara, things begin clicking together in Aeserast's mind.

For as long as Aeserast has been contracted, he has wondered why Darion has had such an extensive knowledge on the Da'ruha, the ancient past, and even old, forgotten words from the language before Voyana's explosion. He has always been suspicious of Darion's 'adopted' surname Bronzec, as well as his familiarity with *so many* Eleth guards and souls from the realm of death. It is as if...

As if he had lived during the time of the Ecalain families.

A cold shiver slides down his spine. No one should ever live that long; even he, who has been in contract for almost three thousand years, is already looking for his replacement so he may retire. Having that much knowledge of the turn of the realms is... unfathomable.

And incomprehensibly desolating.

Aeserast falls to his knees. "That's why you get that look on your face," he breathes, his eyes wide. "You're trying to redeem yourself, aren't you, Darion? But... what? What did you do that was so horrible you cannot bear the thought of letting it go and moving on?"

The darkness surrounding him swallows his whispered words.

— ◆ —

Darion walks along the pathway, baffled. Mara's Source permeates the air, turning the once colorful, glowing forest into gloomy, haunted woods. Even the exquisite blue flowers had turned black; only a fine, silvery dusting of pollen remains to hint at the once-beautiful forest that had been a mirror image of the duir'raz'ne's grove in Alamirana.

"Follow the darkness." The odd woman on the Tower had said that, but Darion is not sure how following Mara's remnant power will do him any good when it is permeating the air like this. As he continues through the blackened trees, he has a nagging sense that he has seen a different yet equally dark Source act like this before.

Seeing a grove of glowing trees, he heads for it, hoping

this is the "light" the cryptic ghost had been talking about. Catching movement along the ground, he looks down to find the black sand creeping over the glowing grass, absorbing the colorful shine. He stares, enthralled.

A blue-haired elf peeks around a still-glowing tree. "Darion? Thank the flow! Something weird is happening. This black Source is devouring the entire forest."

Darion exhales slowly, restraining his irritation. Of course the head of the sorceral wing is here; she has been trying to harvest the Silver Mirrored Forest's power for years. "Vierna, give me a report."

Zain peers around his instructor. Seeing Vierna floundering for words, he whispers, "The black Source is devouring any external energy it runs across; even the emergency access boxes we designed to open teleportation holes have been destroyed."

"This black sand eats everything thrown at it – literally!" Vierna spits out, trying to kick the sand away from the colorful grove. "All of my research has been ruined by it. I can't even use the data I have for the Academy. It's all that girl's fault."

"What girl?" Darion asks, his voice harsher than intended.

Chief Wizard Vierna points deeper into the woods. "She headed toward the lake; we didn't pay her any mind at first, though she had seemed pretty skittish."

"It wasn't until she ran that we saw the first bit of the black Source," Zain admits. "We were monitoring its progress, thinking it was just an anomaly when the plants… *disintegrated*." He points behind Darion. "Much like that tree is."

He looks over his shoulder as a tree collapses in on itself, falling into a huge mound of sand without a sound. It shifts and rolls to its next target. "How long has this been going on?"

"About… four days, I believe?" Vierna calculates,

frowning. "It already ruined our timekeeping devices, and we're afraid of losing the data in our units if we feed Source into them. When we tried calling for help, it destroyed our transponders. This stuff is attracted to *any* external Source, so be careful."

Darion steps into the shrinking silver glade, watching the black sand as he finds a fissure in the membrane and opens a portal for them. "Alert Timian of the situation; I will find what is causing this."

"Thana baro, my 'Lord." Zain jumps through.

Vierna pauses before following after her assistant. "I mean it when I say be careful. The black Source is acting scarily like Voyana; it doesn't just change the color. It's converting the forest into itself."

The portal closes behind her, leaving Darion with more questions. Is this really Mara's doing? Why is she absorbing the Danti Cauerr'ien's power? Is it because it used to be a part of Eliara and the Essence?

He follows the dark Source through the trees, noticing how its movement patterns change the closer he gets to the lake. By the time he makes it to the shore, his expression is grim as he stares over the blackened surface of the once blue water. He watches the black surface for movement, but it is as still as a marsh.

Only a few glimmers of color can be seen through the trees where parts of the forest resist the black sand's consuming appetite. One glowing tree remains on the edge of the lake, illuminating the dark form resting beneath it.

He wades through the thick sludge on the shore, noticing how it temporarily clings to him before falling off. It seems to know he contains an exorbitant amount of Source, but it doesn't seem to know how to access it. *Let us hope it does not figure that out,* he thinks, shivering at the thought of his Source being stripped from him.

Within minutes, he is close enough to the glowing tree to see black veins tracing their way through the bark and leaves. The silver dusting on the bark pulses in time with the black.

That is the heart of this forest, he realizes, feeling slightly nauseated. *The very thing that keeps this entire area safe.*

He peers around the tree trunk at the still form resting underneath the dimming branches. His breath sucks in as he recognizes the hazelnut hair.

He kneels next to the slumbering mage, shaking her shoulder. "Mara, wake up."

She doesn't stir. He glances at the approaching sludge and sand, wondering if it really is her Source. If so, why is it eating the forest? Why is it converting –

"Power," he breathes, staring at the glowing tree laced with black veins. "Mara, you need to stop."

She curls up tighter, mumbling incomprehensibly in her sleep. The tree above her pulses brightly as if responding to her, and he can see the faint tilt of her lips in a smile.

Darion leans against the trunk, frowning. "This used to be a beautiful forest," he says absently, a deep sadness welling within him. It feels as though he is seeing Eliara's forest burn down a second time. "You should not destroy something like this on a whim, Mara."

Mara curls against his leg. Surprised, he glances down to see her still fast asleep. Sighing, he rests his hand on her back.

"Wake up soon," he murmurs, returning his gaze to the lake just in time to see black versions of the pseudo-sprites that used to dance across the surface. They briefly twirl and jump before sinking back into the sludge-like surface.

———◆———

Mara curls against the warmth, feeling colder than she has ever been in her entire life. How can she even be alive while still feeling this cold? Or is it the opposite: is this what being dead feels like?

She wraps her arms around the warm presence, feeling

as though it can protect her and banish the horrendous chill that seems to have settled over her. The soft, jade green color pulses in rhythm with her breathing as she slowly becomes aware of her surroundings.

Opening her eyes, she stares at the black sleeve in front of her face. Still half asleep, she traces her finger over a wrinkle in the fabric. Coming to the end of the sleeve, she touches the tanned, callused skin there. The muscles twitch when she brushes her fingers across the palm. Her eyes follow the arm up to take in the tanned features and bronze hair of the handsome elf.

Carefully, she backs away from him, already shivering as the chill in the air pierces her. He opens his eyes, catching her in his jade green gaze. "Mara," he breathes in relief. "Thank the flow you are awake."

"Darion, I…" Guilt spears through Mara as she glances around. Her eyes widen, and her mouth falls open as she takes in the desolate, bleak landscape. "What… happened?"

"Your Source devoured the Danti Cauerr'ien," he whispers, glancing above them into the black branches of the tree. "This tree had been the last thing to go. How are you feeling?"

Wordlessly, Mara stands and picks up her robe, slinging it on. She walks along the edge of the lake, appalled at its reduced state of a sludge pit. She covers her mouth with a hand, her fingers shaking. "I-I didn't mean to do this. I was just trying to get somewhere safe until I felt better. The dream-eater had sapped my strength."

"You fought a dream-eater again?" Darion demands, his voice bordering on a note of panic.

"I wasn't hurt – at least, not much," Mara admits, gesturing to the water. "I ran this way and ended up in the water before I could stop. When I came out, I was soaked and tired, so I… stretched out underneath the tree."

She rubs the back of her neck, continuing down the 'beach.' Something drags at her legs and robe; looking down, she sees the black sand creeping up her shins and sinking into her clothes. She doesn't feel it at all, though. Staring in rapt fascination, she kneels down and touches the black sand only to yelp in surprise as it sinks directly into her hand. "Is this normal?"

Darion shakes his head. "Did you not know your Source was changing the forest?"

"No." She runs her hand through the sand, watching it stream toward her. She does not feel afraid as it piles up around her feet and robe, making her feel heavier than before. "I thought… I thought my Source was just rubbing off and then spreading. I didn't realize it was *changing* anything."

Darion frowns. "While it is unusual for someone to sleep in a form created by Carni Matter, it seems as though your Source was putting you into a type of stasis to help you recover after your fight." He pauses. "Do you feel any different?"

"Heavier," she admits, clenching her fist. "I remember having a dream that I was on the edge of this lake, speaking with a reflection in the water. She was telling me she can help me."

Darion glances back at the tree Mara had been resting under. "You could have met the embodiment of this forest. It would look like – "

"Eliara. Yeah, I figured that out." She takes a deep breath. "Do you remember when you stopped me after the Ecalauna meeting?"

His cheeks redden slightly in remembrance as he glances away. "Yes. You had… surprised me."

"I apologize, Darion. I shouldn't have run from you."

Darion shakes his head. "You should not have to apologize. We were the ones who should not have pushed you so hard."

She takes a deep breath, staring into the sky. "No, I shouldn't have run. It was cowardly of me. I had been scared of my own emotions, though, and I wanted answers. I was tired of being in a constant state of confusion."

He watches her, holding his breath. "And... now?"

She shifts her gaze down, smiling. "It turns out the answers I have been looking for have always been inside myself." Her fingers dig into her robe as she laughs self-consciously. "It's quite ironic, really. I came into Carni looking for answers to questions I could have answered on my own."

"Sometimes, one must come into Carni to realize they have the answers they have been seeking all along," he whispers, his eyes full of understanding. "So... you have a purpose?"

"Mostly." She faces the lake, although she does not miss the frown he gives her. "There is one more thing I'm missing. I don't know where I can get it, but... I know I need it before I can leave." She looks at him over her shoulder. Her smile wobbles in uncertainty. "Can I be a little selfish, though?"

"Anything," he says immediately.

"Will you accompany me?"

"Of course, Mara."

"Thank you." She turns back to the blackened beach, taking a deep breath. "Let me finish cleaning this mess up, and then we can get going."

"How do you intend to do that?" he asks, curious. His eyes widen in alarm as she steps into the lake, sloshing through the black muck. "Mara, I do not believe that is wise. Absorbing that much Source at once could blow you apart."

"I'll be all right, Darion," Mara reassures him, sparing him a quick glance over her shoulder. She is now up to her waist in the sludge. Once she is up to her chest, she stops. "This... should do. It shouldn't take too long, and then we can leave."

"Mara —"

She dips underneath the surface, submerging her head. Darion rushes forward, ready to drag the foolish mage to the shore.

A wall of black sand swells up and blocks his path.

Gritting his teeth, he strikes it with a raw jade sphere of power. It absorbs the blast, converting it into more sand. He punches it with his fist, but it merely shoves him back onto the beach.

"Carc'ra," he swears vehemently, glaring over the lake. "If you die, Mara, I swear I will drag you out of Eleth myself."

Black sand coalesces on the sides of the beach, merging with the sludge around Mara. It grows, forming an enlarging sphere around the mage; soon, it is several feet taller than him. He moves away from the edge of the lake.

He watches in morbid fascination as what had once been an entire forest piles into a huge semblance of a sphere in the middle of the lake. "This... this cannot be her Source," he whispers, shocked. Mara has a large amount of Source, but her lack of control has made it seem larger than it really is; in reality, she is approximately a rank six or seven when it comes to the amount of Source she has, which is only slightly higher than average. This, though...

This is on par with a full-blooded Alkinian from six thousand years ago at a level eight or nine.

He reaches for one of the many rifts inside of Carni separating the realms from one another. However, his senses encounter nothing; it is as if the coalescing power in front of him has managed to mend the rifts in the surrounding area.

Collapsing onto the ground cross-legged, Darion glares at the orb. He will make sure to thoroughly lecture Mara after she is done, whether or not she survives – and Voyana help him, he will make sure she *does* survive.

Pulling out his reki, he hesitates as a black tendril inches by him. Maybe he can send out a distress signal fast enough before it breaks the reki.

He takes the chance. Feeding his Source into the reki, he presses the first contact on his list: Air'Lord Tyson Mills. He feels the signal blast out just as a black tendril attaches itself to the reki, instantly converting the Source.

He shakes it off, staring at the cracked communication device. At least the emergency signal had reached Tyson; he should be able to trace the origin and relay the information to Timian and the others.

Darion watches the huge sphere of power; it has barely decreased in size. Sighing, he stretches out on the now-bare ground, resting his bag behind his head like a pillow. This might take a while.

———◆———

Eliara shoots up in bed, gasping for breath while clawing at her throat. She gulps in air as she tries to calm herself from the nightmare.

Rubbing her forehead, she questions why the Essence is giving her flashes of previous vessels' lives despite its shattered state. "*You should be focusing on healing yourself rather than making me dream of these awful things,*" she chastises it.

It doesn't respond, barely holding itself together by floating in Eliara's Source as the seal containing the Hemius restricts it, as well.

Sighing, she walks to the balcony, throwing open the bay windows. It is nothing like her old view from Alamirta that had overlooked the twisting spires and curved buildings of the Alkinian sanctuary. It is also nothing like her small balcony in Eleth that occasionally had a different drab scenery on some mornings.

She stares at the horizon, almost unable to look at the vibrant colors of the early morning. The sprawling city interspersed with green trees below and blue sky above is exquisite, a sight she has not seen for millennia. Despite the overstimulation of so much color, she has come out onto the balcony every morning since the first day she had entered the mage's room. According to the others, Mara used to do the same whenever she could.

Propping her elbow on the balcony railing, she rests her chin on her hand. She finds the similarities between them strange despite them being two completely different people.

A breeze shifts her hair off to the side, reminding her that she needs to tie it up. She closes her eyes, enjoying the sensation a little longer. She does not understand why Mara despises her hair; it is so beautiful and healthy. She wonders if Mara will let her style it when she is back.

Her eyes snap open as she blushes at this thought. Of course Mara won't let her style it; she is nothing like her younger sister, Kyrina, who would always let her play with her long, wavy locks of hair. She is also nothing like Rinali, who had such a pretty singing voice and would not hurt a single insect, let alone...

Hot tears sting her eyes. "Sister..." she breathes.

A sharp rap on the door to her chambers has her wiping away the tears and clearing her throat. "Come in," she forces out, turning to the balcony doors.

A female guard steps in, shutting the door behind herself. She bows to Eliara before she can see her face, remaining in that stooped position. "My apologies for the intrusion, Voi'duir'stra Danarko. I have important news from the Highlords."

Eliara's brow creases. *I suppose sending guards is the new method of transferring information,* she rationalizes. "What is it?"

"A particular individual that has been rumored to be in Carni has been located; the Highlords are sending backup to retrieve her," the guard explains, still bent over. "If you don't mind me asking, Your Grace, is this related to your recent return from the Corridor Realm?"

Eliara nods, recognizing part of the explanation Timian

and the others have been giving everyone in regard to Mara's sudden escapade inside the Corridor Realm. "Y-yeah, of a sort."

The woman partially straightens. "Might that individual be… Mara?"

Eliara squashes her alarm and frowns. "What *are* you talking about? I'm standing right here."

"Indeed you are." The woman takes off her helmet to reveal straight black hair and vivid blue eyes. She grins wolfishly. "But based off your expression, *you* are not Mara."

The Essence sparks weakly, and one of Mara's memories flit through her mind. "Desdemona," she gasps, staggering back. "How-how did you get in here?"

"Ohhh, just a bit of mind manipulation." She examines her gloved fingers. "Fooling the guards was the easy part. I never thought I would be able to fool you, too… Essence, was it?"

She does not know, Eliara realizes, sinking into a defensive posture. *I may manage to get out of this alive.*

"You see, a little birdie told me Mara had been ripped free of you, thus leaving you in a pretty broken state," Desdemona explains, reaching down her collar to pull out a dragon fire opal necklace. "I will admit, though, you're functioning a lot better than I expected. No matter; the Da'ruha will enjoy the company."

Eliara grits her teeth. "You won't get away with this," she stalls, backing up to the bay windows. Perhaps she can escape over the balcony and float to the ground; she has enough Source for that, at least, even though she has been dutifully purifying Gamerog these last few days.

"Ha!" Desdemona bares her teeth. "The only thing *I'm* getting away with is this hunk of armor. Da'ruha will have all the fun in the world *here,* with you. The insolent fletchling that had shattered my sister is gone, and you're sealed to that body. There is no escape this time."

She disappears.

Eliara glances around, confused. *Where did she go?*

"Srui," Desdemona whispers behind her, slipping the necklace over Eliara's head. "You fell for that a lot easier than I thought."

As soon as the necklace touches her collarbone beneath the Alamiran crest, Eliara knows the Da'ruha is contained within. "*I apologize, Essence. I will find help.*"

She forces her way out of the body just as the slimy presence of the Dark Warrior slithers out of the pendant. Barely holding her form together, she slips out the balcony window, hiding around the corner.

"How does it feel?" Desdemona asks eagerly.

"Hmm…" Eliara holds perfectly still; she begs the surrounding Voyana to mask her Source signature. "It is as our informant had said. There is a seal binding the Essence to this body. However…"

"Is something wrong?"

"No. Leave, Desdemona, before you are discovered. Father would be upset if he lost another daughter."

"Of course, sister." The soft clink of armor and click of the door alerts Eliara of Desdemona's departure.

Eliara creeps over the edge of the balcony, having trouble controlling her form in the material world. While she had mastered her spirit form while in Elethanos and Eleth, trying to maintain it in the physical world is much more difficult.

I… I need someone to shelter me, she reluctantly thinks, her mind racing. *Someone similar enough to me so I do not strain their mind.*

As quickly as she can, she makes her way to Cerlail Academy; she knows the hard-working Kimala will be there despite the early hour. She freaks out a few strong-blooded and powerful Alkinians, Quanarets, and elementals on the way who can see her ethereal form; luckily, none of them seem to know who she is and simply believe she is a renegade soul that had escaped Eleth prematurely. By the time she makes it to the correct floor, she is exhausted and can barely keep her form from spreading until it hits the walls.

"Kimala…" she breathes, trying to get the young medic's attention. She gathers her strength, worried that the young medic is not strong enough to hear her weak cry.

Kimala's head snaps up, hearing Eliara's feeble whisper and proving to the duir'raz'ne that the medic has a potent Source. However, she does not look behind her. "Who's there?"

"It is I, Eliara," she gasps, resting a half-formed hand on Kimala's shoulder. The medic's eyes widen as she feels the shock of the ancient duir'raz'ne's Source touching her own. *"Please, help me. Mara's body has been compromised."*

Kimala twists in her seat, staring at the softly glowing blue form. "What happened?"

"Please." Her control partially slips, and she winces as she draws her power back around her, solidifying her form once again. *"I cannot hold on much longer."*

Kimala straightens, pausing for only a moment before holding out her hand to Eliara. "You need a body, right? I-I can try."

That is all the encouragement she needs. She slips inside the willing mind, sighing in relief and allowing herself to relax. Her Source spreads out, complimenting Kimala's silvery-blue Source as it settles alongside it. Her shock is mirrored with Kimala's as they realize how *comfortable* it is to rest alongside one another.

"I apologize for startling you," Eliara says, letting her guilt resound through her Source. *"I did not want to impose on you. However, Mara's body – "*

"The Dark Warrior possessed her, didn't she?" Kimala whispers, surprising Eliara. "I had a bad feeling this would happen ever since I found out she was Lost. No offense to you, Your Highness."

"*None taken.*" Eliara's mind works on overdrive. "*We must come up with a way to drive her out of Mara's body without causing damage, though. I do not believe the Da'ruha will destroy her body; it seems as though she needed a material form to stay in, just like me.*"

Kimala shivers. "What about Mara, though? Do you think she will be able to drive the Dark Warrior out?"

"*Possibly,*" Eliara admits hesitantly. "*We shall have to wait and see. She does not seem to be ready to reveal herself, and it sounded like someone had given them information on Mara's state.*"

"An informant," Kimala whispers in realization. "Eliara, we need to tell *someone*. Maybe — "

The door slides open. Kimala whirls around, her heart pounding.

Chapter 10
The Split City

Ezra frowns at the medic's terrified expression. "Are you all right, Kimala?"

Kimala sags in relief, touching her chest lightly. "My apologies, Aunt Ezra." She pauses, a thought crossing her mind. "Actually, I have a question. How did you find out Mara wasn't... Mara?"

"It was her Source signature; the moment I touched her, I knew. Why?" Ezra asks, curious to know about Kimala's sudden interest.

"Tell her," Eliara orders, sensing Kimala's uncertainty. *"She needs to know so she is not surprised when she encounters her."*

Kimala chews on her lip. "I know, but..."

Ezra's frown deepens. "What's going on?"

Kimala squeezes her eyes shut, blurting out, "The Dark Warrior took over Mara's body, and Eliara is in me now." She opens one eye, sparing a glance at Ezra.

She is staring at the young medic in shock. "No... that can't be," she breathes, turning on her heel.

"Stop her!"

"Aunt Ezra, wait!" Kimala grabs Ezra's arm, and the medic advisor's eyes widen at the familiar Source signature. "Please, don't go after her! You could put yourself in danger if you approach her directly."

Ezra's shoulders slump. "You're... right." She eyes Kimala. "How did Mara's body take the transfer? Is it all right?"

Kimala glances away, listening to Eliara's apologetic response. "We're... not sure. Eliara slipped out before the Dark Warrior even knew she was there; they didn't seem to know she had been maintaining Mara's body. However, it doesn't seem like she wants to *destroy* Mara's body; just-

just use it."

Ezra sighs. "That's all we can hope for right now." She frowns. "I wonder how she even knew…"

"Eliara said she overheard Desdemona and the Da'ruha talking about some informant," Kimala says, her mind whirling as she tries to come up with some sort of plan. She is distracted by Eliara's swirling emotions. "What should we do now, though?"

Ezra taps her lips with a finger. "We should report this to Timian; he is the only one I know for certain not to be the traitor."

"*I agree*," Eliara concedes. "*Uncle Timian will be able to help us.*"

Kimala blinks. "Uncle?" she repeats. "That's what Mara calls him."

She can feel Eliara's surprise at this. "*Truly? How… interesting.*"

"Hold off on the chitchat for now," Ezra warns as they enter the platform lift. "It looks a bit suspicious. Do you know mindspeech, Kimala?"

Kimala shakes her head. "Not yet. I've been focusing on my medical studies."

Ezra holds her hand over the control panels, and the platform descends. "Timian should be able to teach it to you while we are there; if Mara managed to figure it out on her own for the most part, I am sure you will be able to learn it within a day."

The young medic fidgets, feeling her chest tighten. She suddenly understands why Mara kept to herself about all the Essence stuff now. She will have to give her cousin a proper apology when she returns.

Ezra frowns as the lift makes a mandatory stop at one of the levels. The doors open to reveal Evan leaning on his crutches while Jayden and a medic tail behind him.

Evan's smile wobbles a little as he asks, "May we join you?"

"Of course! Come on in," Ezra encourages him, stepping to the side to allow them in.

Kimala shifts slightly to the side as Jayden stands next to her. He beams at the medic. "Hi, Kimala!"

"Hello, Jayden," she greets, returning his smile. While she still does not like Evan, she enjoys the company of his energetic younger brother. "How are those documents I gave you?"

"I love them!" He pulls out his tablet, flipping through it expertly. "I have them right here in a category. Evan understands them better than me, though; I think I want to study in the sorceral wing. I want to build things!"

Kimala giggles. "You should talk to Wizard Narbundel, then. I am sure he would like to know what you want to study."

"That is where we are headed," Evan murmurs, glancing at his brother. "They thought it would be good for me to leave my room for a bit, too."

"How is the therapy going?" Ezra asks, and Evan turns to her. Kimala listens in, noticing how the young man seems comfortable talking to Ezra. Every other time she has seen him, he is skittish and anxious about nearly every little thing; she is relieved to see his mental state is doing better.

However, she can feel Eliara's uneasiness seep into her; the duir'raz'ne had interacted with both of them several times as 'Mara,' and her anxiety seems to be conditional at this point.

Kimala feels some of the tension drain away once they part ways in the library. The two medics step past the guards and enter the lift to go to the lower levels. It stops quickly, sliding open to reveal a short hallway leading to the Time'Lord's office.

The door opens on its own as they approach, and Kimala follows behind Ezra as they enter the well-lit office. Books, papers, and electronic records are shoved onto the shelves alongside one another with no apparent regard to order.

"Ezra," Timian greets, giving them his usual friendly smile. "To what do I owe the pleasure?"

"Timian, I need to talk to you about the Academy again. The structure of this building is just horrendous."

Kimala glances at Ezra in surprise at the sudden random accusation of her own late husband's magnificent architectural work.

The smile immediately falls. Timian takes a deep breath, expelling it slowly. "The room is soundproof."

Both Kimala and Eliara are both utterly confused as Ezra takes a seat in one of the two armchairs across from Timian's desk. "I apologize for suddenly intruding like this, but the situation is dire."

Eliara stirs in Kimala's mind, and Kimala senses the duir'raz'ne's unsettled shock. For some reason, she recognizes something in the way Ezra is speaking.

Timian clasps his hands in front of him, his expression grim. "What happened?"

Ezra takes a deep breath, explaining everything to the Time'Lord. "Eliara is currently within Kimala; she reports an insider gave the Dark Warrior information on Mara being in Carni, but they did not seem to know Eliara was keeping the body stable. We're not sure if the Dark Warrior sensed her presence before she managed to escape, though."

Timian frowns, clasping his hands on his desk. "This is indeed disturbing. Admittedly, we have known we have an insider, but I have been keeping confidential information limited. Only Darion, Aeserast, Shaniel, Lilly, and us know the true state of Mara and Eliara."

"*There might be others,*" Eliara murmurs, deep in thought.

"Do you... do you want to tell them?" Kimala asks. Timian and Ezra glance at her curiously.

"*I do. Perhaps... I could speak with them directly?*"

"That's not a problem." She gives Ezra and Timian a self-conscious smile. "Eliara has something to say."

Between one eye-blink and the next, Eliara sighs, flexing her fingers. "I will admit, Mara has never been this lenient," she murmurs absently. "I will make this quick for Kimala's sake. I believe we should look into Headmaster Folion, Duir'ne Alec, and Illusionist Quora. They were suspicious of me when I had been impersonating Mara."

"It can't be Alec!" Kimala immediately argues defensively from the back of her own mind.

"We have to cover anyone possible. It could just be that he had mentioned my odd behavior to someone else, and that *person could have been the informant without him even knowing it."*

"I... suppose so."

"Headmaster Folion..." Timian repeats, not knowing of the argument going on in front of him. "When did you speak with him?"

"Shortly before Kimala found out," Ezra says.

"He had come to me later that day with concerns on Mara's Source and her recent actions," Timian informs them. "I had told him of Mara's escapade through Carni, as he has never once faltered in his loyalty to the Ecalauna. However, I shall speak with him and make sure he has not spoken to anyone else about it, including Quora."

"Thank you," Eliara whispers, closing her eyes as she relinquishes control back to Kimala.

"It is a start," Timian admits grimly. "One I will not look forward to exploring." He frowns as another thought crosses his mind. "Is Gamerog still in the room?"

Kimala relays Eliara's words. "Yes; it's in the closet, the one Mara doesn't tend to use."

He rubs his chin. "I will see about retrieving it before she discovers it; Wester can safeguard it for the time being."

Ezra exhales slowly. "Let us hope we are not caught." She reaches over and pats Kimala's shoulder. "In the meantime, though, can you teach Kimala the basics of mindspeech? I don't want her accidentally giving away Eliara's presence."

"I would be glad to." He turns to Kimala, his usual kind smile back. "What do you know of mindspeech, fletchling?"

<hr>

Mara exhales slowly, brimming with energy. She feels the hard-packed dirt underneath her feet and the tingling sensation as something brushes across her face. Opening her eyes, she briefly catches a glimpse of bright sunlight in the form of currents before it fades away like an afterimage.

Her eyes fall to the ground, staring at the cracked earth so unlike the glowing green grass or crystal pathway she has grown used to seeing in this strange realm. Only a faint, silvery dust blows across the barren lakebed. *How long have I been here?* she wonders.

"Mara...?"

She allows her gaze to wander upward. At the top of a steep slope, Darion stares at her, concern etched on his face. She smiles at him. "See? I told you I'd be all right." She takes a step toward him.

The ground rumbles.

Huge cracks and fissures form across the dark dirt. Mara's legs buckle, and she falls onto her knees. She watches in horror as the ground crumbles underneath her hand, revealing dark purple swirls below.

"Mara!" Darion slides down the slope and sprints across the dry lakebed. He staggers at an upheaval, sparing a glance into the swirls below the cracked earth. He hurries to Mara's side and wraps his arm around her waist, dragging her upright. "We need to go."

"But — "

"The entire forest base is collapsing! If we stay here, we will fall deeper into the Treavaun."

She staggers alongside him, twisting around just in

time to see a glowing white flower trembling in the middle of the lakebed where she had just been. "No, Darion. We can't leave yet!" She pushes away from him, rushing to the flower and collapsing next to it. She gently cups its petals.

Its glow brightens to illuminate her face.

"Mara, there is no time! Forget it!" Darion panics, tugging on her shoulder. His eyes flit around them, looking for the safest route out of the lakebed.

"I can't... it's..."

"*Please... take me...*" The voice of the reflection from her dream – the forest's pseudo-consciousness – whispers in her mind.

Tears well up in her eyes as she chokes on a laugh. "Of course. Of course I will." That's right; she had made a promise. She refuses to break it.

He twists around to look at her just as the ground underneath them crumbles away. They fall into the swirling clouds beneath them.

Darion pulls Mara against him, barely registering she is clutching the white flower to her chest. Looking down, he doesn't recognize the scenery. "Carc'ra," he hisses, manipulating the Carni Matter surrounding them.

They land softly on the dark pathway. The flower pulses, emitting light and illuminating the path. Darion stays close to Mara, glancing to the side, behind, in front, *above* – every direction.

There is no hint of an exit.

"Mara," he starts in a low voice. "I need you to tell me exactly what you had been thinking of while we were falling."

Mara frowns. "I was remembering the promise I made to the reflection I had seen in the forest; she had wanted me to do one last thing for her."

A terrible sense of foreboding sinks into him like oil. "What was it?"

She holds up the flower, a soft smile on her face. "She

wanted me to place this on the cliff overlooking the unreachable split city."

Darion's breath whooshes out. "Hariana."

Mara's eyes fill with alarm at the name. "*Hariana?* But I thought it was in Eleth!"

Darion shakes his head. "There are two sides to Hariana. We created the portion of Hariana on the jethel – living – side, which then created the mirror image in Eleth. We made it so the entrance can only be accessed through Elethavi, though the physical location is deep within the worst part of Carni, locked behind a myriad of seals, barriers, and shields so no one can ever enter or leave Hariana through the Corridor Realm."

Mara takes a deep breath, letting it out in a whoosh. "I guess I need to get as close as I can, then."

"Mara, we need to focus on finding a way out."

"Not before I plant this flower."

"Plant...?" He glances at the white per'lusa in her hands. He feels the last remnants of energy from the Danti Cauerr'ien radiating off of it. It suddenly strikes him what the reflection Mara keeps talking about wants her to do. "You are relocating the Danti Cauerr'ien."

Mara frowns. "I... suppose that's what I'm doing. The reflection wants to see the split city that travelers talk about."

Darion shakes his head, unable to fully believe this. "I do not understand how it is that you can converse directly with Source, yet you cannot even see Voyana."

"Let's just go," Mara grumbles, starting down the path. The flower lights her way.

As she walks, though, a snarl erupts from behind them. Darion whirls around, spotting three sets of glowing white eyes. "Cerberus," he whispers, sinking into a defensive posture. "The scent of our Source must have attracted them. Mara, stay behind me."

"Can't do much else," she exclaims. She shifts the

flower to one hand as a black blade materializes in her hand. She faces three more sets of eyes in front of her. "There's another one here."

"You will have to cut it – "

"Down the middle; I know. I met one in Dounta."

Darion bites back the question burning inside of him at that casually mentioned fact. Aeserast didn't tell him that she had also faced off against a cerberus – unless, of course, she hadn't actually *fought* it.

Striking between the eyes of the middle head and pushing down, he smiles grimly as he hears the cerberus's pained yelp before the creature collapses into a mass of Carni Matter. Grabbing Mara's sword-wielding hand, he sprints down the path, putting distance between them and the other monsters.

"D-Darion! I had it!" Mara complains, quickly releasing her materialized sword so she doesn't hurt him.

"Cerberus travel in packs inside Carni," he huffs, glancing behind them. "Trust me, Mara; you do not want to meet their alpha."

Mara remains quiet, suddenly happy for the darkness as Darion continues to tug her along. After a while, he slows down, glancing around before releasing her hand. "We should be all right now. Cerberus packs are extremely territorial and will not leave their area; as long as we do not run into another pack, we should be fine."

"Okay."

The flower illuminates their way, guiding them through the dark, swirling Treavaun. Mara remembers what Lunesh had told her in the abandoned village, and her curiosity gets the best of her.

"Darion, I…" She clears her throat. "I found Lunesh again before I went into the Danti Cauerr'ien."

He glances at her in the dim glow of the flower. "I am glad you were able to see her again."

She fiddles with one of the flower's leaves. "Yeah…"

164

"Is something wrong?"

She shakes her head, staring at the glowing petals. "I do have a question, though."

He waits for a moment, but she doesn't continue. "What is it?"

Her eyes flick to his face. She cannot see his features clearly in the darkness. "She told me you sometimes come out here to Hariana or the Danti Cauerr'ien. Is that true?"

He stops on the pathway to stare at her. "That pesky Creation... what else did she tell you?"

Mara's eyes drop to the ground. "That you believe you're atoning for some sort of crime, although she doesn't think anything is wrong." She pauses before whispering, "Does it have to do with Eliara? She had been your fiancée, right?"

Even though she cannot see his features clearly, she still catches the motion of his jaw clenching. "While it is true that we had once been betrothed, that was nearly six *thousand* years ago. I barely remember what happened two hundred years ago, let alone all of my memories from her time. Even now, I have to read my own reports on certain events, as I have subconsciously deemed them unimportant and have forgotten about them. Eliara and I are merely acquaintances now, Mara; nothing more."

"Then why do you always get this look on your face anytime you speak to her?" she asks softly. Even in the dim light, she knows he has that anguished, guilty look on his face once again.

He turns away. "It is one of the few things I still remember; an inconsequential vow, but nonetheless, I... I broke it. I broke my vow to protect her with my life. I could not kill her sister – but neither could I imprison her. I had failed."

"Darion, you didn't – "

"You do not understand." He stalks down the path, and Mara hurries to keep pace. "Based off of my own reports of the situation, I had noticed Rinali was acting odd the moment she had returned; it had been my obligation to detain her. Before I knew it, she had already killed Codimus, an elemental ambassador whom she had supposedly loved, and my brother, Cain; it should have been enough, but… I did not stop her. I was a coward."

"I'm sorry."

It is as if he cannot hear her. He continues, his voice becoming more bleak as he confesses to the darkness of the Treavaun. "It was my fault the Da'ruha killed Eliara; if I had stopped her back then, none of this would have happened. Codimus and Cain would not have died; Carni would not have disappeared; Kyrina would not have lost her memory; Eliara would not be in the state she is in now; and the realms would have progressed more naturally without the influence of the Highlords' endless feud."

Mara's lips part in a temporary moment of silence as she struggles to say something to the elf who believes he had inadvertently caused the beginning of *everything*. "It's not your fault, Darion," she finally breathes. "It was the fault of the ones who decided to attack. You had known how much Rinali meant to Eliara; anyone with a good conscience would have hesitated."

He takes a deep breath, chuckling incredulously. "The worst part about it is I am glad it happened. I am *glad* the Alamir family died, Mara. If they had not, I would have never known the history of the Ecalain families, nor would I – nor would I have met you."

She stares at his back as they continue walking. It is as if the darkness is a blanket, making it safe for his whispered words. "When Eliara woke up inside your body and you were gone, I was furious; all I could do was worry about *you*. Even when Eliara was having a seizure, all I could think of was keeping your body alive so you can return to it." She glimpses his clenched fist. "It was the first time I ever truly resented Eliara for anything."

166

Her footsteps slow until she stands on the path, her vision blurring. "Darion, I – "

He turns around. "I do not expect anything from you," he whispers, and she sees his smile in the dim glow of the flower. "All I desire is your safety and happiness."

"But… you loved Eliara," she breathes, unable to control the tears racing down her cheeks.

"That was six thousand years ago," he explains gently. "We have both moved on."

"Then what was Eliara saying about the – " Suddenly, everything clicks together. She chokes between a laugh and a sob, feeling like an idiot. "The vow… It was a vow to *protect* her, not marry her."

He nods, closing his eyes briefly. This time, she *does* see the flash of pain and guilt – but now she knows what it is directed at.

She reaches up, wanting to comfort him somehow. Touching the left side of his face, she feels uneven skin along his jawline close to his earlobe; following it up to his temple, she realizes what it is. "Darion – "

He grabs her hand, stopping her. "It is proof that I failed my duty," he murmurs, squeezing her fingers. "I must never allow the mistake I made in the past to repeat itself."

"And you won't," Mara says, more emotion behind her voice than either of them expected. She tightens her grip around his hand. "I know you won't, Darion, because you are not the same person you were back then."

He gives her a heart-wrenching smile. "Thank you, Mara."

"Let's finish this so we can get out of here," she announces, holding his hand as she continues down the path.

I will protect him, she vows to herself. Her fingers can still feel the scarred skin where a blade must have sliced into him. She will ask him later to remove the illusion over it. *I will make sure he never feels this crushing guilt ever again.*

Her fingers constrict around his hand, but he doesn't say anything as they walk down the path in silence. Mara stares ahead, holding the flower close to her heart while never letting go of Darion. Her thoughts are centered around planting the flower on the cliff overlooking the unreachable prison.

Just as Mara sees the vague outline of a walled fortress, Darion sucks in his breath in recognition. "Hariana," he breathes. "I am surprised we made it so quickly... we must have been deeper in the Treavaun than I thought."

She glances at him. "I thought your thoughts are what lead you through Carni."

Darion shakes his head. "There are sections of Carni that are static, such as this fortress and the surrounding land." He points ahead. "If we keep walking that way, we will be able to overlook the valley and Hariana."

They walk for a couple of minutes before reaching a slight embankment. Trudging up it, Mara suddenly stops as she looks at where the hill drops away into purplish-black swirls, marking the end of solid ground. Experimentally, she holds her foot over the empty space.

The crystal pathway does not form underneath her foot.

"Mara, be careful," Darion warns, tugging her back. "Carni will not allow anyone or anything passage to Hariana via this route."

"Then..." Mara struggles to understand. "Is this the closest you can get?"

"Yes." He points at the ground. "This is the ridge over-looking the valley Hariana was placed in. This is where you wanted to go, correct?"

"Yeah," Mara breathes, still staring at the fortress. The walls stretch up dozens of floors, curving inward almost like a dome. Only a single spire rises out of the middle, looking oddly like a watchtower – or a single cell. She can see the top of the squat fortress just beneath the curved wall, allowing no entry or exit of any kind – not even a place to look out except for that lonely tower.

It's so desolate, she thinks to herself, taking a deep breath as she kneels in the purplish-black grass. It turns a bright lavender in the light of the flower's glow, banishing the darkness as well as a nagging feeling of recognition within her at the sight of the fortress. *But if this is where the last of Eliara's Source wants to be, then… so be it.*

"I hope this is what you wanted," Mara murmurs aloud, setting the flower down. White roots extend into the ground, pushing their way into the soft dirt and taking root. The grass around it brightens, taking on the same glow that the Danti Cauerr'ien had had before Mara had absorbed it.

Darion watches the glowing plants, understanding dawning in his eyes. "Mara, the Source you absorbed… was it sentient like the Essence?"

Mara shakes her head. "Not… quite. It was like it was on the border; it was curious to know what everyone in the forest had been talking about, but there was no emotion behind it. When it talked to me…" she trails off, staring at the blooming per'lusa.

"When it talked?" Darion repeats softly, urging her to continue.

Mara smiles lopsidedly at him. "It asked a lot of the same questions Auntie did in the gold and green forest. That's how I knew it wasn't like the Essence."

Darion takes a steadying breath. "So you spoke with the Will of Carni."

She frowns. "Lunesh didn't call her that…"

He shakes his head. "The manifested creations call the Will different things; mother, aunt, ruica, grandmother, werui… however, they all refer to the realm itself, which has gained sentience since its creation. Thousands of years of existing seems to do that to external Source without an owner."

"Like the Essence," she whispers.

"Indeed." He squeezes her fingers lightly. "Is there anything else you must do here?"

Mara shakes her head, turning away. A sprout pushes out of the ground to form the beginning of a tree. "Not here. I-I do need something else, though."

Darion frowns, but he does not argue with her. "Where must you go, then?"

She stares at their joined hands. "Don't... get mad at me, all right?"

"I am here because I am supporting your decisions, Mara. Do not be afraid to tell me what it is you need to do to no longer be eiv'ra."

She glances into his eyes in the strengthening glow. While he does look concerned, there is also trust in his gaze.

I don't deserve that trust. At least... not yet.

"I came to Carni so I could figure out why the memories and my power were going haywire," she whispers, barely able to keep the tremble out of her voice. "Instead, I found out it wasn't the realm at all. It was *me*. I was the one doing this to myself."

She can tell he wants to say something, but he clenches his jaw in silence.

"I want – no. I *need* to do this. I'm willing to do what it takes, too." She takes a steadying breath, giving him a shaky smile. "I don't want you to hurt anymore because of me, Darion. I wouldn't be able to live with myself."

His eyes widen before hooding in determination. "What can I do to help?"

She chews on her lower lip. "I don't know where to go from here. I know what I need to do, but I also know I'm not... ready. Does that make sense?"

He smiles in understanding. "More than you realize, Mara. Think of your goal and what it is you need to finish up here in Carni. Carni's Will can sense your desires, and it will lead you to them — even if you are still not sure exactly what it is you need. That is the power of this realm."

Mara releases her breath, giving him a genuine smile. It feels like the one true smile she has been able to give anyone since Codi had died. "Thank you, Darion."

His breathing hitches. He bows, whispering almost reverently, "It is my honor, Mara."

"Please… don't bow to me." She touches his jaw, pulling his face up. "I don't want you to ever bow to me, Darion."

Uncertainty flicks through his eyes. "Then what — "

She presses her lips against his. Her fingers rest on his shoulder as he slowly relents, his own hand hesitantly sliding around her waist.

For a brief moment, Mara cannot comprehend anything other than his lips, his hands, and the beautiful jade green Source she can sense churning within him. Her emotions make her own Source dance as her feelings are reciprocated, and in that brief moment, she can only think of one thing:

I will protect him.

Breaking off, she stares at him, still giddy from the kiss. He is taken aback by the passionate blaze in her eyes. She tugs on his hand. "Let's hurry; I want to go home."

He laughs incredulously. "Mara, how are you still able to shock me so?"

"Maybe because I'm not like anyone else you have ever met before?" she teases him, smirking.

"That is for certain." His mood sobers as he focuses on why they are on this pathway. "Just be sure you keep your thoughts centered; Carni will take you as a whole person and break you down, forcing you to choose whether or not you will accept different parts of your own self. You must be careful what you *do* choose because Carni has the ability of solidifying your choices and ingraining them into your very nari. These choices cannot be changed later if you decide otherwise."

She stares down the pathway. "I want the power to protect everyone."

His eyes widen at her bold statement, slightly shaken at her sudden resolve as well as how true her words hold to her original personality. "Mara, are you certain this – "

"I can't let anyone else die because of me." Her voice is barely above a whisper. "My father, Codi, Thanos… even Naiya. They all died because I was too *weak* to help them. I couldn't protect them. In every case, I was powerless to give them the support they *deserved*. I was too young and naïve to help my father. I couldn't control my powers in time to save Codi. I was too easily manipulated by Rath, and both Naiya and Thanos suffered for it. I-I didn't have confidence in myself nor the power to help any of them."

She clenches her empty hand, staring at her fist. She remembers Thanos's form disintegrating in her arms as she had begged him to stay. She knows he is still alive and recovering, but it doesn't dismiss her actions in his fight with Rath.

"I will not allow another person to suffer just because I am the Essence's Vessel or an Ecalain. It's time I stop cringing over all of these stupid titles, too, because as much as I hate them, they will give me the power I need to protect those I love."

Darion slowly exhales. "Power is not everything, though, Mara; you can have all the power in the world, and things can still go wrong. Please remember that."

She gives him a wry smile. "I know, Darion. However, if it's the difference between hiding behind you because I am afraid or standing in front of you as a leader to block a fatal blow, I will always choose the latter."

"I would rather be by your side than behind you, though."

She laughs, self-consciously rubbing the back of her

neck. "I-I suppose that's all right."

He squeezes her fingers once again. "I understand what you are saying, though, Mara. As for your status as Ecalain, you do not have to decide right now; that can wait until you reach Alkinian age."

Mara shakes her head. "No, Darion. That's only a year away. I need to – " She stops, racking her brain for any semblance of timekeeping. "What is today?"

Confused by the switch in topic, Darion shifts his bag off his shoulder and digs out a tablet. He channels his Source and inspects the date on the device. "It is the twenty-fifth of Tora. You have been in Carni for over half of a month, Mara."

Mara groans, rubbing her face. "You're kidding me. I know it's felt like a long time, but I didn't realize it was *that* long." She glances around, searching for an exit. "I guess there's no way for us to get back before my birthday…"

"When is it?"

"The twenty-seventh," she responds, walking forward with a newfound determination. She will finish doing whatever she needs to do so she can get back to her friends and family.

Darion sighs. "It will take at least a day to leave this Treavaun area, and I will need to rest soon. I am in a material body."

Mara whirls to him, suddenly worried. "Why didn't you tell me sooner? What if you had gotten hurt, Darion?"

He shifts the bag onto his shoulder again. "I will be fine; I am trained in traversing the Corridor Realm. It is *you* I am worried about."

Mara continues down the path, grumbling to herself about the unfairness of everything. Darion chuckles, amused.

Chapter 11
Holographic Design

Kimala picks at her food, feeling more nauseated than anything as Alec converses with "Mara" about the strategy game Siege. "*I don't know how much more of this I can take,*" Kimala complains mentally to the duir'raz'ne, having already gotten the hang of mindspeech after the quick lesson with Timian yesterday.

"*Only a little longer, Kimala,*" Eliara responds, morbidly curious of the conversation. "*It seems she is trying exceptionally hard to fit in, but what would her motive be?*"

"*Who knows.*" Kimala risks a glance at Mara.

She is caught in the curious gold eyes. "Everything okay, Kimala?" she asks, shoving a large bite of omelette into her mouth. It is exactly like what the real Mara would do.

Kimala gives her a weak smile. "Yeah, just a bit tired. I was studying late last night." She forces herself to take a bite of her biscuit.

"Oh, have you heard?" Alec suddenly says, lowering his voice to a hushed whisper. He grins at Mara and Kimala. "My father said Teresa succeeded in recapturing Alamirana! They are currently trying to unseal the teleportation platform so they can set up an anchored portal. Can you imagine? After a hundred years, we finally have control over Alamirana again! We get to see what the Alkinian city looks like!"

Kimala's breath hitches as she feels Eliara's deep longing to return to Alamirta. "That sounds amazing," the medic admits, smiling at her beloved. She remembers him gushing about his older sister a couple weeks ago when she had first set out with her troops to break the cracking barrier over the ancient elven city. "When will they be able to finish the anchoring?"

"I don't know," Alec admits. "Father didn't tell me. However, my sister has already started straightening up the city; apparently, it was trashed from when Paro'ki Naiya had been there."

"Alamirana…" Mara mutters. Kimala glances at her, noticing the mage's face is scrunched up in uncertainty and worry.

"What's wrong?" Alec asks, but then looks away. "Oh, right. I apologize, Mara."

Mara forces a smile on her face. "If you go, I'll accompany you. I just… don't want to go into the throne room or the dungeons."

"Was it really that awful?" Alec whispers. "I mean, I know it was, but… I've heard Erimentha took down the drapes and pulled up the rug. The throne room looks nothing like it had before."

Mara's smile wobbles. "If that's the case, then… maybe. It would be nice to have a different memory of that room."

"Different than when she had stabbed Codimus and tossed Kyrina through the portal?" Eliara grumbles sarcastically, her tone poisonous.

Kimala stands up rapidly, trying to disguise her sudden hatred toward Mara. She really needs to learn how to control the emotions rolling off of the duir'raz'ne. "I'm going shopping," she exclaims exuberantly, grinning at them. "Do you want to come with me, Mara?"

The possessed elf hesitates, staring at Kimala a little longer than normal. Right before Kimala's smile can crack, Mara warily says, "No, thanks. You might want me to wear dresses or something."

Kimala rolls her eyes, able to mask Eliara's irritation easier this time. "Dresses look *cute* on you, though, Mara!" She gives Alec a quick kiss on his cheek, smiling flirtatiously at him. "Want me to get anything in particular for you?"

He grins at her lopsidedly. "Surprise me. I always love your gifts."

She gives him a final kiss before rushing out the door in feigned excitement for the upcoming trip. In reality, though, she is panicking inside.

The Da'ruha wants to go to Alamirana; she just knows it.

Covering her nervousness with a hum, she heads for her chambers. Eliara's curt tone in her mind nearly causes her to go off-tune, though. "*How can you act so calmly around her?*"

"*What happened to you feeling sorry for your sister?*" Kimala retorts, closing her bedroom door behind herself and heading for her closet. "*When you first told me about it, you seemed more upset than angry.*"

"*The Essence's memories started surfacing while I had been in Mara's body,*" she admits. "*I was also reading up on the history I missed while resting in her room. I truly wish Darion had told me of the awful things she has been doing.*"

Kimala changes into a simple yet pretty top that shimmers blue in the light and a pair of snug white pants that compliment it well. "*Get it under control, Your Highness, or our little secret will be blown. I am not used to keeping my expressions schooled like Mara.*" She swirls on her second rank medic robe.

"*I apologize,*" Eliara whispers, chagrined. "*You are right. I will try to control myself.*"

"*Perhaps the shopping will help you feel better, too,*" Kimala reassures her as she tucks her money purse into her pocket. She steps out of her room and nearly runs into Mara.

"Highlords, Mara, you nearly gave me a heart attack," Kimala gasps, clutching at her chest. "Are you feeling all right? Your headaches aren't returning, are they? You should have Lilly check on you."

Mara shakes her head, eyeing Kimala's appearance.

"It's nothing major. I'm just a little tired, so I'm going to lay down. Are you really going into town right *now*? What about your studies?"

Kimala shrugs, ignoring the fluttering in her chest as she smirks at Mara. "Today is my self-study day, but I already completed everything required. Even my field and surgery reports for Lilly and Ezra are finished. Plus, with the trip coming up, I figured I would need to be presentable to meet the guardian of the city!"

Mara shifts her gaze down the hall. Kimala barely catches the mage's muttered words, "She isn't that impressive…"

"Huh?"

Mara shakes her head. "Nothing. Have… fun, I guess."

Kimala watches the mage walk down the hall and open the door to her room. She frowns, addressing Eliara as she walks down the corridor, *"It's spooky how much she is able to act exactly like Mara does. It's like… like she studied Mara. I don't understand how that would be possible, though."*

"I do not know," Eliara admits. *"However, we should inform Timian of this recent development."*

"Not now; it might look suspicious if I suddenly go to the Academy for no reason after I told her I'd be going into town."

"True…"

"Ah, Kimala! There you are." Kimala pauses, turning around to see Adul'ne Cleo Roanoak and a black-haired woman approaching her. "Do you have a moment?"

"Of course, Your Majesty," Kimala immediately says, bowing slightly to her. Even though Alec's mother had insisted on Kimala to not bow, she still feels obligated to do so considering she is the ruler of the country.

"Come inside," Cleo encourages, stepping into the sitting room she and the woman had exited from. Evan is lounging on the couch, resting; he keeps his place in a book with a finger. "This is Michelle, our ambassador. I am sure you have heard from Alec by now that we have reclaimed Alamirana, correct?"

Kimala fidgets. "I-I – "

Cleo chuckles. "I am not upset; in fact, I am under the assumption that he is interested in visiting the Alkinian city. I have already assigned Michelle to travel there to watch over the restoration. If you would like, you may accompany her to Alamirana tomorrow – it would be like a birthday present of a sort. She will be taking supplies, as they are in desperate need of assistance. The teleportation engineers will be anchoring a portal outside the city."

"Um…" Kimala chews on her lip, torn about sharing this bit of information, but feeling as though it will be more suspicious not to. "Alec had told both Mara and I…"

Cleo laughs. "The invitation extends to all of you! Evan said he will see if any of the engineers and medics are willing to lend a hand in revitalizing the city, so it won't only be the three of you."

Kimala turns to Evan, tilting her head as she asks in polite curiosity, "Are you not coming with us?"

Evan shivers. "Highlords, no. I'm *not* ready to see those halls again." He rises to his feet and props his crutch underneath his arm. "If you are heading in the direction of the Academy, I will accompany you."

"All right. Thank you, Adul'ne Roanoak!" She bows deeply to Cleo. Suddenly, a thought crosses her mind and she pauses at the door. "Is there any way Ezra can come with us since Mara will be going, too? I'm still worried about her health."

Cleo nods. "Of course; I will ask if she can spare the time. I am sure she would be concerned for her daughter, as well."

Evan and Michelle frown. "Mara?" Evan murmurs, a little alarmed. "What happened? She hasn't said anything to me."

"She stumbled into Carni, and her Source was damaged

in an attack," Cleo simply explains. "She has been limited to simple exercises and regular checks until the medics have determined she is well enough to resume her studies."

"I see." Evan rubs his chin, looking concerned. "I can speak with Ezra when I return to the medical ward."

Michelle crosses her arms. "If it helps, I can ensure she does not strain herself while she is under my care."

Kimala beams at them. "Thank you! That would be much appreciated. I will come back a little later." She steps out of the room as Evan follows behind, limping a little as he uses his spring-based crutch to keep up with her.

"*You should not have said anything about Mara,*" Eliara snaps, her nerves frazzled by the new information. "*This is all falling into the Da'ruha's hands. We need to alert Timian!*"

"*We will be talking to Ezra,*" Kimala states simply, careful not to speak out loud so Evan doesn't know of their current predicament. "*As soon as Ezra hears the plan and that 'Mara' is going, she will alert Timian to make sure he knows.*"

"*We need to find this traitor so we do not have to be so secretive about this,*" Eliara grumbles. "*I am getting sick of having to sneak around every corner and trust the flow that the Da'ruha will not find us out.*"

"*It will work out,*" Kimala reassures her, but even she doesn't believe her own words. They are playing a risky game; a game that, if even one piece is out of place, the entire board will tumble into the enemy's hands.

She glances at Evan. For all she knows, he is in on the entire thing. However, after a moment of examining his pained expression, she cannot help but ask, "Why were you in the room with Adul'ne Cleo and Michelle?"

"I was asked to divulge everything I knew of the castle and the city," he admits, giving her a tight smile. "They offered to come to the medical wing, but I thought the walk would be good for me."

Curiosity gets the best of her. "What did you tell them?"

"The defense system, all the traps and snares I knew of, major changes I knew Mother or Rath had made," he lists off absently, having to pause to adjust the settings on his crutch. The springs straighten and the entire unit grows an extra inch at the push of a few buttons. "I knew more than I had let on while in that castle. I don't know if that's a blessing or a curse, but if it will help the troops reclaim the City of Energized Glass, I will tell them everything."

"That's very kind of you," she murmurs as they begin walking again.

He watches her out of the corner of his eye. "I'm not expecting anyone to trust me," he whispers. "I won't be surprised if I am banished from this city soon. However, if it means that wretched man is thrown into Hariana for what he did to Mother, then I will tolerate any judgment the Roanoak family casts on me."

Kimala glances at him sharply. She has heard of this individual only briefly via the others talking around her, but she hasn't heard any details. "What did he do to her?"

His face scrunches in disgust and revulsion. "He gave Mother a phan'stra pill; I could see it was destroying her from the inside, but I couldn't do anything to stop it. The one time I tried to help her, I was locked in the phobia manifestation cell."

Kimala feels her stomach churn at this. Phan'stra pills are a failed experiment from millennia ago to help a woman have a child when there was no other way for a couple to conceive one, as Alkinians have an extremely low birth rate. The reason they were banned was because many couples were forgetting the critical step shortly after the phan'stra pill activated: DNA strands need to be implanted into the preprogrammed fetus to keep it from draining the mother's Source levels and to help it develop like a normal baby. This step had been commonly ignored, and the mother's Source would be drained into creating the pseudo-child. Many died before they gave birth because the DNA procedure was not done.

'Shadow child,' or phan'stra, became an apt name for such an abomination.

"My condolences," Kimala whispers, now understanding the rumored whispers behind Naiya's suicide. Many mothers of a phan'stra go crazy from their near-empty Source levels, and many of them want to either kill the baby or themselves — anything to get away from it. Shadow children are never normal, not even after they are born. They are made up of too much condensed bio-chemical, thus giving them an odd hue about them even if the proper procedures are used.

Evan gives her a bitter smile. "Rath was only using her. She knew it, too, but couldn't do anything about it. Hopefully, everything that has happened recently has put a dent in whatever twisted plan he had."

Kimala nods, finding herself hoping the same thing.

Once they make it back to the medical wing, Kimala accompanies Evan back to his room on the long-term patient floor. Ezra chats with Jayden inside the room, both looking concerned.

As soon as she sees them enter, Ezra rushes over to Evan. She holds up her reki, exposing a frantic, hasty message on the crystal's screen. "Your medic said you returned before him. What were you thinking? What if you had another one of your spells?"

Kimala glances at Evan. *Is he still having anxiety problems?* "I was with him the entire way back," Kimala defends him. "If I had known he had been accompanied by a medic, I would have relieved him of his duty since I was going with him."

Ezra glances between them, still disgruntled. "I suppose I cannot argue with that, but it is Evan who should have informed his medic he was returning with you."

Evan hangs his head. "My apologies, Advisor Ezra. I won't do it again."

Ezra places a hand on her hip, giving Kimala a knowing look. "So? What is it you need?"

"Alec, Mara, and I were invited to go to Alamirana," Kimala says bluntly, knowing Ezra despises people beating around the hedge. "I wanted to ask if you or someone from the Source specialization ward could accompany us since Mara is still recovering from her tromp through Carni."

"Of course; I just need to speak with my assistants and Lilly," the medic advisor says coolly as she gestures to Evan. "Let's see how you're doing right now, though. How have your walks been?"

"Very nice," he admits, giving a wobbly smile. "Though also tiring. I never noticed all the colors and shapes until recently; I do not know how I had missed everything before."

"It's common for people in your circumstance to notice more than the average person," Ezra passes off as her butterscotch-colored Source cascades over him. "It seems as though the walks are helping you regain your strength, though, which is good. Keep it up, and you will be back to health in no time."

"Thank you, Ezra," Evan says sincerely. "And thank you for accompanying me back, Kimala."

She waves to the disowned duir'ne and his brother as she steps out of the room. After a few minutes, Ezra exits with a huff. As soon as the door shuts, she turns to Kimala with a worried expression. "I am surprised you walked back with him. If you have a trip coming up, shouldn't you be packing?"

Kimala meanders down the hall with her. "I can pack later tonight," she says, waving it off as she keeps up the charade of nonchalance. "I wanted to invite you along since Mara is involved, and I know how you have been worried about her recently."

"I appreciate the invite." Her eyes narrow ever so slightly. "Where are you going right now?"

"Shopping!" Kimala beams at her aunt. "Would you like to accompany me?"

"Let me drop by Lilly's office and inform her of the sudden travel plans; I'm sure she can find someone to cover for me. After that, I would be happy to join you." She pauses for a moment before adding, "Do you want to meet in town?"

"Sure!" Kimala agrees, and they pick their usual place at their favorite seamstress's shop.

By the time Ezra arrives, Kimala is almost done browsing the new selection of patterns inside the shop. They meander through Quasala, picking out a few clothes and chatting more about the occurrences in the medical wing, especially a particular 'difficult patient' who has been under the illusion of being someone else. Under this pretext, they come up with a plan to keep an eye on Mara during the trip.

Despite all of their planning, Kimala has trouble sleeping that night. Her dreams are plagued by Mara's haggard appearance when she had tumbled through that portal with Desdemona hot on her heels.

The next day, it takes all of her willpower to get up as if nothing is wrong. She has a horrible feeling everything is about to fall into the Da'ruha's hands.

———— ◆ ————

Lavender and teal colors swirl and twist in the sky as Darion pauses on the glistening pathway. "Mara, I need to stop for a moment."

Mara pauses, frowning. "We haven't been walking that long, have we?" she asks as he sits down on the pathway and digs through his bag.

He glances at her briefly as he pulls out a shiny silver

packet. "About five hours," he informs her as he rips open the food pack. He bites into the hard, flat rectangle inside the packaging.

Mara takes this brief respite to examine him. He looks exhausted; he struggles to keep his eyes open while his shoulders sag forward. Her fingers involuntarily grip her robe in concern for the elf. "Did I... keep you up last night?"

"It is not your fault, Mara," Darion quickly says. "I appreciate you taking watch all night; I just do not sleep well in Carni."

She doesn't look at him. Her Carni-manifested body does not need to rest or eat, and ever since her respite in the Danti Cauerr'ien, she has not felt tired at all. According to Darion, her need for rest back then was because her Source levels had been low and not because she had actually been tired.

He pulls a crystal tablet out of his bag, handing it to her with a small smile. "Here."

Seeing it, she grins and takes it. Plopping on the crystal pathway next to him, she quickly activates the tablet's holographic system and sets it on the ground, allowing it to expand into the air in front of her. She flits through the applications and opens the building software she had been messing with while on guard duty last night. A multi-tiered city layout appears, tall buildings extending between layers of platforms and supporting the entire infrastructure of the massive city.

"You have gotten good at working that," Darion grunts in pleasant surprise as he chews another bite. Mara is oddly reminded of a granola bar and is curious to know what the meal replacement tastes like.

"Six hours of nothing else to do will do that to you. Definitely an interesting way to spend my birthday," she admits, tweaking the placement of a road a few degrees so it has a slope. "It's been fun, though. I almost have the city design done."

"What is it for?" he asks in curiosity.

She shrugs. "Just for fun. Maybe later, we can turn it into a multiplayer Siege game; I'm sure I can transfer the data onto the fae'reth in Danarkana."

Darion smirks. "Your father and I have already designed a multiplayer version of Siege; I am sure we can integrate it into this." He pauses, frowning. "What city is this design based off of?"

"Maybe a bit of Lunesh'kun's influence for the multiple levels or other city designs I've seen, but other than that, it's just some stuff I've had rolling around in my head recently." She laughs self-consciously. "I'm becoming like my dad… designing Siege board games for fun."

He gives her a gentle smile, his eyes soft. "You seem much more relaxed now."

"My head *is* a little clearer," she admits dryly. "I think I needed this time apart from it to process everything I had already recollected. I miss the Essence's company, though; I've grown so used to it being with me."

He frowns. "You still hold the Essence's memories?" She nods. "That is odd… The Essence's memories should not have bled into your consciousness like that. If anything, they should be shadowed, as if you had watched them from afar."

She shrugs. "I can tell you that's not the case; it's like I had lived them." She returns to her hologram, adding a billboard sign in the sky and tweaking the settings so it floats and rotates around a tall building. "Though I have noticed a difference between how I 'remember' the memories and how other vessels have."

Darion watches her construct the holographic city. "How so?" he asks, absently taking a bite out of his meager meal as he racks his brain. He has definitely seen something like that setup before, but he can't place where.

"What you said about the memories holds true for

them," she explains, scrolling through the options for transportation and finding the older versions of Alkinian vehicles. "I never noticed it before, but since I've actually had time to mull over the different memories without being bombarded with more, I've been able to differentiate them. Selena's are a great example."

She catches a glimpse of his worried expression. "What about her?" he asks warily.

"She remembered them like a holographic movie," she explains simply, pausing in her designing to look at him directly. "She felt like she was there, but she was also aware of herself. However, because of that, she was exposed to it *as herself* but also as someone else, leading to confusion and eventually... well, she didn't know what was real in her own head anymore."

Darion takes a slow, deep breath. "And... you?"

"I seem to be experiencing them how the Essence had." She turns back to her holographic designing. "It's like I was there, living as that person – not segregated from the memories. I think that's the key to remembering them properly; now that I have had time to sort through them, I have noticed little nuances in the different vessels, and I am better able to differentiate them from myself."

Darion rubs his chin. "So you are saying that because the previous vessels were remembering the memories as themselves, they were confusing them with their own lives?"

Mara nods. "I was doing the same before I came here, but now that I've gotten them under control, I'm able to confidently say that those lives are not my own because those vessels are nothing like me. Sure, I may have experienced them all firsthand when I saw their memories for the first time, but it was like *I* was *them* – not the other way around. Looking back, I now know they were not me."

Darion stares at her for a long moment. "How many had you remembered before you came here?"

"Hmm…" Mara uses both hands to adjust the positioning and size of a new building. "About… twelve complete vessels, I think, with some bits and pieces of an additional eight or so." At Darion's silence, she glances over to see him gaping at her. "It's not *that* impressive. Now that I've had time to process it all, I treat those memories as if… as if they're part of my imagination, really. It helps me separate them from myself even further."

Darion shakes his head, amazed. "The way you are able to handle these memories is phenomenal, Mara," he admits, holding his hand out for the tablet. "We should continue on, although I would like to continue this conversation."

"Give me a moment…" she murmurs, carefully placing a thin, spiraling building on the topmost platform of the holographic city. She switches on the gravity function to ensure the building will not collapse. Grinning, she turns to Darion. "Pretty cool, huh?"

He stares at it, even more certain now that he has seen this city design before. He glances between the floating billboard and the spiraling building, his mind racing. "Indeed, it is."

"I feel like something should go here, but I can't find a building design I like…" Mara admits, pointing to an empty space by a water fountain. The floating billboard circles the large building, facing Mara's pointing finger for a brief moment. "Maybe… a medical facility? But it would have to be crescent-shaped, and I haven't seen any designs for that in the program."

Unsettled, Darion murmurs, "Mara, that building style… It is from Alkina before Voyana's explosion."

She laughs, a bit self-conscious. "Maybe I saw it in a book, then. I know I had been reading a lot of old history before I came here, including stuff before the Fall of Alkina. I was hoping it would help me with the memories." Saving her design, she closes it and powers off the device.

"Thanks for letting me play with it. I guess my ideas aren't as original as I thought."

"That is not necessarily a bad thing, though," Darion says as they stand up and walk down the pathway again. "I had been wondering why the city you were building looked familiar, and now I know why; it looks much like a city from that time on Alkina. You might have seen images of it within one of the books you had read. It was one of the major cities that collapsed when Voyana exploded; it had contained one-twentieth of the entire world's population within its levels."

"Wow," she breathes, vaguely remembering the city by the description. "Yeah, that does sound familiar…"

He glances at her curiously. "However, for you to be so meticulous in the design…"

She shrugs. "I have a weird kind of photographic memory. Show me a picture, and I'll remember it subconsciously."

"I suppose that could be it."

* * *

Kimala stares up at the glimmering crystalline castle, awed at the spectacular sight of the towers spiraling into the sky. Curving pathways and stairs connect one tower to another, creating an almost maze-like system over the buildings on which they sit.

Riley walks behind the group as he converses with Rick, a loyal guard originally from Veera who had started his service in the Quasalan palace a year ago thanks to Aeserast's recommendation. Alec murmurs with Michelle about the seal on the teleportation platform in Alamirta's courtyard as they walk down the main road.

A wave of nostalgia courses through her. Turning inward, she asks Eliara, *"Did you miss Alamirana?"*

"Yes," she responds simply. *"Even though where I had stayed in Eleth was a mirror image of my city, it was still not the*

same."

Kimala's eyes trail down from the towering spires to examine the neka-style pillars supporting the entrance of the castle that looks more like a miniature city. She has already conversed with Eliara about Eleth and how the duir'raz'ne had lost track of time in her bland room. She cannot fathom the patience the ancient Alkinian must have developed over these thousands of years of simply… existing. At least when someone is reborn, they forget about the bleak loneliness of Eleth.

"We'll be staying in a vacant house right outside of Alamirta," Shaniel explains, his hands shoved into his pockets as he slows down to walk alongside Kimala. "Michelle wants me to go through the castle one more time to make sure there's no lingering traps before we move in."

"Sounds great," Kimala says, distracted by the surroundings. They pass by a shop with pretty Alkinian-styled dresses, and both Eliara and Kimala sigh wistfully in unison. Kimala has to fight the giggle from this coincidental synchrony between them; she enjoys the duir'raz'ne's presence.

"Hello, my little fletchling! It is so good to see ye again."

Kimala looks ahead, the thick Xharos accent startling her out of her thoughts. A black-haired woman with silver eyes and light brown skin grins at Mara, heading straight for the mage. Kimala's eyes flit to her cousin-but-not-cousin, wondering how the Da'ruha will take this random person.

"H-hey, Erimentha," Mara stammers, forcing a tight smile.

Kimala's eyes widen as she glances at the woman who looks to be in her late twenties or early thirties. Making a split-second decision, Kimala steps forward, gasping in respectful awe. "Erimentha Alamir? It is an honor to meet you in person!" She bows deeply in respect, allowing her excitement to show for meeting the woman well-versed in the medical field. Supposedly, she had been the one to tutor Eliara in the healing arts.

"*She was,*" Eliara confirms Kimala's thoughts, sounding a little smug. "*Take her hand; she likes physical interaction.*"

Erimentha chuckles. "And who might you be, fletchling?" she asks in amusement.

Peeking in front of herself, Kimala sees the woman's callused, tanned hand reaching for her. Blushing, she takes it.

Erimentha stares at her, startled. A jolt goes through their joined hands. "You…"

"I'm Kimala Brunet, Mara's cousin," she introduces herself, a big grin plastered on her face as she glances at Mara. Her gold eyes are narrowed ever so slightly. "Mara, you should have told me you knew the guardian of Alamirana! Or was this my surprise birthday gift?"

She can see the tension drain out of Mara's shoulders as she shrugs awkwardly, giving a forced smile. "Uh… sure. Erimentha, meet Kimala. Kimala, meet, uh…"

"You didn't even know, did you?" Kimala mildly lectures her cousin before turning back to the Alkinian. "Ecalain Alamir – "

"Please, jus' call me Erimentha," she corrects her, placing her hands on her hips. "I see yer burnin' with a question. What is it, fletchling?"

Kimala taps her fingers together, a little self-conscious. "Could I ask you about past healing techniques sometime while we're here? I'm studying to become a medic, and I have read extensively on your expertise in the field."

Erimentha's eyes sharpen on Kimala. She shrugs. "Why not now, then?"

Shaniel sighs. "Erimentha, we are heading to – "

"I *know* where yer heading to." Erimentha takes Kimala's hand, linking arms with the young medic. "Can't two medics chat for a bit before gettin' down to business? It's the fletchling's birthday, after all."

Michelle rests a hand on Shaniel's shoulder, stopping his retort. "Please do not keep her too long, City'Lord," she says coolly. "I am sure she will want to tour the castle once Shaniel is done searching it one final time."

"I'm tellin' ya, I'm not an official Ecalauna," Erimentha grumbles. She glances at Mara. "We will chat later, fletchling; I look forward to gettin' to know ye more than the last time you were here."

Alec sighs. "Kimala, it truly would be best if you would – "

"It's quite all right," Erimentha reassures him, patting Kimala's hand as she leads her away. She examines Kimala's robe. "In my last incarnation, ye had to be trained under a high-ranked official to become a medic, ye know. 'Tis phenomenal that today, anyone can work to the rank ye are now, little one."

Kimala's cheeks turn pink as they walk down a road, moving away from the group. "Th-thank you. Ezra Danarko and Life'Lord Lilly Mirana are my main instructors."

"Some of the best, I have heard." Erimentha gives her a sidelong glance. "Perhaps you wouldn' mind explainin' why my niece is hitchhiking in ye?"

The flush quickly disappears from Kimala's face. "Y-you could tell?" she squeaks.

Erimentha rolls her eyes. "Jus' as much as I could tell that mage wasn't Mara."

"*E-Eliara, help, please?*" Kimala begs, suddenly having no clue how to deal with the Alkinian who obviously knows more than just healing techniques.

Eliara sighs as Kimala recedes into the safety of her mind. "Vara tir'rani, Werui Erimentha," she greets her reincarnated aunt. "I was originally in – "

"Oh, my little fletchling!" Erimentha exclaims, cutting

the duir'raz'ne off. She hugs the girl tightly, grinning. A couple people down the street pause and glance at them before recognizing Erimentha and continuing on with a chuckle. "How long it has been! You will not *believe* the amount of srui I have met over these millennia."

Eliara sighs heavily. "While I know of your xhuri rehkava, I have never understood how you have not *forgotten* everything, werui."

Kimala struggles with the older Xharos words. Even though she is bilingual in Xharos and Blazhreian Common, she is still studying Old Xharos. She recognizes werui; it is Xharos for aunt. However, the other one is completely foreign. Hesitantly, she asks, *"What is xhuri rehkava?"*

"Soul promise," Eliara reluctantly admits. *"Admittedly, mine was broken right before I died, thus the reason why the Essence and I are not one and the same anymore."*

This knowledge rocks through Kimala. Everything she had known from the history books seems to have been... *warped.* If Eliara's soul had been fractured from a broken promise as opposed to the way the Dark Warrior had killed her, then what had actually happened to the ancient duir'raz'ne back then?

Chapter 12
Deception

Erimentha waggles her finger at Eliara. "It is my *duty* to protect this city from being destroyed; you know this, fletchling." She exhales, her shoulders slumping. "It just seems as though my rehkava is strong enough that I retain my memories even when I am reborn."

Eliara taps her chin. "Darion never informed me whenever you passed through the Mavi, so I was never able to talk to you."

"I asked him not to." Erimentha pokes Eliara's cheek. "I knew you would worry for me. How is your xhuri?"

Eliara gives her a tight smile. "Still… broken." Kimala feels her pain from admitting that about her soul. "The Jethel Vortex shot me into Mara, but despite us having similar goals, we do not… get along."

Erimentha narrows her eyes. "Is that who I think it is currently in Mara?"

Eliara nods, not looking at her. "I apologize. I was too afraid to face her."

"Mara will stop her."

Eliara glances at her aunt, surprised at her conviction. "How are you so certain?" she asks, disconcerted. "She is but a child."

"I have seen her Source before." Erimentha stares ahead; they are nearing a plaza with a beautiful, crystalline water fountain. "This is the first time the Essence has chosen her, but it chose well. I have a feeling this battle will finally end." Erimentha grins. "And then I can finally rest assured my brother's city will never be destroyed with *her* watching over it."

Eliara stares at Erimentha. The same question races through both her and Kimala. "Who… was she?"

Erimentha waggles her finger. "You always forget that it is not who she *was*. It is who she decides to *become*."

Eliara dips her head. "My apologies."

Erimentha taps the bottom of her chin, making her look up again. "I could never see you sticking with Mara," the Ancient murmurs, smirking. "She was too stubborn."

"She's telling us," Kimala grumbles, irritation spiking through her. "She does not listen, ignores our help, trains and studies when she needs to rest, ignores my medical advice – "

"Is that you talking, or is it Kimala?"

Kimala blinks, realizing she is in control. Everything she had thought she had been grumbling about to Eliara had actually been spoken *out loud*. Eliara cackles in the back of her mind, completely agreeing with Kimala's statement of Mara. "I-I apologize! I did not realize she had..." Kimala clamps her mouth shut, her cheeks reddening.

Erimentha chuckles, patting Kimala's shoulder. "No worries, fletchling. I am glad you and my niece are getting along; you seem like a better match for her than Mara."

"I would hope so," Kimala mutters. "Unlike Mara, I *like* her. According to Shaniel, Mara had fought with her from the moment they met."

Erimentha chuckles, but then her expression sobers. "So tell me, what is the Da'ruha planning? Is she trying to infiltrate?"

Glancing around, Kimala hesitates.

"Do not worry, fletchling. No one has been able to see or hear us since I hugged you earlier."

Kimala stares at her; she had felt absolutely no surge of energy come off of this woman at any point of their conversation. Despite the Alkinian's words and the lack of people on the street they happen to be on, she is still uncomfortable. "I-is there nowhere else we can go?"

Erimentha watches her for a moment before leading the medic through an alley. On the other side, there is an

194

empty plaza sequestered against a wall. A large fountain splashes in the middle. "This is my own personal space," she tells Kimala. "No one else really comes over here, not that many even know about it."

They sit on the edge of the fountain. Kimala takes a deep breath, staring at the falling water for a moment before explaining simply, "I don't know exactly what it is she wants, but she seems to be keeping Mara's body preserved. We think…"

"Go on," Erimentha encourages her.

Kimala hesitates. Is she even allowed to tell Erimentha any of this? Timian didn't say she can't tell the Alkinian, but then again, he also didn't say she *can* tell her.

"If we cannot trust Erimentha, then this world is already doomed," Eliara whispers. *"Both Erimentha and Artemis are from my family, Kimala, not the Da'ruha's family."*

"But… the Da'ruha is your sister, isn't she?" Kimala asks, suddenly confused.

"It is too complicated to explain right now. You can trust her, Kimala."

Kimala takes a steadying breath. Erimentha patiently watches her. "We think she is trying to infiltrate Alamirana again," she whispers. "We can't figure out anything else, though, without the risk of giving away that we know she is possessing Mara's body."

"Do the Highlords know?" Erimentha asks, her voice low and serious.

"Only Timian, Lilly, and Shaniel. Aeserast and Darion are in Carni searching for Mara." Kimala bites her lip, another spike of concern going through her.

Erimentha exhales slowly. "So the welp is back," she breathes, her eyes flicking to the huge fortress-like crystalline castle. "Now I understand why she hasn't been tossed back into her cell. Does Darion at least know of the situation?"

Kimala shakes her head. "Probably not. Timian had

told me not to tell anyone."

"*She can be trusted,*" Eliara repeats.

Erimentha pats Kimala's shoulder, smiling softly. "He already informed me of the situation. I was just hopin' there had been new information since then." Standing up, she offers her arm to Kimala once again. "Now that business is out of the way, how about I give you a personal tour?"

Kimala blushes. "I don't want to impose – "

"Yer not! Let's go back to the others and see if any of them want to join."

Erimentha leads Kimala through twists and turns until the young medic is so lost she doesn't even know which way the entrance into the walled city is. Walking up to a building near a side-entrance to the castle, she knocks on the door.

Shaniel opens it, blinking at Erimentha. "You have one crazy sense of timing. I just got back from the castle."

"I can tell. Yer Source reeks as usual," Erimentha comments, pulling Kimala into the Alkinian house.

The young medic glances around, trying to take in as much of the house as possible. Curved entryways, seamless walls, and elegant slopes create a sophisticated design where one room flows into the next without pause. She feels as though she is in New Atlantis again; everything is designed to be efficient in both architecture and technology.

"Does anyone want a tour of the city?" Erimentha announces to the room, a mischievous smile resting on her lips as Alec peers around the corner. "It hasn' changed much over the years, but if ye never been, then I suppose it's all new te ya."

Mara-but-not-Mara looks slightly uncomfortable as she steps out from the other room with Alec. "I-I don't know…" she mumbles, rubbing her arm. Kimala tries hard not to act surprised at the unusual move; she is certain this is a direct habit of the Da'ruha herself, as Mara

196

has never expressed discomfort in that way before.

"I'll make sure not to go to the places we were," Erimentha reassures her as Air'Lord Tyson steps out of the kitchen. She frowns. "An' who might you be?"

"Air'Lord Tyson Mills," he greets, dipping his head respectfully as he gives the Alkinian a relaxed smile. "My contract started twenty years ago; it is nice to finally meet you. Timian has told me much about the Ancients."

"Oh, so now we're Ancients?" Erimentha mutters to herself. Shaniel rolls his eyes, and she directs her next question at him. "Does this fletchling even know what the term originally referred to?"

Shaniel shrugs. "We still call them by their Xharos name, Erimentha. It's only old reincarnations such as yourself who are referred to by the Common term now."

"Ha!" Erimentha jabs a finger at the laig'hius. "You callin' me old, kitten? I should get Artemis here to set ye straight."

Shaniel's face pales. "N-no need. She's already done enough damage."

"You bet she has," Erimentha grumbles, straightening. "So what'll it be? Tour or no?"

Alec glances around the oddly tense room before hesitantly raising his hand. "I will accompany you." He walks to Kimala, linking his hand with hers. She gives him a wobbly smile, feeling a bit claustrophobic from all the tension in the air.

"Come now, Mara," Erimentha says gruffly, grabbing Mara's hand and pulling her out the door. Kimala catches a glimpse of pure panic cross the mage's face before switching to befuddlement as if she had expected something to happen.

Their eyes meet.

Kimala smiles at her 'cousin,' trying not to give anything away. "Come on, Mara; you can't tell us you weren't thinking of it. You're *always* interested in new things."

"Y-yeah." She turns those wary gold eyes onto the black-haired woman dragging her forward.

Tyson strolls alongside Shaniel, still smiling. "I myself have not been able to see Alamirana yet. Mind if I tag along?"

"Of course not," Erimentha says, releasing Mara's hand as they walk down the street. "By the way, fletchling, I noticed yer Source seems to be acting up again."

Kimala holds her breath. *Why is she approaching her right now?!* she panics, involuntarily squeezing Alec's fingers. He glances at her, startled by the sudden movement.

Mara shrugs as if she expected this question. "Carni did something to it; seems like I never get a break." She laughs, rubbing the back of her neck.

Erimentha shrugs. "If ye say so." She slings an arm over Shaniel's shoulders, and the laig'hius flinches. "Say, pirranki. Have you ever been to the slums of Alamirana?"

"Don't call me that," Shaniel mutters, slipping out from underneath the Alkinian's arm after being called kitten in Xharos. "And what's it to you? Is that where Artemis is?"

"Ye think I know where my elusive sister is?" Erimentha laughs loudly. "You know better than me! Say, didn't she steal yer best knife set a few months back? She sent me a message about it, you know."

"That thieving, backward, conniving…" Shaniel takes a deep breath, gritting his teeth. "Next time you send a letter, tell that redhead to give those back to me! They were my best pair!"

Erimentha waves her hand. "In due time, in due time. She said she's *alterin'* them for ye." She gives him a sly grin.

Shaniel stares at her. "*Artemis* is? But… why? She hates me."

Erimentha rolls her eyes. "She never said she *hates* ye, kitten. She jus' likes toyin' with ye. We get bored, too, ye know – especially her."

Kimala watches the interaction between them, curious. She knows of the Ancient named Artemis from the history books, but the elusive reincarnating Alamir has not been to Quasala for decades. Eliara's swirling emotions catches her attention, though. "*What is it?*"

"*Werui Artemis might remember some of what had happened during my time,*" Eliara explains. "*I have never been able to talk to her directly about it, and the Eleth'Lord has never elaborated.*"

"*Artemis helped Da'neka Kyrina regain her memories,*" Kimala explains, but then hesitantly adds, "*Or… at least, that's what the history books say.*"

Eliara settles for this tidbit of information, going silent. Kimala finds it disconcerting that the duir'raz'ne is growing quieter and quieter as the days go by; she hopes nothing is wrong.

Erimentha guides them around the city, pointing out specific spiraling buildings and noting their historical significance. They enter an older portion of the town where the labyrinthian streets twist and turn so much that even the inhabitants of the ancient city can become lost.

"These here roads have held up ever since the city was built. It's all thanks to Alamirta's power hub and repairing seals. The buildings… not so much." Suddenly, she turns around, looking guilty. "My deepest apologies, Mara. I told you we wouldn't come here, but…"

Mara frowns, glancing at the half-collapsed building in front of them. "What are you talking about?"

Erimentha narrows her eyes, *truly* looking suspicious now. "Don't ye remember this, Mara?"

Mara's eyes snap down to Erimentha, startled. She gives a small embarrassed laugh. "S-Sorry. It's a bit of a blur…"

"Ye woke up in that building, screamin' and whimperin' about the Da'ruha. We all thought you were possessed."

"Erimentha," Shaniel starts, glancing at Mara. "Take

it easy on her."

Erimentha glares at Mara, jabbing her finger at the mage. "That isn't our precious fletchling. It's the *welp* that killed my niece."

The smile freezes on Mara's face. Her head tilts down, and she gives a low chuckle – a sound that Mara has never emitted before. "I knew coming to Alamirana would be a risk," she murmurs to herself. Tyson takes a slow step away from the mage. "You set up traps to seal me here, didn't you?"

"Yer smart as usual," Erimentha snarls, curling her finger into her fist. A circle materializes and spins about Mara's feet. "This barrier cannot be broken from the inside. That should hold ye until Darion can toss ye back into yer cell."

Shaniel's breath whooshes out. "Phew… at least I can stop pretending. It was downright creepy, you know."

The Da'ruha glances around, noticing that Tyson and Alec are the only two who seem shocked. She focuses on Kimala, her gold eyes narrowing. "So you knew, too, huh? That doesn't surprise me. You reek of Alamir scum."

Kimala shrinks behind Alec. He puts a defensive arm in front of her, glancing at Erimentha and Shaniel. "Will someone tell me what's going on?" he asks, his voice quavering.

"Jus' a little trap for the Da'ruha," Erimentha cheerily says, her eyes full of hatred. "Ye really went off the deep end with this one, Da'ruha; not the smartest decision trying to sneak in amongst Highlords and Source-readers."

"The Da'ruha?" Alec breathes, his eyes widening. "I-I didn't even know."

Mara's face twists into an unfamiliar sneer. Her eyes swirl a temporary purplish-red. "I have already succeeded in acquiring what I came for, though." She splays her hand across her chest just beneath the Alamiran crest. "This."

Erimentha frowns before gasping. "No!"

"Yes," she whispers, smirking. "I will admit, this is the best vessel I have inhabited in *centuries*. She can truly contain a lot of power; it is quite phenomenal when considering how little Source she actually had. I have enjoyed walking around like a regular Alkinian these past few days, but I suppose it is time to return to Father."

"Ye won't be going anywhere but Hariana," Erimentha spits as Tyson steps forward, his hands raised as if to fight. She frowns. "Tyson, step back; the barrier will break from physical contact on the outside. She is not goin' anywhere, though, so ye don't need to worry."

The Air'Lord spares a glance at her, his lips twitching into a smile. "Truly?" he murmurs.

His hand strikes the barrier, and it shatters. Erimentha falls to her knees, gasping in pain.

The Da'ruha grabs his arm, giving them one last grin as he tugs her through the warped air and disappears. The emergency portal shrinks, vanishing as fast as it had appeared. Not even Shaniel can move fast enough to stop them.

"Carc'ra!" the laig'hius curses, gritting his teeth as he glares at where the teleportation hole had disappeared. "Where's Aeserast when we need him?"

"More importantly," Erimentha forces out as she staggers to her feet. "It seems as though we've found yer elusive traitor."

Shaniel freezes, the situation finally sinking in. He groans loudly. "Tyson." He slaps his hand against his face, dragging it down. "Of all the Highlords… it has to be the *Air'Lord*."

"Go; inform Timian," Erimentha orders, her expression and tone losing all aloofness. "I will call for Artemis."

Shaniel stares at Erimentha. He seems torn between confusion and concern. "I thought she hates being involved in Ecalauna business," he says, though there is a questioning tone to it.

Erimentha shakes her head. "Normally, I would agree; but this involves the one person she has been trying to catch for centuries to interrogate." She gives Shaniel a grim smile. "Darion always gave Da'ruha the easy way out; Artemis will not be as nice."

Shaniel exhales slowly, glancing at Kimala. "Take care of them. I'll... inform Timian."

Erimentha grabs his arm. "This isn't yer fault, kitten," she says in a low, steady voice. "Tyson was not Wayne. Don't beat yerself up over it."

His shoulders relax as he nods. Within seconds, he is gone, sprinting faster than possible to the entrance of the city.

Erimentha claps her hands together. "Let's go to the castle; it's the safest place right now."

"How long has the Da'ruha been impersonating Mara?" Alec demands, rattled.

Poor Alec, Kimala thinks, wincing. *I guess he hasn't been informed of the situation...*

— ◆ —

Darion and Mara continue down the crystalline pathway through the twisting swirls, bouncing between topics to alleviate the dullness of the walk. After several more hours, she grumbles about the 'drab view,' which has him laughing and explaining the odd swirling colors of the realm, which are visible clumps of Carni Matter forming and blending into one another.

The purple and dark blue colors churn around them as Carni's Path glistens beneath their feet, looking almost like nighttime. According to Darion, this is the realm reacting to his sense of time and how he knows it is late evening in the material realms.

She glances at him, concerned. They had been walking for the entire day yet again with little to no change in scenery to alert them of their progress. She finds it very disheartening and wishes there is an easier way to traverse the shifting realm.

As they pause on Carni's Path, Mara glances around once more. If there is some type of *tangible* goal she can see in the distance, she will feel better about the supposed progress they had made that day. She takes a few steps forward, making her head hurt with how hard she focuses. Just as she is about to return to Darion, she sees a thin line of darkness on the horizon. "Do you know what that is?"

Darion frowns as he squints, identifying it. He huffs in surprise. "The entrance to the Tower of Discord. Aeserast is most likely still there; we could stay at his place for the night."

She nods, walking forward. Within minutes, she is staring down a long staircase into a twilight region covered in a lavender-hued mist. The top of an enormous structure peeks through the hazy air and darkness, suggesting a monolithic building emerging from a seemingly endless pit.

They walk down the stairs. "Be careful around the Tower, Mara," Darion warns. "It has a tendency to draw in eiv'ra."

"All right." She scours the mist atop the tower, sensing something familiar.

It's here. What I'm looking for… it has to be here.

She gains speed as she descends the staircase, ignoring Darion's warning to slow down. She peers into the center of the mist, knowing deep within herself that whatever it is she needs is *there*, in the middle of the huge space.

On the third step from the bottom, she jumps the rest of the way down and lands with her knees bent. As soon as she hits the surface, the mist recedes as if fleeing from her.

She stands on an enormous clock face and is awed by the sheer size. She quickly steps over the second hand as it creeps around the clock in its predetermined path; gears buzz in the center while a faint, off-rhythm *tock, tock, tock, tock* echoes in the empty space. Based off the multitude of sounds, there must be many unseen clocks on the sides of the tower, as well.

At the Xharos sigil for the number twelve, a bridge connects the clock face to a single door that seems to float in the middle of darkness. She steps toward it, momentarily distracted from her goal by her curiosity.

The door opens, and light from the inside spills out as Aeserast steps onto the bridge while tugging on his blue-streaked lavender robe. His alarmed expression turns to one of shock as soon as he sees her standing in the middle of the clock. "Mara?! How did you get here? Are you all right? Are you hurt?"

Mara glances around the huge clock, intrigued by it. "Yeah, I'm fine. So this is the Tower of Discord?"

"Yes," Darion calmly answers her question, stepping onto the clock tower. "There are countless clocks covering the surface; whenever one chimes, we log the amount of tolls. Based off of these calculations, we know something of a certain magnitude will happen in one of the realms. There are more clocks than there are realms, though, so we are not always certain of which realm it might be."

"Fascinating." Mara kneels next to the center unit that holds the hands of the clock. "So it senses when things are going to happen. That's cool."

Aeserast shifts closer to Darion as they watch Mara. He is unnerved by her pitch-black apparel. "Is she still eiv'ra?"

"Somewhat." Darion looks directly at Aeserast. Mara glances at them, ready to explain to her guardian, but Darion beats her to it. "She knows what her purpose is and somewhat of what she needs to do. I do not know why the Path led us here, though."

"Perhaps she needed something from the Tower of Discord." Aeserast shrugs, finally shifting his gaze to Darion. "Many eiv'ra come here; helping them finalize their journey is one of my tasks as Creation'Lord, after all."

Darion rubs his jaw. "I understand that, although based off my understanding of what she is looking for, I do not see how the Tower can help her." He exhales in a huff. "However, since we are here, I need to make a report to Timian. Mara absorbed the Cauerr'ien."

Mara blushes, feeling a mixture of guilt, shame, and embarrassment. She walks over to one of the runes, pretending to examine it with intense curiosity. However, after a brief moment of staring at it, her interest is piqued as she recognizes the Old Xharos shapes for the numerical system.

Aeserast's eyes widen. "She did *what?*" His voice cracks on the last word. "How is that even possible? That was nearly a third of the duir'raz'ne's original Source!"

"I do not know," Darion murmurs, watching Mara crouch next to the Xharos number eight. "It seems to be her Source's innate ability, though."

She tunes them out, seriously examining the Old Xharos numerical runes. She is a bit disconcerted that she can read it without the Essence being there to translate it for her. She steps over the hour hand, noticing its position at the number nine. *I wonder if the time on it is accurate*, she wonders as she meanders closer to the pathway stretching from the number twelve.

"It is beautiful, is it not?"

Mara whirls around at the soft murmur. A woman stands by the Xharos number for two, staring at the clock's face. A brilliant glow emanates from her; it is soft enough not to hurt Mara's eyes, but it shrouds her features.

Glancing at Aeserast and Darion, she catches Aeserast's reassuring smile. *She must be trustworthy, then*, Mara thinks, turning back to the odd woman. "Who are you?"

The woman chuckles, and Mara's eyes widen as she recognizes the sound. "You have already met an image of me, albeit a slight deviation from myself. What is it you seek, Mage Danarko?"

Mara straightens, her voice firm yet oddly muted by the surroundings. "I need the power to protect my friends. People have died for me, and I refuse to let it happen again. I want the power to protect them. All of them."

"That is a high goal." The woman shakes her head. "The only way to achieve it is by getting stronger and becoming a leader, both of which will cause you to walk a fine line."

"I don't care."

"Be careful of what you say, little fletchling," she warns, but Mara can see a hint of a smile on her face. "Your Source may be like none other in that it can devour other Sources, but you should never be reckless with it. Too much power used the wrong way will be your downfall."

Mara takes a deep breath, settling her nerves at that casually mentioned fact. *So that really is my Source's ability,* she thinks to herself. "Is it wrong to want to protect my friends?"

"There was one other who had a similar goal," she murmurs, her head tilting to the side as if in thought. "He did everything imaginable to keep those he loved safe, even becoming one of the monsters he feared the most. He has killed and destroyed just to keep his family together. How do I know you will not do the same?"

Mara pauses, her lips parting in surprise. She had never thought of that; never thought someone would take the simplistic desire to protect to such an extreme. "I don't want anyone else to hurt because of me," she finally admits softly. "Not even the Da'ruha. I want all of this fighting to end, and if I can make it end, then I will do

206

everything in my ability to do so."

The woman stares at Mara for a long moment. "Just know you are not alone; those around you wish the same for you, as well." She holds out her hand. "However, I believe you will benefit from the power of this Tower. Allow me to show you the door to that which you desire."

Mara hesitates, her mind flashing to Lunesh's blackened hand. "I'm not going to... hurt you, am I?"

She chuckles. "While your Source was tailored to mimic that of Voyana itself in order to absorb and convert another's Source, I do not have anything you can take from me."

Mara stares at her, shocked at this simple yet clarifying explanation of her abilities. *Is that really what I can do?* she wonders to herself, stunned. "How do you know that's what my Source does?"

"I have seen it before," she answers, a simple yet vague explanation. Standing at the edge of the clock tower, she gives Mara a friendly, caring smile. "Are you ready?"

Mara nods, feeling no trace of maliciousness from this woman. She intuitively knows she can trust her; perhaps she will also answer the mage's questions about her strange ability. "Yeah."

She takes the woman's hand.

Across the tower, Aeserast frowns at the interaction. While the Tower's ghost talking to an eiv'ra is not uncommon, physical interaction is a strange occurrence. "Mara, what are you doing?" he calls out to her, but his voice is oddly muted.

The Tower is suppressing the noise around them.

"Carc'ra," he curses, walking forward. "Mara, stop. I don't know what she has said, but — "

Mara glances back at him. Her eyes meet his startled gaze as she steps over the edge of the Tower.

"Mara!" they both cry, racing to the edge only to be knocked back by the invisible wall.

Mara feels the gravity shift underneath her. She glances at her feet, surprised; it is as if the center of gravity is the Tower itself. Seeing the woman walking ahead of her, she hurries to catch up as she glances around at the myriad of clock faces stretching across the side of the tower. "This is amazing…"

The woman chuckles. "It is certainly an anomaly. Normally, I do not allow anyone down here as it is dangerous to traverse the Tower too far; however, where we are going is not much farther."

After a few seconds of silence, Mara clears her throat. "I… have a question," she admits as they skirt around a clock face about six feet in diameter.

"You may ask."

She chews on her lip. "You said my Source mimics Voyana, but why? Why can I do that but no one else can?"

The woman gives her a mysterious smile. "Souls go through a cycle of jethel er eleth, my fletchling. Your particular soul is from the time of Voyana's initial explosion; you had been one of the few who survived. However, your task after the Fall of Alkina had not been easy. Too many were corrupt, and the only way you were able to stop them was to listen to Voyana's orders and use your gift to take away the power they were using for ill intent."

Mara touches her chest, her lips parting as something about the woman's words echo deep within her. She knows a bit about reincarnation and rebirth – the main difference between the two being if the soul keeps the memories of its past lives or not – but she has never studied it seriously. All she really knows about jethel er eleth, or the cycle of life and death, is that Eleth is like a mirror reflection of Jethel, the living realms, and souls are in a constant state of cycling back and forth between the two. However, the woman's comment on her supposed 'past life' has her questioning the legitimacy. "How do I know you're not making it up?" she asks stubbornly, not willing to fall for another manipulative scheme.

The woman turns to her, the glow significantly receding to reveal light hazelnut hair, swirling blue-purple eyes, and tanned skin. "You may be an older soul than I, but I have witnessed your rebirth time and time again. Your stubbornness has never changed, just as your xhuri rehkava to protect those you love has never once wavered." She gives a soft yet sad smile as she touches Mara's face. "This is the first time the Essence has chosen you as a vessel, and I am glad it has; you will work well together despite being the definition of danra er vuti itself. I have been waiting for this moment for millennia."

Danra er vuti... white and black. Taking a deep breath to settle her rattled nerves after this mental translation, Mara follows the woman farther down the clock tower. As she walks, though, she feels gravity shifting yet again, pulling her almost at a slant so she is hiking upward despite facing what should be down. "Wh-what's going on with the Tower?"

"The center of gravity is underneath Alkina's Clock," the woman murmurs, turning and walking perpendicular along the Tower. "This is what I wanted to show you."

She walks around an odd platform jutting out of the ground, and Mara follows. The woman pauses at a plain, wooden door with a brass knob leading into the side of the tower. It is unremarkable by itself, although it looks misplaced against the gears.

Mara stares at it, disconcerted. In relation to her knowledge of what is right-side-up, this door is upside down, yet according to gravity, it is leading into the slanted ground.

"Part of what you seek is inside," the woman murmurs, sinking through the wood as if it isn't even there.

A chill slides down Mara's spine. She hopes her nagging suspicion of the woman's identity is incorrect. Stepping onto the platform, she cannot help but look down the way they had come from. She swallows hard, trying to wrap her mind around the notion that she is actually looking *up*, though the gravity pulling at her is telling her otherwise. Leaning forward, she grasps the handle of the door and pulls.

The door doesn't budge.

Confused, she pushes instead. The door remains closed, the wood not even creaking from the strain. She examines the edging, looking for any sign of hinges or an indication of which way the door should open. She even tries to slide it open like many of the entryways in Cerlail Academy and New Atlantis.

Still nothing.

Huffing, Mara holds her hand near the door knob. Pitch black power coalesces, twining around her fingers and reaching for the wood. Startled by how *dark* her Source is, she pauses, briefly confused. She had absorbed a whole forest-worth of bright, colorful Source; it shouldn't be black. But here it is, darker than any color could ever be.

She holds her Source in her hand, her thoughts churning. *If the color of someone's Source reflects their ideals, why is mine black? Isn't black… death or something?*

Surely, that would have changed her Source color to some extent. Frowning, she thinks about what the woman had said a moment ago; supposedly, she has always had her Source and the ability to convert other Sources into her own.

Have I absorbed that much over time?

Her hand trembles. Clenching her fingers, she watches the black tendrils drape themselves across her knuckles. She slams her fist into the door, emotionally void as it blasts apart from her Source exploding outward.

Chapter 13
Awakening

Exhaling slowly, Mara straightens and walks onto the platform inside the tower. She feels the gravity shift with each step until it is nearly directly beneath her.

The woman stands on the stairs off to the side, not surprised at the destructive way Mara had entered. The mage turns to her, unable to look directly into the woman's face. "Tell me one thing."

"If I have an answer, I shall."

"Was I… evil?"

The woman chuckles, amused. "If you mix every possible color of paint together, you will get black. Does this mean it is evil?"

Mara's shoulders slump. "No," she breathes, glancing at the descending staircase before looking "up" into the darkness. "But what does it mean?"

"My dear Mara." The woman steps forward and touches Mara's face. "Black is merely the compilation of *all* the colors in the universe. It means you contain every trait possible: kindness, loyalty, strength, joy, ambition, anger, perseverance, determination, confidence… There is only one color that can reflect all of these at the same time, and that color *is* your Source. Your Source is extremely rare and unique in that it is compatible with *every other Source* except one."

"What is it?" she whispers, although she has a nagging suspicion she already knows.

"White; it is the absence of every color. But white also compliments black." She taps Mara on the nose. "While black symbolizes knowledge, wisdom, and power, white represents innocence, naivety, and purity. Remember that when you reunite with your companion."

Mara's eyes widen. "The Essence? But… it's silver. That's not white."

"It has darkened over these past several thousand years because of the sheer amount of knowledge it has gained; the color white cannot exist when innocence is lost. The reason it is sharing its knowledge with you is because it wishes to return to its original state: innocence and purity. It is the only Source you will be unable to absorb, simply because it is not a color."

"So… you're saying it hasn't been shoving its knowledge into my mind," Mara slowly says, piecing things together. "My Source has been *taking* it?"

She can see the small smirk on the woman's face. "Have you not realized you still contain the knowledge you gained from the Essence despite it not being here?"

"I did, but I didn't think much about it," she whispers, touching her head lightly. "That's why I still have these memories? But… what was driving me crazy?"

"You were absorbing too much too fast," she explains simply. "The Will pulled you into this realm and blocked both you and the Essence to give you time to finish processing what your Source had already taken."

Mara stares at her. "When I go back, will this happen again?"

The woman shakes her head. "Most likely not. You have recovered, correct?"

Mara already knows her mind is calm despite the sheer knowledge she now contains. "So… you're saying my mind hadn't been prepared when my Source had started pulling from the Essence, but now it is?"

The woman nods. "But first, you must make a choice, Mara." She points down the staircase that leads to the top of the Tower and the mysterious, strange gravitational pull. "Up there is power – the power that fuels this very Tower. It has desired only one thing over all of these years: to protect. It will accept the conversion as long as you vow to protect those around you."

Mara waits for her to continue, but she doesn't. She glances up into the darkness. "What's… down there?" she asks, still disconcerted that things are upside down in this tower.

She gives Mara a secretive smile. "You shall discover it shortly. Go; it is waiting for you."

Mara glances at the woman one last time before starting down the staircase. She stares into the depths of the Tower of Discord, trying to see what she is walking toward. She wonders why the woman had told her she will have to make a choice; isn't it simple? She has already expressed what she desires most.

As she draws closer to the 'top,' her body feels heavier and heavier as if gravity is trying to grind her into the steps curving away from the wall. Looking down, she pauses for a brief moment to take in the sight below her.

A huge, swirling sphere of purple and red floats underneath the top of the Tower. The sphere encapsulates a pulsing ocean that crashes against its walls. It is nearly the size of the average sorcery wing planetarium's interactive planets, which is twice as big as herself. Mara squints at it; she cannot tell the color of the water because of the sphere, though she does notice that it is a deep, dark red in the empty space and a dark purple wherever the water is.

Waves crash against the barrier closest to Mara. She jumps, a little unsettled that it seems to know she is there. Glancing up the way she had come from, she doesn't see the glowing woman anymore.

"Cryptic lady," Mara mutters out loud, continuing down the stairs. Eventually, it levels out onto a platform that stretches beneath the huge sphere. Mara kneels on it, once again looking 'up' into what she knows is down.

She realizes why the woman had said she has a choice.

The sphere beneath her splashes with pure energy,

generating its own gravitational pull. If she breaks it, she will be able to absorb that power – however, she will tumble into the bottom of the Tower with no way to catch herself from splatting on the ground. She can also choose not to break it and remain safe, but then she will not have the power that 'desires to protect.'

"I just can't see how an ocean of power like that has a-a will," Mara mutters out loud, unable to keep her skepticism at bay anymore.

The water pools against the side closest to Mara, and she hears the sphere groaning under the pressure.

Dong, dong, dong.

Mara glances to the left, catching sight of the gears slowly coming to a halt as the hands continue to move across that particular clock face. She looks beyond the sphere, seeing the underside of the huge clock face that decorates the top of the Tower of Discord. She can see the vague shapes of Darion and Aeserast, both of them pacing and walking to the edges of the Tower.

Searching for me, she realizes, feeling a pang of guilt. *I had walked off the edge of the Tower, after all.*

Mara sighs, standing up again. "Hey, you big ball of gravity," she shouts down at the sphere. The sloshing water stills, and Mara has the uncanny feeling that it is listening to her. "I can tell you want to be free, but I need to know you're not going to go rampant on me. Because if you do..." She punches her fist into her hand, feigning a toughness she doesn't quite feel while facing this orb. "I *will* reseal you in here."

From the still surface of the water, a single form rises and shapes itself into an elfin woman in a dress. She bangs her fist against the side of the sphere. Even though there are no colors other than purple, Mara recognizes the outline of the young woman.

She is the same as the reflection in Danti Cauerr'ien.

Her hand is already moving before she thinks of what

she should do. Black Source pools at her fingers, twining in on itself to make a beautiful black per'lusa rose. She releases it, watching the flower bud fall onto the sphere.

Boom.

The entire tower shakes, making all of the clocks ring from the disturbance. However, not a single scratch mars the surface of the sphere. She makes an even bigger bomb, taking a deep breath before releasing it to drift down and explode against the barrier.

The platform underneath her quakes, nearly sending her over the edge. She kneels down, firing a continuous stream of exploding bombs into the barrier in order to free the trapped power within.

Something crashes against the clock face. She squints through the sphere, and the water makes a small hole just in time for her to see an emerald fist smash into the clock tower once again.

Hairline fractures form over the surface of the sphere. Mara whoops, grinning. "Keep doing that! It's working!" she yells before slamming her power into the barrier once again.

There is a pause before another emerald fist smashes into the clock face. Glass falls against the barrier, sticking to the fractured surface. Darion peers through, worry and panic etched on his face.

Mara closes her eyes and centralizes her thoughts, taking a slow breath before holding out her hand. Opening her eyes, she whispers, "Go."

Her black Source streams forward, wrapping around the sphere and squeezing it tightly. She strains to maintain control; the sphere is *huge*, taking all of her concentration not to let a single tendril slip out of her control. The black Source completely encases the sphere, twisting and writhing to find a way to slip by the cracks. Mara squeezes her fingers together and yanks her fist back.

A loud *crack* resounds inside the tower.

Just as the barrier is destroyed, Darion punches another hole in the ceiling. Glass rains down the endless tunnel as the ocean of pure Source explodes outward, washing over Mara and sending her into the darkness.

"Mara!" Darion shouts, but she is submerged under the lapis blue water as she free-falls. She squeezes her eyes shut, hoping she hasn't made the wrong decision.

She feels a breeze on her face; water tickles her dangling foot. Opening her eyes, she finds herself back in the Danti Cauerr'ien, but this time, the lake is a beautiful lapis blue. Looking down at her own reflection, she expels her breath as her suspicions are confirmed on the identity of the power inside the sphere.

The missing portion of Eliara's Source.

Her face relaxes. She looks up at the sky, completely content now. She *can* trust this power; after all, the duir'raz'ne had wanted to protect her family and loved ones. She never wanted to hurt anything, not even her own sister.

That had been her downfall.

Mara stares into the sky, a small smile on her face. *I'm not like the duir'raz'ne,* she thinks firmly. *I will fight to protect my friends.*

She lays back into the hued grass, enjoying the peace inside of her own mind for a moment longer before closing her eyes. Leaving the deep recesses of her mind, she becomes aware of air rushing by her as she free-falls through the Tower of Discord. She will reach the bottom, and she will land with her arms stretched out wide.

When her feet touch the ground, a ripple of energy extends from her. It is a simple disturbance in the calm water lapping over her ankles, yet all of the realms feel this wave of power.

She moves through the darkness and steps onto the platform she knows is there. Kneeling on the mossy exterior, she touches the cold, damp stone.

"I'll set you free," she whispers.

Her power extends to the surrounding area, absorbing the remnant lapis blue Source that had fallen from the Tower. It whispers to her, telling her what she needs to do next.

———•◆•———

Darion and Aeserast stare into the innards of the Tower of Discord, unable to figure out what had just happened. The shattered clock face drops into the seemingly endless void, disappearing into darkness.

"How will I be able to explain this to Timian?" Aeserast mourns, covering his face with his hands. "I'm going to lose my position after this. Maybe even get thrown into Hariana."

"If anyone will be tossed into Hariana, it will be me," Darion snaps, searching the darkness for any sign of Mara. "Now tell me what that was, Aeserast, before I wrangle it out of you."

"According to previous Creation'Lords' reports, something was sealed inside the Tower of Discord before the Ecalauna were formed; no one, not even Timian, knew what it was. We figured it was something really terrible considering the Tower itself can predict the occurrences of events across the realms."

"Aeserast."

He groans. "What now?"

"That power was not evil. It was Eliara's."

Aeserast's eyes pop open and stare at Darion. The certainty in his voice unsettles him. "B-but how are you so certain? Why would the ancient duir'raz'ne's remnant energy be sealed inside an endless tower in the Treavaun?"

Darion stares into the tower, his jaw tense. "Carc'ra. I never thought of this… it all makes sense."

"Darion, what are you keeping from the Highlords?" Aeserast demands. "You have been acting oddly ever since the duir'raz'ne came back. What do you know?"

Darion meets Aeserast's eyes. "If you want to know that badly, Aeserast, go read Timian's personal records on the Alamir incident. I am sure if you ask about them directly, he will allow you access." He jabs his finger at the hole in the clock tower. "In the meantime, *I* am going to deal with the more pressing matter at hand – Mara's sudden desire to *destroy* the Tower of Discord."

Just as he says that, a wave of pure energy courses over them. The Tower trembles, and the surroundings shift to a lush green forest with multicolored vines and gold-veined plant life.

"The Will's Forest," Aeserast breathes, walking to the edge to look down into the tree canopy. "Something… something landed down there, Darion."

Darion frowns, looking down into the tower. It is still pitch black. "Perhaps we should – "

The Tower of Discord crumbles, falling apart.

"Carc'ra!" Darion curses, grabbing Aeserast's arm as they begin falling. "Aeserast, help me out here!"

Aeserast blows the rubble away. He glances at the ground far below them, losing his stomach. "Darion."

"Wait for it…"

"Darion, I really don't want to die."

"You will not die. Now shut up."

"Darion, I never told you, but I'm afraid of falling from high places!"

Darion shoots Aeserast an irritated look before holding his hand out. His jade green Source melds together with Voyana, churning in the air to create a beautiful emerald color. Their descent slows until they float the remaining few feet to the ground at the edge of the Tower's remaining inner wall. They slosh through the vivid blue water, and Darion shivers as he feels the raw energy tingling against his skin.

Mara kneels on a large rectangular box covered in moss

and grass. Her black Source radiates out from her like vines, coating the ground and pulsating like a heartbeat. The lapis blue water recedes as the black tendrils absorb it.

Aeserast watches in rapt fascination, his mouth falling open. "I knew you said she had done this with the Danti Cauerr'ien, but to actually see it…"

"I had never suspected her Source had this odd ability," Darion admits quietly, staring at the dry grass and moss around them.

Mara's head is tilted forward, and her eyes are closed. She is on her knees, her fingers digging into the soft moss coating the rectangular box.

The black Source around her creeps down her back, rippling like a cloak as it extends over the rectangular platform. The black melts away to reveal colorful shimmers that form the silhouettes of objects. Stars twinkle into existence behind the blue and purple bands dancing in the sky. Green trees appear on a light, blue-grey ground, forming a snowy slope and mountains in the background.

"An Ecalain robe," Aeserast breathes in awe. "I have never seen one for myself."

"Stop her."

At Darion's order, Aeserast shakes his head. "Darion, you know we are not to interfere – "

"She needs to stop right now," he says, a twinge of panic in his voice. "That is not an Ecalain robe; it is not a Voyana robe at all. That is her *Xhuri* Robe."

Aeserast stares at Mara, shocked speechless. He has only ever read of the mythical Xhuri, or Soul, Robes from ancient historical tomes; the only two that had been even remotely mentioned in any detail were the Soul Robes of Eliara and Kyrina before the Da'ruha's initial attack. Soul Robes are created when an individual makes a vow to uphold a single desire throughout all of their lifetimes, no matter if they have memory of this vow or not. He finds this quite hard to fathom; after all, how can someone know to follow a vow they do not remember?

The mountains on the robe glisten, looking like snow on a dark night. The robe extends to the ground, and the colors form the top of an arching handle.

Mara opens her eyes. Her left eye is a vivid lapis blue while the other is a dark brown, almost black. She smiles gently at them. "It's all right. I'm almost done."

He shakes his head. "No. You must not do this, Mara. If you break your rehkava – "

"This is not a new promise, Darion. This is a vow I have made before."

Darion's jaw snaps shut. She closes her eyes again as the design on her back ripples, nearly finished.

Aeserast examines it, feeling as if he should be afraid of whatever this is based off of Darion's reaction – but all he can feel is the *sheer desire* to protect radiating off of it.

The design completes itself. A glowing woven basket rests in the snow on a dark hillside, and pine trees lead into the mountains and star-lit sky. The light emanating from the basket moves and shifts, cycling through all the colors of the spectrum. The bottom of the robe keeps growing, wriggling into the cracks and fissures in the rubble as it roots itself into the ground like a tree. Mara slumps forward, exhausted.

Darion hesitantly reaches out and pushes back her hair, exposing her strained expression. "Mara, please do not do this to yourself. You do not have to put your own soul under this much stress."

Aeserast feels the energy levels in the air spike as the robe continues to grow. "Darion, is it normal for there to be so much Source inside the robe?"

"Mara, please," Darion begs, his voice cracking. "Creating this will only bring you pain, just as it did for Eliara."

Aeserast's eyes widen at Darion's words. Before he can question the Eleth'Lord, he has to stagger out of the way as the robe rapidly expands to the edge of the tower's remaining walls. It pulses with power, forming an intricate pattern of multicolored veins along the ground.

Mara opens her eyes again, smiling tiredly at Darion. Both of her irises are gold again. "I'll be all right, Darion; this robe won't hurt me."

"No, it will," he chokes, his words cut short. "Do not – do not finish making it. Please, Mara."

She touches his face, running her fingers over the scar she can feel underneath the illusion of smooth skin. "Can you help me down?"

Darion supports her by the waist as she jumps off the stone, pulling the robe taut.

It rips apart.

Mara collapses against him, gasping for breath as the tattered cloth sways about her ankles. A chill slides through Aeserast as he stares at the basket that remains attached to the floor, perfectly torn from the robe still on Mara. Not a single tree or mountain had been damaged on the intact robe; it is ripped perfectly along the bottom. Now that Mara is no longer on the stone, he sees the rectangular shape she had been kneeling on.

It is a *tomb*.

"Mara?" Darion exclaims, supporting her as she leans against him heavily. "Mara, tell me what happened. Are you hurt?"

"I'm fine," she breathes, her arms slowly creeping around him to hug him tightly. "Thank you for helping me, Darion."

He settles a hand on her back, tangling his fingers in her hair. He kisses her forehead gently. "I told you I would."

Aeserast cannot tear his eyes away from the moss-covered stone. He creeps closer to the tomb, noticing where Mara's fingers had dug into the moss. Scraping it away, his eyes widen at the faded name that had been carved in a single Xharos rune on the stone along with a plethora of sealing and binding spells.

"This… this is impossible…"

At the base of the tomb, the ripped cloth roots itself to the stone. The glow from the basket settles on gold, slowly growing brighter and brighter. It begins pulsing rhythmically, slowly picking up pace.

Turning her head, Mara catches sight of Aeserast standing by the stone slab. Her breathing catches. "Aeserast, get away from there!" She tries to move toward him, but her legs cave underneath her. Darion catches her, glancing at the Creation'Lord in alarm.

The glowing woman appears in front of Aeserast. She smiles at his wide eyes as she shoves him away from the tomb.

The pulsating basket explodes.

Darion tosses up a barrier shield, redirecting the explosive blast to the side. When the smoke clears away, they are on top of an undamaged clock tower resting above the green-and-gold canopy of the Will's Forest.

Aeserast sways on his feet, collapsing to his knees. He looks down at the undamaged clock tower, his eyes wide in the revelation of the ghost's true identity.

Mara forces herself upright, shuffling over and touching his shoulder lightly. "Aeserast…"

Aeserast turns his face upward, revealing the tears streaking down his face. "You… you knew who she was, didn't you, Mara?"

Mara pauses. Of course she knows. She had guessed it before she had opened her eyes and had seen the name carved on the tomb.

"She's free now," Mara says simply, giving her friend a smile. "She is no longer imprisoned. That is what is important."

Aeserast stares at the tower's surface again. "I never thought… Not once…" His fingers tangle in his hair. "I'm such an idiot."

She kneels next to him, squeezing his shoulder. "You will meet her again. I'm sure of it, Aeserast."

He nods, his eyes tightly shut. "Just… give me a moment."

Mara stands up and faces Darion. He wears a quizzical expression. "The ghost of the Tower… was that her tomb down there?"

Mara shakes her head. "It wasn't a tomb; it was a prison. She had been sealed inside that box." She takes a deep breath, closing her eyes briefly before opening them again to smirk at Darion. "Being in Carni is nice and all, but I really miss Blazhreia."

Darion's brow creases in concern. "You made a Xhuri Robe, Mara. You should rest for the time being." He glances at Aeserast briefly. "I need to finish speaking with Aeserast, anyway; he had been about to give me his report when you decided to destroy the Tower."

Mara winces. "My apologies. I never meant to disrupt your conversation."

Darion gives her an odd look, noticing the difference in her speech patterns. Before he can ask her about it, Aeserast stands up, clearing his throat. "Yes, the report… Things took a bad turn on Blazhreia, and I had been attempting to get a hold of you. Did your reki break?"

Darion nods as they walk toward the path leading to the door floating in midair. "I tried sending a distress signal to Air'Lord Tyson, but I suppose it never got through. What happened?"

Aeserast clenches his jaw. "No, I am sure it *did* go through. Tyson was the insider. Not only that, but he apparently had an access stone for Alamirana; he was able to open a portal and kidnapped Mara's body. There is no trace of them anywhere, either."

Mara snorts. "Sounds about right. I wouldn't doubt it if the Da'ruha had somehow found out and possessed my body somewhere in the middle of all of that, too. Eliara is a wimp, so she probably abandoned my body *and* the Essence."

Aeserast exhales slowly as he opens the door. "That would make sense... Timian did say there was more to the report, but he claimed it can't be sent over the Ecalauna transponder network."

They step into the Alkinian-styled home. Aeserast absently takes off his robe and hangs it on the hook near the door before stepping into the kitchen. Mara follows Darion around the corner into the cool-toned living room. They sit at the bar and watch Aeserast pull down three cups as some water heats over the Voyana-powered stove.

"Who is the extra cup for?" Mara asks, curious.

Aeserast glances at her, surprised for a brief moment before realizing his mistake. "Ah, my apologies... it's a habit." He puts one of the cups back. "Darion, you look exhausted; try sleeping a bit after a cup."

"I think I shall," he breathes, crossing his arms on the bar and resting his head on them.

Concerned by the uncommon move, Mara hesitantly touches his shoulder. "Are you all right, Darion?"

He turns his head toward her. "I will be; these past few days were exhausting. A little sleep will help."

Aeserast shakes his head as he sets a cup of swirling purplish liquid in front of the elf. "A little? You need more than that, Darion. You can use the spare room; I'll stay with Mara."

Darion gingerly cradles the cup, nodding mutely. He takes it with him, sipping the liquid as he walks down the hall.

Mara watches him, even more concerned now. "Was he really that exhausted?" she murmurs to her guardian.

"We have been looking for you for days." Aeserast comes around the bar and sits in the vacant seat next to her. "Darion has barely slept this entire time."

Her eyes drop to the ground. "He didn't sleep much

on the way back, either."

"He will get some rest, and then we can see about returning. In the meantime, do you mind me asking you something?"

She smirks at him. "Let me guess: Have I found what I'm looking for yet?" She stares at her hand. "Yes."

He exhales in relief. "That is a step, then. So what is all of this?" He gestures to her robe. "I have never seen one of these before. Quite honestly, I thought they were myths. Not even real."

Mara picks at the robe where the trees meet the aurora dancing in the sky. The colors never remain still; the bands in the sky slowly dance like the real thing. "I'm... not quite sure, honestly. Ever since the Danti Cauerr'ien, I've felt like I have been on the verge of remembering something very important."

Aeserast waits patiently, but she doesn't continue. "It is obvious you know *something*, though. After all, you did say it was a promise you had made before."

She stares at the twisting aurora. "A promise... from before..." she murmurs, a small frown creasing her brow. A shadowy memory lingers in her mind, almost like trying to look at a hazy image underneath the water's surface. "It was something to do with... an explosion. I wanted to protect everyone, and then I woke up." She rubs her temple. "It's weird. I'm almost remembering something, but I know it isn't from... my life? Does that make sense?"

Aeserast slowly exhales as he suspects the problem. "Mara, may I examine your mental state?"

She visibly shrinks away from him. "No."

His eyebrows snap together in concern. "Why not?"

"It's... my Source. I don't want to hurt you." She stares at her hand again. "I have so much now, but it won't stop. It doesn't know how to."

He holds out his hand. "If I feel as though I am in danger, I will pull away," he reassures her. "However, it is imperative that we know what is going on with you before we return to the material realms."

She hesitates for a moment before placing her hand in his. "Just be quick. Prolonged exposure to my Source will increase the risk."

As soon as she touches his hand, he instantly wants to yank away. Her Source level is significantly higher than ever before, which is impossible; an individual's Source level cannot change so drastically. If they are an average level five, then they will never be able to do complex tasks unless in conjunction with someone else.

However, Mara is close to a level nine out of ten.

She didn't just absorb the Source from the Cauerr'ien and the Tower; she converted it into her own core, he realizes, shocked. *No one has ever done that before.*

"Um… Aeserast?" Mara interrupts his thoughts. "You're looking at my Source core."

"My apologies," he murmurs, focusing on the spark of consciousness within the personal black biochemical – her mind. Within seconds, he discovers his suspicions are correct, and he withdraws. "You know of the difference between reborn and reincarnated souls, correct, Mara?"

She nods. "Yes. One remembers the previous lives they had lived, and the other doesn't."

"That is the easy explanation." He holds up his hands, pressing them together at the index and thumb to create an almost teardrop shape of space in the middle. "When a soul exits the Jethel Vortex – the vortex of life – it goes through a thin film. Most souls are coated by this film, thus 'covering' the old memories of their previous lives and experiences so they can live again with no influence of the past. However, the souls that shake off this film remember their past since the memories are no longer buried."

Mara taps her finger on the counter. "Do you think I'm 'shaking off' this film you're talking about?"

He nods. "If this is to happen, normally it occurs early on in the individual's life, such as Artemis and Erimentha; they realized who they were at an early age, and so they were unable to have a normal childhood. There are exceptions, though; extreme trauma can tear the film off, and at times, being told about a previous life can cause rips, as well. It is a very fragile film, and anything can start the process of wearing it off."

She struggles to understand what he is trying to get at. "So these new shadowy memories are actually *my* past lives? They're just still stuck behind this film?"

He nods. "It is stretched extremely thin, but what surprises me is that it is still there at *all*. Based off the remnant Vortex Matter still in your mind, there had originally been a strong film there." He pauses. "It is almost as though the Vortex had taken extra precautions to keep you from remembering the other lives."

She sighs. "I can see why, though. My Source's ability isn't a pretty one, and I'm sure I had done stuff in the past I won't be proud of today."

He frowns. "Mara, who you were in past lives does not matter; the reason why there *is* such a thing as vortex film is so that the individual can live and grow as a person living that life with no influences of past experiences; because of this, no soul can be condemned for the actions of merely one lifetime. The actions of a *reincarnated soul* are the ones in jeopardy of being incarcerated simply because their actions are more consistent and stuck in one way than that of a reborn soul with the vortex film in place."

She scratches her head, confused now. "So I might get into trouble now? But with who? Darion?"

Aeserast sighs heavily. "No, not Darion. It is when you *die*. The Elethani may be widely unknown to us, but what we have noticed is that they have an uncanny ability to know which souls need to be incarcerated for a time."

"Hmm..." Mara mulls over this, now insatiably

curious. "How long do you think it will take for the rest of the film to wear away?"

He shrugs. "It depends on what happens between now and then. I know that if you focus on it enough, it has a chance of wearing off faster under the pressure." He watches her for a moment. "It might be best for you to meditate on it for a while. By focusing on your own past, you might be able to understand your Source better and have a clearer grasp on how to control it."

Mara's eyes alight with excitement. "Do you really think so?"

He nods, standing up. "We can start the process now. Let's return to the middle of the Tower; that way, if your Source runs a bit rampant, you won't hurt anything. Once we get a grasp on how you react to the deteriorating film, we can return to the others."

"This is a hilarious ending to my birthday," she says sarcastically as she follows him. "First a new power, then a new robe, now new memories… I wonder what's next?" She hesitates. "Will I… still be me even if I do manage to do it?"

"Of course, Mara. Who you are will never change," he lies, knowing that telling her the truth right now will only make matters worse.

He can tell the film over her old memories is deteriorating at an incomprehensible rate. Unbeknownst to her, she has already begun changing; her speech pattern is only the beginning. Once it is completely gone, there is a possibility she may not even be the same person. He will have to remain near her for the next few days to ensure the 'awakened' Mara is not a threat to the realms.

If she is, he will need to seal her the moment she begins to show those tendencies.

Chapter 14
Strange Arrival

Kimala stands beside Erimentha, a little nervous as they wait by the open gate. "Are you sure she will be here today?"

"I'm certain of it," Erimentha says, her arms crossed as she leans against the entrance. "The Da'ruha is involved."

Kimala stares out the gate at the grassy expanse of empty land beyond Alamirana's walls. According to Erimentha, Artemis Alamir has been hunting for the Da'ruha for as long as the Ecalauna have been; however, her reasons aren't as noble. Artemis wants to interrogate the Da'ruha into spilling all of her secrets, and if what Erimentha says is true, she has a nasty way about getting what she wants.

"Boo."

Kimala shrieks, leaping away. Whirling around, she sees a wickedly grinning red-headed girl standing where she had been, her hands on her hips as her vivid green eyes spark mischievously. Her brown skin is covered with gold runes that disappear underneath the mahogany sleeves of her shirt. A brown belt with an ornate gold rune as the buckle keeps the billowy cloth about her waist. A collection of knives, vials, and small packs are strapped over her brown leggings, and even her boots are decked out with gold rune etchings.

Erimentha sighs, eyeing the newcomer who can't be much older than Kimala. "Have ye been using potions again, Artemis?"

"And what if I have?" she shoots back, shoving a hand through her hair to expose pointed ears. Her accent sounds more Common than Kimala had anticipated, although she can hear the faint intonations of Xharos underneath. "I can't be getting old; I look the best at this age!" She holds her arms out. The sleeve on her shoulder slides off, exposing more runes on her skin.

Erimentha raises an eyebrow at the obviously oversized shirt.

Clearing her throat, Artemis quickly adjusts her shirt, grumbling, "Fine; I did. It didn't age me as much as I wanted, though. I was shooting more for twenty-five, not-not *eighteen*."

"Quit playin' with potions and age like a normal person," Erimentha grumbles, stalking down the road to the castle.

"Say that to my parents; as soon as I started remembering, they wanted me to just grow up and move out." Artemis rolls her eyes as she walks alongside Erimentha. Leaning forward from the waist, she peers around. "Where's my kitty?"

"Inside Alamirta."

"I'm not going in there."

"Yes, you are."

"You can't make me."

Erimentha cocks an eyebrow at the rebellious elf. "Tell that to your niece."

Artemis's eyes narrow as she glares at the castle. "How fitting; which room?"

"I meant *this* one." Erimentha reaches over and wraps her arm around Kimala. She squeaks in surprise. "Come on, fletchling. Speak up."

"H-hi," Kimala stammers, nervous under Artemis's calculative gaze.

"Nice to meet'cha," the dark-skinned redhead greets, holding out her hand.

"Nice to – "

Erimentha pulls her away from the elf's hand. "Artemis, what is that rune?" Erimentha demands, glaring at the glowing gold sigil on her palm.

"Oh, this?" Artemis waves her hand in the air, showing it off with a grin. "Makes the person I touch speak nothing but the truth!"

Erimentha sighs, releasing Kimala. "While normally I would be thrilled to try somethin' like that out, now is not the time, Artemis. This is Kimala Brunet, and our dear Eliara is coexisting with her at the moment."

"Ooh, fascinating," Artemis breathes, tapping her chin as she stares intently at Kimala. "If you're really Eliara, then why am I not being peppered with a thousand questions?"

"She's a bit… speechless," Kimala admits in a quiet voice, earning a surprised look from both of the Alkinians. "She wasn't expecting you to look so, um…"

"Beautiful? Young? Energetic?" Artemis scrunches her wavy hair, smirking.

"Cursed."

Artemis stares at the medic. Her expression darkens as she recognizes the look in the girl's eyes. "Not many know the look of a cursed soul," she whispers. "But I believe I could say the same about you, Eliara."

"What happened, Artemis?" Eliara asks, her voice barely a breath as Kimala allows her to have control for the time being. Her vision blurs. "What happened to Rinali?"

Artemis points at her. "*That* is why I want to catch the Da'ruha myself. Rinali had left my care as planned, perfectly happy and excited to return to the castle. Next thing I knew, I was coming to visit to find my brother and his wife weeping over the tragedy." She shakes her head. "When I found Kyrina, I did my best to help her regain her memories, but even she didn't know what had happened to Rinali. It's a pity that *guard* was the one who found her in the end; I would have liked to get some information out of her before she had been tossed into

Hariana."

Erimentha sighs heavily. "You have already ranted about it several other times. No need to go into it again."

"You're right, you're right." She glances around again. "So there's no chance my kitten is hiding from me? I made a toy for him."

Erimentha smirks, pointing to the castle. "He's at the fae'reth with the others."

"Goody; my only favorite place in there." She rubs her hands together, giving Kimala a wicked grin. "I have news to report, anyway."

"Hopefully, good news," Erimentha says, glancing at her sister.

"I don't know." She sobers, staring at the ground as they near the castle. "I'll wait until everyone is gathered before I share."

Once they are in the upper right spire of the castle, Artemis sniffs the air and grins. Pressing a finger against her lips, she winks at Kimala and Erimentha before sneaking forward and cracking the door open. "Uthu morla ikuta, pirranki," she singsongs, tossing two knives into the room.

"A-Artemis?!" Shaniel yelps as two metallic clatters echo out of the room. "Bloody Elethavi, are you *trying* to kill me?"

She giggles, leaning against the door while twirling another throwing knife between her fingers. "Those are for you."

Kimala stares at the woman with wide eyes. Cautiously peering into the room, she sees Riley, Michelle, Teresa, Timian, and Alec giving Shaniel a wide berth as he hesitantly picks up the knives she had thrown at him. "These are amazing," he breathes in awe, glancing at her. "Are they really... mine?"

"The ones you had before were *awful*," she says, cleaning underneath her nails with her knife. "I tossed them in the ocean while I was in New Atlantis."

Shaniel's face changes color as he fumes, "Those were custom-made! Go fish them out, thief!"

She sticks her tongue out at him as she approaches the fae'reth. "Nope. Don't feel like it." She waves at Timian. "Yo."

"Hello, Artemis," Timian says stiffly. His expression is relaxed, but Kimala can see the tightness around his lips. "Would you mind quitting the antics until after the meeting?"

"Sera, sera," she mutters as she fiddles with the fae'reth's design. "You're as fun as usual. I have a report for all you kranluk-heads, anyway."

Kimala follows Erimentha the rest of the way into the room. Stopping next to Alec, she isn't surprised when his blonde sister leans toward her and whispers, "Who is that?" She is dressed in shimmering dragon armor that had been custom-made for her when she had visited the Northern Dragon Clan in the Gwynhavo Mountains over the past year. Her clear, sky blue eyes and features reflect that of Alec's, but Kimala has learned that Teresa can be much sterner than her younger brother.

"Artemis Alamir," the redhead answers the duir'ne absently, somehow hearing the question. "Fourteenth reincarnation; my birth name is Rayne Lieuss. I was in Male'stra examining some *beautiful* ruins when this lovely group strolled by and almost trampled me."

She pulls out a flat disk from one of her various pouches. Tapping the fae'reth's surface, a small section folds away to reveal an indent the same size as the disk she holds. She places it inside the niche, and the entire table flickers before displaying a colored map of Saheir.

"It looked like an entire village's population of about seven thousand," she says as a red dot appears in the southeastern corner over the shattered islands that make up the Male'stra Strand southeast of the Heramus. "They were moving north, so I thought they were just fleeing from some wildfire or something that had happened to their island. But then the oddest thing happened."

She flicks her wrist, revealing a picture of a man with a deadpan expression. His eyes are void of emotion.

"When I approached them, they didn't respond to my presence," she informs them. "Didn't blink when I waved my knives in their faces, and didn't speak even when I used my runes. However, as soon as one of my blades accidentally nicked one, they were on me like a pack of cerberus."

Timian frowns, staring at the image of the man. "Where were they when you came here?"

She flicks back to the map, pulling up controls to manipulate the movement of the red dot. "I left a tracking rune on a few of them before I escaped," she admits with a wolfish grin, her Xharos accent temporarily becoming thicker. "It was a bit fun dodging all their attempts to try to kill me."

They watch the units move north above the tree line before cutting west. Riley points to a spot on the map. "Is that where they are now, then?"

"Supposedly." Artemis zooms the image out a bit to reveal their position farther west on the continent. "If they keep the pace they have, they will be on this side in about a week."

Kimala stares at the crystal fae'reth, her stomach dropping. "So they're moving closer..."

Shaniel crosses his arms. "Are they armed?"

Artemis nods as she sweeps up her hair and pins it into a messy bun with three different spikes from one of her leg holsters. "Unconventionally, but yeah. None of them seemed to be right in the mind, either."

"My battalion is stationed along the wall. If they try to attack, we can stave them off," Teresa exclaims.

Artemis glances at her. "I like you," she says, a hint of

respect in her voice.

"Wait a moment," Riley exclaims, holding up his hand. "While I know yer troops can hold 'em off, how do we even know these folks aren't just *escaping*? After all, they're comin' from Male'stra."

The red-haired Alkinian shakes her head as she snaps, "You think I haven't considered that, grunt? Bloody Elethavi, this is why I don't like dealing with you Ecaulana. You're all about *redemption*."

"Settle down, Artemis," Timian murmurs to the young-looking Alkinian. "Duir'ne Teresa, I appreciate your forward thinking; however, I fear your troops will not be enough based off Artemis's observations."

Teresa nods. "The other half of my battalion is currently in Quasala; if Alec could take over these troops, I can return via portal and get my other team battle-ready in five days."

Michelle, who had been leaning against the back wall, now straightens and gives Teresa a grim look. "Unfortunately, we are still having a hard time with the seal placed on the teleportation platform. You would have to trek back by foot."

"You can't get a blasted seal undone?" Artemis exclaims, giving her sister an incredulous look. "What *happened* to you?"

"Don't you give that to me," Erimentha snaps back. "What happened to *you*? Bloody Elethavi, Artemis. Ye look like a half-baked welp!"

"Male'stra has great tropical weather," Artemis snaps. "Not only that, but Raz'hai has *amazing* views from the ocean!"

"I'm talkin' about yer *age*," Erimentha snaps. "Though if ye want to go into that, let's! Yer worse than our brother when it comes to the sun. Yer gonna get radiation poisoning again if you spend too much time in Male'stra."

Artemis sticks her tongue out at her supposed sister as

Shaniel tugs Erimentha out of the room. "Let's work on the teleportation platform," he suggests. "Maybe they could use some help, Erimentha."

As soon as they are out of the room, Timian sighs. "Erimentha is right, Artemis. You should be more careful in Male'stra; the high concentration of Voyana can still alter you." He eyes one of the runes on her skin. "Let me guess. You tried an age-enhancing rune, but it did not work properly?"

"Maybe," she grumbles reluctantly.

"You have probably already absorbed too much radiation from the area. Try avoiding it for a few years."

"Where should I go, then? Huh?" Artemis snaps, crossing her arms. "Artemana is no longer inhabitable because *someone* broke my terraforming platforms, and I'm not welcome in Aihalia for at least another few hundred years."

"Move back here," Timian says gently. "I am sure the inhabitants will welcome you with – "

"And deal with *that* every day?" She jabs her finger at the door. "No. I will not put up with Erimentha's nagging." She leans heavily against the fae'reth and stares at the map. "Forget it, Timian. Once this is over, I'm disappearing again – and depending on if I capture the Da'ruha, perhaps for good this time."

"The Da'ruha is inhabiting the body of the Essence's Vessel," Timian says grimly. "The true owner's name is Mara Danarko, and we are searching for her in Carni as we speak. We cannot have you damage that body, Artemis; it is too valuable."

Kimala swallows the lump in her throat; she doesn't like how Timian is speaking of Mara. Alec, seeing her conflicted expression, squeezes her hand tightly in sympathy. He and the others in the room had been filled in on the situation earlier that morning.

Artemis throws up her hands in exasperation. "Of all

the things Voyana flows through, I can't touch *her?* Bloody Elethavi." Suddenly, she whirls toward the door, her knives at the ready.

Shaniel bursts into the room, his eyes wide as he gasps, "The seal… something broke it from *the other side!*"

"What?!" Timian exclaims, standing up quickly. Everyone is startled by his rattled expression. "But that is impossible!"

"No, it is not," Artemis whispers as a familiar wave of power ripples through the room. "It seems as though we have guests."

Kimala trembles at that powerful surge. She knows it but doesn't at the same time. Before she even registers what she is doing, she takes off down the corridor at a run. Shaniel and Riley quickly follow, staying by her side.

"Kimala, I don't think – "

"It's her, Shaniel. It-it has to be." *It has to be Mara,* Kimala thinks to herself, an unexplainable tightness forming in her chest. *Out of everyone we have gathered in these past few hours, Mara is the one we need the most right now.*

Eliara silently guides her through the castle to the courtyard containing a huge marble platform with runes etched along the rim. A dark portal opens itself over the platform, stabilizing on its own. The portal engineers and sealing experts stand several yards away, terrified; only Erimentha stands close to the portal, grimly holding two glimmering scio'thi in her hands.

"Stay back, fletchling!" Erimentha yells over the high-pitched whistling of the portal, not even glancing at Kimala. "There's no tellin' what is coming through here!"

A black boot pushes out of the portal, setting down onto the ground. A gritty black smoke emanates off of it ominously.

"It's a spirit," Erimentha growls, crouching into a defensive posture.

A tanned hand appears, grabbing the side of the portal

to pull itself through. The sleeve of a black robe comes next, decorated with a multitude of colors. Finally, a hooded head pokes through, the features of the individual shadowed as the person grips the other side of the portal and tugs the rest of the way through.

As soon as the other boot strikes the ground, a ripple of power extends outward from the crouched individual. Black smoke fizzles and snaps ominously about the mysterious, cloaked person. The robe extends to the ankles, and as the person straightens, Kimala can see a multicolored design extending around the sides of the robe to the front. It looks like a starry sky with mountains and trees.

The hands rise, pushing the hood back to reveal dark hazelnut hair and gold eyes. Mara blinks in surprise as she glances around. "I never thought I would be greeted by weapons." Catching sight of Kimala, she gives a lopsided grin and waves. "Hey, Kimala."

Kimala can only stare. *This… this* feels *like Mara, but it's different.*

"That is a Xhuri Robe," Eliara whispers in the back of her mind, explaining before Kimala even has to ask. *"It is a robe created when a soul of an individual vows to uphold a single desire for its existence. Mara did not just find who she is; she* dedicated *herself to it."*

Glancing at the portal, Mara suddenly steps to the side. Darion stumbles through, frantically glancing around until he sees Mara. "Next time, wait until Aeserast checks the connection. You could have – "

Aeserast falls into him, and they tumble onto the platform. "Carc'ra, Darion! You *knew* I was coming through behind you."

"Do not get upset at *me,*" Darion snaps back. He focuses back on Mara. "How are you doing? Any trouble?"

Aeserast frets over Mara's shoulders. "It seems as if you're holding up well… Luckily, you grasped the concept of condensing matter about you fairly quickly. How are the memories? Any different?"

Mara examines her hand as everyone else from the tactical room catches up and stops to stare at the new arrivals. "Not really; I was hoping *something* would have changed, though. Guess I'll have to work on that later." She steps off the platform toward the others. "So what did I – "

Teresa leaps forward, leveling her sword at Mara. "Stop right there," she demands, her eyes hard. "Da'ruha, you are under – "

Artemis bursts out laughing, cutting off the duir'ne. "If that's the Da'ruha, then we're all done for!" She grins at Mara. "A Xhuri Robe? Never thought I would see one of those during these times. Care to share the meaning?"

Mara twists about, and they all see the shimmering multicolored designs of dancing lights and snow-covered trees. The bottom is ripped as if it had torn away from something. "It's nothing new…"

They stare at her, dumbfounded. Kimala finally regains her voice. "Nothing *new*? Mara, you have been gone for nearly a *month*, and then you show up with a-a Soul Robe? Those things are serious business! What if you break the rehkava? What will you do then?"

Now it is everyone's turn to stare at Kimala. "What is she even talkin' about?" Riley whispers to Shaniel, who shrugs.

Mara stares at Kimala for a long moment, her gaze softening as she catches glimpses of Eliara's lapis blue amidst Kimala's silvery-blue Source. "Ah, I see now. I'm glad Eliara is all right." Clasping her hands together, she ignores the next round of confused, shocked looks that are exchanged. "Back to business; a little birdie told me Da'ruha took off with my body. Where is she? I need to teach her a lesson about possession."

Everyone reacts to this; those who did not know of the possession gasp in shock while others shift uncomfortably.

"Unfortunately, we do not know," Timian admits.

Mara's hands fall to her side. "Of course not," she mutters, glancing back at Kimala. The medic's fists are balled so tightly her knuckles are prominently on display. "If you want to slap me, now is the time."

Kimala stalks forward. Aeserast quickly steps in front of her. "Kimala, it would not be a good idea for you to – "

"Move out of my way."

Kimala physically pushes Aeserast aside, stepping onto the platform in front of Mara. She raises her hand, and everyone flinches in preparation.

Kimala inspects the robe, fiddling with the black cloth and the shimmering designs. A *zing* goes up her arms at touching the mage's Source directly through the condensed form, but she ignores it as she lifts Mara's arm. Momentarily impressed that her cousin had managed to condense all of her Source to the point of visibility, she steps around the mage to examine the pattern on the back. Kneeling down, she tuts over the ripped seam. "What *happened*, Mara? Why did it rip?"

Mara looks over her shoulder, surprised. "It was supposed to."

Kimala – no, *Eliara* straightens, huffing at her. "Xhuri Robes do not just… just… *rip*. You *did* something to it."

"So what if I did?"

Her fingers twitch, clenching into a fist as she splutters over words. "You could have *hurt* yourself by ripping your own robe!"

"I know that."

"Ugh!" She shakes her head incredulously. "You are even *more* intolerable now!"

Mara smirks, a smug look that only infuriates the duir'raz'ne even more. "That's just me. Deal with it."

The medic turns to Darion, giving him a piercing glare. "What happened in Carni? Did she lose her sensibility while there?"

"She – "

Mara holds up her hand, willing Darion to remain silent. "It ripped," Mara begins softly, "because I wanted it to. That was part of my Xhuri Rehkava, and thank the *flow* it *did* rip, else I would probably be *dead* if I still had that dratted piece attached to me."

The medic's shoulders slump. "The memories of your failures," she whispers, her gaze shifting to the ground. "Of… of course. That makes sense."

Mara snorts, and Eliara glances at her with narrowed eyes. "Geez, you love jumping to conclusions, don't you? It had blown up; nothing else." She pats her shoulder, giving the medic a big grin. "Now it's your turn to answer *my* question: What did I miss?"

Her eyes fall to the ground as she shifts uncomfortably. "I apologize, Mara," she whispers, too low for anyone but Darion, Aeserast, and Mara to hear her. "I… I could not face her. I let her take your body and the vessel."

Mara squeezes her shoulder. "I'm not mad at you," she murmurs, just as quiet. "In fact, I'm glad you're all right, Your Highness."

"Do not call me that," Eliara breathes, tears forming in her eyes. "It sounds weird coming from you."

Mara smirks. "You're right, it does." She pats the medic's shoulder once more. "But I see that you're doing well with Kimala. That is good."

Eliara nods, closing her eyes briefly. When she re-opens them, Mara is surprised by the hard slap to her cheek. She flexes her jaw as Kimala chastises her, "We were worried about you! Not only that, but do you know how *hard* it has been these past few days trying to fill your shoes? We're not strategists; we're medics!"

Mara rubs her jaw, taking a deep breath. "Strategist?" she repeats, feeling as if she is missing something important.

"Yes! You!" Kimala grabs Mara's wrist, ignoring the

zing from touching Mara's condensed Source again. She drags the mage across the courtyard. "We need you at the fae'reth. It looks like a large group of people are on their way here; we have some troops in place, but — "

"Hold up, Kimala." Mara yanks her hand back, stopping in the middle of the courtyard. Taking a deep breath, she pulls her cousin into a tight hug.

"What — "

"Someone I met wanted me to give you this. He says happy birthday." The medic stills at her quiet words. "He's proud of you and your progress in combating Hemius."

Pulling back, she ignores Kimala's questioning expression as she turns to the unfamiliar individuals. She glances between the red-haired elf and the wary blonde in armor. "I apologize for my entrance; I probably startled some of you. I'm Mara Danarko."

The elf's eyes sharpen on the mage. "Artemis," she greets, thrusting out her hand. "I do not believe we have met."

Mara grasps her hand, quizzical as Artemis's eyes widen in recognition. "We haven't? How strange; you seem familiar."

Kimala stares at her cousin, wondering what is going on with her.

"I see what the others mean about you," Artemis finally says, regaining her composure. Her eyes spark in curiosity. "Am I safe to assume the rehkava is not new?"

Mara shakes her head, turning to the woman in armor. She gives the blonde a calculative look. "Are you... Duir'ne Teresa Roanoak?"

Teresa straightens at her title, looking regal in her glimmering dragon scale armor. "Yes. I apologize for the way I addressed you earlier; I knew the Da'ruha had taken your physical body."

"It's all right." Mara bows slightly to her. "I would have done the same, Your Grace. It's a pleasure finally meeting you."

Teresa quickly bows in return. "Thank you, Your Highness."

"Ye worried us, fletchling," Erimentha murmurs, approaching her. "T'was unpleasant seeing that welp using yer body. I jus' wish we had caught her."

"I agree with Erimentha," Riley rumbles, looking as though he wants to hug her but restraining himself. "Ye had us worried, Mara."

"I'm better than ever. As for the Da'ruha, she will get what's due to her soon enough." Mara turns to the approaching Time'Lord, noticing his quizzical look. "Is something wrong, Uncle Timian?"

"Welcome back, Mara. It is good to see you doing so well." He eyes the front of her robe. "Would you mind turning about for me? I would like to see the back design," he requests.

"Sure." She shows him the back as she asks the others, "What's this about an army? Is the Da'ruha making this easy for me?"

Artemis shakes her head as Timian walks over to a calm Darion and fidgeting Aeserast. "I did not see any trace of the Da'ruha or anyone who looked like you," she admits as she leads Mara down the hallway. Erimentha follows close behind. "The group had come from Male'stra, heading north for a bit. At first, I thought they had been heading for the mountains, but then they turned west."

"They are about a week out from here," Teresa informs her with a grim expression. "Now that the portal is up, I should be able to get my troops here and battle ready within five days."

Mara rubs her chin, thinking. The black aura surrounding her briefly intensifies; unsettled, Teresa steps away. Artemis seems unfazed. "I'll fix the portal after I see the fae'reth. I didn't break all of the seals on it; just the one that stopped the connection to Carni. As for this group, how do you know it's an army and not simply people leaving an area?"

Behind her, Riley clears his throat. "They're armed," he explains in his thick Scottish brogue. "Not only that, but it seems a little too coincidental that the Da'ruha and the traitor disappear right when this large group is on its way."

"It's not lining up…" Mara murmurs, her mind racing. "Why would they attack Alamirana? What's *here* that they would want?"

"Not much, really," Erimentha admits, shrugging. "There's the power hub underneath the throne room, but that's sealed shut. Only Ecalauna and Ecalain have access to it."

"Power hub?" Mara inquires, curious. Something nags the back of her mind; she had known about this power hub, but she doesn't remember much. *It must be another buried memory,* she thinks.

Artemis snorts in amusement. "Looks like you don't remember everything, then," she comments dryly, earning a few odd looks from the rest of the group. "Back when this city was first created, an enormous amount of energy was stored inside the hub to keep the city maintained and to stop it from collapsing. Every couple hundred years, it needs to be replenished and repaired, but this is why the castle has not fallen."

"What happens if it *is* taken?"

Artemis and Erimentha exchange looks. "Eventually, the city will not be able to withstand the elements and will crumble," Erimentha says softly. "Even Voyana does not want that; it also replenishes the hub when we open it."

"That's what they're after," Mara announces, glaring straight ahead. "More specifically, that must be what *Rath* is after."

"Rath?" Artemis repeats, a sharp tone to her voice. "Is that who I think it is?"

Timian, overhearing the conversation, breaks away from Aeserast and Darion to walk alongside Mara and Artemis. "Unfortunately, yes, Artemis. It does seem as though the same man who altered your memories is still around."

"That man never knows when to give up…" she mutters. "Do we know what he looks like now? Not just a pitiful sketch?"

Mara holds out her hand. Black sand collects in her palm, extending upward to shape a small model; the sand rolls off to reveal a pale face, grey hair, ice blue eyes, and a gold-lined black suit. "I can't replicate the hair color," she admits regretfully. "It's more of a platinum color than grey, but – "

"Cronus," Artemis hisses, her eyes dilating. For a brief moment, they glow a bright peridot green.

Chapter 15
A Complete Circle

"Of all the Ecalain," Erimentha exclaims, staring at the figure. "I never even knew he was still *alive*."

Even Timian seems rattled. "Mara, are you *certain* this is what he looks like?"

Mara frowns. "Aeserast looked at my memories; he saw the man. Didn't he show you?"

Timian shakes his head. "He told me the description matches that of the white-haired man we have been searching for, and that was all I needed to know at the time." He narrows his eyes at the model. "He looks to be exactly the same as back then... not even a rebirth difference. How is this possible?"

"Cryo-sleep?" Artemis theorizes, tapping her lip. "Coulda made a concoction like me. Or – "

"Could have experimented on elementals and figured out how to change his genetic code," Mara whispers, remembering what Lyon had said before Rath had blasted a hole into his chest.

Timian gives her a sharp look. "Mara, what you are suggesting is – "

"Illegal, I know," she whispers. "But I remember Lyon talking about it. He had accused Rath of experimenting on an air elemental and the subsequent child, but maybe he was also experimenting on himself."

Timian's jaw tenses. "If so, then he will be much harder to capture than I had ever anticipated." He narrows his eyes, giving Mara a look. "Lyon never revealed that information in a report to me, though. How did he know about it?"

Mara shrugs. "I don't exactly know." She feels an ache in her chest at the thought of Thanos fading away in front of her. Taking a deep breath, she mentally berates herself; it is better that he is not here for this. If he dies for good, she will never be able to forgive herself.

Once they finally make it to the fae'reth, Mara is awed by the hologram-projecting table made out of crystal. Its sleek, curving design compliments the smooth, seamless walls and simplistic chairs.

Mara is careful not to touch the edge of the fae'reth. "So what is the plan?" she asks, glancing around as everyone settles into their seats. Kimala leans forward and deactivates the holograms.

"Teresa has some troops out front, but it won't be enough to hold them off," Riley admits. "I have some soldiers over in Danarkana; we had been training just in case anything like this ever happened."

Mara rubs her jaw. "It will be a three to four day trek from Quasala. It's pushing it, but…"

"We do not have much of a choice," Teresa says, her eyes hard. "Alec can take over my troops here; he is already familiar with my captain."

Alec dips his head respectfully. "It would be my honor, sister."

Teresa smirks at him. "I heard you have been training hard in the tactical wing. I am sure you will do great."

"What am I, chopped liver?" Mara mutters to herself, earning an odd look from Teresa. Clearing her throat, she announces, "I have an idea."

Darion is already shaking his head. "Mara, now is not the time. Allow us to – "

"Let me speak, Darion." Mara's hard gaze has him snapping his mouth shut. "Geez. I'm gone for a month, and all of you forget I have the Essence's knowledge in me? To top it off, I *did* come back with my Xhuri Robe and more memories. Give me a bit more credit."

Kimala gives her a confused, guilty look. "But… Mara, the Essence is still sealed in your body."

Mara shakes her head. "I still have the knowledge I learned from it, including memories of previous wars." She smirks at Timian's startled, unnerved expression. "You're getting that look a lot with me, Uncle Timian."

"It is phenomenal that you are in so much control," he murmurs. "I would not have expected you to be able to hold together your form as you are now. Everyone can see you, after all."

Mara raises her hand, examining it. A bit of black smoke rises as if she is some type of shadowy creature, but overall, she looks almost exactly like she does in a regular body.

Almost.

She knows a major difference that no one else has commented on yet, and she doesn't need a mirror to see it. Her ears are pointed, and her eyes are more slanted than usual. Her skin is also darker. *Perhaps they are still too shocked to see me to catch these differences,* she thinks to herself, crossing her arms. "Renewing my Soul Promise put a couple things into perspective. First off, I want to clarify one thing: no, I do not remember my own past lives. I know *of* them and I may get flashes, but I do not outright remember them. As for my Xhuri Rehkava..." Her eyes flick to Kimala, knowing Eliara is listening. "I made a vow to protect those I care about, so with or without your permission, I *will* be helping out during this fight."

A quiet murmur ripples around the table. Teresa's short, dry laugh cuts through it, though, as she comments, "That was a stupid vow; we are going into *war.* People get hurt and die."

"And I understand that," Mara responds in a low voice, giving her a serious look. "That is why my last Xhuri had been broken; I was stupid and naïve to think that everything rested on my shoulders. Now, I better understand that people have their own will; I cannot help or protect those who do not want it."

Kimala exhales slowly, her eyes sinking to the table as Mara's words resound within her.

"*I* will fight," Mara clarifies. "I will do everything in my power to protect and assist all of you. Whatever you need me to do, I will do it to the best of my abilities." She smirks. "And I have a few new ones since Carni."

Timian, Erimentha, and Artemis are torn, knowing the implications of upholding a Xhuri yet not wanting to put Mara in danger. Riley, Michelle, Teresa, Alec, and Shaniel look dubious. Darion and Aeserast give exasperated huffs of disapproval.

Kimala is the only one with an understanding look on her face as she asks, "What do you have planned, Mara?"

Mara eases onto one of the backless chairs, careful not to sit down too suddenly in case she causes an energy current. "Nothing right now. I wanted to hear your plans before I made any suggestions." She rolls her eyes at their shocked expressions. "I didn't come in here to take over the meeting."

Once the meeting is over, Mara meanders out of the strategy room with the others, beginning to feel the strain that Darion and Aeserast had been worried about. Before they notice the tension in her expression, she excuses herself by claiming she wants to explore the castle a bit on her own.

In reality, she is drawn to a particular spot: the grove-like courtyard the teleportation platform is in. Stepping into the sunny area, she takes a deep breath out of habit and is surprised when she can smell the earthy scents and old stone surrounding her.

A portal engineer holding a tablet eyes her warily. "You're... Mara Danarko, correct?"

She nods, assuming he is the head engineer. "Yes; I apologize for giving all of you a scare earlier. Was anyone hurt?"

He shakes his head. "Most of them had been taking a

break around the time you came through; Erimentha and I were the only ones close enough to be affected." He glances at the portal. "What did you do, anyway? It doesn't seem to be anchored to a physical location, and we aren't able to pass through it."

"I just broke the seals that kept it from connecting to Carni," she admits, drawing closer.

He frowns as his screen flashes. He taps a few buttons and shakes the unit. "I apologize, but I think our equipment is too sensitive for you to get near it."

Mara pauses as he moves a few paces away. Tapping her chin thoughtfully, she suggests, "Power it off and hand it to me."

He hesitates for a moment before following her instructions. As he steps toward her, though, he pales as a cold sweat breaks out on his face. He dabs his brow. "I apologize for this, but your Source is overpowering the area. I can't get closer."

Mara glances down at herself. Black smoke trails off of her like sand, giving her a permanent dark aura. She closes her eyes, centralizing her thoughts and focusing on drawing in the straying energy. She knows why it is slipping; the strain is wearing down her mental state.

When she opens her eyes again, she sees the engineer staring at her. He hands over the tablet wordlessly.

"What's your name?" Mara asks as she turns the tablet back on, careful not to overpower the unit until she lowers the Source sensitivity.

"Yander, Your Grace," he introduces himself, awkwardly shifting on his feet. "Is 'Your Grace' acceptable?"

"I would prefer it if you call me Mara," she absently murmurs, scrolling through the data about the teleportation platform. "I don't care much for titles."

Kimala walks into the courtyard, catching Mara's words. "At least that hasn't changed about you," she comments.

Yander quickly bows to her. "Your Grace! I do not

recommend coming any closer; the portal is still unpredictable."

Mara presses the tablet against his shoulder; he straightens and takes it from her, confused. "It won't be in a moment," she tells him, eyeing the platform. "Keep your distance; I don't want anyone getting hurt once this thing is cut loose."

Yander backs up until he is next to Kimala. "Is this far enough?"

Mara eyes the distance; it is several yards from the platform. "Maybe… a little farther," she admits. She knows that the portal's pull won't be enough to harm them from this distance, but that isn't what she is worried about.

Once they are far enough away, Mara walks to the platform and examines the Old Xharos sigils decorating the rim. She kneels next to one, feeling an odd sense of déjà vu. She has stood next to this very platform before, but not in this exact position.

Her eyes are drawn to a rune five sigils over. Stepping around the platform, she traces the Old Xharos rune with her finger as she takes a slow, deep breath.

She can sense her own Source inside of this rune.

She swallows hard. *I must have been in this castle before,* she realizes, her fingers pressing on the rune a little harder. *That would explain why I keep getting these weird memory flashes.*

"How long has this seal been here?" she asks Yander, keeping her voice flat; she doesn't want them to see how shaken she is over this newfound knowledge about herself.

"According to Erimentha, about five hundred years," he answers her, frowning at his tablet. "There's more information in here, but I-I can't activate it. If you don't mind me asking, what did you do to it, Your Grace?"

"It's Mara." She straightens, glancing at Kimala. "I decreased the Source input sensitivity levels. Have Kimala channel it; she should be able to help reverse the settings."

Turning back to the platform, she stares at the sigil. Her

emotions swirl dangerously, threatening to break through her self-control and reflect their agitation through her Source. She crosses her arms, feeling as though her gaze will drill a hole through the sigil and reveal its history if she stares at it long enough.

"That sigil won't be movin' even if ye look away, fletchling," a familiar voice says. She turns around to see Erimentha passing by Yander and Kimala working together to fix the settings on the control panel.

The Alkinian glances at the teleportation platform as she draws closer. Keeping her voice low, she asks, "You know who placed that, don't ye?"

"I have a suspicion," Mara admits, returning her gaze to the sigil. "It's the 'why' that I don't understand yet, though."

Erimentha's eyes flick between Mara and the seal. "Her name was K'sanri," she murmurs, and the harsh name has Mara shivering in recognition. "She was a spy from the country Mishir; they don't like Alkinians, ye see, an' they were trying to start a war with Saheir back then."

Mara frowns. "If they didn't like Alkinians, then why wasn't she killed? Wasn't she... Alkinian?"

Erimentha shakes her head. "Have ye heard of the Erus?"

Mara shakes her head. "I don't think so. Who are they?"

"More like *what*," Erimentha corrects her. "They're an aquatic bipedal species with both lungs and gills. They can survive out of the water for up to a week before they need to be submerged in freshwater again. They were affected by Voyana, but they are in permanent denial of its effects; those who can use Source are called warlocks."

Mara raises an eyebrow. "So they're... fish people."

Erimentha snorts. "Something like that." She gestures to the platform. "Five hundred years ago, their ruler got it in his head that if they destroyed Alamirana, no more

Alkinians would come to Blazhreia. He sent his most talented warlock to thwart the rechargin' process of the castle."

"Was that… K'sanri?" Mara fumbles over the name, having trouble pronouncing the 'k' at the beginning.

Erimentha nods. "She was definitely a clever one. She realized that even if she did manage to stop the Alamiran ceremony, it wouldn' have stopped the Alkinians from having access to this realm. She sealed the teleportation platform with old techniques from her country, techniques I haven't managed to crack yet despite workin' on them for over two hundred years." She sighs. "I jus' wish she had stayed. She had so much potential here; she seemed to be interested in our ways, too. Found 'em fascinating."

Mara examines the teleportation platform with new interest. "She sealed it as a compromise?"

Erimentha nods. "If ye know how to break it, then by all means, do it." She grins. "An' then tell *me* how ye did it."

Mara laughs a little self-consciously, rubbing the back of her head. "It's a bit hard to describe…" Kneeling next to the sigil, she points at it. "The main anchoring unit is here, but the problem is that this is an infusion method; only the caster can break this type of seal because they actually have to *pull* the Source out of the stone, not break the anchoring units. If someone else does it, there is a chance some Source can be left behind."

Erimentha frowns. "We've tried that technique, though… all it does is sap at our Source, as if it's fuelin' the seal."

Mara shakes her head. "It's not fueling the seal; it's fueling the Source itself." She hesitates before admitting, "I recognize the Source because it's just like mine."

Erimentha's eyes flick to hers. "I had a feelin'," she admits, sighing. "Ever since you came through that portal earlier, you have given off the same Source signature as

K'sanri. In fact, it was so different than yer Source from before that I didn't recognize you until you let down yer hood." She grows quizzical. "How did you make that portal, anyway?"

Mara walks around the platform, stopping on the farthest side from the entrance to the courtyard. She glances into the 'back' of the swirling dark portal before looking down at the rune. "This is where external portals from Carni were not allowed to come through," she tells Erimentha. "The only way to break it *is* in Carni, though; that's why I was able to create it. All it takes is the same Source that had made it to crack it, and it shatters."

Erimentha exhales, realization dawning on her face. "So you've suspected this all along."

"Something like that." She steps onto the platform, walking to the portal to place her hand in the middle. It encounters an invisible wall, unable to pass through. "However, the reverse seal is still in place, thus we cannot travel *back* to Carni. That seal should be…" She looks in front of the portal, scouring the runes. Kneeling next to one, she presses a finger on it. "This one."

Crack.

The portal emits a loud whistle that quickly diminishes as the invisible barrier tumbles into it, cracked and useless. Mara steps off the platform before she is sucked into it.

Erimentha whistles, impressed. "Fer not rememberin' everything, yer doing great, fletchling."

She shrugs self-consciously as Darion and Aeserast meander into the courtyard. "It's like it was… ingrained in me. I just *know* what to do."

"Keep doing it, then!" She gestures to the rest of the platform. "What's next?"

"The seal on the anchoring unit." Mara points at the sigil she had been standing by earlier. "Once we break that one, we will be able to anchor portals to the platform."

Erimentha eyes the portal swirling in the air. "How's

this one here, then?"

Mara glances at it, a bit disconcerted. "I… don't know, honestly. When I made it, I just did it."

"The data we've been collecting on it finally came back," Yander informs them, staring at his screen. "According to this, it anchored itself into the ground and it's holding itself together by… the surrounding Source?!" He backs up from the platform, horrified. "No wonder our Source levels have been depleting rapidly! It's using *us* to hold itself here!"

"Of all the random techniques for me to use." Mara shakes her head, walking to the edge of the portal. "Everyone with a Source rank of six or lower needs to leave. Now."

"Six?" Yander repeats, unsettled. "But… that's all of the engineers, including myself."

She shoots him a dark look, her eyes temporarily swirling purple. "Then *leave*. This isn't going to be pretty."

Erimentha slowly backs away from her as the engineers exit the courtyard. "You all right, fletchling?"

She nods. "I know you're powerful, Erimentha, but I prefer for you not to be affected by this, either. Can you move closer to the entrance?"

"And what about you?"

"It's my Source; it can't hurt me."

"That's a foolish thing to think, fletchling," Erimentha murmurs, but she walks over to where Darion, Kimala, and Aeserast are standing.

Darion takes a step forward, concerned and worried. "Mara, if it puts a strain on – "

"It's all right, Darion." She smiles at him, her eyes gold again. "Just… stay back, all right? I don't want you to get hurt."

She closes her eyes, allowing her Source to expand and cover the entire platform and portal. She winces as the portal's anchoring system switches its focus to her

Source, sucking it into the rim and darkening the area even more.

She glances at the rune to her left, her semi-corporeal hand reaching for it. She knows that once she breaks this, she will need to act fast. Black sand tumbles forward, coating the platform. She clenches her fist.

Crack.

The portal in front of her wobbles, unstable as it tries to latch onto the platform beneath it; however, the last rune on the right is still blocking it. She repeats the same action: reach, grasp, *crack.*

Using both of her hands now, she grabs the edges of the portal, manually stabilizing it as the anchors migrate to their respective positions and lock into place via the platform's own energy entrapment system. Exhaling, she draws in her Source as she backs away from the portal to reveal the swirling, clear disk. A strand of black clings to the edge briefly before dissipating, falling onto the platform as black sand. It creeps toward Mara.

She kneels down and brushes her fingers over the platform. She frowns, standing up and glancing around. "There's another seal here somewhere; it's blocking the portal from locking onto a destination."

Yander peers around the corner of the entryway, his eyes wide. "Th-there's a control unit over there," he informs her, his voice shaking as his trembling hand points to the right of the platform.

Mara glances over. A shimmering stone pulses weakly on the ground, hidden behind the wild grass. She glides to it, placing her hand over it and *yanking* the seal off. It shimmers multiple colors in her hand for a brief second before being absorbed into her already-enlarged Source.

The semi-precious stone rises, tilting to reveal a control panel that lights up and projects holograms and figures into the air directly in front of it. Mara immediately checks the status of the newly-anchored portal, refining the connection and ensuring stability.

"It's safe," she calls over, setting the anchored portal's destination to connect to Cerlail Academy's platform. It loads the connection as Yander approaches. "I apologize if you felt dizzy; I tried to restrain the reach of my Source. Once it connects, tell Engineer Tyrmas I said hi."

Yander stares at the screen, scanning over the information. "This... this is amazing..." he breathes, his fingers brushing over the edge of the built-in crystal slab. "The channels are undamaged after all of this time..."

"Of course they are," Mara huffs, walking over to Darion and the others. "It's Alkinian tech. What did you expect?"

Darion glances between her and the platform now crawling with engineers and researchers. "What you did was phenomenal," he murmurs.

"Truly," Erimentha concurs, grinning as she claps. "To think that the one who had originally created those seals is the same one who breaks them. The irony."

Darion, Aeserast, and Kimala stare at the Alamir. "What?" they chorus.

Mara sighs, waving at them. "I'll let you fill them in, Erimentha. I'm going to sit down."

"Have fun, K'sanri!" Erimentha calls to her cheerily.

"It's Mara," she retorts half-heartedly, her irritation thwarted by her own tiredness. "Quit calling me by different names, werui."

Erimentha gasps. "Did you hear that? She called me aunt! We're closer already!"

Walking through the courtyard, Mara sees an archway leading to another area. Curious, she enters the smaller grove. It looks somewhat like the Danti Cauerr'ien, and she wonders if this is the recreated Duir'raz'ien she had read about in the history books. She sits beneath a tree that reminds her of the one she had rested underneath inside of Carni. She closes her eyes briefly; unsealing the portal had taken more out of her than she had anticipated.

Her mind wanders to the meeting from earlier. She had sensed that everyone has questions for her, although no one had said anything at that time.

This is hilarious, she thinks to herself, opening her eyes to stare at the walled corridors encapsulating the grove. *They still think I might go over the deep end if they ask me the wrong thing. They don't realize I'm back to normal now. Or... at least, as normal as I can be.*

She sighs, looking up at the branches. She is relieved to see it is regular bark and leaves; no Source-creations that her Source can devour. Despite having used it several times by now, she is still having a hard time wrapping her mind around her Source's ability.

It converts external Source into itself.

No wonder it never took long for it to replenish itself, she grumbles inwardly.

Catching movement out of her peripheral, she turns her head to see Kimala hesitantly walking toward her. She glances at the tree, looking a little disturbed.

Mara wonders why before she remembers this is most likely where Eliara had died. She distracts the medic by saying, "Did you know there was a tree a lot like this one in the Danti Cauerr'ien? It was beside a lake. Really pretty, too."

"I-is that so?" The medic sits down, folding her legs underneath her as she sits a few feet away. She examines Mara, concern creasing her brow. "Mara, I need to tell you something. I think Eliara is fading."

Mara rests her head against the tree. "I guessed as much."

Kimala's eyes drop to the ground. "I... I apologize."

"Don't. I never would have been able to get along with her. So she's sharing her memories with you?"

"Yes." Kimala sighs. "She hasn't been speaking as much recently, though; she only says something when it directly involves her, or she feels a lot of emotion. It's beginning to concern me."

"Don't let it. It's normal." The mage eyes her cousin, a serious look in her eyes. "Kimala, I need your help."

Kimala's breath catches in horror. "Mara, you can't be – "

"I'm not dying, srui." She spots Aeserast and Darion entering the garden. Not seeing anyone else, she continues, "After this war and I have my body back, I'm going to need your help learning about my duties and titles. I've decided it's the way I want to help protect everyone, but I can't do it on my own – not after all the kranluk manure I went through to get back home with my mind still intact."

Aeserast, hearing the last part, snorts in amusement. "I'm pretty sure you *did* lose it a few times. You had insisted on opening the portal yourself, after all."

"W-we don't have to talk about that," Mara mutters, her cheeks reddening.

Darion smirks. "Let us not forget that you blew up the Tower of Discord." Kimala's eyes widen at this.

"We don't need to talk about that, either!"

"Oh, but wait…" Aeserast taps his chin dramatically, almost looking like Shaniel with that simple motion. "Didn't she *already* absorb the *entire* energy supply of the Danti Cauerr'ien except for one flower? Glutton. You're worse than my sister."

"Now you're just antagonizing me."

"Of course we are." Darion ruffles her hair.

"I thought it was impossible for someone to convert another's energy into their own," Kimala exclaims, her eyes wide. "We can only mix Voyana with our own. The closest is using someone else's Source. How did you… did you really… destroy it?"

Mara stares at Kimala for a long moment. Again, she has a nagging sense that it is Eliara's concern influencing Kimala's speech. Holding out her hand, she allows her

Source to coalesce into a harmless sphere. "Have you ever wondered why my Source is black?"

"Because it's the color of your soul," she mutters. Darion and Aeserast shoot her startled looks at the rather harsh insult.

Mara smirks. "Actually, you're onto something there." She allows the sphere to disintegrate. "At first, I thought black was evil, too, until the lady on the clock tower explained it to me."

"The ghost," Aeserast breathes.

Mara nods. "That's a bit more fitting," she admits. "She explained that every color represents a core aspect; for example, blue is a common color that represents the desire to heal. It's also a color of calmness or nurturing. Black, though, is commonly misconstrued."

Darion eases onto the ground cross-legged next to Mara. "How so?"

"Well, black often means death, right?" At Darion's and Kimala's nods, Mara shakes her head. "Think about how you make the color black when drawing or painting, though. You have to mix nearly every possible color together."

Realization crosses Darion's face. "So your Source is a combination of *all* of the possible Source colors."

Mara nods. "It means I am also compatible with all Sources except one." She looks down at her robe sleeve, staring at the rainbow-like colors. "White."

"The Essence?" Aeserast queries, confused.

"Somewhat. That's something else I learned; as I've said before, I still have the knowledge and memories I had gained from the Essence. My Source's ability is to take all external Source and convert it into itself, including whatever knowledge is stored away within it – such as the Essence."

They now look confused. "But… you said you can't do that with white," Aeserast points out.

"Nope, I can't." Mara grins. "White is the absence of any color, but the Essence isn't purely white; it's a shade of grey. It's been tainted with its own experiences; joy, happiness, love, anger, *everything*. What my Source was doing without me even realizing it was *converting* the Essence's knowledge and storing it away directly inside of me. I wasn't just accessing the Essence's knowledge; I was gaining it for myself."

Aeserast's eyes widen as he fully understands the implications of this. "So… if you merge with the Essence…"

"I'll absorb all of its memories and knowledge," Mara finishes, her lips quirking up. "The Essence will be reverted to its original state – a clean slate with no taint of a single color or emotion. It makes sense, really."

Chapter 16
War Preparations

Darion looks torn. "But you were having trouble with the memory lapses before. Are you sure it is wise?"

Mara nods. "Yeah, I'm sure." She knocks her fist against her head. "I know who I am now; there's no more question about it. That was my main problem before."

Kimala chews on her lip, staring at the grass. "But the memories were the reason why you went into Carni. You couldn't stand them. What if…"

Mara's eyes soften. "It wasn't Carni that had been causing my lapses after porting," she murmurs. "Whenever I teleported, a fragment of the broken seal in my mind would break away, and my Source would flood a new region of the Essence. That's why it seemed as though I kept lapsing anytime I went through a portal."

Aeserast slowly exhales. "This explains… a lot." He glances at Darion. "What do you think?"

Darion stares at Mara for a long moment. "Do you know how to control when and what your Source devours?"

Mara flinches. "Somewhat; I'm still getting used to it. Even though I renewed my Xhuri Rehkava, it's still taking a bit of getting used to. Apparently, I've had this trouble ever since Voyana exploded, though."

They stare at her, dumbfounded.

Mara glances between them. "What?"

"Mara…" Darion fights to find the right words. "Have you remembered more since the Tower?"

She scratches the bottom of her chin. "It's… hard to explain. It's like I just woke up; I know that I've been reborn before with no previous memory, but I can't always tell you who I had been or what I had done." She pauses, mulling over a particular tidbit of 'knowledge.' "However, there is *one* that I remember pretty well. It was… it was waking up after the Voyana explosion. I thought I had died. When I looked around, though, the entire city had collapsed; the reverse-magnetized platforms had crashed to the ground, and the barriers keeping out the pollution were shattered. I wasn't wearing a protective suit, either." She laughs in realization. "Actually, now that I think about it, that city design I was piddling with on your tablet is the same one as from that memory."

Darion's breath expels slowly. "Do you remember the name?"

Mara's eyes briefly flash a dark smoky blue. "Zandria." They return to gold. "But… I don't remember the last name."

"The Kuri'Voyana," Kimala breathes in awe. At Aeserast's confused look, she quickly explains, "It was a name from Eliara's time. Zandria was one of the first Ecalain after Voyana's explosion; it was before they were even *called* Ecalain. The legend is that she would stop rampaging Alkinians who had lost their mind due to the explosion by taking their Source away from them so they could not harm anyone. Back then, the high volume of energy was reanimating those who had died; if it was taken away and they were killed, they… did not come back."

"Devourer of Energy is a bit of an exaggeration," Mara mutters at the title she had called her. "But… yeah, that sounds about right. She would take their Source to stop them from hurting her comrades. She was the one who made the Xhuri Rehkava the first time; I know she died shortly after, but I don't know how."

"This is phenomenal," Kimala whispers. "Do you know if you can fight like that, though, Mara? You do not have a body."

"If there's one thing I've learned, it's keeping my form together," she answers shrewdly, grimacing. "I have this nagging feeling I got lost in Carni before, and then had to find where my body was… Something about a coma." She yawns. "But enough of that. Any word about the troops?"

Darion shakes his head. "Duir'ne Teresa already left; it will be several days before she returns with reinforcements."

"According to Shaniel and Artemis, the approaching legion hasn't changed pace at all," Aeserast adds grimly. "We're at a bit of a standstill as we wait for both our allies and our enemies to get here."

Mara rubs her chin. A dark aura of smoke slowly coalesces around her as she ponders out loud, "They came from Male'stra… but why? What's there? It's only ruins with excessive amounts of Voyana now."

"There were some people who would seek shelter in the Alkinian ruins," Darion says, shrugging. "It has never been a surprise to find people inhabiting the old buildings. According to some scouts' observations, it looks as though the people heading this way really are from Male'stra."

"Perhaps… no, it can't be." Mara shakes away the thought; there is no way all of those people are controlled by one person.

"What is it, Mara?" Aeserast asks, leaning forward.

"It's not possible to mind-control that many people, is it?"

Aeserast exhales slowly. "No, but it *is* possible to manipulate and alter their minds, although it is illegal." He stares at her for a moment. "You don't think…"

"If it's possible, that might be the case," she whispers. "Rath won't stop. After what happened in Dounta, I'm surprised Desdemona and Rath didn't hunt me down in Carni to kill me."

"You didn't kill Naiya, though," Aeserast says, confused.

"Desdemona thinks otherwise," Mara points out, leaning against the tree again. "As for Rath, well… he's a bit crazy. He didn't want to hurt me, but he has some sort of end goal. I just need to figure out what it is he wants."

Darion shakes his head. "It is not safe for you to put yourself directly in the middle of this war, Mara. You should stay back and – "

"I will not." She glares at him. "I swore I would do *everything* in my power to protect those I care about, and if I stand back and watch all of you fighting when I could be helping, I might as well throw myself through the Elethavi now before my rehkava is broken a *second* time."

Stunned, they stare at her. "You really made a soul promise on that?" Kimala whispers.

Mara nods. "There is a difference between this promise and the first one I made, though. I can't help things that are out of my control no matter how hard I try." She holds up her hand, watching her Source flex lazily about her fingers.

Kimala stands up, brushing off her skirt. "If that's the case, then I guess we can't do anything about it," she says brusquely. "A rehkavi is a rehkavi. We have no choice but to try to help you not break it."

Mara smiles wryly. "Thanks… I think."

Kimala stalks into the corridors of Alamirta. Aeserast stares after her, glancing at Darion and Mara. "I'm going to follow her," he mumbles.

Darion watches Aeserast leave before turning to Mara. He gives her a long, hard look. "There is no way I can persuade you otherwise, is there?"

Mara shakes her head, leaning against the tree and closing her eyes. Despite being in a semi-corporeal form, she is tired. "Nope. You're stuck with me being stubborn on this one."

He sighs heavily. "I just worry about your state right now. It would be too easy for…" He trails off, looking as though he wants to say more.

Mara frowns, peering at him with one eye. "For what? What aren't you telling me, Darion?"

He glances around before resting his hand on hers. It is an odd sensation having him touch her semi-corporeal form, but she struggles not to yank away from him as he telepathically explains, *"There have been incidents surrounding the Da'ruha's escape. The guards in Eleth are either completely shattered or their minds are wiped. Because you are also in your non-corporeal form, I fear the same might happen to you if you encounter her."*

Mara smirks at him, responding with the same method. *"I'm stronger than that, Darion. I was the one who shattered the Da'ruha, not the other way around."*

He shakes his head. *"It is not her I worry about; it is her accomplice."* He pauses. *"We are almost certain it is Rath since he is directly associated with the Shasta family and matches the description we have been provided."*

She mulls over this, remembering the weird spell in Dounta where she had slipped into the role of nanny and guest without question. *"It's a possibility. He is a phenomenal mind-weaver; I did not even notice when he had altered my own mind."*

He sighs. *"Exactly."* His thumb rubs over the back of her hand, sending an energetic tingle up both of their arms. "How are you fairing? Are you sure you are doing all right?"

She nods, closing her eyes. "I'm just getting tired; the mental strain is getting to me a bit."

"Perhaps Elethanos can help," he offers. "We can go to the Chamber and let you rest before the battle; Elethanos can also create a temporary form that you can operate much like a regular body."

Mara wrinkles her nose. "That sounds weird..."

He chuckles. "It is a simple process; Elethanos uses some of the material stored away in its inner chambers to construct a temporary body for situations such as this so the strain on the soul is not as bad. As soon as you are in your own body, the constructed body will return to Elethanos."

"Definitely weird." She shivers. "But… yes. We can try that."

He takes her hand, guiding her to her feet. "Allow me to inform the others, and then we can be on our way."

"All right."

He pauses. "Your speech patterns have changed since you acquired that robe," he murmurs, his eyes hooding.

Mara's smile is tired. "Have they? I… have not really noticed." She flexes her hand once again. "I don't feel much different, either, other than the obvious lack of a material form."

"I suppose that is a good thing," he murmurs. "I will be back shortly. Would you prefer to accompany me or meet by the teleportation platform?"

"I will wait." She strides to the grove's entrance, glancing back to see him watching her closely.

Entering the larger courtyard, she waves at Yander standing at the control panel. He smiles as she approaches. "Your Grace – I mean, Mara, I managed to figure it out! The control unit is a little outdated since the most recent teleportation tech, but it still functions like any other unit."

"I'm glad it is working for you," she says, eyeing it curiously. "Would you mind programming it in advance for Elethanos, then? Darion and I are going there for a bit."

He glances at her in concern. "Are you feeling all right, Mara?"

"Yeah," she waves off, shrugging. "Just tired. We're thinking it will be less exhausting for my mental state."

"Ye *are* struttin' about in yer soul form," Erimentha points out as she walks over from the platform. "Be careful; time moves differently there."

"I figured as much," Mara admits. "I'm sure we will

be back in time, though."

Darion enters the courtyard, glancing between Erimentha and Mara. "Are you ready?" he asks, offering his arm to her.

"As ready as I'll be," she says, wrapping her fingers around his forearm. "We will be back shortly, Erimentha."

"Ye better be," she mutters as they move to the platform. "This war isn't gonna win itself."

They step through the portal.

Mara squeezes her eyes shut; it is disconcerting feeling every particle of her semi-corporeal form passing through the membrane, though she does notice it is different from every other porting experience she has had before. As soon as her foot strikes hard stone floor on the other side, she sighs in relief, already feeling better… and heavier.

"Elethanos, could you construct her a temporary body?" Darion asks the dark chamber as he walks forward.

"*Already done,*" echoes throughout the large room. "*It should hold up for a day or two in the material realms.*"

Darion frowns. "We need one that will last longer."

"*Her Source's ability restricts the type of body I can create to withstand energy pressure.*"

Mara smiles at him tiredly. "At least I can get some rest."

He beckons her to the left wall; they walk around a pillar and into the half-hidden entry leading to his living quarters.

"Elethanos can prepare a room. Make yourself at home, Mara," he encourages her, pausing by his wiry assistant standing at the entrance to the kitchen. "I need to speak with Mornak for a moment."

She nods, following the hallway deeper into the chamber's living quarters. A few paces down the hall, a door to her right swings open. She enters to find the exact same setup she had the last time she had stayed there. "Thank you, Elethanos," she says sincerely.

"My pleasure. If there is anything you need, do not hesitate to ask." At that, the door swings shut behind her, and she has an odd sense of being alone.

This must be Elethanos's way of giving me privacy, she thinks, crawling underneath the covers. She is relieved to discover that she isn't getting weird tingles anytime she touches something. Within seconds, she is fast asleep. It feels as though barely any time has passed when Darion's voice stirs her awake.

"Mara, we need to head back to Alamirana."

"Give me five more minutes, please…" she mumbles, curling into the pillow.

He sighs heavily. "Mara, it is only a day until the army reaches the walls. We need to return now."

She blearily looks up at him as Erimentha's words come back to her. *Time really does move differently,* she thinks, sitting upright and yawning.

Darion is dressed in armor very similar to her own back in Quasala, although his is black-scaled with gold edging and highlights. His black and gold Highlord cloak rests on his shoulders, clasped in the front with a brooch that looks like the Elethavi. Scuffs and nicks decorate the surface of the worn dragon armor.

She looks down; she is still in the same clothes as before. She hesitantly sniffs at herself, disconcerted that she doesn't smell any different.

"It is not a real body," Darion explains, noticing her concern. "You will be fine in it after you leave the Chamber, but we need to hurry."

She takes his offered hand. The same zing goes up their arms despite the mage being in a body. Their eyes lock.

"Elethanos, what type of body did you construct for Mara?" he asks, suddenly pushing Mara's hair to the side to examine her ears. They are pointed.

"One that would reflect her xhuri the most," Elethanos

responds. *"Her xhuri is an old, powerful one, so this was the best I could do."*

Darion's fingers linger on Mara's face as he glances off to the side with a frown. "But it looks as though you put her into an adult Alkinian body from the first era."

"I did."

"But she is not an adult yet."

"This Alkinian body is the best I could construct to contain her power, and even then, it is not enough. I cannot generate a body strong enough to withstand the pressure of her Source; only special circumstances give her xhuri an opportunity to be reborn into a living body that can withstand her power."

"It's true," Mara whispers, her fingers wrapping around Darion's and pulling his hand away from her face. "While my personal Source might start out small, my ability to convert other Sources and absorb them gives me a unique advantage – yet it can also strain my body." She gives him a reassuring smile. "I'll be fine, though. I lasted a day without a body on Blazhreia; if this one fails, then I will just have to find my own body that much faster."

Darion's fingers constrict around hers as he gives her a concerned look. "If you say so…"

"We need to go, right?" she says, standing up. She rolls her shoulders, feeling a bit stiff. "Let's go, then."

He nods. "I already contacted the others at Alamirta. Ryutaro and Twyla have arrived and are preparing the Northern Dragon Clan and some Ruha Coven troops." He pauses. "The soreia sisters are there, as well, to help you into your armor."

Mara nods, remembering Ryutaro mentioning them the first time she had put on the armor to go to Thalak with him. These particular soreia sisters' duty is to apply the dragon armor to the wearer; according to Ryutaro, they had chosen their own profession and take pride in tending to the armor.

As they walk into the main chamber, Mara glances

around. "Where's Mornak?"

"Sleeping," Darion says, pausing in the middle of the room. "He will be watching the Chamber while we are in Alamirana. Hold onto my arm, Mara; the transition might be rough on the constructed body."

She links her arm with his, ignoring the odd tingles. It feels as though he is touching her Source directly even though she is in a physical form again; she hopes this doesn't mean anything too terrible.

As he had warned, the portal tries to resist her as she passes through. After a brief moment, it gives in, and they step onto the other side of the portal.

As soon as their feet touch the stone platform, Erimentha immediately snarls at them, "Cutting it a little close, don't ye think?"

"I apologize for the delay," Darion says sincerely, Mara's arm looped through his. "We had some complications with the material form Elethanos had constructed for Mara."

"Uh-huh." Erimentha eyes them, her gaze lingering a little longer on their linked arms. "Complications. Of course."

Darion gives her a disapproving look as he leads Mara past her. "Still holding up?" he asks in a low voice.

"I-I think so," Mara says, wincing as her foot strikes the ground. She feels as though she is wearing a skin-tight outfit that is too small.

He glances at her, noticing her pained expression. He stops; Erimentha nearly runs into his back. "It is not working," he breathes, looking distraught.

"I'm all right, Darion," Mara reassures him, forcing a smile. "It's just a little... snug. I see what Elethanos meant now."

"Hopefully, it will last long enough," he says grimly as they continue to the strategy room. They walk in on a heated discussion with a letter resting on the unlit fae'reth.

Everyone goes silent at the sight of Mara and Darion. Standing off to the side, Ryutaro shifts uncomfortably, looking unnerved at Mara's appearance. Kimala is the only one to hurry to her side. "Mara, how are you feeling? Did Darion manage to help you?"

Mara nods. "Yeah. What's going on here?"

"We received a letter from an anonymous individual," Riley says curtly, gesturing to the paper in the middle of the holographic table. "We think it's the Da'ruha, but we're not sure. It's sayin' that if we hand ye over, Alamirana and Danarkana will be spared."

"We also have news of the troops," Alec announces, leaning on the edge of the fae'reth. "Somehow, they got their hands on some of the Quasalan armor – the newest version, too. They look like our troops now."

Mara rubs her jaw. "They have to be connected," she murmurs. "There's no way this is all a coincidence."

"Our spies have not been able to pinpoint the leader of the group," Shaniel admits, scratching the back of his head. "Not only that, but they have picked up their pace. By new estimations, they will be here by late afternoon."

"Has anyone been to Male'stra since the troops have been on the move?" Darion asks.

Aeserast nods. "A few scouts, but none of them reported anything amiss. However, Male'stra is huge; they would not be able to cover all of the islands in a couple of days."

"Check the ruins in the middle and along the southern mountain range," Darion suggests. "Those are natural Source-shielding areas. If there is any place the Da'ruha would hide, it would be in one of those in order to disguise her Source signature."

Mara focuses on Alec. "How fast can we alter the troops' uniforms?"

"Within a tock or two," he says confidently. "Teresa and the extra troops have not returned yet. I know we have the Danarkana troops as well as the Ruha Coven and Gwynhavo Dragon Clan now, so they may take longer."

"We should be all right if we move quickly," Mara reassures him. "Stain all of the soldiers' uniforms; however, don't make it obvious. The enemy's are new, correct?"

Shaniel nods. "They look like they came straight from the crafters. They could even be illusions for all we know."

"As long as we can distinguish our own from them, we should be all right."

"I'll help with the troops," Riley says, following Alec out of the room. "We should take some scrub and…"

Shaniel smacks his fist into his hand, glancing at Aeserast. "How do you want to cover Male'stra? Should it be sorcerers or spies?"

"Both," Aeserast says, tapping his chin with a finger. "The spies will be able to hide the sorcerers, and the sorcerers can find the hidden locations."

Ryutaro, who had remained silent during the meeting, steps forward. "The soreia sisters were brought here along with the armor," he informs Darion and Mara. "I recommend we apply it soon in preparation. Blacksmith William Wester brought Gamerog, as well."

Darion nods. "Where are they?"

"Follow me." They follow the dragon duir'ne down the corridor as he leads them to the residential area of the fortress-like castle. They take several turns before finally arriving in an oversized section of the castle that Mara intuitively knows is for larger guests such as the dragonkin.

Opening a door, he greets three young women of varying skin, hair, and scale designs and colors. The only similarity between them is the simplistic design of the clothing they wear. "These are the soreia sisters," Ryutaro introduces them. "This is the armor's new wearer, Mara Danarko. She needs to be fitted immediately."

The dragonlings hesitate, unnerved as they stare at Mara. The one with bright red hair whispers, "She is not in an original body." Her fiery-scaled tail flits about her nervously.

"That does not matter," Ryutaro says curtly. "The enemy is on our doorstep, and Mara needs to be protected."

They bow and scamper around the corner, returning with the familiar silver rainbow dragon scale armor Mara had received just a little over a month ago from Ryutaro and Twyla. The silver armor glints as they fit the tunic over her head before strapping the pieces to her. Within seconds, she is completely decked out from head to toe in the dragon armor.

"Pardon me," the red-haired soreia mumbles as she pushes aside Mara's hair to access the back button for the armor to connect to Mara's Source. However, she gasps and yanks her hand away from Mara's skin. "I-I cannot. It is unnatural, Your Grace."

Ryutaro frowns. "What is?"

"Her Source."

Mara has the odd sensation that something like this has happened before. Frowning slightly, she tries to pinpoint why she has a strange, foreboding feeling about activating the armor. She reaches behind her neck, feeling for the button. "I'll do it. Step away from me."

Alarm sparks in Ryutaro's eyes as the soreia sisters hesitantly shuffle back. "Mara, if the soreia sisters say something is wrong, then – "

"It will be fine. I know what's wrong; I just need you to move away from me." As the dragonkin back up, she glances at Darion. "You, too." Frowning in concern, he follows after Ryutaro and the soreia sisters.

She clicks the button.

Just like last time, a hungry, cold presence enters her mind, searching for her Source. Expelling her breath, she slowly feeds her power into the armor, giving it more and more as the entire suit creaks. The weight increases before adjusting, the process repeating over and over again as she adds more Source to the armor. Black tendrils ooze out of the cracks, questing over the darkening scales until she is wearing a black-scaled suit of dragon armor that could have been cut out of the night sky itself.

When she had first applied the armor, the Essence had fed itself into the hungry maul of the Source-fueled armor, pulsing brightly like a star's heartbeat. Now, it radiates a blackness so complete it emits a dark aura around her, shadowing her features. Dark vines wrap around her arms, extending from the armor in a protective cocoon. She takes a deep breath, now certain she has worn armor like this before – armor she had activated with her *own* Source, not the Essence's.

Ryutaro and the three dragonlings stumble away from her. "Mara, your Source – " Ryutaro chokes, horrified.

"This is *my* Source," she explains, holding up her hand. "When the armor had been applied before, the Essence had fueled it."

Darion keeps his distance, staring at the armor. "What is wrong with it?"

Mara glances down, watching the black vines questing over the darkened armor. "It's looking for the origin of the armor's power, I believe. I don't recommend anyone coming near me while I am like this, though, especially if they are using Source."

Curiosity sparks in Darion's eyes. "Is this what you meant by you cannot fully control it?"

Mara nods. "Pretty much. Once it's questing, it won't stop until it finds something to devour." She smirks grimly. "The enemy won't know what is about to hit them, though."

Ryutaro shivers, his jaw tensing. "Refough Graeun," he whispers in Dragonir, the guttural language of his kind. His eyes rake the ground. "The only one who was not supposed to have the armor…"

Mara looks at him, curious. The words sound vaguely

familiar. "What are you talking about, Your Grace?"

Ryutaro stares into her eyes, noticing they are a dark smoky blue. "Two thousand years ago, there was an Alkinian who was goindun among the dragonkin. She was gifted dragon armor much like the one you wear now, but as soon as it was activated, the soreia attending to her were killed by her Source, which devoured others' Sources – thus named Refough Graeun. Since then, we had sworn never to give dragon armor to anyone of the same Source. I-I never even knew yours was of the type."

"Again, with that title…" Mara mutters, realizing the phrase means 'Energy Devourer' in Dragonir. "Listen, Ryutaro. I'm fighting on your side here, but if you would feel better about it, you can have the armor back. Just let me fight with it tonight. Please."

Ryutaro stares at the dark elf standing regally in the blackened armor and twining Source. For the first time, he notices the pointed ears. Expelling his breath, he nods. "I will return the armor to the vault after the war, but… please be careful around others, Mara. The last time someone with your Source wore that armor, she killed both friend and foe simply by walking near them."

She nods. "I will." She glances around. "You said William also brought Gamerog. Where is he?"

"Assisting the troops," he says, regaining his composure as he points to a bundled item resting in a chair near her. "He left Gamerog in our care."

She picks up the swathed sword, uncovering it to reveal the glimmering metal. Unsheathing it, her eyes widen at the pretty blue blade. It shimmers brightly, and the sword chirrups happily at her touch. The stone on the hilt has an exquisite, clear crystalline sheen. "What happened to it?"

"Eliara," Darion breathes, awed. "She must have purified it while we were gone."

"I'll have to thank her," she murmurs, strapping it around her waist and smiling at the dragon duir'ne. "I'll

276

see you later, Ryutaro."

She turns on her heel, stepping out of the room. Darion follows close behind, concern warring with wariness. "Mara – "

"I think he's right," she whispers, glancing at her gloved hand. "What he said earlier sounds familiar."

"Timian himself had taken care of that incident," Darion informs her, frowning. "Perhaps he will know how to keep that from happening again."

"Maybe." She stares down the hallway. "Darion, I need you to promise me something."

"What is it?"

"Don't die." It barely comes out as a breath. Her vision blurs ever so slightly.

"It is my duty to protect you, Mara," he murmurs, his voice soft. "However, I will do my best to uphold your request; I cannot help you from the other side of the Gate, after all."

"Srui," she breathes, swiping the tear away as her vision sharpens.

"Mara." He gently takes her hand. She glances at him, a spike of fear slashing through her; however, her Source isn't reacting to the physical touch. He squeezes her fingers, his smile gentle. "Do not worry about me in this battle. I will be all right."

I can't lose him, pops into her head as her lips meet his. It is over as fast as it had begun. She walks down the hallway, leaving the stunned Darion standing there to rush after her.

"Mara, that just now – "

"I can't lose you, Darion."

He stares at her, speechless.

She doesn't look at him right then. How can she? She cannot stand the thought of him dying to protect her. "I want you to stand by my side after this war, too, Darion. You're not allowed to die. This is an order."

His lips quirk up in amusement. "Yes, Your Highness."

"Quit calling me that," she mutters half-heartedly.

His fingers brush against hers, temporarily linking together as they walk down the corridor.

Chapter 17
Chaos

They find Timian in a small, secluded reading room working on a multi-screened holographic terminal. A rectangular box rests on the desk next to him. As soon as the door opens, he switches off the screens and glances at them. His shoulders sag as he exhales in recognition. "Ah, it is just you."

"Is everything all right?" Darion asks, concerned.

He nods, his eyes on Mara as he lowers the terminal screens to the desk. "Yes, I just did not recognize Mara for a moment. It seems as though I have gotten used to the Essence's Source signature within her own."

Mara frowns at this. "I think something like that happened in Danti Cauerr'ien, too; Chief Wizard Vierna didn't recognize me." She watches her Source twine around her gloved fingers. "Is it really that different?"

"Imagine a starry sky," Timian suggests, lacing his fingers together on the desk. "The brilliance of the stars brings a beauty to the darkness that nothing else could. Now, imagine there are no stars, and you can hear thunder in the distance foretelling an awful storm. It is quite foreboding, Mara."

She shifts her weight, and the armor clinks softly. "It's not *evil*," she murmurs, glancing down at the armor. "Sure, it's dark, but that doesn't mean anything."

"No, you are right." Timian sighs, glancing at the platform he had been working on. "It is all on how an individual utilizes the power, thus dubbing the user good or evil. However…" His eyes narrow on her. "I have seen a similar Source twine about armor like that before."

"That's what we came to talk to you about," Mara admits, not moving closer as Darion sits in the chair across from Timian. "Ryutaro mentioned someone called the Re-refog – "

"Refough Graeun," Darion says helpfully as he leans back in his seat. "It sounds much like the individual Erimentha and Eliara had called her: Kuri'Voyana."

Timian rubs his chin thoughtfully. "Erimentha had told me she has the memories of the Erusian spy K'sanri from five hundred years ago buried in her subconscious." His eyes flick to Mara. "It seems as though we are beginning to see a connection between all of the Vuti Voyana."

Black Energy.

Mara takes a deep breath at this Xharos phrase. "Do you think it was me?"

Timian shakes his head. "Of course not." He holds up his hands, pointing to the ceiling with his index fingers. "When a soul is reborn, it is as if the memories of that soul are repressed; this way, the soul can theoretically live a new, fresh life as a different individual. This is how the soul itself can learn from past mistakes."

Mara mulls over this. "So you're saying even if I had committed crimes in a past life, that doesn't... define me?"

"Most likely, no." Timian flattens his hands on the table. "By what I know of the souls connected to the Vuti Source, all of them had a deep sense of obligation to protect those about them; however, that is where the similarities end. Different species, different worlds, different *moral* codes; they all varied." He eyes her curiously. "But now..."

"What?" Mara isn't sure she likes the way the Time'Lord is staring at her.

"The Essence most likely knew of your particular soul. Now that I am certain your soul is in the Vuti Voyana class based off Darion's and Aeserast's reports, it bears the question as to *why* the Essence would choose such a volatile Source type to be its host."

"I don't know," she whispers, her gaze dropping to the ground. "This-this is the first time I've even heard of my Source being called Vuti Voyana. What does that even mean?"

"It is a term I have given it," the Time'Lord explains, his voice gentle. "It goes off the basis that your Source acts much like Voyana in that it converts chemicals within the air, shifting the anatomical state around until it mimics itself. However, what makes yours different from Voyana is that it converts other *Sources*, not chemicals. The color is used merely as reference."

"That… makes sense," she admits slowly, daring to look at Timian again. "So what happened with the-the Energy Devourer found in the dragon clan?"

Timian gestures to the seat next to Darion. "Please sit down, Mara. There is no need for you to stand." When she glances worriedly at the terminal still active next to him, he powers it the rest of the way off. "Is that better?"

She nods, easing into the chair. She monitors her Source warily, making sure it doesn't decide to do anything on its own.

Timian eyes her armor curiously. "I will admit, the last time I saw a Vuti Source in dragonkin armor, it went rampant and ended the life of the wearer," he tells her matter-of-factly. "Once we got there, she had already been run through several times by those who had withstood her Source long enough to kill her. She was still alive, though, despite her injuries."

"What did you do?" Mara asks.

Timian links his fingers together on the table. "We had no choice; the only way to stop her was to kill her. If I remember correctly, Darion had accompanied me and ran her through with Karakeit." At Mara's shocked expression, he gives her a reassuring smile. "It was how she wanted to go. She was going to die some way or another; better it was quick than the slow death that would have been in store for her had we spared her."

Darion rubs his forehead, trying to dredge up the memories. "I vaguely remember this… A lance had gotten under the dragon armor, correct? I had been shocked that anything could have gotten through that armor."

Timian nods, booting up one of the terminal screens and scrolling through the files. He opens one and skims the contents. "Her name had been Raegan. The lance had struck her heart, but her Source kept healing it. Darion had tried to heal her, but her Source kept taking his." He leans back in his seat. "Once she realized what her Source was doing, she requested to be killed instead of saved."

Darion sighs. "I cannot believe I forgot such an important moment." His eyes flick to Mara. "That must be why I recognized the armor once you activated it. It looked like Raegan's armor."

Mara shifts uncomfortably. "That wasn't *me*, though, right? Just-just someone else who had the same type of Source as me."

"You are mostly correct." Timian presses two fingers on the table. "Source is linked with a soul; the ingrained morals the soul learns over time is what colors the Source. You may have the same soul as Raegan, but you are not her. The personality and demeanor between a soul's different lifetimes can be drastically different; for example, Raegan was a brilliant, cool-headed diplomat. She did not have quite the stubborn, impulsive streak that our dear Mara has."

Mara's cheeks darken as she slumps in her chair. "Geez, thanks for the encouraging speech…"

Timian chuckles. "I am merely pointing out the differences to show you that who you were in past lives is of no consequence."

"You are forgetting an important detail about Raegan, though," Darion points out darkly, now glaring at the older Alkinian. "It is the one thing I remember clearly of that incident."

Mara glances between them, frowning. "What's that?"

Timian sighs, shooting Darion a disapproving look. "I had my reasons for leaving that out, Darion."

"She deserves to know," he snaps, looking directly at Mara. "After Raegan died, I returned to Elethanos to help guide her through the Mavi. When she entered Eleth, the Elethani guards were there, waiting. They threw her into Hariana where she remained imprisoned for over five hundred years."

Mara shakes her head, confused. "Wait, they did it on their own? I thought they worked for the Ecalauna."

"The Elethani work alongside us, not for us," Timian corrects, tapping his fingers in irritation. "Even now, they do not fully disclose why they do some of the things they do. Raegan's imprisonment was one of them; they would not even allow Darion to question her, and as soon as she was released from Hariana, she was sent through the Jethel Vortex almost immediately."

"Who *are* the Elethani?" Mara asks, confused. "I thought they were… well… dead guards in Hariana."

Darion shakes his head. "They seem to be a species native to that dimension. It is completely separate from our own realms and even Carni." His eyes flick to Timian.

Timian clasps his hands together again and gives Mara a small smile. "How much do you know of Eleth, Mara?"

"It's the realm of death," she states flatly. However, at Timian's unwavering expression, she second-guesses herself. "Isn't it?"

"Of a sort," he admits, curling his fingertips on the table. "The scientists on Alkina and only a few individuals other than Highlords on Blazhreia know the exact specifics, but it is not because it is classified; quite the opposite, really. Many are easily confused by the differences between *dimensions* and *realms*."

Mara frowns. "So… what's the deal?"

"Imagine that the realms we know of being inside a seemingly endless yet flat bubble called Jethel," Darion explains. "Now think the same of Eleth – it is yet another bubble. There is nothing but void between these two bubbles, except for a few gateways called Elethavi and Jethelavi respectively, with a chamber named Elethanos connecting these gateways together."

Mara struggles to wrap her mind around this. "So… you're saying that our universe is inside of a realm, and all of the realms are inside of an even bigger space?" Darion nods, and she huffs. "Let me guess; Eleth is a perfect mirror image of Jethel, then."

"Indeed," Timian says, grinning at her as if she had won some prize. "Anything that happens in Jethel is subsequently mirrored in Eleth – the reason why Hariana is in both our Carni and inside of Inrac, which is Eleth's version of the same Corridor Realm."

"Creative," Mara mutters, giving Timian a deadpan look. "So how does this relate to the Eleth guards?"

"They are the only native inhabitants that we know of in Eleth," Timian informs her, his expression suddenly turning serious. "They were the original guards of Ele-thanos and Elethavi before Darion was appointed the Ecalauna over that jurisdiction in order to monitor the Da'ruha. They share little to no information about them-selves with anyone; not even the name of their species. We have called them Elethani simply because we have no other name for them."

"I have spoken to the same collection of guards over the past thousand years," Darion murmurs, shaking his head. "I still do not know their names, even though we are on amicable terms now. There are even times they come through the gate whenever they are on 'break' from their duties to join me in a strategy game, and according to Shokain, they go out of their way to make sure he is doing well in Eleth." He hesitates before adding, "They even protected Eliara and helped her feel at home inside of Eleth's version of Alamirana. They are not mindless creatures; they have their own will. We just do not know what drives them."

"Wow," Mara breathes. "So when Raegan was imprisoned, that was all the Elethani's doing?"

Darion nods. "I have seen them do this countless times, though; in Eleth, they use the vast Hariana as a sort of… prison system for those who commit heinous crimes. We believe they have even expanded upon the structure, because the Hariana in Carni has grown bigger over the past thousands of years – and it was most certainly not our doing."

Mara's eyes widen. "That's possible?"

"Whatever structure is inside one dimension is mirrored inside another," Timian informs her. "Hariana is called the 'split city' by many because it seems almost as if the sides of the two versions of the prison system are touching. Many who have walked the corridors of the Jethel side of Hariana claim they have heard echoes down the halls that sound like the souls imprisoned on the Eleth side."

Mara shivers at this, unnerved at the thought.

Darion glances at her, noticing the small movement. "It seems as though each time a soul with black Source ends up in Eleth, they visit the Hariana – whether from within a cell or not. Raegan's 'visitation' was the longest, though."

"There, you are wrong, Darion," Timian whispers, his tone somber. "The longest term was served by Zandria, who had taken it upon herself to work for the guards in order to pay for the crimes of her own species." He shakes his head sadly. "The woman was as stubborn as you are now, Mara; I knew her when I was but a child, but despite the millennia that has passed by, her harsh gaze still bites into me." He pauses, his eyes widening as he stares at Mara.

"Wh-what?" she stammers, glancing between the two Highlords.

"Your eyes are the same color as when you had absorbed the Tower of Discord's power," Darion says softly.

Mara frowns. "What color is that?"

"Dark smoky blue." He glances at Timian.

The old Alkinian clears his throat, looking away. "I am sure you will be fine, Mara," he says distractedly as he opens the box on the desk and fiddles with the objects inside. "Just be careful with using your Source around your allies. If you find yourself losing control, move away from them; it should settle down."

Mara nods, still confused at the odd look he had given her when her eyes had changed color. "I'll do my best."

"It is all we can ask for." He stands up, tucking the box underneath his arm. "Please excuse me for a bit; I must lock some items in the Sealed Archives before this battle begins."

Darion and Mara rise from their seats, following him out of the room. "We should head to the entrance and see how the troops are doing," Darion suggests, and Mara nods. "Thana baro, Timian."

"I wish you both the best during this battle," he responds, giving both of them a concerned glance. "Please come back alive."

They part ways, walking opposite directions. Mara glances at Darion, noticing his brooding expression. "Is Timian not joining us?"

He shakes his head. "Nearly all of the Highlords will be fighting during this battle; however, Timian is the only person out of all of us who can train a new Highlord in any position. It would be foolish to risk losing *him* on the battlefield."

Mara turns her gaze forward, swallowing a lump in her throat. She doesn't want to think about Timian having to

286

train *anyone* to replace a fallen comrade.

They make their way to the walled entrance of Alami-rana where the allied troops are preparing for battle. The sunset casts an almost eerie reddish-orange light on the gathered people as it sinks lower and lower on the horizon. The twin moons Narien and Naros are low in the southeastern sky, revealing a rare instance of both of the moons being full.

Everyone seems nervous and on edge, their eyes flitting about and small arguments breaking out all over the place as the tension gets the best of them. It is a mixture of different species and even races, ranging from neka and ruha coven elves, dragonkin from various clans, both seelie and unseelie fey, and Blazhreians of varying skin colors and body types.

Mara sticks by Darion's side, watching Alec talk to the commander of the troops. She leans toward Darion, whispering, "Does a pre-war speech normally take this long?"

He gives her a sidelong glance. "No, it does not. However, this would be the first time Alec has commanded a large group before."

"Ah." She imagines she is the one delivering a speech in front of everyone and cringes. She would be nervous and stalling for time, as well.

Alec clears his throat, gaining the attention of everyone waiting. A sorcerer in the grey robes of the Academy steps up next to him and places his hand on the duir'ne's shoulder. It glows a peridot green, and when Alec speaks, his voice is amplified. "While the majority of us have been going about our daily lives, a silent battle for the control of the continent has been going on. I have only ever been on the outskirts of such conversations; now, I am leading those of you who may face a formidable foe that the Highlords themselves have been unable to detain for centuries."

"What is he doing?" Mara asks Darion.

"We granted him permission to explain the situation," the tall elf murmurs. "The more people who have eyes looking for Rath, the better – especially if that army is being controlled by him."

Alec continues over the uneasy murmurs of the crowd. "As many of you know, there is a large group of armed individuals heading toward us. We are still uncertain if they are ally or foe; however, based off of recent circumstances, we are not taking any chances. These people could possibly be accomplices of the man we are looking for, whose name is Rath Shasta. He is an extremely dangerous mind-weaver who can turn you against your allies. He hides on the outskirts, never taking action himself; he has white hair and pale features. If you ever see a man that fits this description, do not engage him. Tell the nearest Highlord or high-ranking official, and we will deal with him accordingly."

A disturbed murmur races through the crowd. Alec holds up his hand one more time, silencing them. "But do not fear! We have not only the Highlords fighting on our side, but we also have the Ecalain with us. We will be victorious!"

The soldiers cheer, but it is a dark and desolate sound.

Before she even registers what she is doing, Mara pushes by the soldiers, working her way to the front. They scramble out of the way, startled by her dark, ominous armor.

Darion follows after her, hissing, "Mara, what are you doing?"

"Giving these people something more to fight for." *And putting a target on myself,* she finishes mentally.

She climbs the platform's steps and stops next to Alec. He stares at her, his eyes wide. "Mara, what happened to your armor?"

"It's my Source," she passes off, turning to the crowd of spectators. For a split second, her entire body and mind locks down when she sees everyone's eyes are on her; she has never been good at public speaking. Taking a quick breath, she opens her mouth and is surprised as the words tumble out. "My name is Mara Danarko, and I am the heir to the Alamiran Ecalain title. I stand here with you today because I believe we can fight off this incoming enemy no matter how large their numbers. They are puppets, and puppets never fight as well as those who were trained since they were old enough to hold a weapon." She raises her fist, a wild smile on her face as her eyes flash that odd smokey blue once again. "And I have been trained since I was born. Let us fight side by side to keep our homes safe!"

The crowd cheers, the sound ringing in her ears. Mara pats Alec's shoulder. "You need to remain positive," she whispers. "You're a duir'ne. Fear in the leaders will instill doubt in the troops."

He stares at her as if she is a stranger. "I never thought you would be one for speeches, Mara."

She snorts. "I'm not. For a moment there, I was afraid nothing was going to come out of my mouth."

Darion gives her a reassuring smile. His smile falls as he looks over her shoulder at something in the distance. "They are here."

She turns around, squinting at the darkening horizon. Sure enough, a large crowd is quickly advancing, the setting sun's rays illuminating their armor. Her breath sucks in sharply and her nerves are rattled at the sheer *amount* of people there must be in the crowd for it to be that large.

"I take back my words," she mumbles to Darion, too low for any of the troops to hear her. Alec glances at her sharply. "That's too many people. I really hope we're wrong and they're refugees."

"Dragons, to the air!" a commanding feminine voice rings across the field. Mara glances over to see Twyla leaping onto Ryutaro's back; the graceful elf is in a suit of dark blue armor much like her own. They lock eyes as

Ryutaro launches into the air, and Mara feels the elfin duir'ne's gaze slice through her.

Michelle steps forward, calling to the rest of the troops, "This is the time we have been waiting for; let us prove our worth to the Ecalain who have taken it upon themselves to join us in this battle!"

This time, Mara freezes as the soldiers emit a loud cry and shift into position. Shields and barriers are erected in the front, forming the first line of defense. From there, everyone falls into their respective places, fitting together almost like a puzzle – a puzzle that Mara does not know.

"Stay with me," Darion murmurs, following Alec into the center of the army. She scrambles after him, carefully restraining her Source from questing out to the soldiers she passes. It seems content to wait, almost as if it knows what is about to happen.

After only a few minutes, she hears the diplomatic team in the front calling out to the advancing strangers to state their intentions; however, based on the lack of a response and unfaltering pace, word is quickly spread to ready all weapons.

As they draw closer, the first line of troops see the happy and relieved smiles on the people's faces. Again, the diplomatic team calls out to them, but there is no response; rapidly whispered comments spread throughout the troops that some of the people are even crying as if in relief at seeing them. None of the advancing individuals appear to have any weapons drawn.

Hearing this, Mara glances at Darion in uncertainty. He meets her gaze, his eyes hard with determination.

"Hold your ground!" Alec calls over the crowd in a firm voice, his eyes steely. "It could be a ruse to drop our guard!"

"Darion…" Mara starts.

"I know, Mara." She feels his armored glove briefly touch hers. Raising his voice, he calls out, "Prepare yourself; the enemy will not fight fair!"

Darion's voice echoes oddly over the troops as though he had amplified it. Mara hears the decisive clank of armor as the troops shift into defensive postures, preparing for the first attack.

On the front lines, one of the soldiers shakes his head, breaking formation by lowering his shield. "This is wrong," he whispers to his partner as the sun dips below the horizon, casting the surrounding land into a cool, dusky blue. "They are not even *armed* properly."

A spear slips past his half-raised shield, piercing his chest. He stares at the smiling man who laughs as if he is reuniting with an old friend.

Chaos erupts.

Disconcerted by the elated enemy, the allied troops stave off the attack the best they can while recovering from the grinning faces of the attacking forces. Within mere minutes, the entire army's formation is ruined as skirmishes break out deep within the allied forces.

"They are trying to split us down the middle," Darion snarls, leaping forward and cutting down the first smiling enemy that makes it to them.

Mara throws her arm up, slicing through the wooden handle of the axe and narrowly dodging the falling blade. The man, still grinning maniacally, swings the broken handle at her, crazed with… something.

Darion's giant garonita, Karakeit, emerges from the man's back. He falls, dead.

Mara expels her breath, swallowing her bile. *This is wrong*, she thinks. *They're puppets; you can tell by looking at them. We shouldn't be killing them. We should be* saving *them*.

Darion yanks on Mara's arm with his gloved hand, pulling her behind him as he smashes his sword against an enemy's laser gun. The man accidentally shoots himself in the foot, but he doesn't utter a breath of a scream.

Mara takes this moment to glance around at the moon-lit battlefield. Their allies are rattled by the arrival of the grinning enemy; while they had been warned that they could be puppeteered, no one had expected *this*.

Alec grits his teeth, sweat dripping down his neck. Despite the guards surrounding him, he still has to fight – the enemy's smiles belie their relentlessness and ferocity.

Darion once again spins Mara around, guarding against another attack from behind; it is as if the elf has eyes in the back of his head. She blocks an attack that would have injured his non-dominant hand, though, and he glances over his shoulder at her. "Thank you."

"I'll cover this side," she responds, standing back-to-back with him as three enemies approach.

Suddenly, Aeserast is beside her. He throws out his hand, shouting, "Quelara!"

A man charging at them suddenly stops, blinking in confusion. He stares at them, dumbfounded, until one of his 'comrades' runs him through with a grin.

Mara cringes, appalled. "Tearing away the mind-warping film doesn't help?" she asks, recognizing the Quanaret word for *awaken*.

"No," Aeserast snarls, snapping yet another enemy out of his mind-controlled daze only to watch that person get run through, as well. "They seem to know the difference between their own and those not being controlled by the film."

"I am about to hunt for this puppeteer," Darion hisses, taking out two men at once with a fatal sweep of his blade. "This is getting ridiculous."

"I agree." Aeserast glances around. "I'll scour for the source of this; the puppeteer *has* to be nearby to keep up this farce."

Darion nods. "Good idea."

Aeserast disappears.

Disconcerted that her friend and guardian had suddenly vanished in front of her, she is forced to fend off yet another attacker. After she takes him out, she glances up to check on the dragon troops circling above.

She watches Ryutaro dive through the moonlit sky, two smaller dragons flanking him in perfect synchrony as they extend their claws. Their Source overflows, melding with whatever element they are trained in and raining down on the enemy below.

Aeserast floats high in the sky, his Source piled around him like two ethereal, purple wings. Concentrating deeply, he spreads his Source out like a net, encompassing the entire battlefield.

"Carc'ra," Mara curses under her breath, dodging Aeserast's Source in hopes her own Source won't latch onto it. "What is he doing?"

"Trying to find the puppeteer," Darion explains, grabbing Mara's wrist and tugging her through a gap in the skirmish near them. "Do not worry; he should not be in any danger unless someone tries to attack him directly."

"I'm more worried about his Source getting caught in *mine*," she snaps back.

He looks up and notices a hole in Aeserast's net right above them. He grins. "It seems as though he has already taken that into consideration," he informs her as he defends against a smiling woman.

Seeing an enemy trying to use Source, Mara latches a black tendril on him. He emits a muffled grunt as he collapses, dazed and disoriented from having all of his Source drained at once.

Darion spares a glance at Mara, startled at the way she is utilizing her unique ability. "You took – "

"We need to keep going," she barks, pushing him forward. Suddenly, her leg gives out from under her, and she falls to her knees.

He fends off a downward-arching sword, protecting her. "Are you all right, Mara?"

"Y-yeah," she says, catching a glimpse of color in the corner of her eye. She turns her head, her eyes widening in horror as she sees the familiar robe design of Cerlail Academy's tactical wing just as the person falls to the ground, dead. Shaniel, who had been battling alongside the mage, yells in anger and attacks the killer with rapid strikes, but the grinning enemy throws up a sparking orange barrier and forms a deadly sphere in his hand.

Mara sends out another black tendril, hoping to make it before he releases the deadly spell on Shaniel.

The sphere barely digs into Shaniel's shoulder at the same time Mara's Source swallows it. Shaniel staggers back in pain, gasping for breath as he watches the black tendrils cocoon the man; he collapses to his knees, his eyes wide and unseeing. After a few seconds, he slumps over.

Alarmed, Shaniel glances around. His hand covers the shallow wound in his shoulder as their gazes meet. Eyes hardening in determination, he nods to her before diving back into battle.

Chapter 18
Rage

After Shaniel disappears into the melee, Mara grits her teeth as her entire body aches. She knows what is happening; the body Elethanos had made for her is failing. The more power she absorbs, the more she strains the capacity of the temporary physical form.

She releases her breath, allowing her head to fall forward. "Darion, move away from me."

He glances back at her in alarm. "Mara, I will do no such – "

"This body is failing!" she snaps, glaring at him. "I can take out several enemies at once, but I won't risk you being caught in the blast."

He stops a sword from striking her back. "How far?"

"A few yards." Mara closes one eye, barely restraining her power from breaking free. *Just a little longer…* "I'll only catch the ones immediately around me."

He finishes off the enemy, glancing at her one last time before leaving the vicinity. Mara takes a deep breath, crouching on the balls of her feet and looking into the sky. She smirks at the advancing enemies.

"I hope you're watching, Rath," she whispers.

She sends out her Source, and the stormy cloud encompasses seven men and women closing in on her. Darion steps farther away, narrowly escaping the Source-draining cloud. When it recedes, Mara is on her feet and rolling her shoulders as she glances at the moaning individuals slumped on the ground, depleted of their Source. She steps over them and walks over to Darion.

He stares at her with wide eyes. "The body – "

"Gone." She touches the armor. "I'm managing to keep this on, though. I guess it's because it is fueled by my

Source."

He nods. "Most likely." He defends against a lance, sliding his blade along the wooden shaft as he reaches under his cloak and whips out a black laser gun. Two shots zip out, and the man falls.

Mara tilts her head to the side, sensing a large amount of Source heading their way. Narrowing her eyes, she grabs Darion's arm and yanks him behind her as she crouches into a defensive position.

Someone crashes next to them, groaning. Darion rushes to the laig'hius's side. "Kyle, what happened?" He asks the fallen Shape'Lord.

"She... killed them." Kyle coughs, blood seeping into his beard. His breath is labored and wet. "Rachel and... Esme. They are dead."

Rage boils in Mara at these words. Before she can ask Darion how the burly Highlord is, a downward surge of Source has her raising Gamerog to block a lethal, blood-red blade.

Her own face sneers back at her, the once-gold eyes flashing red. The usual illusion spell is gone, putting the Hemius on prominent display. The ugly, bruise-like marks cover the entire right side of her face as thin, bruised veins trace over her nose and forehead. Her hand is completely covered in dark purplish-red colors.

"Well, hello," the Da'ruha greets in a sickeningly sweet voice. "You should have stayed in Carni; I hear there is a lovely forest with an amazing view over a lake."

"Been there, done that," Mara spits out, gritting her teeth against the strength of the Da'ruha pressing down on the scythe. "In fact, I relocated it to an even better view."

Her face scrunches in confusion, the right eye swirling with Hemius colors. "Have you gone mad?"

"Maybe." Mara shoves the Da'ruha back, her voice smooth. "I'm surprised Desdemona isn't here; I thought she would want a chance at my head."

"She had to babysit," the Da'ruha says, twisting Mara's face into a sneer. "We couldn't leave our newest sibling unattended."

"Aww, a pity. I was looking forward to fighting *her.*" Mara lunges in with the blade pointing to her body's stomach. Darion scrambles to his feet, preparing to leap forward and stop her.

"If you kill this body, you will die!"

The Da'ruha's screech has the mage faltering, and the Da'ruha dodges the lethal blow.

Seeing an opening, she kicks out, grinning as her knee strikes the armor and knocks Mara back. "Silly welp. Just give up; you are never getting your body back. You are better off in Carni."

"No, thanks," Mara rasps, straightening and shrugging the armor back into place. She swings her sword at her own body.

The Da'ruha blocks it, laughing darkly as she performs several punches and kicks that drive Mara back. She kicks out one last time, knocking the mage onto her back. She presses her foot against Mara's neck, leaning over to whisper, "Give up."

"Mara!" Darion yells, charging at the Da'ruha.

The Da'ruha bares her teeth, twisting Mara's face into an unrecognizable expression. "Interfering, meddlesome elf; you have gotten in my way long enough!"

She swings her scythe around. It slices through the air, nothing but a blur.

Darion cries out, staggering back as he clutches his upper arm. Blood seeps through his armor.

The Da'ruha giggles. "Look who's not so tough anymore," she singsongs, smiling down at Mara. "This is the end. I tried letting you live, but you're just too stubborn for your own good."

The scythe falls toward her neck.

Mara catches it, barely keeping it from slicing her apart. *Why do I even care?* she realizes, staring up at the Da'ruha possessing her body. *It's not like it will kill me. In fact...*

"Heh. Heheh."

The Da'ruha's smile falters at Mara's laugh. "What are you laughing at?" she demands, pressing on the scythe harder. It doesn't budge. "You shouldn't be laughing! I'm about to kill you!"

Mara stares into those blood-colored eyes. "No, you aren't."

Her Source hungrily creeps up the blade, turning the red weapon pitch black. The change is barely visible on the moonlit battlefield.

The Da'ruha narrows her eyes, feeling a subtle change in the Source-generated weapon in her hand. "What are you doing?"

"Stopping you," Mara whispers. She releases the blade, watching it crumble into black sand that falls onto her armor and sinks underneath the scales. She stands up, swaying; she feels giddy with the amount of power she has absorbed in the past few minutes.

The Da'ruha drops her Source-manifested weapon, staring at Mara in fear. "You... you cannot be Mara."

Mara feels her control slipping as her Source whips about her, questing for more. She cannot help the grin that spreads across her face as the black aura around her strengthens. Darion, seeing Mara's state, quickly glances around before evacuating nearby soldiers, leaving only the enemy.

"Oh, I am," Mara says confidently. "In fact, I've never been so sure before." Gamerog trembles in her hand as it absorbs her Source, and a loud creaking emanates from it as the arcing spikes that make up the guard lengthen. The tip of the sword gains a serrated edge along the back side. The newly-purified blue blade turns black within seconds.

The Da'ruha sinks into a crouch, snarling, "You cannot

beat me! You don't even have a body!"

"I don't need one." Mara tilts her head to the side, her eyes narrowing as her lips tilt into a curious, almost playful smile. "You know what it feels like to be free of the constraints of a body. To *never* have to worry about getting hurt."

"This will hurt you," the Da'ruha snarls, holding out her hand. A blood-stained salev'i appears, the red stone on the end pulsing weakly. "Gameleth can injure even spirits."

Mara narrows her eyes. "I took that sword from you."

"But not the scabbard!" she cries as she lunges forward.

Mara stops the downward thrust, but she is barely able to block the kick to her armor. Digging her gloved fingers into the soft flesh of the knee, she hears the Da'ruha grunt in pain.

"It's over," Mara whispers.

"Indeed."

Mara's eyes widen as she quickly releases the Da'ruha to dodge the blow from behind. Twisting around, she stares at Tyson Mills, the Air'Lord who had betrayed them. He is dressed in a black robe bordered with gold that looks exactly like the one Rath had been wearing when Mara had first met him.

The Da'ruha rolls her shoulder, standing behind the traitor. "Thank you for the save, Tyson."

"Allow me to assist you, Your Highness."

Her eyes flick to the side before narrowing. "Keep her busy, then."

Mara glances to where the Da'ruha had looked, seeing Darion kneeling next to a fallen Bojek and attempting to heal the fey's wounds. "Darion, watch out!" Mara cries, moving toward him.

Tyson appears in front of her, his face expressionless as a strong breeze whips by her. "I've read reports on you," he murmurs, his eyes narrowing. "Such strong potential…

yet *wasted.* You should have taken Rath's offer, Your Highness."

"How can you even *listen* to him?" she snarls, and then gasps. "He brainwashed you. Tyson, snap out of it! He's manipulating your mind!"

Tyson laughs as two thin scio'thi appear in his hands. The long blades shimmer, looking like glass. "It is pitiful how wrong you are."

Mara dares a glance off to the side in time to see the Da'ruha fighting against Nature'Lord Derak as Darion struggles to his feet. She winces as Tyson's invisible blades clang against her armor.

"If you are not careful, your head might be chopped off," he warns, narrowing his eyes at her. His arm muscles twitch, and the swords disappear.

Hearing the telltale whistling noise, Mara drops to the ground, dodging both of the twisting blades. "What are they?" she asks rhetorically, leaping away as they twist through the air and come after her again.

They clang on the ground where she had been.

"Source blades fused with elemental properties," he says simply, smiling. "Rath taught me this technique."

Mara's eyes narrow. "Did he?" Closing her eyes, she listens for the whistling noise. After a brief moment, she hears it. Moving faster than possible, she catches the Source-blades out of the air.

"But how?" Tyson cries, his eyes wide.

"They make too much noise," Mara informs him, standing up as the blades temporarily turn black before dissolving into sand that floats about her.

He grits his teeth, holding his hands out. Multiple blades form, more visible than the ones she had destroyed. "Let's see if you can block all of *these.*"

She grins. "Sure; let's play." He hesitates, unnerved by the hungry look in her eyes.

That is all the pause she needs.

Her Source swarms forward, encompassing the swords and instantly sapping the energy from them. Tyson tries to back away, but the black sand stops him. "No. No! Stop it!"

"I'm sorry," Mara whispers as she feels her Source taking everything from him. She enters the dark cloud, thrusting her sword forward.

The swirling sand drops to the ground to reveal Tyson slumping over. Blood drips off Mara's blade as she turns to her comrades.

Darion slashes at the Da'ruha with Karakeit, barely restraining his rage. Derak lies on the ground a few feet away, his green Highlord robe completely soaked in blood.

The Dark Warrior spares a glance over at her. Her eyes widen in horror at the dead Air'Lord. "You *welp*!" she screeches, lunging at her. "To Hariana with what Father wanted. I will throw you through the Elethavi myself!"

Mara waits patiently, watching the Da'ruha charging at her in a blind rage. Her mind is icily clear as a plan falls into place. "You're the one who will pay," she breathes as the enraged woman steps into the black sand.

The Da'ruha's face pales as she is suddenly paralyzed, cocooned by Mara's power. Her arms are flattened to her sides, and she struggles to breathe as Mara crushes her. "Go ahead; kill me," she rasps.

Mara stands in front of the Da'ruha, allowing a bit of her rage to show. "That's too nice for you," she snarls. She squeezes the cocoon even tighter, watching the red eyes widen at the crushing force of Mara's Source. She grits her teeth, trying to hold back a scream of pain.

"Mara, do not kill her! She is in your body!" Darion cries, limping toward her.

Mara narrows her eyes at the Da'ruha. "I don't care." She raises her hand, touching the side of her body's face. "I'll drag you to Hariana myself if I have to."

Pure terror flashes in the Da'ruha's eyes the moment

Mara sinks into her own body; the abandoned dragon armor clatters to the ground, no longer supported by her Source. Before the mage can stop her, the Dark Warrior flees, narrowly escaping Mara's energy-sapping prison.

Mara collapses to her knees, gasping for air as excruciating pain dominates her senses. She groans; she hadn't realized she had been squeezing her body *that* tightly.

Darion rushes to Mara's side. He catches her as she begins to slump forward. "Mara? Mara, can you hear me?"

"I'm… all right." She takes one gulp of air after another. Her good right arm wraps around her waist. "Just… give me a moment, Darion. I-I think I dislocated my shoulder and broke my ribs."

He exhales in a huff, giving her a reprimanding look. "Stay still; I will need to bind it so it does not move and injure you even more."

"At least I'm not dead," she points out, impulsively trying to wrap her left arm around herself. The resulting agony from trying to move it makes her head spin. Her vision temporarily blacks out. "Ugh…"

He keeps her upright, glancing around. Catching sight of someone through the crowd, he waves. "Shaniel! Over here!"

Within seconds, Shaniel is on the other side of Mara. She blinks at him, her breathing short and clipped.

"Hey, Danarko," he says softly, glancing over her. "You still with us?"

"Never better," she rasps, temporarily closing her eyes in pain. She can hear cloth ripping. "Do-do you know where Kimala and Lilly are?"

"Near Alamirana gate." He frowns as Darion brings over large strips of ripped cloth. "What's that for?"

"She broke her ribs," he informs the laig'hius. "Mara, I need you to raise your arms the best you can so I can bind your ribs."

"Gotcha." She bites her lip as Shaniel helps her. A

moan slips out, and her breathing comes in short gasps. "H-hurry, please."

He reaches underneath her robe, moving in close so he can wrap the cloth snugly around her back before bringing it around the front. She breathes shallowly as he tightens the bandages, wrapping them around a few more times before carefully tying them in the front. "Now for your arm."

A strangled yelp comes out of her as they bend her arm into position and form a makeshift sling for her. She feels Darion's hand against her face, and she gratefully leans into his cool touch. "You are already running a fever... Carc'ra."

"Darion, I'm not sure we'll be able to walk her across the field like this," Shaniel says grimly. "This may be a dead area, but there's heavy fighting closer to the city."

Darion huffs. "I know."

A gust of wind has them looking up as Ryutaro lands next to them, sweeping some grinning enemies away with his tail. Atop his back, Twyla fires one shot after another from her sonar gun, keeping the advancing enemy at bay. Seeing the fallen dragon armor back to its original state, his eyes narrow on Mara. "*I sensed your loss of control. Did anyone —*"

"None of our allies were injured," Darion quickly informs him, gesturing to the armor. "However, it would be most helpful if you can reclaim the armor now instead of later. We need to get Mara to the medics near the gate."

Ryutaro nods, shifting to the side to let one of his guards land and grasp the light grey armor in his claws. "*Twyla, ride with Garov and help the reinforcements.*"

Twyla pauses in her shooting long enough to leap from Ryutaro's back and land on the other dragon, already firing at the enemy again.

Ryutaro crouches low on the ground, allowing Darion to climb on. Shaniel helps Mara up, and she nearly passes out from the simple movement. "Carc'ra. Darion, I don't think she – "

"I see that." Mara feels Darion's Source encapsulate her, lifting her into his arms. She groans as he gently holds her to him.

"Thank you," she rasps, dazedly looking up into his worried eyes.

Ryutaro tilts his head back, examining Mara's face. *"Will she be able to withstand me lifting off?"*

Darion glances into the melee. "If you can do so gently, then perhaps," he says. "Try not to turn or land too abruptly."

Despite being as gentle as possible, Mara temporarily blacks out from the pain that comes from Ryutaro lifting off the ground. When she regains consciousness, she cries out in agony as her bones pop into place.

"Bloody Mavi, Mara," Lilly's voice exclaims above her. "I can't believe you did this to *yourself.*"

"The Da'ruha had been in her when she did it," Darion says; Mara can feel him squeezing her right hand.

"I don't bloody care *who* was in her body; this is just-just ridiculous." She cups Mara's face, looking into her pupils. "I need you to focus on me, Mara."

"Ungh…" she squints, the chief medic advisor's features swimming into focus.

"Carc'ra. She tore some ligaments in her arm when it dislocated. As if fractured ribs weren't enough."

Mara's head lolls to the side. She stares blearily at the elf beside her. "Darion…"

He squeezes her hand. "I am here, Mara."

"Are you… still hurt?"

A string of curse words flow out of Lilly's mouth; if Mara wasn't in so much pain, she would laugh. "She's *dying,* and she's worried about *you!*"

Darion ignores Lilly's ranting as he clasps Mara's hands in both of his own. "Someone already treated my wounds; you are in worse condition than me, Mara. You need to focus on Lilly."

"But…" She doesn't want to take her eyes off of him. She is afraid he might disappear if she does.

Lilly glances at Mara's face, irritated – and then notices the way Darion is clasping the elf's hand. She takes a deep breath. "Keep eye contact with her, Darion," she instructs, refocusing on setting the bones back into place and sealing closed her punctured organs. "Whatever you do, keep her awake. I still need to clear out that concussion."

Mara frowns, her eyes drifting off to the side. Darion's hand on her cheek has her looking at him again. "Concussion? I-I didn't…"

He shakes his head, looking guilty. "No, I… hit the Da'ruha over the head when she stabbed Derak."

Lilly pauses for a brief second before resuming work. She clenches her teeth, exhaling sharply. "I will be glad when this war is over."

"I apologize," Mara whispers, tears forming in her eyes. "I… I didn't want to…"

"You did what needed to be done," he comforts her, his thumb brushing across her cheek. "Without you, I am sure there would have been more casualties. Just remember that *she* was the one who killed them, not you."

"I killed Tyson, though."

"He made his decision," he murmurs, unfazed by her confession. "Just as you said before this war started, Mara – you cannot save those who do not wish to be saved."

She sighs, leaning against his hand. "You're right." She blinks, her mind suddenly feeling a little clearer. The deep ache in her head abates.

"Done," Lilly murmurs, sighing. "You have really out-done yourself this time, Mara. I wish I could ban you from ever fighting again."

Mara gives the Life'Lord a sheepish grin. "I wish it was as simple as that." They ease her upright, and she is relieved that she no longer has that breathless pain in her abdomen anymore. "Where's Kimala?"

Lilly glances around; medics rush about, treating the wounded soldiers as fast as they can. "She's…" She pauses, puzzled. "Huh. She's not here."

Alarm shoots through Mara like an icy arrow. "The Da'ruha," she breathes, appalled.

Hopping off the field cot, she sees Gamerog on a supply crate nearby. She snatches it as she walks through the arch into the still-raging battle.

Darion hurries after her. "Mara, you should not rush out like that! You only just regained your body; give yourself time to – "

She deflects the sword blow of a grinning soldier and kicks his stomach. Within seconds, he is slumped on the ground at her feet.

She takes a deep breath, wincing as her head aches; she recognizes the sensation of the Essence's power being sedated. "Blasted seal," she grumbles, touching her temple lightly.

"Do not break it," he warns. "It is keeping the Hemius mostly sedated."

"*Hang in a little longer, Essence,*" she mentally tells the fragmented Source underneath the seal. She can feel her Source chipping away at it; she needs to hurry and find Kimala before the Hemius has free reign once again.

They fight their way through the crowd, trying to catch sight of a medic's white robe in the ocean of bloodstained armor. Mara deflects another strike to her neck, narrowing her eyes as she scans the crowd.

She is out of time.

"Darion," she calls over her shoulder, her back pressing against his as they each stare down their respective enemies.

"What is it, Mara?"

"My Source is destroying the seal; I can't stop it."

He glances at her, alarmed. "How much longer do you

have?"

"I don't know." She grits her teeth as another spear of pain pierces her head. She blocks a grinning soldier's attack and slashes out. He collapses as her vision temporarily goes black. She staggers, falling to her knees.

She can hear Darion fighting above her, protecting her from any stray swords. "We do not have *time* for this."

She agrees with him. Despite this, though, she sinks into her mind and finds the entrapped Essence. She nudges her Source to the weak points of the already-crumbling seal; it falls apart, unable to withstand the added pressure.

Her Source encapsulates the Essence, completely devouring it as though it is starving.

She collapses, blacking out as silvery sparks flit erratically around her. Information floods her mind, and for the briefest of seconds, she feels as if she is living dozens of lives simultaneously.

Just as fast as it had happened, it is over. Her head spins as she stares at the grassy earth, her fingers curling into the dirt.

The Essence thrums within her, filling her veins as it quickly puts a halt to the Hemius's movements. It grows brighter and brighter, her own Source sapping away every bit of blemishing color – every bit of knowledge – from the ancient fragment of a soul and finishing what it had started before.

Mara clutches her head, overwhelmed with the onslaught of knowledge. A strangled grunt erupts from her lips as she staggers to her feet, trying to focus on her present situation.

The memories do not matter; they are *memories*. She can deal with them later. All she needs to know at that moment is who she needs to hunt down.

The Da'ruha.

Her vision swirls with multiple colors as she involuntarily slips into runkare, gazing at the twining strands of

Source and Voyana around her. Darion shines a bright jade until he mixes his Source with Voyana, turning it a brilliant emerald.

More importantly, though, she sees the blood-red Source of the Dark Warrior deep within the crowd of enemies.

She holds out her hand, summoning Gamerog to her. It nestles solidly in her palm, humming in excitement. She takes a step forward when a blast of air has her shielding her face.

Ryutaro lands next to her, snarling menacingly at the surrounding soldiers. He swings his tail around, sending them flying before they can even raise their weapons. "*Mara*," he rumbles, his fiery eye meeting hers. "*Do not go. Your mind is unstable right now.*"

Mara. That's… my name.

She touches the side of his face. He flinches, but then relaxes as nothing happens. "I need to," she whispers, her fist clenching against his scales. "Fly me over there."

Darion turns around, glancing between Ryutaro and Mara. "Ryutaro, get her out of here!"

Ryutaro scoops Mara up with his head and deposits her on his back. She nearly topples off as he whips around and wraps his claws around Darion's waist before beating his huge wings and lifting them into the air.

"Nice save, duir'ne," Darion calls up to him. Realizing they are heading deeper into the battlefield, he exclaims in alarm, "Where are you taking us?"

"*The Ecalain desires to fight,*" he responds, pausing over a particular fight between Kimala and some of the soldiers. "*It looks as though Kimala is —*"

"Thank you, Ryutaro," Mara murmurs, patting one of his protruding spikes. "This is good."

She leaps from his back.

"Mara?!" Darion shouts, shocked as she plummets to the ground several stories below her.

The shadow of her Xhuri robe whips behind her as she holds out her hand and generates a scio'thi made out of Source. She slams into the ground next to Kimala, her sword plunging deep into the earth.

A shockwave of pure energy ripples outward, knocking back the surrounding soldiers several yards.

"Wh – " Kimala starts.

Mara lunges and thrusts her sword at the medic.

Kimala closes her eyes, too stunned to do anything else.

Mara bypasses her, stopping the blow from a soldier that would have killed the medic. The soldier bears down; she grits her teeth as she struggles against his strength. He pulls out a gun from its holster and rapid-fires against her unprotected chest.

Shing, shing, shing.

The energy beams ricochet off a curved blade a hairsbreadth away from cutting into her. The chains attached to the hilt clink softly as the weapon withdraws; Shaniel's expression is dark and foreboding as he turns the small twin salev'ra onto the man, slicing him across the throat and an unprotected spot in his stomach armor all at once.

He whirls around, facing Mara. "Are you all right?" he demands, looking her up and down. "Did Lilly fix your ribs and arm?"

Mara nods, taking several deep breaths as she regains her composure. She sways on her feet.

Shaniel looks over Mara's shoulder and tosses one of his chained salev'ra. The chain pulls taut as it lodges in the chest of a soldier attacking Kimala. "Tein'stra, I know you wanted to save them, but it's too dangerous."

"I-I wanted to try!" she says, tears welling up in her eyes. "I can't bear to see anyone else die."

Mara whirls on Kimala, grabbing the front of her robe. "You can't fool me," she hisses, her Source whipping around both of them.

Shaniel's eyes widen. "Mara, let her go!" He pauses, paling. "You're not – "

"Shaniel, move three steps to the left or Darion is going to land on you," Mara barks, not breaking eye contact with Kimala. The medic's eyes are blue, but she knows the Da'ruha is barely managing to keep the red from swirling up.

Darion's soft *thud* to the ground signifies his arrival. He glances between Shaniel and Kimala with narrowed eyes. "Were you with her the entire time, Shaniel?"

"Y-yeah," the laig'hius says. "She asked me to accompany her out here; she had heard some of her friends had – "

"We do not believe that is Kimala."

Shaniel's eyes widen. "No-no way," he breathes. "But Eliara is in her right now."

Chapter 19
One Life for Another

Mara glares at Kimala, ignoring their banter. "This is pretty low, even for you."

"Mara, what the Bloody Mavi are you even talking about?" Kimala whines, wincing as Mara's hand tightens on the cloth. It constricts around her throat. "Pl-please stop…"

"Get. Out. Of. Her." Each word is enunciated and sounds more and more like a snarl. Both Darion and Shaniel sink into a crouch, preparing for a fight. "I don't care if I have to stab her to get you to leave."

Kimala forces a smile as a flicker of red flashes across her eyes. "You… wouldn't," she chokes out.

Gamerog presses into the unprotected side of the medic. "Try me."

Pure fear enters her eyes now as they clear to a perfect lapis blue. "Mara – " Eliara starts.

Her sword lowers as she hesitates. She can't inflict the same wound on Eliara that had killed her six thousand years ago; that will be too traumatic to the already broken soul of the ancient duir'ne.

The Da'ruha sneers. "I didn't even know she had returned. She will die again, I assure you – and this time, I will make it *permanent*."

"No!" Mara shouts, tightening her grip – but it suddenly slackens as Gameleth bites into her side. She stumbles backward, gasping and clutching at her hip. *Maybe I really should quit fighting,* she thinks, gritting her teeth through the pain. *I'm getting sick of all these near-death experiences.*

The Da'ruha turns to the defensive Shaniel and Darion while Mara struggles to remain standing. "Now, which of you two to pick off next?" she murmurs, grinning dement-edly. "I assure you, it won't be a pleasant death."

Shaniel charges forward, swinging his salev'ra with expert moves.

"No," Mara says weakly, stepping forward and falling to her knees. "Don't…"

Darion charges in after Shaniel. The Da'ruha dodges Shaniel's strikes, slicing Gameleth across his arm before kicking his back. He sprawls on the ground, and she raises the sword over his head.

Darion swings Karakeit at her, but a blood-red shield suddenly materializes, forming between the two of them. She smiles sweetly at Darion. "Here you are, trying to *kill* the woman you had once loved. What happened between you two? A lover's spat?"

"Kimala is not my betrothed," Darion snarls.

She dodges his strike. "I think it would be quite fitting for you to end her life one final time. Don't you think?"

"Darion, no! Get out of there!" Mara screams, lurching to her feet. She needs to stop both of them before they kill each other.

Darion's eyes widen, realizing the Da'ruha's plan. He hesitates, pulling his sword back – but it is too late.

The Da'ruha throws herself onto it while thrusting forward with Gameleth.

"Bodies are disposable," she says raggedly, smirking at Darion's shocked, appalled expression as they both fall to their knees. "But souls… are not."

Mara's hands shake as she gathers her Source and focuses on her wounds, closing them just enough so she doesn't bleed out. She doesn't have time to properly heal them, but at least this will keep her from dying in the next several minutes.

She staggers forward, briefly sparing Shaniel a glance. His arm is sliced from the shoulder down to his elbow, but there doesn't seem to be any Hemius infection. His eyes meet hers as his breath hisses in and out. "Help them," he rasps.

She grabs the back of Kimala's robe, yanking her off of Karakeit's blade. Gameleth slides out of Darion, thumping on the grass. He slumps to the ground, his hand curling around the wound as he immediately begins trying to close it.

Kimala's eyes are unfocused as she gives Mara a dazed smile. "You cannot stop me," she giggles, her eyes turning a dark red as blood drips from the corner of her mouth. "I will kill… everyone you love, you… Alamir scum."

"I'm not Alamir," Mara snarls, plunging her Source into Kimala and forcefully yanking out the Da'ruha. "And *you* don't belong here!"

Holding the writhing core of intertwined Sources, she closes her eyes and searches for the hairline seams that separate them from one another; they are small and nearly impossible to find, but they are there.

Unlike the Highlords, *she* is not afraid of damaging either one of them. Unlike the Highlords, *she* does not have her position to worry about if she breaks their rules. Unlike the Highlords…

She just doesn't care.

She rips the two Source-cores apart, separating the souls of an Alamir and a Danarko.

The resulting screeches echo over the battlefield, sounding like two banshees wailing over loudspeakers. Even Mara is overwhelmed with the volume and pressure they are putting on her. Naturally, the ocean blue and blood-red Sources fight to merge back together to fix their near-fractured state, but Mara cocoons them separately with her Source.

She collapses to her knees, gasping. Her side throbs painfully as she squints, trying to focus on her surroundings. Her vision is hazy, the colors in her right eye warping and fluctuating.

A familiar presence grips her shoulder. She looks up and can barely make out the vague form. "Darion…"

"Can you go through the portal?"

She nods, forcing herself to her feet. She takes a deep breath, focusing in front of her. Glimpsing the warped air, she clenches her fists and shoves the two orbs through, quickly stepping after them. Darion follows behind her.

She feels the membrane slide across her skin, the sensation drastically different to the previous times she has passed through a portal. She winces at the painful jab in her side as her foot slams on the teal stone of Elethanos.

Glancing at the two orbs, she sees an unconscious dark-haired girl in one. In the other, a raven-haired girl with swirling red eyes pounds on the thick, smoky orb imprisoning her.

"Let me go!" the young-looking elf screams, barely able to sit up inside the orb. Her arms look cracked as if she is falling apart. "Let me out right now!"

The Elethavi groans open, a vortex swirling in anticipation. Mara smirks; even Eleth has been waiting for this moment.

Mara walks up to the vortex, barely seeing Hariana through the swirling air. At least ten mysterious guards wait on the other side; all of them hold an assortment of unfamiliar weapons, each sparking on the tips with some sort of electrical current. They wear the same unfamiliar armor and have the same expressionless look on their faces. The blue-grey monotone colors give the entire scenario an eerie vibe.

"You better wipe her memory," she yells at the swirling air, and she feels a tug on her robe as the currents grow stronger.

She releases the screaming Alkinian first, watching her tumble into the vortex. Their eyes meet, and Mara can see pure hatred in her gaze.

As she sets down the other girl, the vortex calms,

showing a simplistic yet grey visage of Alamirana. Frowning, Mara looks down just as the girl stirs.

Stormy blue eyes meet hers, blinking as she looks around dazedly. Her eyes water as soon as she sees Darion. "Is it… over?" she rasps, sounding as if she had been screaming for a long time.

Darion kneels next to her. "Yes, Your Highness," he breathes, carefully taking her cracked hand. "You must enter Eleth now before your soul fully fractures, though. The separation… damaged you."

"Darius." She touches his face lightly. Her eyes water. "I keep seeing Codimus, but she kills him over and over…"

He clasps her hand firmly. "You will find him again, Your Highness. I am sure of it."

"Thank you." The membrane of the gate reaches out and cradles her, pulling her through. She glances at Mara, giving the mage a grateful smile. "I hope we can meet more properly in the future, Mara."

She bows deeply to the *true* Da'ruha – Rinali Alamir. "I am sure that day is not far off, Your Highness. Eleth is not unfair with its terms."

"So I have heard."

She disappears.

Mara gives into her wobbling knees and sinks to the stone floor, expelling her breath in a pained hiss. Darion approaches her, kneeling to examine the wound in her side. "It needs to be treated," he murmurs, his fingers gentle as he touches her side.

"Darion, I brought bandages and salve," Elethanos says curtly, walking up as the little girl with a frustrated look on her face as she kneels next to him and promptly begins bandaging his wound.

Mara lurches to her feet, her side throbbing painfully and her head spinning. She knows she has already lost a massive amount of blood, but she cannot focus on that right now.

She needs to save Kimala.

She reaches forward, involuntarily slipping into runkare state. The sunlight currents trickle throughout the chamber, and she sees them warp around certain areas at the front of the room. She staggers toward them, her vision wobbling.

"Mara, stop. Allow Elethanos to treat you," Darion orders, trying to get up. Elethanos pushes him back down, keeping him from moving.

"Kimala was stabbed, too," she rasps, clutching her side. She can feel the wound seeping as it reopens, but she doesn't care. "I need to help her."

She hooks her fingers around one of the rips, opening it and sticking her hand into Carni so she can open a subsequent one leading to Blazhreia. She focuses on Kimala, pinpointing her location so she can step through to the medic's side.

"Mara, please. Allow Elethanos to – "

"Kimala was nearly cut in half!" She spares him a glance. "At least I can walk. Kimala…" Her breathing hitches, remembering the large blade piercing through the medic's torso.

He exhales slowly. "Go. I will be right behind you."

She steps through.

The battle looks to be over; the enemy troops that are still alive are on their knees, looking dazed and frightened at the multitude of soldiers hovering over them. Now that the Da'ruha is gone and the puppeteer has cut all of his strings, the war is over.

A few feet away, Shaniel cradles Kimala's head as Alec speaks softly to her, trying hard not to cry – and failing. A cloud covers the moons overhead, casting the grim battlefield into shadows. Only Mara's weakly sparking Source casts light on the scene, revealing the growing pool of red liquid underneath the medic.

Mara collapses to her knees next to Kimala, staring

dully at the blood. Bright blue eyes turn to Mara, and the dying medic smiles up at her, her eyes already glazing over. "Mara… you're all right…"

"You will be, too," she says hoarsely, holding her hand over the wound.

"You don't know this level of healing," Kimala says weakly, her eyes sliding closed. "Not even… I do."

"You don't know everything about me," Mara retorts through gritted teeth, her vision blurring. Tears spill over her cheeks as her black Source pours from her fingers, pure white sparks edging it. "Drat it, Kimala, where are your harsh quips now?"

The clouds move, and the twin moons illuminate the small group. Kimala does not breathe again.

"Mara, stop," Shaniel whispers quietly as Alec sobs. "She's already gone."

"I won't!" She yells. Her voice is barely a breath as she leans over her cousin's body. "I won't…"

She clenches her fist over the wound. *I won't let her die,* she swears, renewed determination flaring within her. *I've fixed wounds like this. I've* felt *wounds like this heal on* me *before!*

She closes her eyes, digging deep within her own subconscious as her Source sinks into Kimala. An old, old memory bubbles to the surface – not a memory that the Essence had experienced, but one her own soul had.

————◆————

Despite being unconscious, she can still feel her skin knitting back together. She wants to die; the pain is unbearable. She had been fired at repeatedly, and then someone had rushed in and hacked at her. Even her head is nearly severed; only her spinal cord is intact, which, when it all boils down to it, is all she needs to revive.

Stupid radiation, she manages to think as she feels the muscles thread themselves back together with the help of the biochemical. Little nano atoms fuse the tissues, nerves, skin, and joints, healing her to nearly tip-top shape.

———◆———

Mara takes a deep breath. She knows what happens next.

Pop.

Kimala gasps, her eyes flying open as she moans in agony. "M-my ribs..." she whines, her hands flying over where her shattered and crushed bones had popped back into place after being welded together. Her eyes fly to Mara.

Her eyes are open, but instead of them being their usual burnt gold, they are a deep, dark smoky blue. Her expression is slack, her eyes glazed over. For a split second, Kimala wonders if she is lost in a memory when those unfamiliar eyes meet her own.

"I am glad... you're all right..." Mara breathes in Old Xharos before collapsing on the ground next to the medic.

Kimala struggles to sit upright, immediately reaching for her cousin. "You can't keel over after doing that, Mara! Tell me what you did!" she demands, flipping the young woman onto her back.

She closes her eyes, scanning the mage for injuries and missing Alec's and Shaniel's stunned expressions at her sudden revival. As soon as she finds the internal bleeding caused from Gameleth's gash in her side, her eyes fly back open.

"No, no, no..." she breathes, straightening Mara's arms and pressing her head against her cousin's chest. Her heartbeat is faint but still there. "Shaniel, I need you to get Lilly. Alec, come and help me."

Alec snaps out of his stunned state and rushes to his betrothed's side as Shaniel sprints away. Just then, Darion topples through a portal, wincing as he forces himself to sit upright. "Mara – " He freezes as he sees Kimala holding Mara's leg knife over the mage's abdomen.

318

Leaping forward, he holds Kimala's hand at bay, his eyes wide as he meets her startled gaze. "What are you doing?" he demands, his voice shaking.

"She has a huge amount of internal bleeding!" Kimala exclaims, yanking her hand free. "Not only that, but the Hemius is corrupting the cells around the wound. I need to cut it off and help it heal properly."

He slumps onto the ground, staring at Mara before glancing at Kimala. "You-you were almost dead when we left," he murmurs, confused. "Did Mara…"

Alec glances at Darion, still in disbelief. "She *was* dead," he breathes, his tears leaving wet stains on his face. "Her heart… her heart had stopped beating when Mara…"

"Stop talking, Alec," Kimala snaps, though his words shake her to her core. She remembers that terrifying moment after Mara had stepped through the portal. She had been in so much pain; she had closed her eyes, wanting the agony to end… and it had. It was replaced by a darkness so complete it had begun swallowing her whole. However, after what had felt like days yet was mere seconds later, she had regained consciousness after an odd pop in her ribs and a tingling jolt to her heart that felt eerily like pure energy.

Lilly rushes over, staring at her for a long moment before focusing on Mara. "What happened?"

"Internal bleeding," she quickly reports, moving out of the experienced medic's way. "The Hemius is corrupting the edges of the wound, too. It's impeding new cell growth."

The Life'Lord drops her medical bag and rips Mara's shirt away from the wound. "Kimala, I need you to – "

Kimala is already digging inside of Lilly's bag. She hands the Life'Lord scissors and an odd cylindrical tube with a funneling system within it.

Lilly takes the items, glancing at Darion. "Do not stop me, Darion," she warns, pressing the tube against the wound. "Timing is critical, and I cannot have you interrupting me."

Darion rakes his hand through his hair, looking away. Catching sight of the wound underneath his shirt, Kimala frowns. "You… you were stabbed, too, right?" she suddenly says in alarm.

"Yes." Darion lifts his shirt hem enough to reveal the bloody bandage. "Elethanos patched me up temporarily, so – "

"Kimala, tend to him," Lilly barks, her fingers flitting over Mara's wound. Her Source coats the young mage's stomach in a steady light as she works.

Kimala gestures to the ground. "Lie down."

Alec and Shaniel step back, keeping out of the way. Alec bites his lip, resisting the urge to sweep Kimala into a tight hug. For a brief moment, he had truly thought he had lost her forever.

Shaniel pats the duir'ne's shoulder. "Hold on just a little longer, Your Grace," he murmurs.

Alec gives him a wobbly smile. "Thank you." He glances at Mara, who must be in a critical state based off of the intensity of Lilly's Source and how fast the expert woman is working. "Do you think she will make it?"

"If she doesn't, then I'll be beating her up in Elethanos over letting herself get this bad off," Shaniel mutters, crossing his arms.

Lilly huffs, cursing under her breath. Glancing at Shaniel, she orders, "Get over here and block her Source. She's-she's sapping mine away."

Shaniel kneels next to Mara, frowning. Stroking her hair back, he delves into her mind, trying to take a look and see what is happening to her Source.

What he sees shocks him to the core.

The black Source completely engulfs a white core in the middle, enormous and teeming with power. Tendrils lash out, latching onto any small amount of external energy.

Lilly's warm-colored Source works overtime to lower the injured mage's core body temperature and heart rate via an access point within Mara's mind, but the black Source chips away at it.

Shaniel wrestles against the black tendrils, trying to contain them. As soon as they touch him, he feels as if he had expelled a large amount of Source. Horrified, he watches the magenta-colored energy darken and fall into the growing mass of black Source.

A white Source deep within suddenly rears up, breaking through the encompassing tendrils to form a perfect, impenetrable sphere around the rampant black Source. Shaniel yanks himself out of Mara's mind, gasping and shaking.

What was that?

Lilly exhales slowly, her hand now covering the wound. She spares a glance at Shaniel. "Thank you."

"It wasn't me," he whispers, staring at Mara's relaxed face. "It was something else. Something... white."

Darion tilts his head to the side, trying to look at Shaniel as Kimala finishes sealing his wound. "The Essence, most likely."

Shaniel shakes his head. "The Essence is silver. This... this one's white, and it's solid, not... shattered."

"It is the Essence," Darion says firmly, sitting upright with the assistance of Kimala.

"I healed it the best I could, but take it easy," she warns him.

"Thank you, Kimala," he says gratefully, moving to Mara's side. "Mara had told me the Essence had not always been silver, nor had it always been in that fractured state."

"You can ask her yourself in a minute," Lilly grumbles, sweat rolling down her face. "I'm almost done."

Suddenly, black tendrils encase Lilly's hand, latching onto the woman. Her eyes widen as she tries to yank free, but she cannot move.

A pure white ribbon curls around the black, forcefully pulling it back to Mara's right arm. The black Source latches itself onto the skin, pulsing like a dark heartbeat. The white Source brushes against Lilly's fingers, and she gasps in surprise.

"What just happened?" Shaniel asks, unnerved by the sight of it.

"It saved me," Lilly whispers, pressing a finger against the white Source. She smiles gently. "Thank you."

It sinks into Mara's wound. The skin knits itself closed, leaving a faint blemish of a scar. They all stare at Mara; Lilly hesitantly touches the wound, frowning.

"Is it healed?" Kimala asks, her voice shaking.

She nods, glancing at Mara's face again. "I do not understand why she is not waking up, though."

Darion rubs his chin thoughtfully. "Perhaps she is still healing…" At Lilly's odd look, he clarifies, "Right after we rejoined the battle, she broke the seal on the Essence. Perhaps…"

"They had merged?" Shaniel finishes.

Darion shakes his head, something else nagging at him. "I do not know; let us return for now." He gently lifts her up, carrying her back to Alamirana.

The moons hide behind the clouds once again.

———◆———

Mara stares up at the colorful sky, resting on an embankment of silvery-green grass. She takes a deep breath, inhaling the scent of the multitude of flowers growing within the forest. The lapis blue lake glimmers in the dim light, reflecting the glowing forest.

She closes her eyes. She needs to come here more often; it is the one place that memories and knowledge do not encroach on her mind. She can think for herself here.

She finally found her haven.

Sitting up, she looks down at herself. She is wearing her Xhuri robe, but the bottom edge of it is no longer torn. It is complete – all thanks to reuniting with the Essence.

She smiles, looking back up into the sky as brilliant white stars appear. "The other side of the coin," she murmurs, thinking of the meaning of her own name as one of the stars falls into the lake. It reemerges as a white figure mirroring her own image.

"*Mara.*"

"Essence." She dips her head respectfully. "It's good to see you again."

"*We have been reunited,*" it says in a happy voice much like Hope's.

She chuckles. "So you still have access to the memories?"

"*As long as I am with you, yes.*"

"I am glad." She closes her eyes briefly, taking another deep breath. "Do you like my haven?"

"*Yes.*" The white figure tilts her head to the side. "*I sense that you are at peace. Have you managed to control the flow of knowledge?*"

"Yeah." She stands up, brushing off her robe. "I think I'm ready to go back."

"*We should come here more often. I like it when you are happy.*"

Mara laughs. "It's certainly a nice change, Danti." She pauses, staring at the form the Essence had taken. "I… guess Danra is more fitting of a nickname, though, seeing as you're no longer silver."

A thoughtful expression crosses the white Mara's face. "*I still prefer Danti,*" it admits. "*Would you rather me call you Vuti instead of Mara?*"

She laughs. "No, thanks." She holds out her hand, grinning lopsidedly. "Will you be the half that completes the whole, though, Danti?"

The white form mirrors her perfectly. "*It would be my honor to.*"

As soon as their fingers touch, Mara knows intuitively that she never has to fear her own power again; she can trust Danti to help her control it if it ever goes rampant. Danti is the only one who cannot be devoured by her Source, so it is only natural that it is the one thing that can stop her from ever hurting her friends again.

———————•◆•———————

Mara slowly opens her eyes, blearily looking around at the concerned faces crowding her vision. She recognizes the ornate walls of the medical ward inside Alamirta.

"Mara," Darion breathes, relieved. "How do you feel?"

She opens her mouth, but before she can get a single word out, she goes into an awful coughing fit. She clutches her chest, her eyes widening as something constricts her heart. *Drat it*, she thinks. *Why did this have to happen now?*

"The Hemius is reactivating!" she hears Lilly exclaim, trying to pry Mara's arms away.

"What about the Essence?" Darion demands, alarmed. "It has always moderated it."

"It doesn't look like it is helping this time!"

Don't worry, she tries to tell them, but something coppery floods her mouth. She coughs out the liquid.

Blood.

Gritting her teeth, she forces herself onto her knees on the cot, determination burning within her. She *refuses* to let this pitiful remnant of the Da'ruha defeat her.

Lilly takes one look at her fierce expression and backs up, shaken. Darion stops her. "What are you doing, Lilly? Help her!"

"I-I – " Her hand shakes as she points at the mage.

Darion stares at Mara, his mouth falling open.

The mage cocoons her right side with her Source, completely encapsulating her skin with the black energy. *Feed*, she orders, forcing the devouring energy onto the Hemius; it is just another form of energy, albeit an invasive kind.

Her black Source rears back, refusing to absorb the poisonous energy. She forces it forward, gritting her teeth as she feels the Hemius travel throughout her whole body, turning her skin a blackish-purplish color as the Hemius infects her to the core. She chokes, feeling everything tighten as the Hemius tries to crush her from the inside.

Her black Source finally concedes, encapsulating the parasitic energy. Its survival instinct kicks in as it sucks in all of the Hemius, *choking* on it as it struggles to convert the corrupted Source's nano-atoms.

She squeezes her eyes shut and curls in on herself as she waits out the agonizing conversion process. Her face sinks into the pillow, hiding her pained expression.

To the others, it looks as though her skin turns from a dark bruise to pure black within the span of a minute. Within another minute, it fades away, leaving unblemished skin in its wake. Yet another minute passes by before Mara suddenly sucks in a huge gulp of air, her eyes popping open. Her gold eyes flit around, dazed and unfocused.

Darion helps her sit upright. "Mara, what happened?" he whispers, checking her all over for a single blemish. "The Hemius…"

"It's gone," she croaks. Clearing her throat, she says in a clearer voice, "I got rid of it."

They stare at her in disbelief. "That is impossible," Lilly breathes. "No one has ever been able to… to… *rid* themselves of it."

Mara sways slightly, almost falling over. Darion quickly catches her before she topples off the cot. "When you break it down, Hemius is Source-corrupted water. Quite honestly, I'm surprised my Source hasn't devoured it before; it did seem to have an issue with it, though."

"Did you say… devour?" Kimala repeats, her eyes wide. "You converted the Hemius into your own Source?"

Mara takes a slow, deep breath, checking her lungs.

They work fine now. "I've told you what my Source does, Kimala. It shouldn't be a surprise to you."

"You just took the most dangerous substance in the *realms* and absorbed it into your own Source, Mara!" Kimala yells, reaching her breaking point. Her fists ball against her sides as tears race down her cheeks. "What if it was more powerful than you? What would you have done if it had consumed *you*, instead?"

"Absorbed... the Hemius?" Lilly repeats, having a hard time processing the information.

"And what would you have done if you found yourself choking on Hemius and the Essence couldn't help you moderate it anymore?" Mara snaps back at the medic, anger bubbling up. She sits upright, no longer leaning on Darion. "It was either try that or die, Kimala. Luckily, I didn't suffocate in the process, as it took longer than I expected."

"The Da'ruha had been inhabiting the body," Darion murmurs, calculating. "It could have added more to the Hemius than what had originally been there."

"It did." Mara rubs her face, closing her eyes briefly. "How long was I out?"

They exchange glances. "A couple hours," Lilly murmurs. "Alec and the others are still counting the dead."

Mara closes her eyes, remembering the fallen Nature'Lord. "Did Derak..."

Lilly's eyes drop to the ground. "We could not save him in time."

Mara stares at her lap. She has on black leather pants and a dark red silk top; the choices of the Da'ruha, most likely. She glances around, trying to block out the memory of her screaming as she had tossed her into the Eleth Vortex.

She feels something warm brushing past her cheek. Frowning, she touches her face, but there is nothing. "What the..."

Darion tilts his head to the side, curious and slightly confused. "Did you feel something, Mara?"

She nods, feeling the odd 'breeze' at her elbow now. "Is there a window open or something?"

Lilly's eyebrows shoot upward. "No, but the Voyana currents *are* shifting around you. Perhaps you feel them?"

Mara's eyes narrow as she reaches forward, grasping at the air. For a brief moment, her irises glow the same color as the bright, sunlight-colored currents flowing about her. This time, when she feels the brush against her arm, she sees the current rushing by her. "Oh… I see what it is."

Darion's eyes widen. "I did not realize you can see Voyana now."

"Yeah." She frowns, watching some of it swirl around her finger briefly before joining the major current sweeping by them. She looks in the direction it is flowing. "Is it normal for it to go in one direction like this?"

"No, it is not," Darion admits, eyeing a particular current. "I shall check it out. Mara, stay – "

"No; I want to try something, anyway." She gets up, and he is quick to support her. "I need to be in the court-yard with the portal."

He hesitates a moment, his eyes flicking to Lilly. She sighs in resignation. "Let's see what she has planned."

Chapter 20
Altered Memory

They meander their way to the courtyard. Mara's brows furrow together as she watches the currents of golden sunlight; she feels as though she should be in awe, but it just feels so familiar. Not only that, but the singular direction it is flowing in has her concerned.

As soon as they stop in the courtyard, she takes a deep breath. "Thank you, Darion," she says sincerely, stepping away from him. "If this works, then it shouldn't take long."

She concentrates, forming an orb in her hand and raising it above her head. Her Source feeds off of Voyana, growing exponentially in the span of a few seconds. They are all stunned as they watch the black Source sphere expand rapidly, rising on its own and floating along the current. It heads toward the outskirts of the city's wall as it grows bigger and bigger.

Mara watches it for a moment, calculating the point at which it should be over the area where the battle had taken place. "*Will you do the honor?*" she asks the Essence, now a silky white ribbon twining through her mind.

It thrums, elated to still be of use. She points to the sphere, and a pure white arrow shoots from her fingers and pops the large sphere. It explodes over the field.

Mara's eyes slide out of focus. For a split second, she is everywhere that the faint black mist of energy is; she sees the other Sources in the area and how Voyana's currents are flowing over the land, depleted due to the battle.

She is looking for a specific Source signature, though. An unmistakable one.

On the outskirts of her Source's reach, the blood-red Source stands out like a thorn; her own Source recoils from it after briefly touching it. It sends a familiar chill down her spine – but now she knows it is more than the previous vessels' memories of the Da'ruha. She herself has met this person before and knows for a fact his Source is not natural.

Her eyes fly open, temporarily swirling red. Everyone takes a few steps back, alarmed at the sudden color. "Uthu morla ikuto, *Rath*," she hisses out loud, tightening her Source over that one energy signature.

She feels the alarm rolling off of him; he recognizes her. More than that, she can tell he recognizes her Source's ability and what it can do to him. She attempts to cage him in her Source before he leaves the range of her net. However, in that split second, he yanks open a portal and escapes.

"Carc'ra!" Mara curses under her breath, darting for the anchored portal on the platform. She focuses on the tainted Source as she reaches for the swirling air, briefly connecting with Carni. Before anyone can stop her, she jumps through and barrels into the white-haired man on the other side.

They tumble onto the crystalline pathway in Carni, and Mara's landing sends a large, radial crack through Carni's Path. It creaks like grinding stone under the pressure of her Source.

Rath scrambles to his feet, staring at Mara with a look of dread. "You," he breathes, appalled. "How did I not realize it was *you?*"

Mara raises her fists, narrowing her eyes at him. "You're not getting away this time, Rath," she whispers, looking much older than her physical body right then. Her Xhuri robe flares about her, whole and untorn.

He holds up his hands, his fingers splayed wide. "Please wait, Mara." An idea sparks in his eyes. "Help me get my wife out of Hariana, and you will never have to see us again."

"You think I'm going to free someone from that

prison system?" Mara asks rhetorically, incredulous. "You're even more insane than I thought."

"I am not the one insane!" he cries, desperate. "It is the other families that are. Always babbling on about Voyana and how it dictates us; now it even has soldiers, the Ecalauna!"

"Quit making riddles to confuse me, Rath."

"I am talking of the other Ecalain families," he murmurs, his hands slowly lowering as he straightens. "The Alamir family was *brainwashed* by the chemical. The Danarko family – *my* family – were next. I tried to salvage our name after the incident, but nothing worked! Everyone thought of us as evil and crazy. They did not understand. But you... you have the soul of a Viridian, one of the originals. You must understand our plight. Please, Mara. Help us! Help your family!"

She narrows her eyes. "Why have I never heard of the Viridian family?"

"We made it disappear," Rath quickly explains. "It would not have done us any good if my wife's name had been tarnished, as well."

Mara's brow furrows as she recalls Darion's and Eliara's explanation of the feud between Danarko and Alamir, though the name Viridian had never been mentioned. "You're making no sense. I would have heard of it."

He shakes his head. "No, you wouldn't have." He stares at her, pleading. "Please, Mara. My wife and I just want to be together again. Once she is back, we will leave; you will never have to see us again."

Mara stares at him, everything snapping into perspective. Morrigan. His excitement over the birth of his daughter, Reivin. His stubbornness on bringing the Da'ruha back time and time again, targeting the Essence's vessels for her to inhabit. Wanting to be with his wife.

"You're trying to bring your family back?" she asks,

her voice low.

He nods. His icy blue eyes spark with hope as he holds out his hand to her. "Will you… help me, Mara?"

She remembers another pair of those eyes. They had stared into hers as his body disintegrated underneath her hands.

"I'll bring your family together," she finally concedes, taking his hand.

He exhales, relaxing. "Thank you, Mara."

"In Hariana." Her Source lashes out, moving as fast as a lightning bolt.

A blood-red barrier blocks the strike, and her Source flinches away, refusing to touch the corrupted energy. Mara staggers back, wincing; she feels as though she was punched in the shoulder.

Rath straightens, drawing back his fist. She stares at him, her eyes wide; she had not seen him move. The calculating, cold look in his gaze accentuates his ice blue eyes as he promises, "You will regret this, Mara."

His form disintegrates into red particles, disappearing.

Mara slumps to her knees, taking one deep breath after another. She places a hand over her pounding heart, trying to control not only the painful throbbing from where he had punched her shoulder but also her swirling emotions. She doesn't notice the lingering red dust about her.

She finally processes the entire conversation. "I was… a Viridian?" she murmurs out loud, a deep frown marring her face. She feels as if something had been off about the whole conversation. Shaking it off, she pushes it to the back of her mind to deal with later.

She stands up and reaches forward, looking for the rift that will take her home. Her cousin's half-dead state flashes through her mind as she passes through the portal, and she hopes she is all right.

As soon as her foot touches the platform in Alamirta's

courtyard, she is bombarded with an irate Kimala. The rising sun splashes reds and oranges over the ground, making the blood on Kimala's robe stand out starkly.

"Bloody Elethavi, Mara, where did you run off to this time? You could have still been injured! Who were you even looking for? Why didn't you take someone with you?" She stops, sucking in air.

Mara stares at her, blinking at the sudden onslaught. "Breathe, Kimala. I'm fine." *At least I know she's all right,* she thinks to herself.

"You better be!" she snaps. She crosses her arms over her torn robe and shirt. "What happened after we healed you?"

Mara sighs. "I went after Rath. I almost had him in Carni, but he… got away." She scratches the side of her jaw, a bit embarrassed to admit her failure.

Kimala gasps. "Rath?! But that's the man we have been looking for! Mara, you should not have gone alone!"

Erimentha enters the courtyard and crosses her arms. "I agree with her; that was a stupid move goin' after him alone." She pauses. "Darion is mad with ye, fletchling."

Mara flinches and hurries past the Alkinian. "I should apologize."

Erimentha shakes her head as she falls into step behind the mage. "He's probably already here."

Kimala whirls toward the old Alkinian. "He isn't supposed to leave the medical ward!"

Alarm spikes through Mara. "What happened? Was there more fighting after I left?"

Kimala crosses her arms again, glaring at her cousin. "He punched a wall; put a huge crack in it. Erimentha beat him up before making him fix it. I managed to heal him, but he's still recovering his depleted Source levels." Glancing ahead of them, she stomps forward. "Darion, get back to the medical ward right now, or so help me, I will sedate – "

332

Darion rushes by her, not even listening to the irate medic as Shaniel and Aeserast trail behind him.

He crushes Mara against him, burying his face against her shoulder. "Mara… you are all right…" Pulling back, he cups her face and stares into her eyes. "Are you injured?"

"No," she responds, touching his hand lightly before pulling it away. She glances around self-consciously, but neither Kimala nor Erimentha seem surprised. However, Shaniel and Aeserast have different reactions.

Shaniel stares at them with wide eyes, his mouth hanging open. "He – he –"

Aeserast glances at his friend, silently reaching over to press his finger underneath the laig'hius's jaw to close it. Glancing back at Mara and Darion with a curious gaze, he says, "We should speak inside one of the rooms."

Darion quickly drops his hands, realizing now that he had been a little too familiar with Mara. As they walk toward the castle, he hisses at her, "Why did you go by yourself? What if you had been hurt?"

"I'm fine, Darion." She gives him a reassuring smile. "Really. I am."

He huffs. "I do not want you doing something like that again. I cannot – "

"Protect me if I'm on the other side of the Gate," she finishes. "I get it. Next time, I'll just drag you with me."

He exhales in another huff, glancing at her. "Yes, please do."

Shaniel glances between them as they walk down the corridor. "In the courtyard…"

Darion glances away, slightly embarrassed. Mara twists her finger in her Xhuri robe. "You do realize I almost punched you, right, Darion?" she tries to cover up.

Aeserast gives her a stern look. "Quit trying to hide it. You were *not* about to punch him, Mara."

She sighs. "Fine, you're right. I suppose you have questions, then?"

"How long has this been going on?"

They glance at one another. "A month…?" Darion says, sounding doubtful.

Mara shrugs. "Not even, I think."

"But… you kissed me before you went to Carni."

She blushes. "That-that was a distraction so you didn't follow me."

Aeserast's eyes widen as he stares at Darion. "She *kissed* you? Why didn't you tell us that when you gave your report?"

"Like she said, it was a distraction, and I fell for it," Darion stammers, raking his fingers through his bronze hair. He winces, knowing he is only making matters worse with this nervous gesture. "I did not want to admit that, though."

"Oooh," Shaniel breathes, slinking alongside Mara and glancing at Darion. "Darion likes our little Danarko!"

"Don't call me that." Mara's tone is harsher than intended.

"Mara, what's wrong?" Aeserast asks, concerned.

She hesitates. "It's… something Rath said before he disappeared."

"The last time you allowed him to talk to you, he manipulated your memory," Aeserast points out, his eyes narrowing. "When we get to the room, I want to check your mind for damage."

Mara nods. "Please do; I am concerned about that, as well."

Once they reach the sitting room, Mara immediately sits down and leans back in the chair. Aeserast stands behind it, reaching around to press his fingers against her temples. He frowns at Mara's open eyes; they are a dark smoky blue. "Mara – "

"Just ignore it." She closes her eyes, intuitively knowing they are a different color. "I think my Source changes the color whenever I recollect something specific from…

from a different life."

Unnerved, he scans her mind, looking for any corrosion or alteration. As far as he can tell, there is none. Huffing, he withdraws. "I can't find anything."

Mara touches her temple, frowning. "No. Something is wrong."

Darion kneels next to her, watching her intently. "What is it?"

"I can't place it." Her eyes slide out of focus as she racks her brain. "I'm forgetting something important; I just know it. Aeserast, look again."

He does. This time, he uses his knowledge of Mara's past to try to pinpoint what it is the young mage might be forgetting. He sucks his breath in, shocked. The alterations are seamless; if he hadn't been there for some of the memories, he would not have been able to pinpoint exactly where the changes had been made.

"Your memories of Thanos are *gone*," he whispers in disbelief.

Darion stares at Aeserast, startled. "Thanos?" he repeats. "But why would Rath take those memories?"

Mara frowns. *Thanos*, she repeats inside her mind, vaguely recognizing it. *It sounds so familiar…*

Aeserast shakes his head in disbelief as he continues scouring Mara's mind. "This level of mindweaving is inconceivable. He managed to alter or replace *every memory* of him."

Darion shifts in front of Mara, clasping one of her hands. "Mara, do you remember anything of Thanos?"

She stares at him. She feels as if something is swallowing her whole; her vision blurs as she touches her head. "No…"

He takes a slow, deep breath, his fingers clenching around hers. "What about Lyrik? Do you remember him?"

Her eyes slide shut involuntarily as she dredges up a single memory. Hope was kneeling in the grass, eating a sandwich next to…

Next to whom?

Her eyes fly open as pure rage churns within her. Aeserast quickly backs up, startled at the sudden emotion. Darion doesn't move.

"He took them," she breathes. "He took Hope's memories."

No one takes Hope's memories.

She stands up, and Darion releases her hand as she moves by him. "*Would you keep them safe while I do this, Danti?*" she asks the white Source twining around her own.

"*Of course*," it responds.

She sits in the middle of the room, her eyes that dark, smoky blue color again. "Don't step over the circle," she warns them, closing her eyes.

Before they can ask her what she means by that, a large white rune of containment manifests itself around her, glowing as it sinks into the carpet. As soon as it is complete, her hair and robe float about her. It is as if gravity has no meaning inside of her area of imprisonment.

Timian opens the door just then. He opens his mouth to ask a question, but both Aeserast and Darion motion him to remain quiet.

Mara picks through her mind, now knowing what the little seams in her memories look like. However, try as hard as she might, she cannot rip the seal placed on them; she grits her teeth, frustrated. Because her Source is even more revolted by Rath's power than the Hemius, she cannot expect her Source to chip away at it over time like it had done with the Essence.

One memory stands out to her, though. Lyon dies in her arms, his form flaking away. For some reason, she feels as though that one is both a truth and a lie. She had known Lyon; she had trained with him. He had been in Dounta. He had saved her. But…

That pesky memory-replacing film is over this particular memory.

She had known something else, too. Something about… Rath. Something *important*. Frowning, she focuses on the memory from earlier that day when she had encountered Rath in Carni. He had wanted something; he had wanted…

She can't remember.

"Carc'ra," she spits. "What was it?"

Darion hesitantly shifts closer. "Mara?"

"Not now." She focuses on the memory, trying to decipher the message. She replays it over and over in her mind's eye, scouring for the seam to tear it off and reveal the true memory that must be behind it.

——◆——

"Mara, you must understand," Rath says desperately, holding his hand out to her. His eyes are pleading. "I only wanted my daughter back. But I have her now! Please; I will not attack you any more. Just spare me so I may raise my daughter."

Mara hesitates on the crystalline pathway. "Where is she, Rath?"

He shakes his head. "Desdemona is keeping her safe for the time being. How could I have brought my new babe to the battle? That would have been such an awful experience for her."

She grits her teeth. "Rath, tell me where she is. We will raise her properly while you pay for your crimes. I don't care how much you love your daughter; your time here is over."

His expression hardens. "I will not let you take my child from me." He backs to the edge of Carni's Path. "I would rather die than give away her location."

"Carc'ra," Mara hisses. "Are you really going to do exactly what Naiya did?!"

"She was weak." He narrows his eyes at her. "And

you… you will never take my family from me again." He disappears in a cloud of red sand.

———◆———

Mara opens her eyes, slamming her fist down on the ground. The white seal underneath her shatters into tiny white fragments before dissipating. "Bloody Elethavi, what did he *mean* by that?"

Darion reaches forward. "Mara, what is it? Did he tamper with other memories?"

She shakes her head. "I'm not sure. I think so, but I can't break any of the tampering seals. He's too good at what he does." She rubs her temple. "I think the best way to break it is to just… find whoever Thanos was and get him to talk to me. That's the best way to break these types of seals, right?"

"Sometimes," Aeserast admits, crossing his arms. "You also don't remember Lyrik?"

Mara shakes her head. "He didn't hide that one very well, though I don't think he *could*; Hope was so attuned to him." She racks her brain. "He was an elemental, correct? Class unknown?"

Timian nods. "Indeed; he had been my informant."

Mara glances up, startled at the sudden arrival of Timian. She fidgets nervously, earning several odd looks from the Highlords. "U-Uncle Timian. When did you get here?"

"Just a moment ago." He watches her closely, his eyes slowly narrowing. "Why does my presence make you uncomfortable, Mara? It never has before."

She glances away. She feels as if she had failed the singular task of capturing Rath, as if it had been her mission or something of the sort. "I apologize."

He stares at her for a long moment, noting her dark blue eyes. "Mara, tell me," he encourages her in a low voice. "Whatever it is, I am sure I can forgive you."

She squeezes her eyes shut. "I apologize for not capturing Rath. I feel like I was supposed to, and I failed."

Timian frowns, kneeling next to Mara. He stares at her Xhuri robe for a long moment, noticing the edging at the bottom. He touches one of the trees, exhaling slowly. "Zandria's mission... it makes sense now."

Everyone stares at him in surprise. "Did you know her?" Kimala asks.

Timian laughs, tousling Mara's hair. "Indeed. And as for your apology, I accept it. You do not need to worry yourself over her failures, Mara; Zandria's mistakes are in the past and should not define you."

She stares at him for a long moment, her eyes slowly narrowing. "You knew who I was all along, didn't you?"

He continues smiling, patting her head. "I had my suspicions, but I was never certain of it until yesterday when we spoke in the library. I have been logging all of Zandria's rebirths to ensure her Source did not go rampant – which she did, twice. Her own power consumed her both times before the Highlords could intervene. When I suspected you were her rebirth, well..." he shakes his head, sighing heavily. "I knew it would be an interesting combination, the Essence with Zandria's odd ability."

"You... *do* realize what happened to the Essence, right?" Mara starts hesitantly, watching her guardian.

Darion frowns. "What are you talking about, Mara?"

"Her Source's ability is to absorb other Source and convert it into itself," Timian explains to Darion, standing up and walking over to the couch. "In so doing this, it also absorbs that Source's knowledge base. As you know, Darion, your own Source can learn its own techniques, being a sentient biochemical."

Darion nods. "Of course, but what does that have to do with the Essence?"

"The Essence is just Source," Mara says. "More specifically, it was part of Eliara's Source before it was split from her." She glances at Kimala who is standing off to the side, completely quiet during this whole encounter. "Eliara's Source used to be the same color as Kimala's before she died."

Kimala shifts uncomfortably, already aware of this knowledge.

"But when Eliara was shattered," Timian continues explaining, "it ripped her Source into a multitude of fragments, as well. Instead of the colors splitting apart evenly, it separated the majority of them into their base colors: white and lapis blue."

Kimala glances down at her clenched hands. "That... sounds about right," she whispers.

"The white Source had absolutely nothing of the original host's memory." Mara holds out her hand, and little white ribbons twine around her fingers. "It was a blank slate. Eliara had managed to keep all memories, experiences, and knowledge with herself, thus the deep color of her Source — but the portion that was ripped from her knew nothing. The Essence didn't even know it had been of the duir'raz'ne until it inhabited a girl and experienced the aftermath of the Da'ruha."

Her black Source twines with the white, creating an exquisite per'lusa flower on her palm. "And that is how the Essence began," she whispers. "It gained experience, knowledge, and resources *as a biochemical,* but in so doing, it gained color. It was no longer pure energy; it had its own opinion and memories, thus its silvery color. I..." Her hand closes over the flower, crushing it. The two Sources dissipate. "I took all of that knowledge from it. It's a blank slate again."

"So you are saying the Essence remembers nothing now that you have merged with it?" Timian asks, curious.

Mara shakes her head. "Not exactly. It still has access to my Source, so it remembers what it had been, but any knowledge it gains on its own is immediately taken away now."

Darion exhales slowly. "So the memories – "

"They are now a part of me," Mara explains, holding up her hands. "I can differentiate between them, though, unlike previous vessels."

"So when Aihalia activated those slow-release spells on the seals still separating you and the Essence, it made things worse?" Shaniel clarifies, frowning.

Mara nods. "My Source grows and gets bigger when it absorbs other Sources, so it had more volume to encompass the Essence, thus… speeding up the process." She taps her wrists. "The bands I had used to restrain it had limited its motion, thus cutting back on the memories – but when I took them off, my Source would suddenly flood over the Essence. That's why I always seemed to regress anytime I took off the bands."

Kimala creeps to one of the chairs and sits down. "But… how are you different from Aihalia, then?" At Mara's quizzical look, she clarifies, "Aihalia takes Source in order to survive. Isn't that similar to what you're doing?"

Mara shakes her head, holding up her hand. The silver and black twine together again. "Aihalia needs some type of consistent flow of Source through her body; it doesn't matter what type it is, and it doesn't have to be her own. She may take others' Sources, but she cannot convert it into her own. Who knows? Looking back on it, my Source could have converted a good portion of whatever she had lying around, and she probably didn't even notice."

Aeserast rubs his jaw. "No, I think she would have, but she must not have found it concerning enough to report it." He snorts in amusement. "In fact, she might be experimenting with it right now. It would explain her sudden desire to be in her lab for so long."

Shaniel shivers.

Mara shrugs. "Regardless, it's not the same. My Source doesn't cycle through the other Sources before dispelling it; mine converts." She holds her hand out to Darion, and the two strands twine about lazily. "Make a sphere with your Source."

"With or without runkare?" he asks, already lifting his hand.

"Without."

He does; a pretty jade green orb appears, looking hollow on the inside. Everyone sees Mara's black Source immediately encapsulate the external Source. It churns, receding to reveal nothing left in Darion's palm. The black tendril twines about the white again, though now it is nearly twice the size of its counterpart.

Darion drops his hand, staring at the black Source. "So that is how you absorbed the Danti Cauerr'ien," he murmurs.

"I still cannot believe the forest is gone," Timian admits, looking rattled. "It has been there for several thousand years."

"I relocated it," Mara quickly explains. "It wanted to overlook the chasm between the cliffs and Jethel Hariana. It's growing a new forest now."

He slowly sits back down, looking disturbed. "I am concerned over how much power you are containing right now, Mara."

She laughs. "Don't be. I expended most of it getting my body back, reviving Kimala, and purging my Hemius."

His eyes widen. "Your Hemius is *gone*?"

She grins. "I told you I would do it – somehow." She raises her right wrist, exposing the scar-like blemish around it. "Though apparently, it left this."

Kimala's eyes drop to the floor. "That... must have been my mistake. I did my best when I healed you in the Heramus, but back then, I hadn't been good at repairing tissues without touching the wound. I apologize, Mara."

"I don't mind." She touches it lightly. "It's a good reminder for me."

Timian sits forward, watching Mara for a moment. "I remember you speaking of your memories. Were they in relation to Rath?"

She nods. "It seems like he did something to me again when I faced off with him in Carni."

Timian straightens, looking unsettled. "When did this happen?"

"Right after we defeated the Dark Warrior." Mara yawns. "I chased him into Carni, but he… he ran, I think."

"You think?" Darion repeats, confused. "Did he tamper with that memory, as well?"

"I can't tell," she admits, sighing. "I… think so, but I haven't been able to break the seal on any of them."

"Let me try again," Aeserast murmurs, stepping forward.

"No, Aeserast." Timian rubs his jaw, eyeing Mara curiously. "Do you remember Wizard Berin?"

Mara nods, catching onto Timian's idea. "If he can take a look, we might be able to determine how to reverse the effects."

Timian smiles at her. "I shall send word to him to immediately come to Alamirana, then. He can also examine your Source so we can understand it better and possibly help you find a way to control it." He looks at Aeserast next. "If you could bring Aihalia here, that would be fantastic. This way, both Berin and Aihalia can work together to help Mara."

Aeserast nods, striding out of the room. Timian pulls out his crystal communication device as he walks to the other side of the sitting room. He murmurs to someone in thick Xharos on the other side.

Darion gestures to the vacated couch. "Mara, I… need to know something."

She sits next to him, her brow furrowing in puzzlement. "What is it, Darion?"

"It is… about your time in Dounta." He meets her

eyes, and she can see the concern warring with his resolve. "We found Naiya's body and a crib. Aeserast wrote a report based off your memories, and Evan gave us more details about the situation there. However, is there anything else you can tell us about Naiya's death or the babe?"

Mara mulls over it, remembering the dark halls and the tired yet seemingly kind woman. "She was different than when I had met her in Alamirana," she admits. "Even now, it's hard to imagine her being the same person. I did notice she wasn't wearing her necklace, though."

He frowns. "What necklace?"

Mara taps her chest right below her collarbone. "She wore this swirling pendant. When I had been imprisoned here, I noticed it changed colors a couple times. It was blue once, but then it turned red." She shivers. "I think the Dark Warrior controlled her that way."

Overhearing this, Kimala leans forward in her seat. "Eliara saw a necklace like that when they took your body; the Da'ruha was within it."

"The access key," Darion breathes, his eyes widening.

"What's that?" Mara asks, curious.

"It is an item from before the Ecalauna," he admits slowly, glancing at Timian. "Most were either lost or locked deep within Elethanos. I have received reports that this particular one has multiple unique abilities, including the capability of holding a soul within it and shielding it from Elethanos's sight."

"That sounds about right," Mara murmurs. "But it doesn't explain why Naiya had me take off her ring, too."

Darion's eyes darken at this. "When we analyzed that ring, we found it to be an old wedding band from Alkina dating back approximately two thousand years ago. Back then, higher-ranked Alkinians would gift this sort of ring to their partners when assassination had been common; it has multiple shielding and healing spells anchored to the metal, which is infused with a large amount of Source.

However, that particular band had been altered so the wearer could not inflict injury upon *herself*, nor could she remove the ring on her own."

"That's awful," Kimala breathes, appalled. "Why would Rath do such a thing?"

Mara exhales slowly. "To keep her from killing herself."

Kimala stares at her, speechless.

Darion nods. "It seems so; I do not believe you had met the true Naiya when you were here before, Mara. If the necklace she had been wearing is the same one from the Chamber, she could have very well been controlled remotely."

Mara shivers at the thought. "No wonder…" She frowns, remembering another detail. "That doesn't explain why she wanted to kill her own *baby*, though."

Darion grits his teeth. "When the medics analyzed her body, we found traces of an illegal substance," he snarls, surprising Kimala and Mara. "It mimics the same chemical reactions and bonding effects as conception, but the fetus produced from this combination actually draws from the mother's Source and body to grow – even after it leaves the womb. Eventually, the mother *will* die, unless the phan'stra is either killed or the fetus gains living cells to survive on its own."

"Shadow… child?" Mara whispers, disconcerted by the Xharos name for such a creation. "You mean Reivin was *that*?"

"Was that the name of the phan'stra?" Darion asks, and Mara nods. "Most likely, yes. Now that it has most likely been in contact with Rath, though, it will be more like a normal child. The key to making a healthy child that had been conceived as a phan'stra is to put it in contact with cells from another individual, usually the other 'parent,' much like an actual child."

"But the mother could be dead by then," Mara whispers.

Darion shakes his head. "When it was first developed, the Alkinians did not realize the implications. They were attempting to create a way where couples could have their own child, including infertile women. The cause was noble; it was the outcome that revealed the repercussions of the plan."

"I remember those reports," Kimala whispers. "Lilly had me study them when I was working on my second medic robe. The scientists and biologists had created the first phan'stra externally, but because they infused the second set of DNA and cells shortly after the creation of the phan'stra, there were no seen implications." Her gaze drops to the ground. "The reason it is illegal now is because many couples were not following up with the second step, and by the time the mother hit the second stage of pregnancy, she was already too weak. Many died before they hit their third stage, and rarely did any make it all the way through the fourth."

Mara blinks, utterly confused. "Uh… aren't there only three trimesters of a pregnancy?" They both give her a blank look. "Y'know… first, second, and third trimester?"

Kimala huffs. "It seems like in all that knowledge you gained, you learned *nothing*. Alkinians call them stages, and we have one extra pregnancy stage than humans."

Mara scratches the back of her head. "You can't blame me for not knowing. The previous Essence's vessels were never old enough to learn stuff like that."

Kimala shifts uncomfortably. "I… suppose not."

Chapter 21
The City of Energized Glass

Darion glances between them. "More importantly, it seems as though Reivin is another creation of the scientific failure. If my hunch is correct, Rath most likely had been trying to manifest a body so the Da'ruha could roam freely."

"I don't think so," Mara whispers, vaguely remembering what the Dark Warrior had said from within Desdemona's body. "Did Cronus have another child other than Morrigan?"

Darion's eyes slowly widen. "Aion," he breathes, leaning back in his seat as Timian walks over. "Now it makes sense."

As Timian puts up his reki, he catches the Eleth'Lord's comment. "Aion? I have not heard that name in centuries. What brings you to her?"

"Timian, would it be possible to use an access key to pull a specific soul out of Eleth to put into a phan'stra body?" Darion asks, his expression grim.

Timian's eyes flit to Kimala and Mara, both of whom seem confused. "It depends on the access key used," he admits, narrowing his eyes at Darion. "What have you concluded?"

"We know Rath had given Naiya a phan'stra pill," Darion quickly says. "But according to Mara, Naiya had been wearing a necklace that fits the description of the access key we have been looking for. If Rath had used that access key the way we believe he has in the past, would it not be easy for him to free a simple soul wandering about?"

Timian narrows his eyes at Darion. "If that is so, then we must obtain this access key immediately. That much power in that man's hands is catastrophic; if he decides to free his wife, we will all be doomed."

Mara winces as a sharp pain pierces her head; she feels as though she is on the verge of remembering something important.

"Mara, what happened?" Darion asks, his hand lightly touching her shoulder.

"Don't worry about me," she quickly says. "Continue; something about what you're saying is… familiar."

Realization dawns on Timian's face. "The memory block?"

She nods. "I feel like I've talked about something like this with… someone."

He watches her for a moment. "If Rath truly is Cronus, then he is the lesser of two evils. He has an approximate Source level of nine," he informs them, his eyes flicking to Darion. "For comparison, I myself am the same, and Darion is only one Source rank below us."

Mara rubs her chin. "So he's that powerful, huh? What Source rank would I be?"

Timian stares at her. "You are an irregular, Mara. Because your Source levels fluctuate, your Source rank fluctuates." He looks to Kimala. "You know your Source rank, do you not?"

She nods. "I was a six. But… since Eliara has been with me, I believe I can be classified more as a seven."

Timian nods. "I would have assumed as much. What would you classify Mara as of right this moment?"

Kimala stares at Mara, her gaze drilling into her cousin. "A… seven." Her brow furrows. "But… come to think of it, she was more like a nine when on the battlefield."

Mara rubs her jaw. "So my Source rank fluctuates…" She glances at Timian. "Then what was I before I went into Carni?"

"A six," Kimala quickly says in a firm voice. At Mara's disbelieving look, she admits, "We were actually about the same in regards to Source levels, Mara. You just didn't know how to restrain and control it."

"Geez…" Mara rubs the back of her head. "So is there such thing as a ten?"

"Yes." Timian clasps his hands in front of him as he gives her a sobering look. "Although they are rare individuals, and oftentimes, we the Ecalauna are the ones who have to stop them when they act out. I am sure that if you can reach rank nine by merely absorbing Source, it would be possible for you to reach ten, as well – but I do not recommend it. Many have lost their sanity from having so much of the biochemical in their system."

Mara taps her chin. "What was Eliara before she was shattered?"

"A nine," Kimala whispers, surprising them. "Carni, as well. Rinali had been a seven, while Kyrina… ten."

"A ten, huh…" Mara breathes, mulling over this. It makes sense for the youngest sibling, really; it is widely known in the historical records that Voyana itself had powered the young child. "Was Kyrina a phan'stra?" she suddenly asks, frowning.

Timian's eyebrows shoot up, disappearing underneath his bangs. "Of course not; it had not even been created then. Wherever did you get that idea, Mara?"

"Just… crossed my mind," she mutters. "She has so much Source, so I thought…"

"When it comes to the phan'stra's Source, it will have qualities of the host who had first infused the pill the mother would have taken," Darion informs her. "Most of the time, it is the woman's 'partner,' or the individual that will be associated with being the child's second parent."

Mara exhales slowly, her mind whirling. "If that's the case, then I wonder if Desdemona was one."

Timian taps his jaw thoughtfully. "It can very well be possible; she is most certainly nothing like her mother, and her Source has always had traces of the Da'ruha."

"It's not the Da'ruha's Source," Mara corrects him.

"It's Rath's."

They stare at her. "That is impossible," Timian argues. "I remember his Source very clearly; it was a dark red, almost black."

"And Morrigan's was bright orange, correct?" Mara's smile is grim. "What if Morrigan and Rath — or whatever his name was back then — had inhabited the same body for several years? Their Sources would mingle, would they not?"

"I do remember the report on this," Timian murmurs, frowning. "However, I would still prefer to assume this is not the case, because that idea is horrific. It would mean the Da'ruha is directly connected with Rath, and there is even a possibility that their consciousnesses are so intertwined that they cannot be separated."

"Oh, they can be," Mara reassures him. "If I was able to rip Morrigan and Rinali apart, I'm sure I can do the same with Rath and Morrigan."

Timian turns to Darion. "You did not tell me of this," he says in an oddly calm voice.

"It happened during the battle," Darion mumbles, avoiding the Time'Lord's gaze. "It was too late by the time I realized it."

Timian huffs, leaning back in his seat. "How was Rinali? Was she badly injured?"

Darion hangs his head. "She was on the verge of shattering when she went into Eleth. I am sure she is doing better now that she is there."

"How did the Da'ruha take it? Morrigan, you said?"

"Kicking and screaming," Mara says before Darion can speak. "A whole entourage of Elethani were waiting to drag her through."

Timian sighs. "At least their souls are not damaged beyond repair." He gives Mara a stern look. "Do not do that again, Mara. You could have completely destroyed them."

She stares back, unrelenting. "I wasn't about to let the Da'ruha kill Kimala and Darion."

After a long moment, he breaks eye contact. "I will have to consult Twyla on this matter; Ecalauna have no jurisdiction over the actions of an Ecalain."

Incredulous, she demands, "Are you serious? You want to punish me for saving their lives?"

"We needed the Da'ruha in order to interrogate her," Timian snaps, for the first time losing his cool. "What you did, Mara, completely ruined our singular chance of possibly finding the location of Rath. We do not have an access key to grant us passage through Eleth, so we cannot interrogate her directly while she is inside Hariana; it does not help that the Elethani refuse to divulge the information they have gathered on her."

Her eyes narrow. "What is this... access key you keep talking about?"

"It is an item created from the same material of the Elethanos and Elethavi," Timian explains, still looking irritated. "Some have the ability to grant the holder passage through Eleth for a short amount of time without dying; many of the reports of the Da'ruha's escape describe said item, but not the person holding it. This is why we have been unable to catch the Da'ruha's accomplice, or even *name* him." He expels his breath. "And to think that cursed woman almost got out, too... I am certain now that freeing her is next on Rath's agenda, considering how close he came to it last year."

"But who would she be able to possess?" Darion points out, his expression serious and grim. "Naiya is dead, and she is the only one I can think of who might be able to hold her."

Timian rubs his jaw, deep in thought. "If Reivin holds the soul of Aion, and Desdemona had the soul of Morrigan – "

"I think Desdemona is dying," Mara whispers, and

they glance at her in surprise.

"The report did say Desdemona showed signs of Hemius infection," Timian murmurs, frowning. "Although the Da'ruha can control it. Perhaps she was doing just that to keep Desdemona alive."

"Desdemona wasn't in the battle, though."

Silence descends on the group as they stare at Mara in dawning horror. Each of them eventually come to the same realization as her.

Rath hasn't been wanting Mara. No... he wants another *body*.

Timian takes a slow breath, settling his nerves. "Darion, would you check on Elethavi?"

He is already pulling out his reki. "Mornak is already there; I will ask him – "

"I want you to go personally."

Darion meets Timian's eyes. "But – "

"Make sure the Elethani know of the situation and that their intruder may return."

Darion rises to his feet, but he pauses and turns to Mara. "I... will be back soon."

Mara stands up, crossing her arms. "I'll go with you."

Timian glances between them, momentarily looking confused before sighing. "Mara, it would be too dangerous – "

"Elethanos is one of the best guarded locations in all of the realms," she points out, raising an eyebrow. "If I'm not safe there, then there's no hope for me." She takes Darion's hand and pulls him out of the room.

Darion huffs as they trek down the hall. "Mara, while I appreciate the company, it would not be feasible for you to accompany me. Berin is most likely on his way right now."

"I'm not asking your permission." Her hand tightens around his. "I need to ask you something."

"What is it?"

"What is the name of Rath's wife?" Her voice is barely a whisper. "You have been talking about her, saying how she is even more powerful and dangerous than Rath, but… you never once said her name."

"Lilith," he breathes. "Her name is Lilith, and she has a Source level of ten." After a brief pause, he adds, "She is the one who killed Carni Alamir."

"But Carni's soul had been sealed at the bottom of the Tower of Discord."

Darion closes his eyes briefly. "I know. Which means that Lilith must have been the one who created the Tower of Discord."

Mara shivers. "That Tower was a prison, Darion," she murmurs as his fingers squeeze hers reassuringly. "It was never holding something dangerous; it was sealing Eliara's remnant power and keeping Carni in a-a living nightmare."

"I know." He pulls her to a halt, tugging her through an archway into a smaller corridor. His fingers tuck a strand of hair behind her ear. "That is why I am going to Elethanos now, though; I will be checking to make sure there have been no disturbances."

She grabs his hand. "Let me go with you."

He immediately shakes his head. "No, Mara. The Elethani might not talk if there are others around. Do not worry, though; I will return shortly." He kisses her, and she cannot help but grip his shirt tightly as his fingers twine through her hair.

"By the flow," someone breathes in shock at the archway leading down the narrow hall. "Darion? Mara?"

They break apart, both embarrassed to be caught. Berin stands at the arch, his mouth gaping open. Aeserast is next to him, his lips parted in amusement.

"I didn't realize it had gotten *quite* so serious between you two," the Creation'Lord admits, chuckling at their flushed faces.

"I-it's only a kiss," Mara tries to mutter an excuse, her

entire face turning red. She wishes she can hide underneath a mountain.

"Hmm… a year ago, a simple 'kiss' had you breaking Shaniel's nose."

"Tha-that was different!" Mara's voice shoots up several octaves. "He used that move to get the upper advantage, but I didn't let it work!"

Darion clears his throat self-consciously. "I better go." He releases Mara's hand. "I will be back soon."

Aeserast's eyebrows snap together. "Where are you going?"

"Elethanos." Darion sweeps by the Creation'Lord without looking at him. "Timian wants me to check on something."

"All right…" Aeserast watches him for a moment before turning to Mara and giving her a knowing smile. "So?"

"So what?" Mara snaps, brushing by them. "Like I said, just a kiss."

"If you say so."

"I *do* say so."

"Uhm…" Wizard Berin hesitantly speaks up, recovering from his shock at seeing the Death'Lord kissing Mara. "Aeserast brought me here to take a look at your Source, Mara. He didn't give me many details, though; is everything all right?"

She nods as she accompanies them back to the sitting room with the others. "Great, actually; I'm still having some problems controlling it, though."

"Perhaps I can take a look, then, and give some advice," Berin offers.

Mara nods. "That would be great."

———•◆•———

After Berin's initial inspection, he disappears into Alamirta's fae'reth room to do some calculations with Timian and Aeserast. Mara and Kimala take this time to freshen up and change into cleaner, more familiar clothes. After a quick meal, they tour the rest of the castle with Shaniel as their tour guide — not that either one of them *need* one considering the knowledge they both have of the place inside their memories.

As they are walking across the main hallway that leads to the throne room, Darion appears from a half-hidden archway. "Timian said you were walking about," he says as he tucks his hands into his pockets. "Do you mind if I join you?"

"That was a fast trip," Mara comments, surprised at his sudden arrival. "And of course. We're heading this way."

He follows them. "The Gate is quiet, and the Elethani have been informed. Mornak is now on the lookout for unusual activity, as well."

"That's good." Arriving at the foot of the staircase leading to the throne room, Mara pauses and takes a deep breath. She has been in that circular room before; it was where the Dark Warrior had tried to possess her for the first time.

Darion pauses next to her, glancing at her stoic expression. "Have you visited the gardens in the back yet?" he murmurs, brushing his fingers over her elbow. "We can go there instead."

She shakes her head. "It's just a room, right? Let's go."

"It has changed a lot since the last time you saw it," Shaniel reassures her as they climb the stairs. "Erimentha threw a fit when she saw what Naiya had done to the Ecalain Tower and would not allow anyone in until she was done clearing away the drapes and rugs."

"Ecalain Tower?" Mara repeats, tilting her head to the side in curiosity. "I'm not sure if I knew that…"

"Probably not." Darion glances at the walls, examining the stones briefly. "It has only been called that amongst the Highlords in the past five hundred years."

"Not only that, but apparently Mara isn't the only one who doesn't study the history books," Kimala adds. "Most of her 'memories' of this place only contain the actual location and *none* of the historical value of it."

"I bet you're a walking history lesson now," Mara shoots back, smirking at her cousin's flushed face. As they near the top, she pauses to stare at the wall to the right of the door. There is a large, radial crack in the crystal.

Darion frowns, seeing the damaged wall. He hurries up the few remaining steps, running his hand across the damage. "Something must have struck it… I wonder if the energy chamber is too drained to repair it."

"That's where Desdemona was slammed against the wall from the Da'ruha's blast when I had escaped." Mara tears her eyes away from it, focusing on the two large doors. They are a pretty silvery-blue and engraved with images of the city's creation.

She doesn't move to open them.

Darion glances between her and the doors. Right when she thinks he is going to ask her about opening them, he says, "Ecalain Alamir had these doors specially carved to always show the history of how this city was created. The design was inspired by the carvings on Elethanos's ceiling; even though the deciphered message made no sense, the artwork was astounding, so he had the finest architects carve these."

"It's beautiful," Mara admits. "I… didn't even notice it the last time I was here. Probably because I was running for my life."

Shaniel's ears flatten against his head. "Hey, Mara, let's go to the side towers, instead! They have this amazing view over Alamirana that – "

"Thank you, Shaniel, but… I need to do this." Taking a steadying breath, she steps forward and wraps her fingers around the engraved handles. She pulls them open.

What greets her is nothing like the dark, foreboding chamber from before.

The crystal floors twinkle with refracted light, glimmering across the walls with all sorts of colors. In the middle, a silvery-blue dragon made out of opals looks as though it is about to rise out of the ground. The lapis background reflects the light, making the onyx talons and glimmering dragon stand out. It is all exquisite.

The eight chairs Mara remembered from before are still there, although they are no longer covered by dark cloth. They, too, are made of semiprecious stones and metals, each of them unique to the individual who had once sat in that very chair. Each one is plush and ornate, looking comfortable and extravagant – fit for the people who had sat in them six thousand years ago.

She is drawn forward, examining each chair; every single one of them is exquisitely fashioned. She runs her hand over the one Naiya had sat in when Mara had first met her; it is a beautiful chair with a silvery leaf engraved along the backrest. Vines climb up the legs, looking as though they are rooting the chair into the ground.

"That was Adul'ne Rhea Alamir's chair," Darion murmurs, a note of respect evident in his voice. "To the left was Eliara's, and the right was her husband's."

Mara's fingers trace over the intricate vines as she turns to her left. She stares out the huge bay windows that let in the light from whatever angle the sun is at; there is even a glass dome above her that allows the light to stream down during the peak of the day.

"Kimala."

The medic snaps her attention from the ornate chair where Eliara would have sat. "What is it?"

"Teach me how to be an Ecalain."

Kimala's face quickly turns different colors. "You-you – no, I won't! I refuse to!"

She raises an eyebrow. "Explain to me why."

"You don't know a thing about the Ecalain position! That should be reason enough."

"Then teach me."

"You really think I can *teach* you about something that people normally train for their whole *life* to do?"

"Yeah. What else were you planning on doing?"

Shaniel leans toward Darion, whispering, "How much longer do you think this is going to go on for?" he asks as the cleanly-dressed medic lectures the mage.

The elf shrugs, leaning against the circular chamber's wall. "It sounds as though Duir'raz'ne Eliara is in control, and according to the historical records, she can hold an argument for *hours*."

"So can Mara." Shaniel sighs. "Maybe we should stop them?"

Darion shakes his head, a small smile of amusement tilting up the corners of his lips. "Let them fight it out. It will be interesting to see who wins."

In the middle of the room, Mara glances at Darion, catching his words. She smirks at him knowingly. Sitting down in the chair, she beckons for Kimala to join her. "Please, Kimala, sit."

"I am not sitting there," she snaps, crossing her arms. "And you shouldn't, either, until you are properly crowned an Ecalain of Alamirana."

Mara props an elbow on Adul'ne Rhea's old chair. She smiles coyly up at her cousin, already knowing her and Eliara are too far merged by now to be able to differentiate between one another; they are already so much alike. Mara truly believes the only difference between them is their memories and how much they dislike Mara.

Not that it matters now, though. It seems as though Eliara's soul has already melded into Kimala's.

"Hey, *Kimala*," Mara starts, cajoling the poor medic. "How will Alec feel about your insistence of becoming the ruling Ecalain? Hmm? I thought you two were getting married once you turn eighteen."

"Don't turn this around on me, Mara. We – " She pales, finally realizing everything she has said over the past several minutes. "Oh. Oh no. Alec. I can't be here; I need to go back to Quasala!"

"Hold up a tick," Mara calls out to the panicking medic. "I'm not even asking you to relocate here to train me, Kimala. Just… give me a cheat sheet."

"A *cheat sheet?*" she repeats, incredulous. "Mara, the Ecalain position is not as simple as some Earthling test! You cannot – urgh!" She stomps her foot in a way that only Kimala can do, proving to Mara that it really is the medic in control.

She glances at Darion, waving her hand at the enraged Kimala. "Do you see this? Kimala won't help me."

Darion frowns, uncrossing his arms and approaching. "I thought you were arguing with Eliara."

Mara shakes her head, nonchalantly grabbing Kimala's wrist as she tries to slap her for ignoring her. "Nope, this is Kimala. Did you really merge together that fast?"

Kimala glares at Mara. "You didn't realize this sooner? By the flow, Mara, I *told* you this was happening."

"I get that," she responds coolly. "But you absorbed her faster than I processed all of the Essence's lifespans – and they both had the same amount of memories and knowledge."

Kimala continues to glare at Mara. "You are intolerable," she breathes.

"You're a little prissy brat," Mara shoots back, her voice surprisingly calm when compared to Kimala's rage. "You'd rather run off with your betrothed and plan a wedding that is in *over a year* than try to give me some pointers on what the Bloody Mavi I'm getting myself into."

"You're in over your head!" Kimala cries, gritting her teeth. "If you can't figure that out on your own, then the

Essence's previous vessels were pretty dumb when *they* tried to take the throne. You shouldn't even be trying to take on the position until you have read all of the history books on – "

"By the realms. *What* is going on here?"

They turn around to see the raven-haired Alkinian woman stride in, a deep frown marring her beautiful Ruha Coven features.

Mara beams at Twyla, glad for the Ecalain's arrival. "Perfect timing. Twyla, will you help me out? Kimala is not being cooperative. I want know what exactly is entailed in regards to the Alamiran Ecalain position."

"It involves overseeing the commerce of the multi-realm cities," she begins slowly, glancing back and forth between Kimala and Mara. "As well as any of the Highlords residing in this realm. You would be reporting on the Voyana concentration amounts and managing reports from other individuals, as well as tracking and following up on cross-realm travel and delivery of various technology and supplies, just to name a few tasks."

Mara's jaw drops. "Seriously? Everyone made being an Ecalain out to be such a big deal. It sounds like corporate business."

Shaniel snorts as Darion sighs.

Kimala makes a small, indignant sound in the back of her throat. "Respect the title, Mara! It is not just about that; you will be carrying out Voyana's requests, too!" Crossing her arms, the medic huffs, "Acting like that... seriously. This realm would be better off if *I* was an Ecalain."

"Uh... Kimala, you *are*."

"She is?" Twyla asks, stunned.

Darion's eyebrows raise in realization. "That does make sense. With Eliara's soul fused to you, you are the third Ecalain of the realms."

Kimala blinks, staring at her palm. "Huh. All right."

Mara sniggers. "That's all you have to say? I freaked

out for weeks when I first heard that, and you – "

"It's because *I* know what it means, Mara!" Kimala snaps, crossing her arms. "It's a mixture of xhuri origin, Source level, birthright, and Voyana's will."

"Voyana likes you," Mara points out, pointing at her cousin. Ever since she has been able to perform runkare, she has been able to see how the bright biochemical swirls around the young medic.

Twyla examines Mara closely. "You have grown used to your powers," she murmurs, smiling in relief. "You seem more comfortable with yourself now. I am glad."

Mara shrugs. "I am who I am. It's as simple as that; no past memory is going to be able to change that." Mara plops back into the chair. "So where do I begin?"

"You should not sit in that chair before you are properly crowned," Twyla says curtly. Embarrassed, Mara stands up, scratching the back of her head.

Kimala sniggers. "Told you so."

"As for you, Kimala, Alec was looking for you. I recommend going to the courtyard before he leaves."

Kimala's breath sucks in. "He's leaving?" she whines, rushing for the door. "No, not yet!" Shaniel sighs, following after her. He gives them a brief wave as he leaves.

Darion walks over, watching Kimala rush down the stairs. "Twyla, Mara truly desires to – "

"You need not speak any more, Eleth'Lord." Twyla turns back to Mara, examining her robe. "I can see very well with my own two eyes. While holding this position may help satisfy your Xhuri Rehkava, know that it could also very easily be your downfall, Mara."

She smirks. "You have to take a risk to be successful, don't you?"

Twyla returns the smile. "Indeed." She clasps her hands together. "For the time being, I have heard Michelle and Erimentha will be restoring the city's commerce. Until you are ready, I will have you return to Quasala so Timian and I may properly train you for this position."

Mara's breath hitches as something squeezes her heart. "Really?" she whispers, unable to fully comprehend that she will be taking steps closer to her new goal.

Twyla nods, holding out her hand. "Truly."

"Thank you, Twyla," she breathes, taking the duir'ne's hand.

She gives Mara a knowing smile. "In the meantime, though, enjoy this respite." She points to the balcony doors. "There is a wonderful view out on the balcony; perhaps you will enjoy it as I speak with Darion for a moment."

Mara nods, walking over to the balcony window. She hesitates a moment before unlocking it, gently tugging on the handle. It opens smoothly, not acting as though it is thousands of years old.

Stepping onto the balcony, she is greeted by a warm breeze and a breathtaking view of the surrounding land. She rests a hand on the balcony rail, her breath leaving her as she gazes over the high view of the city. Following the edge of the balcony, she walks around the outside of the tower until she stands above the staircase that had brought her into the room.

Twyla sighs as Mara disappears around the corner. She looks at Darion. "You care deeply for her, don't you, Eleth'Lord?"

"I do," he breathes, tilting his head forward to disguise his face.

She exhales slowly. "While I am elated to see you find someone to love, I must ask that you remain in your position a little while longer, Darion. We are so close to catching the perpetrators and ending this eon-old feud."

"I was planning to remain, Your Highness."

Her gaze is sharp. "Even if she asks you to remain by her side?"

He freezes. He cannot breathe; if Mara asked him to terminate his Highlord status to be with her...

Twyla's eyes flick to the balcony windows. "I heard from Timian what she had done to the Da'ruha. Since she did not know of the plans we had, she will not be punished; however, I will personally train her in the ways of an Ecalain as well as teach her everything we know of this silent battle." She dips her head down to meet Darion's eyes. "I need to know that you will remain strong in your duties, as well, Eleth'Launa."

"Yes," he breathes in response to his full Xharos title. "I will."

"Good. I recommend you tell her your farewells before you return to Elethanos." She sweeps out of the room, leaving him alone.

Taking a deep breath, Darion steps onto the balcony and walks around the edge to find Mara leaning against the rails, gazing over the crystalline city. The sweeping, elegant spires and curved buildings speak of an ancient civilization that had heavily utilized the sun's rays to empower its technology via small, clear panels on the buildings shaped to expose as much surface to the sun as possible. It is not only a functional design, but an elegant one, too.

He opens his mouth, but the words lodge in his throat. He cannot bring himself to tell her he needs to leave; to return to his job inside the dim Chamber with Mornak and Elethanos as his only company.

"It's beautiful," she whispers, interrupting his thoughts. "I see why it is called Alamirana – a city of energized glass. I'll never get tired of this view."

He props his elbows on the crystal rail. He stares over the city, his gaze hooded and his expression brooding. "This city has seen much over the millennia," he murmurs. "Death. Tyranny. War. Rebirth. Crowning." His eyes flick to hers. "I know you say you have accepted your status as Ecalain, but that does not mean you have to take on the responsibility of Alamirana, as well, Mara."

Mara stares at the multifaceted balcony railing. She

touches it gently, a smile hinting at her lips. "I like old things, though. There's something about them that makes me feel like I can do this." Catching sight of Darion's uncomfortable expression, she blushes. "I-I didn't mean it like *that*." She tucks a loose strand of hair behind her ear. "I want to see what it's like being an Ecalain. Twyla told me I don't have to do it on my own; there are plenty who can help me."

He relaxes, giving her an easy smile. "Indeed, there are. All you have to do is ask."

She avoids his eyes now, her cheeks still red. "Th-then… can you be one of them?"

He stares at her, his lips parting in surprise. He forces out the words he knows he must say. "Mara, I would be honored, but my duties as an Ecalauna come first."

"I don't want you to give up your Highlord position for me," she rambles. "But I don't want you to just be some bodyguard like you have been, either. I know you have your duties, but I… I want…" Her blush deepens a bit more. "I don't want you to leave again. I feel like you won't come back."

"I will. I promise." He places two fingers underneath her chin, and she looks up at him.

His lips against hers slays her doubt.

She hesitantly wraps her hands around his neck. As his arms encircle her, she finally feels at home for the first time since arriving on Blazhreia. She has a purpose, a reason to be here. Not only that, but she is confident she can do this task set before her – as long as *he* is with her.

This is where I belong.

LANGUAGE DICTIONARY

If you would like a pronunciation guide, please go online to the Danarko Vault:
www.maxinastoribrook.com

~ ana	The suffix for *city*.
~ launa	The suffix for *Highlord*.
~ ta	The suffix for *castle*.
~ theia	The suffix for *festival*.
A ik'te	Specifically "you," although often said to a creature of an unknown or foreign species.
Adul'ne	King/queen. Gender neutral.
Alamirana	The first official Alkinian city of the Ecalains and Highlords. It is the largest city in Saheir; it was originally meant to hold the remainder of the Alkinian population 6,000 years ago.

Alamirta	Named after the Alamir family; this castle was built to house the majority of the remaining Alkinian population when they fled Alkina.
Alkina	Home world of the Alkinian species and Voyana.
Ancient	A common term referring to someone or something over two thousand years old.
Ancient Xharos	The main elven language that dates from before the Fall of Alkina when Voyana had exploded 6,000 years ago.
Blazhreia	Home world of Blazhreians and the country of Saheir. It is much like Earth in size; however, due to Alkinian influence, its technological advancements are drastically different.
Bloody Mavi	Bloody Gate. This phrase is used the same way as the British interjection; however, it is not an expletive.
Carc'ra	Kranluk manure. It is used as an interjection.

Carni	The realm between all of the other known realms. | Add'l Names: Corridor Realm; Dream Realm
Carni Matter	Particles heavily infused with Voyana.
Carni's Creation	An entity that had manifested inside of the Corridor Realm. This includes night terrors, dream-eaters, Carni's Children, and Carni's Path.
Carni's Path	A pathway that manifests underneath a wanderer's feet to guide them through the ever-changing realm.
Cerberus	A three-headed nightmare creature from Carni; it was created by the twisted Carni Matter taking people's worst nightmares.
Cerlail Academy	An academy specifically designed to provide a central location for everything learned about Voyana and Source in order to more efficiently put it to use.
Corridor Traveler	An individual trained to walk through Carni with minimal risk of becoming eiv'ra or being attacked by Carni creatures. Also called "Carni

Corridor Traveler	Wanderer."
Creation'Lord	A Highlord whose jurisdiction is over Carni and the Corridor Realm as a whole. His/her main task is to report on the activity of the Tower of Discord. On occasion, they are also called the Dream'Lord.
Da'neka	Light Warrior. In reference to Kyrina Alamir, the youngest of the Four Ancient Sisters.
Da'ruha	Dark Warrior. In reference to Rinali Alamir, the second youngest of the Four Ancient Sisters.
Dan'te	Slang for "silver-blood."
Danarkana	A labyrinthian, multi-layered city built next to Alamirana. It is considered the third-largest city, although many argue it is the second largest. | Add'l Names: Lunesh'kun
Danra	White.
Danra er Vuti	White and black.
Danti	The color silver.

Danti Cauerr'ien	A forest made out of colored Source that has pooled into one region of Carni. | Add'l Names: Silver Mirrored Grove; Silver Mirrored Forest; Danti Ien; Cauerr'ien
Dream-Eater	A nightmare-class creature from Carni that takes on the shape of an individual's worst fears in order to paralyze them and steal their Source. Depending on the victim, this method could kill the dream-eater's prey.
Duir'ne	Prince/princess. Translates literally to "heir" in Old Xharos. Gender neutral.
Duir'raz'ne	First Heir/Princess. A title given to Eliara Alamir, the firstborn of the Four Ancient Sisters.
Duir'stra	Child of a prince/princess. Gender neutral.
Ecalain	Spokesperson (Old Xharos). They are known as individuals who can speak with Voyana and control Source better than the average person. Entire books have been written around the definition of an Ecalain and who they are in history.

Ecalauna	Highlord (Old Xharos). This is a dying term that is mainly used by older elves and certain fey courts.
Eiv'ra	Literally translates to "Lost" in Xharos; it refers to someone who has been affected by Carni's Will and does not have any purpose whatsoever to exist. Due to the nature of the realm, this state of being can be fatal.
Eleth	Death Realm. All who are deceased go here. | Note: "Realm" is used even though this is common improper terminology. It should be "Death Dimension."
Eleth Vortex	A film over Elethavi that transports souls into Eleth.
Eleth'Launa	The official Old Xharos title for the Death'Lord; the only people who use these extremely outdated titles are Alkinian Ecalain or the older generation of Highlords.
Elethani	A mysterious humanoid species native to Eleth; not much is known about them or their purpose.

Elethanos	Death Chamber. Chambers that rest between Jethel and Eleth; all that are deceased and reborn must pass through here. The term is commonly used to refer to the biggest chamber that the Eleth'Lord stays at.
Elethavi	Death Gate. This is the barrier between Elethanos and Eleth.
Eruka'ring	Where is ~ ?
Erus	A bipedal species native to Blazhreia; they are well-known for their aquatic habitats, blue-tinged skin, and their ability to breathe underwater and on land. They are from Mishir.
Eruslyian	The name of the Erus language.
Fae'reth	Tactical table; it can show holograms and 3D images of structures. It is meant for building and designing large-scale projects, although it has historically been used to strategically plan wars and end skirmishes.
Felorna	A green plant that flourishes along high cliffs and along the edges of

Felorna (cont.)	rocks on Quanaris. The Ruaguni Cliffs in particular are renowned for wild felorna and steep drops overlooking the ocean.
Fletchling	An endearing title Alkinians say to their young or those they view as children when compared to themselves.
Gameleth	Blade of Death; Salev'i of Death.
Gamerog	Blade of Foreboding; Salev'i of Foreboding.
Gamlein	The original name of Gamerog.
Goindun	An esteemed title given to individuals who are not dragonkin yet are considered in such high regard by the dragonkin to be one of them.
Guldon	An aquatic animal on Alkina; has six fins that propel it through the thick waters.
Hariana	An advanced prison system that is linked to Eleth and Carni; its physical location is in Carni. It is an artificial 'realm' that had been cre-

Hariana (cont.)	ated for the sole purpose of locking up threats to the realms. The entrance is linked to the Elethavi regardless if someone is going to the Jethel or Eleth side. | Add'l Names: Tartarus
Hemius	Living Curse Poison. It is a viscous Source-fueled liquid that kills its victims.
Heramus	Living Curse Scar. A section of land to the west of Veera infected with Hemius puddles that had been the result of Ecalain War II.
Highlords	Authorities that keep peace between the realms and defend against realm-level catastrophes, such as the Da'ruha.
Ikuta	You (gender nonspecific). Usually in reference to females; used in a 'cute' way.
Jethel er Eleth	Life and death.
Jethel Vortex	A film over Elethavi that transports souls into Jethel.

Jethelavi	Life Gate. Not commonly referred to outside of textbooks.
Kareia	Living metal; it holds a strange symbiotic relationship with its owner. At the expense of feeding it Source, the owner gains a reliable blade that lends power and strength.
Kranluk	A six-legged creature often used for travel and heavy hauling when travel by teleportation hole is unavailable or inconvenient.
Kuri'Voyana	The Xharos title for a specific individual in the history of the realms who has a Source that devours and converts other Sources into itself. Also referred to as "Energy Devourer" and "Refough Graeun" in other languages.
Laig'hius	A creature from Saronis that has the ability to switch between two forms: an animal form and a humanoid form. Oftentimes, the humanoid form contains characteristics of the animal form.
Lunesh	Moon's flower.

Mara	Half of a whole.
Mavi	Gate.
Mind-weaver	An individual with the ability to manipulate someone's mind in some way; usually, they can manipulate thoughts or even memories and can cause people to hallucinate or dream of a specific thing. In special circumstances, mind-weavers can aid someone with a mental illness or a time of grief.
Mindspeech	A method of communication; the speaker uses their Source to directly communicate to the listener's Source. Anyone ranked 5 or higher in Source can learn this ability, though it is not that common of a technique outside of government or higher officials aside from laig'hius and other shape-shifting creatures.
Nari	The feeling people get from someone's Source; it is based off the theory that Source can reflect the ideals and goals of a person. Also known as aura or charisma.
Neivir	A razor-sharp crystal that grows like a weed. It is an illegal substance,

Neivir (cont.)	although it is used in the tools of professional assassins.
Neka	Light (as in sunlight); state of being. Also used as the word for "sun."
Neka Coven	Sun Coven; it is positioned on the side of Alkina which always receives sunlight.
Neka er Ruha	"Light and Dark." In reference to something that receives light, and something that does not receive light.
Night Terror	A nightmare-class creature from Carni that is the manifestation of people's nightmares. This particular type usually only feeds off of a person's fear, so it will use scare tactics in order to feed. Rarely, it needs physical substance in order to maintain its physical form.
Old Xharos	Phrases or words from Xharos that are over 1,000 years old and still in use today.
Olympian	A name usually referring to the Ecalain family, Alamir, who mostly lived in Old Olympus before the

Olympian (cont.)	Fall of Alkina.
Paro'ki	Tyrant. Gender neutral.
Paro'stra	Child of a tyrant. Gender neutral.
Per'lusa	A flower native to Blazhreia; it looks much like a rose, except the tips of the petals have a teardrop-shaped node.
Phan'stra	Shadow Child. The child is created through programmed Source and can bind DNA together. Even after a successful procedure and the child has the DNA of both parents, it will still be different from normal children.
Phan'stra Pill	A medicine created several thousand years' prior to help Alkinians produce offspring when otherwise it was impossible. It was deemed an illegal method only five years after its release because of people misusing it and not following proper procedures. It is named after the child birthed from it.
Pirranki	Kitten; kitty.

Portal	Slang for "teleportation hole."
Quasala	The capital of Saheir and the fourth-largest city.
Quelara	Awaken
Raz	One; first.
Realm	A universe; most realms are named after the known worlds within them.
Rebirth Vortex	A specific vortex in the Elethavi that transports souls safely from Eleth into Jethel.
Reborn Soul	An individual who passed through the Jethel Vortex and has a coat of Vortex Matter covering their previous lives' memories.
Rehkava	Promise.
Reincarnated Soul	An individual who passed through the Jethel Vortex and has shed their coat of Vortex Matter covering their previous lives' memories, thus remembering at least vaguely of who they were in the past.

Reki	A communicative device that is powered by the user's Source; some have cross-dimensional capabilities, such as the ability to send written messages. This small crystal device is the size of one of Earth's cellphones. Also called "transponder" in Common.
Respoura	A type of fey that survives off a constant supply of Source; without it, they will die. They can extract Source from another and circulate it through their own body, but the Source does not become a part of them.
Ruha	Dark (as in darkness); state of being. Can also mean "the side that does not receive sunlight."
Ruha Coven	Moon Coven; it is positioned on the side of Alkina which never receives sunlight.
Ruicov	Grandfather.
Runkare	The ability to mix Source with raw Voyana to amplify and strengthen the individual's energy usage.

Saheir	A country in the northern hemisphere of Blazhreia; it is a large island with a mountain range in the north and coasts in the south, with fields and forests in the middle. Only a thin strip of land connect it to the southern continent Garnesh, which is four times bigger than Saheir.
Salev'i	Scimitar.
Salev'ra	A shorter, chained version of the salev'i.
Scio'thi	Katana.
Seelie	A faction of the fey on Quanaris; it is in reference to their allegiance. Seelie are commonly known for their overall helpful nature, though they can be mischievous.
Sera	Of course. It is used as an interjection.
Siege	A strategy game created by Shokain Danarko; it uses the basic blueprint design of a city as its playing board. Involves two players on opposing sides.

Sital'fu	A mayor. Gender neutral.
Soreia	Profession. Often used as a noun or title.
Source	Voyana that has fused to the genetic code of an individual.
Source Globe	A lighting fixture that senses the usage of Source and reacts to the energy output. Can also be programmed to utilize Voyana in the air, although those models are more expensive.
Srui	Idiot; fool.
Source Inhibitor	A unit that blocks the connective ports between an individual and their Source, keeping them from using their personal energy supplies.
Tein'fu	A duke/duchess. Gender neutral.
Tein'stra	A duke/duchess's child. Gender neutral.
Teleportation Hole	A hole made in the membrane separating the realms from one another; if done properly, this hole can be

Teleportation Hole (Cont.)	used as a transportation method. "Portal" is shorthand for this phrase.
Terular	A sturdy material from the plants in the Black Desert on Alkina. The more advanced types are called Voyana-infused, or Voyana Cloth.
Thana Baro	Safe travels.
Thanos	Chamber.
Therakare	The ability to utilize Source without Voyana's assistance or amplification abilities.
Tik	A measurement of time; approximately a minute. 60 tik = 1 tok.
Tok	A measurement of time; approximately an hour. 26 tok = 1 nuni.
Tora	First month of the year; the middle of the summer.
Toratheia	Summer Festival.
Translocation Sickness	A medical condition in which the individual becomes sick when they

Translocation Sickness (cont.)	pass through a teleportation unit to get from one realm to the next. Medics believe those with unstable Source are more likely to have this condition than those who do not, as the Source moderates how much energy and radiation actually reaches the individual during the translocation process.
Tuatha dé Danann	A supernatural race in Irish mythology.
Unseelie	A faction of the fey on Quanaris; it is in reference to their allegiance. Unseelie are commonly known for their overall malevolence, though they can be benevolent.
Uthu morla a ik'te	Common Phrase: "I found you." Gender Neutral. (See 'a ik'te' for more information.)
Uthu morla ikuto	I found you. (male)
Vara tir'rani er thana baro	Fair weather and safe travels.
Veera	Fifth-largest city in Saheir; also one of the easternmost cities from the capital, Quasala.

Voi ~	Added to the beginning of a title to signify the recognition of or adoption into this rank without proper ties.
Voi'duir'stra	The child of a voi'duir'ne; recognized as duir'stra, yet does not have blood relations to a duir'ne.
Vortex Film	The film-like substance often seen in the Elethavi when it is open. It looks like a soap bubble or rippling water depending on which Vortex is open at that time.
Vortex Matter	A substance that coats a soul when it goes through the Jethel Vortex; it buries the soul's old memories so the individual can be reborn as opposed to reincarnated.
Voyana	Energy (Old Xharos) | A biochemical that devours chemicals and hazardous fumes in the atmosphere that would otherwise kill life. It developed sentience when it was introduced to the atmosphere 6,000 years ago. Those genetically affected by its presence can utilize it as an external energy source.
Vuti'Voyana	Literally translates to "Black Energy"

Vuti'Voyana (cont.)	in reference to the Source coloration of all logged individuals with black-colored Source. Occasionally also called "Vuti Source."
Welp	A derogative version of "fletchling." It expresses the age gap between the speaker and the listener, and putting down the listener for being so young and inexperienced. Classified as both Old Xharos and Dragonir.
Werui	Aunt.
Xharos	The Alkinian language; used as both a spoken language and a way to focus Source. While the runes are no longer used in daily writing, they are still utilized in Source and Voyana techniques.
Xhavio	The equivalence of a soulmate; not many people believe this superstition nowadays. It is based off the belief that two individuals' Source and nari compliment and pair well together. It fell out of style over 2,000 Saheian years ago.
Xhuri	Soul.

Xhuri Rehkava	Soul Promise.

Xhuri Robe — Soul Robe; a special robe that manifests when a soul removes the Vortex Matter and swears on their own soul to uphold a personal belief.

Day		Month
Zanuni	Monday	Tora
Bruanuni	Tuesday	Eona
Denuni	Wednesday	Vuva
Koranuni	Thursday	Sona
Wionuni	Friday	Maua
Senuni	Saturday	Kenza
Xhenuni	Sunday	Alona
		Rawa
		Pina

Season		
Torakonu	Summer	Lefa
Sonakonu	Fall	Fua
Alorakonu	Winter	Zua
Fuakonu	Spring	Owa

* Seven days in a week, four weeks in a month, thirteen months in a year.

Check out the Danarko Vault online for more content. It contains an extensive language dictionary with pronunciation guides, character and world information, and more.
www.maxinastoribrook.com

WANT MORE CONTENT?

Maxina has put much love and effort into this series. She has created an entire website dedicated to the languages, characters, and worlds called the *Danarko Vault*. It is accessible through her main website:

www.maxinastoribrook.com

Maxina also has a Patreon where she posts exclusive short stories, alternate perspectives, novelettes, and even chapters of books she is writing. Patrons get special behind-the-scenes look at her writing, art, and future projects.

The *Sealed Archives*, a Patreon-exclusive website, is treated like the archives of Maxina's Patreon, making it a more interactive platform to read her work. It contains short stories and novelettes based off the Danarko Multi-Realm as well as other exclusive content. Members have access to certain levels depending on their subscription.

Learn more about the *Sealed Archives* and read exclusive stories here:

www.patreon.com/storibrook

ABOUT THE AUTHOR

Maxina Storibrook grew up traveling all over the world. She loved it so much she couldn't be satisfied by merely traveling to all the unknown places across the Earth; she has to discover new places, write about other worlds, and meet amazing, adventurous people.

Maxina has a bachelor's degree in English and a master's degree in creative writing – all for the love of words. The *Danarko Saga* is her first series, and she takes pride in all the effort she has put into her realms.

In Silver Grove Publications, she hopes to bring beautiful content to people's lives.

Her biggest dream? *To tell stories.*

Explore Maxina's written works and learn more about her: www.maxinastoribrook.com

Get exclusive content on Patreon: www.patreon.com/storibrook

Purchase signed copies, find out more about Silver Grove Publications, and explore other SGP Authors: www.silvergrovepublications.com

www.ingramcontent.com/pod-product-compliance
Lightning Source LLC
Chambersburg PA
CBHW030958190726
48285CB00004BB/1372